Praise for the novels of S. Thomas Russell

"Russell's encyclopedic command of nautical lore, joined to his rare ability to spin a ripping yarn, places the reader right in the middle of the action, of which there is plenty. He loves this stuff, and he makes us love it, but does us the courtesy never to oversimplify, never to gloss over the flaws of the officers, the seamen, the politicians and their navy. Out of that ruthlessly clear-eyed vision, he creates characters and situations that stay in the reader's memory even as memories of broadsides and cutlass duels fade."
—Neal Stephenson, *New York Times* bestselling author of *The Mongoliad*

"Fans of Patrick O'Brian's works and other novels in the naval adventure genre will enjoy [*Under Enemy Colors*] . . . A fast-paced and eventful narrative . . . The novel benefits from thorough research and a mastery of the technical details of sailing in the 1790s."
—*Library Journal*

"A colorful account of duty and honor, punctuated by the cannonade of naval warfare."
—*Kirkus Reviews*

"Russell's first-rate debut features taut plotting, liberal action and . . . a complex, sympathetic hero."
—*Publishers Weekly*

"[*Under Enemy Colors*] grips the audience with its insightful look at war at sea. Charles is a fantastic protagonist who keeps the exciting story line together . . . Historical readers will cherish this strong naval saga with vivid sea battles, strong characterizations and a deep sense of time and place."
—*Midwest Book Review*

"Vivid and evocative, especially about what Mr. Russell knows best, the sea and sailing."
—*The Wall Street Journal*

"Late 18th-century naval warfare and the threat of mutiny take center stage in this seagoing thriller reminiscent of Patrick O'Brian."
—*The Sacramento Bee*

ALSO BY S. THOMAS RUSSELL

Under Enemy Colors

A Battle Won

TAKE, BURN OR DESTROY

S. Thomas Russell

BERKLEY BOOKS, NEW YORK

THE BERKLEY PUBLISHING GROUP
Published by the Penguin Group
Penguin Group (USA) LLC
375 Hudson Street, New York, New York 10014

USA • Canada • UK • Ireland • Australia • New Zealand • India • South Africa • China

penguin.com

A Penguin Random House Company

TAKE, BURN OR DESTORY

Berkley trade paperback ISBN: 978-0-425-26853-7

The Library of Congress has catalogued a previous edition of this book.

PUBLISHING HISTORY
Originally published in the United Kingdom under the title *A Ship of War* by Michael Joseph / 2012.
G. P. Putnam's Sons hardcover edition / May 2013
Berkley trade paperback edition / March 2014

PRINTED IN THE UNITED STATES OF AMERICA

10 9 8 7 6 5 4 3 2 1

Cover illustration by Larry Rostant.
Interior text design by Meighan Cavanaugh.

I would like to dedicate this book

to the wise "elders" of our respective families:

my mother, Shirley Russell, and Nori and June Nishio,

my kind father- and mother-in-law

Irish Sea

6°

5°

4°

3°

52°

51°

Torbay

Plymouth

50°

Land's End

Falmouth

English

49°

Ushant

Brest

Belle Ile

Atlantic Ocean

48°

Quiberon

6°

5°

4°

3°

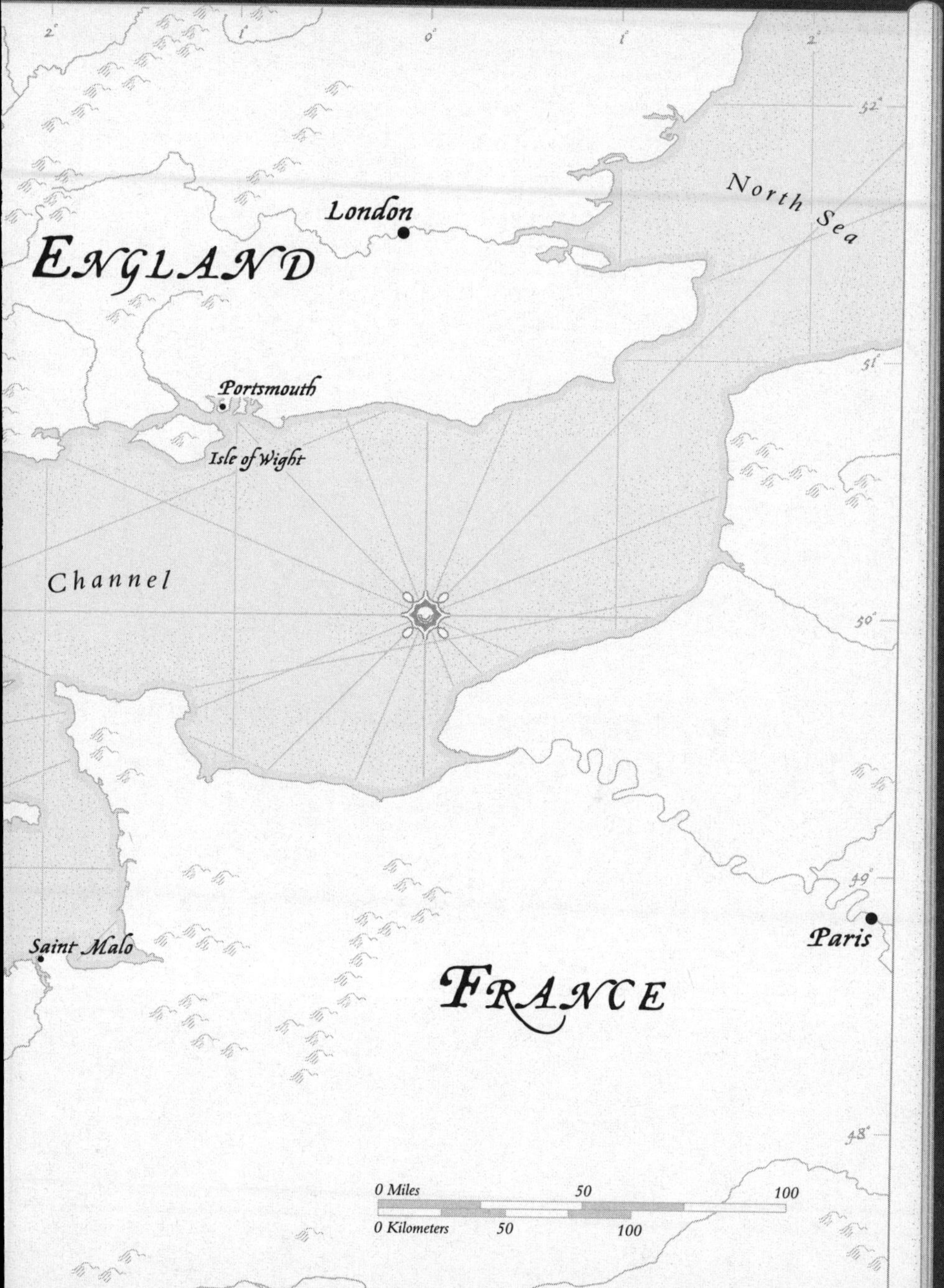

North Sea
London
ENGLAND
Portsmouth
Isle of Wight
Channel
Saint Malo
Paris
FRANCE
52°
51°
50°
49°
48°
2°
1°
0°
1°
2°
1°
0°
1°
2°
0 Miles
50
100
0 Kilometers
50
100

One

They waited upon the Port Admiral for permission to sail.

Seamen came of age comprehending their dependence upon wind, tide, and weather, and so developed a patience for such natural forces that if not saintly was at least philosophical. Being held in port by human agency, however, as Hayden's ship was, provoked quite a different response. Mr Barthe stomped about the decks impressing his juniors with his command of the English language, most especially the strain that could not be used in the presence of ladies. The other sea officers were not so vocal but peevish and too easily vexed, which was quickly sensed by the hands, who modified their behaviour accordingly.

It was Hayden's most urgent desire to get his ship under way on the morrow at first light and be out of Plymouth Sound and into the Channel before the decks were dry. But the forenoon had passed without the awaited permission arriving and now the afternoon was well advanced, the day speeding.

What had the First Secretary said? *I want you at sea—and beyond recall—as soon as can be arranged.* These words sent a little shiver through Hayden's entire being. "Beyond recall" were the words he found most ominous. Beyond recall of whom?

If only the Port Admiral would co-operate. The man's tardiness in granting Hayden's request to sail was madding if not peculiar. It caused Hayden to wonder if the Port Admiral served the designs of the "enemies" Hayden had been informed he possessed and if *that* was the reason the man was so dilatory in granting Hayden's request; orders from Whitehall Street were expected momentarily that would see him removed of his command.

Such were the thoughts that forced their way into a man's mind after the First Secretary informed him that if he did not accept this command it might never be within the First Secretary's power to gain him a comparable appointment again. Such words did speak of secret forces working against him . . . did they not?

Hayden, however, was aware that his mind was not performing as it should and might be making much of nothing . . . or not nearly enough of what appeared to be very little. His estrangement from Henrietta had made sleep all but impossible, his stomach approved neither food nor drink, and his thoughts could hardly be turned to the matters at hand. Some part of him hoped he *would* suddenly be relieved of his command that he might return to London, find Henrietta, and have an explanation with her about the recent false claims of the Bourdages—mother and daughter.

Hayden paced across his cabin, glancing out of the stern gallery windows now and again, across Plymouth Harbour to fields on the eastern shore. The new green of spring grass rippled in the breeze—a fair breeze for Le Havre, to which place Hayden had been ordered to take or destroy a frigate using that harbour as a base from which to harass British shipping.

A knock on his door interrupted Hayden's thoughts, somewhat to his relief, as they had been tracing this same circle for several hours.

At a word from Hayden, his marine sentry cracked open the door.

"Mr Barthe, sir . . ."

"Send him in."

The sailing master, all corpulence and jowls a-jiggle, waddled in, ancient hat tucked beneath his arm revealing a head of red and grey—ash and flame.

"Please do not tell me, Mr Barthe, that you have discovered some fatal wound to our rig."

"Our rigging is all in order, sir, most perfectly so. And our sails are bent and ready to loose, but . . ." The sailing master hesitated.

"Do complete your sentence, Mr Barthe, the suspense is almost more than I can bear."

Barthe smiled. "If we are not to sail this day, sir, Mrs Barthe and my daughters would like very much to visit the ship. Mr Wickham has kindly arranged a boat to carry them out, sir, if that would be acceptable."

"Did Mr Archer not inform you that we have yet to complete our powder?"

Barthe was genuinely surprised. "He most certainly did not, sir."

"For which I have no explanation. The powder hoy is to visit us this very afternoon. I still hope to win our anchor at first light tomorrow and be in the Channel by breakfast."

Barthe did not hide his disappointment at all well. "Perhaps . . . perhaps Mr Archer did inform me about the powder hoy, sir."

"Mr Barthe, it is very obvious that you are attempting to conceal Mr Archer's lapse, but I shall have to have a word with him about it. As to Mrs Barthe and all the Misses Barthe, I am almost as sorry as you that they cannot visit the ship. Please send Mrs Barthe my regrets and explain the reason; I should not want her to feel the least unwelcome."

"I shall, sir. Thank you, sir."

Barthe's ample bottom retreated out of the door. Hayden was sure every man aboard would be very disappointed to learn that Mrs Barthe would not be bringing her handsome daughters for a visit—even Hayden felt a little chagrin.

Allowing the sailing master a moment to make his exit, Hayden then opened the door. "Pass the word for Mr Archer, if you please," he ordered the marine.

Hayden looked at the mass of paperwork that lay in untidy piles upon his desk. If only his mind would consent to focus on it for more than five minutes before returning to Henrietta and his distressing financial troubles.

A respectful knock on the door announced the arrival of Mr Archer. The lieutenant came striding quickly in.

"I am sorry, sir, it was entirely my failure to inform Mr Barthe. He did not for a moment forget."

"And it is a very serious failure, Mr Archer. How is Mr Barthe to plan his work without such knowledge?"

"I do not know, sir. I shall not let such a thing happen again."

"I am quite certain you will not. Fires have been extinguished all about the ship?"

Archer tried not to display offence at this but failed. "All but the lamp in the light room, sir. And I have ordered wet blankets draped about that."

"Go through the ship and be certain that we have no fires lit, Mr Archer. As to Mr Barthe's family, or any other visitors to the ship, I should not want to take the chance of blasting them to hell. Would you?"

"No, sir, I would not."

"Then be about your business, Mr Archer."

The lieutenant went stiffly out. Although Hayden did not enjoy the role of angry captain, he had come to the belief over the years that the occasional upbraiding kept young officers on their toes and alert to their duties. It had certainly had that effect upon him. Archer's pride would be stung for a day or two, but Hayden was certain he would get over it and be better for it as well. There was a small part of Hayden that wondered if he was merely being peevish—a result of his own distress and anxiety about his personal and professional life—and this thought was not easily dismissed. He *was* peevish, he knew; the slightest things sent his choler soaring. But then, Archer's mistake was fairly grave and could not have been passed over without comment. He bloody well *should* have informed the sailing master that the powder hoy was expected. What had he been thinking?

"Perhaps he was distracted by his personal life," Hayden muttered. "As have you been, Captain."

For a moment he sank down on the bench before the windows, his mind deflecting away from duty of its own volition, and wondered again if his letter would reach Henrietta and if she would read it. His greatest worry was that she might simply burn it or toss it away out of anger with him for what she believed was his betrayal—his reputed marriage to a French émigrée. It was a source of the utmost frustration to him that he could not have a five-minute explanation with her that would clear away all misunderstandings . . . but he had not been able to find her while he was in London and neither Lady Hertle, Henrietta's aunt, nor Mrs Hertle, her cousin and confidante, would consent to speak with him.

Yet another knock upon his door interrupted this too familiar train of thought.

"Boat alongside with orders from the Port Admiral," Midshipman Gould reported when the door was opened.

Hayden arose from the constant feeling of enervation and weight bearing down upon him and went quickly up the ladder to the deck, where he found Lieutenant Ransome speaking sharply to an unknown young officer of the same rank.

"The Port Admiral requires your signature, Captain," he said as Hayden appeared. "Mine, apparently, will not answer." Ransome, who had been put aboard his ship by no less a personage than Admiral Lord Hood, had the kind of pride that was rather too easily wounded—a trait that Hayden found aggravating in a lieutenant, and especially so today.

Hayden signed the papers without comment, and discovered not just orders from the Port Admiral but a second letter from the Admiralty. He felt a need to sit, suddenly, and retreated below to the privacy of his cabin.

Sinking down into the chair at his desk, Hayden held the two letters a moment wondering which he would open first. A letter from the Admiralty was more likely to contain bad news.

If only the Port Admiral had given me permission to sail! Hayden thought.

A moment more of wondering, his mind racing, and then Hayden came down on the side of the letter from the Admiralty. It was from Philip Stephens, and in the Secretary's own hand too. It was prefaced as "Most Secret and Confidential."

My Dear Captain Hayden;

You are hereby ordered, at the earliest opportunity of wind and weather, to take HMS Themis *and proceed off the harbour of Le Havre on the night of April the 12th. At two of the morning of April the 13th, at a distance no greater than one mile due west of the headland, you must show a single light, visible to the shore, for one half of the hour. A small boat shall approach carrying an individual who will identify himself as "Monsieur Benoît." He will bear information of a sensitive nature essential to the prosecution of the present war. This intelligence must then be conveyed to the Admiralty with all speed and in a manner that will not compromise the identity of its source. If this task conflicts with previous orders given to you by me, meeting Monsieur Benoît and reporting his intelligence to the Admiralty shall take precedence. These orders should not be communicated to your officers until such time as they require the information and certainly not until you are at sea and well out of sight of our shores.*

The letter was signed "Philip Stephens, First Secretary." Hayden laid it down for a moment on his desk and then cursed loud enough for his sentry no doubt to have heard. It was like the Admiralty to give him additional orders that would make the execution of his previous duties difficult if not impossible. He was also frustrated because taking a frigate could mean prize money, which, given his recent reverses, he desperately required. Meeting a spy did nothing but put his ship in danger, given that the spy could very easily be apprehended and questioned before Hayden arrived and the time and place of their rendezvous then be made known to the French authorities.

He cursed again, this time under his breath. Breaking the seal on the second letter, he found his request to sail finally had been granted. Any thoughts that he might be returned to land and the possibility of a rapprochement with Henrietta must be given over. He was for Le Havre and a meeting with the mysterious Monsieur Benoît. He cursed this particular gentleman in French.

Two

Amalformed moon drifted above the haze and cast a meagre light upon the deck. Beyond the rail, an inky, restive sea rolled and muttered in its bed.

"It is an unwholesome sea." The sailing master appeared out of darkness, stomping the few feet to the bulwark where Charles Hayden stood with a night glass tucked into the crook of his arm.

"Unwholesome? Whatever do you mean, Mr Barthe?"

"It seems like a broth left to stand until it has gone thick and chill." Barthe shivered visibly.

Hayden hid a smile. "I believe you are becoming somewhat of a poet, Mr Barthe. It is just the usual April sea, to my eye. Though the night is too close by half." He raised his glass and swept it very slowly across sixty degrees of arc, then back again, before returning it to its place of rest.

"Three hours yet, Captain, before we have some light," Barthe observed, divining what was in his superior's mind. "Time yet."

Hayden did not think it was near enough time and wanted to be under sail even as they spoke.

"I would rather see them returned sooner than later," Hayden replied. "And as for the other matter . . . That man might be in gaol or on his way to the guillotine. I shall not wait past the appointed time."

A cutter, still painted black from their recent enterprise on the island of Corsica, had set out some hours earlier to enter the French harbour of Le Havre under cover of darkness. Whether the frigate Hayden was to destroy had gone out on the hunt that night, Hayden needed to know. There was no way to intercept it along the British coast, where it stalked its prey under cover of darkness—other than by matchless luck—so Hayden hoped to meet with Monsieur Benoît and then lie in wait for the frigate's return. If, however, the French ship remained in harbour that night, Hayden did not want to lose the element of surprise by being observed lying in ambush. In that case, Hayden would order the *Themis* to slip away long before first light to take no chance of being becalmed within plain sight of the French port.

But for now he must meet this damned "Monsieur Benoît," who, if he had been discovered by the French, could easily give away the time and place of this rendezvous, in which case French ships might keep the appointment instead, which caused Hayden more than a little uneasiness.

"Can you make out the coast, Captain?" the sailing master wondered, his voice suddenly a bit thin. "I fear we are being set to the east. This is no place for a ship on such a dark night. When the Seine fills, upon the rise, the currents can shift inshore, and the duration of high water is often prolonged. I have seen currents set a ship counter to the best pilot's predictions. It is a damned dangerous situation, and I am not pleased with it."

"We are of one mind in this, Mr Barthe, but we have no choice in this matter." Hayden turned about, gazed up into the rigging a moment, and then called up in a low voice, "Mr Wickham? Can you make out the shore? Are we being set to the east at all?"

"We are holding our position most handsomely, Captain," Wickham answered, raising his voice just enough to be heard. "I can make out the lights ashore. Implore Mr Barthe to be at peace on this count. All is well."

"No sign of our cutter, then?"

"None, sir."

"Any other boats?"

"No, sir."

Hayden cursed under his breath, gazed upwards a moment more, then turned back to the rail. Coils of tattered cloud flowed over an indistinct moon, tearing apart any faint light that reached the sea.

"Well, I am still not pleased with it," Barthe declared testily. "By your leave, sir . . ."

At a nod from Hayden, he waddled off forward to see to the trim of the sails.

Hayden went to the binnacle, where the light had been dimmed, and took out his watch—five minutes shy of two. "Pass the word for the master-at-arms, if you please," he ordered a seaman.

Immediately, Hayden returned to attempting to part the darkness. For a moment he imagined he heard the measured dipping of sweeps into the cold Channel, but no boat materialized and the sound eventually blended back into the noises of night and sea.

"Sir?" The diminutive master-at-arms appeared out of the gloom.

"We will show this single lamp for exactly one half of the hour," Hayden instructed.

"Aye, sir."

The signal intended for the French spy was lit, sputtered, then came to soft light. Hayden immediately felt a target for hidden guns or ships lurking in the darkness.

His mind, however, could not be kept on the present circumstances, but was ever drawn back to the troubles that had befallen him upon his recent return to England. Even more than his legal troubles, his estrangement from Henrietta weighed upon him, causing constant distress and drawing his mind from his responsibilities. He needed to be in England, to find Henrietta and explain all that had happened. The discovery of Madame Bourdage and her daughter was of no consequence when compared to this one matter.

You have duties, Hayden reminded himself. The safety of two hundred souls is dependent upon you making decisions with a clear mind.

But his mind was not clear and lack of sleep from worry only reduced its powers more. Added to these personal concerns, he now fretted that, in his preoccupied state, he would commit some error of judgement that would put his crew in danger.

Archer appeared at the head of the companionway, looked about as though confused, spotted Hayden, and immediately crossed to him.

"There you are, Mr Archer. Did you sleep?" Hayden asked, trying to hide away his worries and concerns.

"But poorly, sir."

As Archer habitually appeared like a man just wakened, Hayden could not say if this was the truth.

"No sign of Mr Ransome, sir?"

"None."

Archer considered this news a moment. "What will we do if he does not appear by first light?"

Hayden wanted to reply, "Roast him," but instead paused to consider. "I fear we shall have to assume he had the ill luck of becoming a guest of the French, and we must hope he does not give away our intentions or reveal that the *Themis* was here at all."

"The French will know he did not row across the Channel. What will they assume, I wonder?"

"Any number of possibilities, Mr Archer. That he has come ashore to meet a spy. Or that he has placed a spy among them. We can hope the French might think he planned to cut out some ship in the harbour, for if they think he meets a spy they might become determined to have him name the man." Only Hayden knew the

name of the man they were to meet—and most certainly this was
not the man's *real* name.

Some bitter liquid was pressed up from his stomach into his
throat, and Hayden swallowed it back down, only to be left with a
burning sensation.

"*Capitaine?*" came a whisper almost under Hayden's chin.

"Who is it?" Hayden whispered in French.

"*C'est moi. Benoît.*"

"Come aboard, monsieur."

Hayden could just make them out now. Two men in a small boat,
one at the oars, another in the stern. At the ladder head Hayden
waited, two marines with muskets standing by. A small, well-made
man came onto the deck, leaving the other to tend the boat. He was
dressed as a fisherman but wore a large hat which cast his face entirely into shadow.

"Shall we repair below, monsieur?" Hayden asked in the other's
tongue.

"Let us go to the stern," the other said, eyeing the armed marines. "I will be but a moment."

He might have been dressed as a fisherman, but Hayden knew by
his refined manner of speech that he was anything but. When they
reached the taffrail, Hayden motioned the marines to keep their
distance, allowing the two men to converse privately.

"You speak French very well," Benoît observed, and Hayden
could see this made the man rather anxious.

"I spent some time in France when I was a boy—with relatives."
As he said this, Hayden opened the signal light and extinguished the
flame, feeling a great sense of relief to have done so.

"You are French?" the man asked apprehensively.

"My father was English. A sea officer. I am loyal to that nation,
though many of my sympathies lie with your people."

The man digested this a moment.

"Have you a letter for me?" Hayden prompted.

"I commit nothing to paper. It has been the undoing of too many." Benoît seemed to consider a moment, as though uncertain of Hayden, but then he pushed on. "A large force is being gathered in Cancale, as I have previously reported. But I was wrong as to its objective . . . and to its size. More than one hundred and fifty transports, five, and now I believe six, ships of the line, two razees, and five frigates are there. Presently there are only twenty-five thousand men, but soon there are to be one hundred and fifty thousand."

Hayden cursed aloud—he could not help it.

"The Channel Islands might be the first objective of this armada, as I have informed your people, but their ultimate goal is to land an army on English soil."

"Are you certain of this? Is it not more likely to be Ireland?"

"I cannot tell you how I know, but this information is beyond doubt."

It was Hayden's turn to digest. "When is this invasion planned?" he asked.

"Soon. When your Channel Fleet is at sea, or perhaps if it can be defeated or significantly weakened so that the French fleet can gain control of the Channel for a short time. It requires only the right wind and a single day to transport an army to England."

Hayden felt as though he had suddenly taken ill. Desperately he wanted to shed his coat and loosen his neckcloth. Sweat oozed out of his skin, and he was so overheated as to feel dizzy.

"You must convey this knowledge back to your Admiralty, Capitaine. Immediately."

"I agree, monsieur. Nothing is more important."

"Then I will leave you." Benoît made a small bow and went immediately to the ladder. As he went over the side he stopped. "Good luck to you, Capitaine," he said in English.

"And you, monsieur."

The man went down into the boat and in three silent strokes of the muffled oars the night absorbed him completely.

Hayden stood, staring blankly into the darkness like a man who has learned of a loved one's death—mind empty of both thought and feeling.

Hayden's servant appeared at the moment. "If you please, Captain. Rosseau has your coffee set out in the gunroom, sir."

"Ah . . . Find Mr Hawthorne and ask that he join me," Hayden instructed the boy. Archer was standing silently by the helmsman, watching Hayden. "You have the deck, Mr Archer."

At the foot of the companionway ladder, Hayden was greeted by the sight of the gun-deck cleared from bow to stern, including his cabin and all of its furnishings. Arrayed upon either side were rows of black-barrelled eighteen-pounders, loaded and ready to be cast loose. A moment the young officer stood there, trying to focus his mind, wondering if everything was in its place . . . and nothing more.

Down the next ladder to the lower deck, where the watch below slumbered. Hayden suspected a goodly number slept not at all, but lay awake with the excitement and anxiety that the possibility of action produced. The midshipmen did not even pretend to sleep, but played at cards by a single lantern, jumping up to tip invisible hats as Hayden passed quickly by and into the gunroom.

Herein, seated at the table, he found the ship's surgeon, spectacles perched upon a narrow bridge, a large, bound volume turned towards the lantern and encircled by thin arms. In the warm light his hair, prematurely grey, appeared silver.

"Certainly, you might have another lamp, Dr Griffiths," Hayden offered. "No, no, Doctor, do not stand." Hayden had seen the poor man crack his head upon a beam more often than he wished.

"I am all but finished here, Captain." The surgeon removed his spectacles—they were for reading and such fine work as removing limbs—so that he might see Hayden more clearly.

"Do not feel the need to leave, Doctor. It is your mess."

"Thank you, sir." Griffiths kept his eye on Hayden. "Are you well, Captain?"

"Apart from rather disturbing news just learned, I should say I am."

As Hayden did not offer to share this news, Griffiths did not ask. For a moment neither spoke, and then the surgeon nodded towards the open book. "I swear, I have now forgotten more physic than I presently command."

Hayden was pleased to have the subject changed. "It is too vast a catalogue, Doctor. It would require more than one mind to retain it all."

The surgeon rubbed his eyes. "You are being too kind, Captain. I fear it is merely age, in my particular case, and the common infirmity the reasoning organ begins to exhibit when it is always taxed to its small limit."

"Doctor, your mind seems as clear to me as the day we met. But perhaps a mild stimulant would not go amiss. Would you take some coffee?"

"With more gratitude than I am able to express."

Boots, thump-thudding down the ladder, were followed by the appearance of Marine Lieutenant Hawthorne, red-faced and overly cheerful given the hour and circumstances.

"Do I understand that coffee is being served in the withdrawing room?"

"In the morning room," the surgeon replied, "given the hour." He turned to Hayden. "Have you ever taken note of our lieutenant's mood prior to an engagement? He would appear to be on his way to a ball and all aquiver with the anticipation of meeting young ladies." The surgeon fixed his gaze upon the marine. "One day you shall be carried down to the cockpit with a musket ball lodged in your thigh, and I will tell you, you shall not be so cheerful."

Hawthorne laughed. "I am certain you are right, Dr Griffiths, but, pray, what purpose would be served by my becoming dour and fretful before battle had even been joined? I will save all like emotions for such time as they are needed, and then I will be able to express them in full, for they shall not have been worn thin by unnecessary employment." The marine raised his cup to the surgeon in toast. "I do not think we shall see a great deal of action this night."

Griffiths turned to Hayden. "Are you of the same opinion, Captain?"

"I am always rather embarrassed at how poorly I predict the future. Everyone else seems to do it so well."

"And so often," Hawthorne added.

Griffiths did not smile but seemed to consider these sallies seriously. "Perhaps they should include predicting the future in the training of young officers," Griffiths noted. "Will this French vessel even return to harbour this night . . . assuming it ventured forth to begin with?"

"I do not think it would risk meeting our cruisers by day, and it might very well have a prize or two it would hope to preserve at all costs. So, yes, if it set out to raid our inshore trade, I believe it will return by first light, wind allowing."

"As you have an unrivalled record of estimating what French sea officers will or will not do, I expect we will bring this ship to battle in very short order." The surgeon drained his coffee cup and then patted the volume he had been consulting. "There is nothing like agreement with authority to set one's mind at ease. If you will excuse me, I must return to my patient." He rose, remembering to stoop beneath the beams, and went crouching out.

Hayden turned to the marine, who watched the doctor go with a smile of both affection and amusement. "Does his health seem improved to you, Mr Hawthorne?"

"A little, yes. Even so, he is not himself. Not yet." Hawthorne turned to Hayden, his countenance changing. "Has he told you that his charge has sailed for England?"

"Of what charge do we speak?"

"The woman with one hand."

"Miss Brentwood?"

"Yes, I believe that is her name."

"Griffiths has arranged this?"

"And paid for it, I should imagine."

"Did he not procure a position in Gibraltar for her?"

"Indeed he did, but he is of the opinion she will be more secure in England, where he might stay better informed of her situation."

This gave Hayden pause. "I wonder if that is the whole of it?" he ventured. "Has our good surgeon fallen under the spell of this unfortunate woman?"

Hawthorne shrugged, a look of concern wrinkling the skin around his eyes. "If you can overlook the lack of a hand, she was comely . . . did you not think?"

"A very handsome young woman, Mr Hawthorne, but . . ." Hayden decided against speculating further or passing judgement on the surgeon's actions or motives.

"I am sure my concerns are little different from your own," Hawthorne observed, nodding once. "Let us hope that nothing untoward befalls our surgeon, whose heart, I suspect, is more frail than his health."

"Hear," Hayden intoned, lifting his cup in toast to this sentiment.

Hawthorne sat back in his chair. "I understand we had a mysterious visitor this night?"

"Is my conversation with this man known among the hands?"

"No. Only that a Frenchman came aboard and had a private conversation with you, sir. There is, of course, much speculation as to the nature of this, but it is nothing more."

Hayden sat a moment trying to decide if he would take Hawthorne into his confidence, as he had in the past. The temptation was very great, as he had to make a decision and was, truthfully, uncertain as to the proper course of action. "It would appear, Mr Hawthorne, that there is an army being gathered near Cancale for the purpose of invading England."

"That seems rather alarmist. We have known for some time that the French were planning an invasion of the Channel Islands."

"It would seem that the French would like us to believe precisely that . . . but their real intentions are far grander. My question is, should I collect Mr Ransome and make sail immediately for Portsmouth to convey this information to Mr Stephens, or will that appear to be shying away from the object of my first orders, to destroy the frigate sailing from this port? Certainly, if the claims of my French visitor are not given credence amongst the Lords Commissioners they might think me rather foolish, not to mention shy."

"I hardly think they will believe *you* shy, Captain. Not after all you have done in the past months. But why should it be either one or the other? Can we not take the frigate this night and sail for an English port immediately thereafter? How many hours would we lose?"

"Very few, but one must always consider the possibility that we might be the ship taken. After all, if we were unlucky and lost a mast or two we could easily be the prize. The crew do not appreciate how much good fortune plays a part in every engagement."

A half-amused smile formed on the marine's lips. "I am very doubtful that you will lose such an engagement, Captain."

"But you will agree it is a possibility?"

"A very unlikely one, but yes, I cannot deny it is possible."

Hayden nodded. The odds could not be calculated, but he had less faith in himself than Hawthorne, apparently. Being taken was more likely than the marine realised. The French frigate would very likely be of thirty-eight guns, no fewer than thirty-six, and she was not shut up in port like so much of the French fleet. In fact, she was waging a very successful war against British commerce and her crew were well used to handling their ship and firing her guns.

"What will you do, then, sir?" Hawthorne asked.

"Sail for England . . . the moment we have retrieved Mr Ransome."

Hawthorne nodded, as though he understood even if he had argued the opposite.

There was a little lull in the conversation then, and Hayden believed he could sense the marine lieutenant contemplating the propriety of asking his commander about his personal life. Hawthorne glanced at him and then away, twice.

Determined to forestall any such enquiry, Hayden stood abruptly. "I must beg your indulgence, Mr Hawthorne, for I should return to the deck. I do not want this French frigate to arrive now and catch us unawares."

"Which will not come to pass if Mr Wickham has anything to do with it."

Hayden nodded to his friend. "Mr Hawthorne."

"Captain," the marine replied, standing quickly.

Hayden let himself out, regretting not having more time in the warmth of the gunroom, but he was not willing to discuss his own situation. It was enough that he could barely tear his mind from it—and worse that his thoughts seemed to travel the same cycle, never once finding any sequence of events that he had not previously pondered, any outcome he had not imagined. Hayden was not about to compound this by drawing his officers into the matter. Better he disciplined his mind and put these things aside until the *Themis* was, again, safe in harbour . . . if only he could.

The night appeared unchanged when he took the deck—perhaps a little cooler, but still the same veiled moon and speeding cloud.

"Is the wind making, Mr Barthe?" Hayden asked the sailing master, who stood talking quietly with the helmsman.

"I believe it is, sir, and will continue in this manner for some time yet. We are in for a bit of a blow, Captain. The weather glass is taking a plunge." Barthe looked around as though expecting a hard gale to break upon them at that very instant. "All is not well, sir."

Despite himself, Hayden was unsettled by the sailing master's predictions of impending cataclysm. He turned his head up, removing his hat lest the wind get under it. "Aloft there. Mr Wickham? Any signs of our cutter?"

"None, sir," came the reply out of darkness.

"Blast this night to hell," Hayden muttered. Whatever could have befallen Ransome? Had he somehow been unable to discover the *Themis* on this dark night? Mr Barthe had, rather miraculously, managed to keep the ship in position despite currents and a backing wind. Even an officer as unseasoned as Ransome should not find it difficult to return to this place. Something else had occurred to delay them, and Hayden was beginning to suspect the worst—the cutter had been discovered and taken by the French.

Hayden paced the breadth of the deck, and then back and forth along the larboard rail, the length of the quarterdeck. The moon, though it appeared to be speeding from the cloud flying before it, actually traversed the sky at a pace so languid that Hayden began to wonder if the world no longer spun at its accustomed pace.

Hayden was about to tell Barthe that the moment Ransome was aboard they would make sail for Portsmouth when there was a soft call from aloft.

"*Captain Hayden, sir!*" came Wickham's voice, urgently, from up among the rigging. "I believe there is a ship in the offing—almost perfectly abeam, sir."

Hayden crossed quickly to the starboard rail and peered into the murk. A dull black sea, lifting and easing, low, scudding cloud, and perhaps a shroud of rain not so far off.

Archer appeared at the rail beside him.

"Shall we beat to quarters, sir?" the lieutenant asked, peering out towards the dark Channel, both hands tightly on the rail-cap.

Although Hayden could see no ship, he would not take the chance that Wickham was wrong. "But quietly, Mr Archer. No shouting, no drum."

"Aye, sir." Archer was off at a run.

In a moment, men streamed out of the hatches fore and aft and, at an order from Hayden, cast loose their guns. Below, on the gun-deck, Hayden could hear the same being done, a little buzz of excitement and fear rising up out of the hatches.

Barthe hastened over to stand near Hayden. After a moment of staring intently into the night, his hand shot up. "Is that a light, Captain?"

Hayden swept the area with his night glass. "It is a ship, Mr Barthe. A frigate, if I am not mistaken. Let us hope they have not yet perceived us." Hayden looked about the deck. "Douse these lanterns, Mr Madison," Hayden ordered the midshipman. "And hang a lamp in the larboard quarter-gallery; Mr Ransome might find us yet."

Immediately, the lanterns were extinguished, faint moonlight descrying uncertain shapes upon the deck.

Hayden felt his muscles almost rigid with indecision. Certainly he must let this ship pass, as tempting a prize as it might be. He was more concerned that the French would discover the *Themis*. Would they run their ship under the guns of the shore batteries, or would they make shift to take him?

"I believe this ship will pass astern of us, Captain . . . About three cable lengths." Barthe was shifting from foot to foot in agitation. "If we can discern them, Captain . . ."

"Yes, Mr Barthe, it is almost certain they shall discover us."

What had Mr Stephens' orders read? *If this task conflicts with previous orders given to you by me, meeting Monsieur Benoît and reporting his intelligence to the Admiralty shall take precedence.*

There was no lack of clarity in that sentence, yet . . . to let an enemy ship pass so near and make no attempt to engage her . . . It brought to mind his former captain, Hart, who shied from every action and never without an excuse.

"If they comprehend that we are a British ship, Captain, they might rake us from astern . . ."

"You are correct in every way, Mr Barthe. Just before she draws astern, I wish to put the helm up and shape our course to parallel her own."

"Aye, sir. Shall we close with them, sir?" the sailing master asked expectantly.

Hayden's honour and sense of duty wrestled over this but a few seconds. "That will not be necessary, Mr Barthe. We shall be nearer than I want to be as it is."

"Aye, sir. I shall have the men at their stations ready to brace our yards in a trice." He waved a hand at the darkness. "This Frenchman shall be afforded no opportunity to rake our ship."

Hayden called softly up into the tops. "Mr Wickham? On deck, if you please."

Hayden turned his attention back to the approaching ship. In the dark it was near to impossible to gauge her speed. For some moments he watched.

"There you are, Wickham," Hayden observed as the acting lieutenant reached the deck but a few feet off. "How distant is that ship, do you think?"

"Half a mile, sir, no more," Wickham replied with a gratifying certainty. "And she is carrying the wind with her, Captain. I think she is closing rather faster than we might realise."

Hayden touched a sailor on the shoulder. "Find Gilhooly and

have him snuff the light in my quarter-gallery the moment we begin
to turn."

The man went off at a run.

"Mr Wickham, stand watch to larboard, if you please, and alert
me the instant Mr Ransome heaves into sight."

"He is some hours late, sir," Wickham said hesitantly.

"Yes, but let us not give up hope." Where was that damned fool
lieutenant? If the man had not been a protégé of Lord Hood's
Hayden would have been happily shut of him, but good men accompanied him—among them Childers, Hayden's coxswain.

Rain reached them, carried on the making wind, and for a moment the French vessel dissolved into the blur. As the gun captains
fumbled their lock covers into place, a gust struck the *Themis*, heeling her sharply to larboard.

Hayden took hold of the rail to steady himself, closing his eyes
against the battering rain and wind. A moment the gust mauled
them, pressing the sails and wailing in the rigging. Just as suddenly,
the wind eased and the ship regained her feet.

"Where is the Frenchman?" Hayden whispered. "Can any
man see?"

The question was met by a silence that grew deeper and more
disconcerting by the moment.

"I see 'er, sir!" One of the men at the gun pointed. "Starboard
quarter. 'Alf a league. A mite less."

"I see nothing," Barthe complained. "That gust should have
pushed her past us."

"I have found her as well, Captain!" Wickham stood upon his
tiptoe. "There away. Not quite where I would have expected, but
the current must be setting us inshore."

"This bloody night," Barthe grumbled. "Can't see naught for
nothing, Captain Hayden, and that is giving the truth a little pull
and a stretch."

"Are you ready to brace yards and ease sheets, Mr Barthe?"

"In every way, sir."

Some part of Hayden felt a vague sense of disquiet with their present situation. Despite the darkness and veiling rain, he had been certain this ship had been nearer before the squall struck. "Helmsman, what is our heading?"

"East by nor'east, Captain."

Unchanged, Hayden realised, so the slant of this approaching ship should not be different, even though it appeared to be.

"May I order the helm put up, Captain?" the sailing master asked.

"You may, Mr Barthe."

The helm was put over, sails sheeted, and slowly the head paid off until the backed topsail fluttered, then filled. More quickly now, the wind was brought aft. This evolution, timed to a nicety, set the *Themis* on a parallel course to the ghostly frigate, whose lights winked and flickered through the drizzle.

"Mr Gould! Have Mr Archer stand ready to open larboard gunports. Caution him not to let any man do so until I have given the order."

"Aye, sir," and the midshipman went off at a run.

If the French captain discovered them and decided they were a British ship, Hayden wanted to be certain his guns fired first.

The human silence upon the decks was covered by the sounds of wind, of the bow parting waves as the ship pitched in the small sea. Slowly the moon revealed the frigate, her sails and spars, the wide, pale stripe upon her topsides.

"They must see us, Captain Hayden," Wickham observed in a whisper. "I can make them out most clearly."

"As can I."

Nearer the ships drew to one another. Hayden could distinguish figures moving on the deck.

"Shall we not fire into them, Captain?" the sailing master hissed.

"Mr Barthe, if you please!" Hayden replied, not taking his eyes from the enemy ship. He was not adverse to suggestions or questions from his officers—but a man of Barthe's experience should display better judgement than *that*.

Even through the blear, Hayden could discern an officer, leaning upon the rail and staring intently at the *Themis*. Perhaps he beckoned another, who appeared out of the darkness, affixing his attention upon the British ship with equal intensity. Suddenly, that man turned and ran for the companionway.

Hayden did the same; at the head of the companionway he looked down to find Archer standing on the ladder's bottom step.

"Mr Archer! Open gunports and fire our entire larboard battery."

"Aye, sir."

The bump and screech of gunports hinging up stole a little of Hayden's breath. Apprehending the gunports opening, the French officers turned to shout the alarm, but their calls were lost in the shattering report of British eighteen-pounders. There was no reply from the Frenchman. Musket fire cracked from the tops as Hawthorne's marines began firing at the men scurrying about the enemy's deck.

Immediately, to both left and right, the gun crews went coolly about reloading their carronades. Many were seasoned hands at this now, after their convoy to the Mediterranean. There was no hesitation or confusion, but only a well-greased axle, turning with precision and regularity. The balls and wadding were pushed in together. At the same time, the gun captain uncovered his lock, ran his pricker into the touch-hole, poured a measure into the pan, closed the lock, and pulled back the cock with two thumbs. The carronades were run out on wooden slides, and the gun captain made certain of his target and yanked the firing lanyard with a quick jerk.

Hayden had stepped back from the rail, turned away, and covered his ears just in time. A tremendous explosion tore open the darkness with the muzzle flash, and smoke plumed forth, blossoming up into a weeping night.

In the ensuing silence, Hayden heard officers shouting orders in French. Gunports began to open on the enemy ship. As his own crews were running out their guns, an irregular fire erupted from the French frigate. The always horrifying sound of iron balls rending the air was immediately followed by the crash and splintering of wood reverberating through the *Themis'* deck. A sheet carried away, and sail began to shake and snap.

As was ever the case, the English gun crews fired thrice for every two times the French fired; some crews doubled the enemy's pace. Rate of fire, at short range, trumped accuracy, a fact that Hayden knew well and had led him to manoeuvre his ship so near.

The next quarter of an hour saw an unrelenting fire kept up between the two ships, breaching the oak planking, tearing away shrouds and stays, and ripping through sails. Smoke mixed with rain and low mist to obscure the vessels from one another and hide the true damage being inflicted.

In the midst of this, Hayden glanced shoreward, fearing that they would carry on this battle until they came beneath the enemy's batteries. He must finish this frigate before that could happen. He might yet be forced to lay his ship alongside and board.

Around him, men fell and were carried below or slipped over the side if death was certain. To his surprise, Hayden realised he could now distinguish action upon the forecastle of his ship—dawn was not so far off.

"Captain Hayden . . ." came a call from somewhere forward. "A boat, sir. A cutter, it looks."

"Not a gunboat?" Hayden shouted to be heard above the din.

"I don't believe so, sir."

Ransome would return at this moment!—when it would be worth his life to even approach the ship.

Gould, who had conveyed Hayden's orders forward, came running back along the gangway. "It is our cutter, sir," he called out. "They are pulling for us like madmen and shouting and waving." The boy was flushed and speaking almost too rapidly to comprehend.

"What do they say, Mr Gould?"

"We do not know, sir."

No more explanation was required—the noise of battle was deafening.

"Signal them to stand clear; they will gamble their lives to draw near now."

"I will, sir." And the boy went hurrying forward, apparently oblivious to the cannon balls that hummed over the deck and the musket balls lodging in planking with ominous cracks.

Dawn was still some time off, but morning twilight was beginning to reveal a few shadowy shapes across the deck. From the quarterdeck, the cutter was not yet visible.

Smoke burned Hayden's eyes, and his ears rang from the constant explosions. The French captain, despite being surprised, was putting up a spirited defence and Hayden feared he might yet make the cover of the shore batteries.

As if the French commander had been thinking the same thing, a hoist of signals jerked aloft, the flags mostly obscured by sails. The French officers were hoping there would be light enough for the shore gunners to make out their signals.

"Where is Mr Gould?" Hayden called out.

"Forward, sir."

"Have him run up the French naval ensign and a hoist of flags to starboard. Let us confuse the enemy if we can."

"Captain!" Gould came running along the deck. "Mr Ransome is ignoring our signal to stand clear, sir."

"Well, then he must look to himself. A hoist of signals to starboard, Mr Gould, and the French ensign aft."

"Aye, sir."

A young sailor came dashing up, making a knuckle. A blast of carronade fire completely smothered his words.

"Why are you upon my quarterdeck and not at your station?" Hayden demanded.

"If you please, Captain," the young man began, looking more frightened of Hayden than the French, "Mr Barthe has sent me. Mr Ransome is yelling somewhat about a French frigate, sir."

"'Somewhat'? Whatever do you mean?"

The boy shrugged. "Those were Mr Barthe's words, sir."

Hayden hesitated a second, then made up his mind. "Mr Gould! I am on the forecastle."

He hastened forward in the wake of the running sailor. "What is this about, Mr Barthe?" he demanded as he reached the bow.

Only thirty yards off, Hayden could make out their cutter, the men pulling like they were running from gunfire, not into it. Hayden leaned out over the barricade, half hidden by smoke, no doubt, and waved Ransome away. Spotting his captain, Ransome leapt upon a thwart and began gesturing frantically towards the shore. Hayden's eye was drawn towards France. Out of the mist and morning twilight the sails of a ship materialized, and then beneath these a jib-boom penetrated through the fog.

For the briefest second Hayden's mind went utterly blank, and then he turned to the sailing master.

"Sail handlers to their stations, Mr Barthe," he shouted almost in the master's ear. "The instant Mr Ransome is aboard, we will bring the wind onto our starboard beam, gain way, then shape our course to the nor'west—hard on the wind, Mr Barthe. Do you understand?"

Barthe looked as though he did anything but. "W-We are going to run, sir?"

"Yes, of course we are going to run. Two French thirty-six-gun frigates, sir. What else are we to do? With all haste, Mr Barthe."

Barthe seemed to come suddenly awake to their situation. "Aye, sir." He went trundling off with a rolling run, shouting for Mr Franks to call the sail handlers.

Hayden cursed himself for not slipping off the minute the French ship had been spotted. Ransome could make England in the cutter. Men had gone much further. He cursed himself again.

Hawthorne appeared beside him at that moment, hat gone, face powder-stained, a musket in hand. "Will the Frenchman not rake us, Captain?"

"We are half hidden by smoke and mist. If we are quick, we will have braced our yards and put over our helm before he comprehends what we are about."

Men came running onto the deck and began coiling down ropes as quickly as hands could move.

"With all speed! With all speed!" Hayden called as he hastened down the larboard gangway.

Upon reaching the quarterdeck, Hayden positioned himself a yard from the helmsman. Even though Hayden could see the crew working as quickly as human hands were able, and racing aloft at a dangerous speed, it still seemed that morning light would find them before the helm could be put over.

Defying his captain, the French gunners, and all common sense, Ransome brought his cutter alongside and the men scrambled up to the deck. The first man over the rail staggered back into the man behind, and then fell on his side, bleeding from his chest. The others took him up and bore him quickly below to the doctor. Immediately, Ransome hastened to the quarterdeck, calling out orders to stream the cutter.

Almost out of breath, he touched his hat and began, "I apologise, Captain, for disregarding your orders, but we were trying to warn you, sir, about the frigate."

Hayden nodded. "Yes. I see what you were about. But we must now run, sir, if we are to preserve our ship. Wickham and Archer are overseeing the guns. You will be the lieutenant of the watch until I order you relieved."

"Aye, sir."

Mr Barthe's voice came hollowly through a speaking trumpet. "Ready to brace our yards, Captain."

"Port your helm," Hayden ordered the two men at the wheel— one standing by in case his mate was felled.

The *Themis* was a handy ship and answered her helm readily. Hayden realised that the second frigate would be within range of his eighteen-pounders as they made the turn.

"Mr Gould. Jump down to Mr Archer and instruct him to fire upon the second frigate as she bears."

"Aye, sir."

Hayden turned to watch the French frigate and was gratified to see that he had caught them unawares. They might yet bring guns to bear upon Hayden's stern, but there would be no devastating broadside raking his ship.

Finding the second ship in the murk, Hayden realised that his adversary would not dare to immediately change course to follow Hayden lest he run afoul of the ship emerging from Le Havre. It was a rare bit of luck that would see him jump ahead, for he was confident his crew could make sail more quickly than the French.

Aloft, the hands were making all possible sail, and the *Themis* heeled a little towards France, as though reluctant to let it go. And then the *Themis* was lifted on the wind, slipping into the rain-fog and morning gloom.

When sails were set and drawing, the master came puffing along the gangway, speaking trumpet tucked under an arm, a hand crushing down his hat as the wind freshened.

"We shall haul our bowlines, Mr Barthe. There is Pointe de Barfleur to be weathered, and do not tell me how distant it is. If we are forced to tack ship, we shall have two frigates upon us."

"This wind will go into the north-east yet, Captain. See if it doesn't. We shall easily lay our course for Tor Bay. By midday, sir, I will wager."

Barthe had been involved in sufficient wagering so Hayden did not take this up, but he did hope the sailing master would be proven correct; reaching England was more than urgent.

Archer's head appeared in the companionway, followed by torso, waist, legs, and running feet. He was gasping as he approached and only managed, "Your . . . orders, Captain?"

"We shall race these Frenchmen back to England, Mr Archer, and hope we have the luck to meet one of our own cruisers so we might turn things round on them. If that does not prove possible, we will attempt to fight these frigates off until we can reach the Channel Isles, though we must weather Barfleur to do even that. For now, we set everything she will carry and pray these Frenchmen do not know their business."

The call "belay-o" reached Hayden. "Bowlines hauled, sir" came from the forecastle and Hayden went to the binnacle to discover their course.

"Not even nor'west by west," Archer observed, following Hayden to the compass.

"Let us hope this wind veers, as Mr Barthe predicts." Hayden turned his attention astern, into the drizzle and surface mist. A thin light began to penetrate the low-lying grey, revealing a dull, uneasy sea. A cool April northerly seemed to penetrate through his coat and whistled about his ears, which still rang from the blasting of the great guns.

Thin, grey daylight began to overspread the sea, revealing the coast of France, faintly charcoaled across the south and nearer than

Hayden would like. In no direction was the horizon distant more than half a league. Beyond was obscured by rain and low, scudding cloud. Hayden went to the stern and, as he leaned his hands upon the taffrail, one of the French frigates emerged from a squall of rain. Aloft, French sailors could be seen setting top-gallants.

"Is that not the height of folly?" Archer wondered as he, too, came to the rail. "The horizon is less than half a league distant, and there is every sign that the wind is making and the squalls growing worse."

"It is the height of folly, Mr Archer, I agree entirely. But if he overhauls us before there is another squall . . ."

"Shall I order top-gallants, sir?"

A second of hesitation. "I do not believe we have another choice, Mr Archer."

The second frigate appeared at that moment, a little aft of and to leeward of the first. She was making sail in emulation of her sister. For a few moments Hayden stood at the rail, gauging the speed of the enemy ships. They were closing the gap, though there was some slight indication that the nearer frigate was a little faster than her sister—or so Hayden imagined. If he could but separate them by a league and a half, he would luff and bring this nearer ship to battle. If he could inflict enough damage on her rigging, he might gain some distance on them. But he hardly thought these Frenchmen would be so foolish. His only hope was that they would be separated by fog and he could act before they realised such distance had grown between them.

French ships, Hayden well knew, were reputed to be more lightly built than their British counterparts and notably faster, though Hayden was aware of enough instances of British ships chasing and catching French ships of similar rate that this argument did not impress him overly. The frigates in his wake, however, were larger and longer on the water line, and very likely did have a small advantage in swiftness. This advantage he hoped to overcome by seamanship and sail handling. In this, his father's people did have an advantage, he knew, for the British ships and their officers and crews were at sea in all weather for much of any given year, whereas the French ships languished in harbour bottled up by the Royal Navy blockade. Though, as he had stated to Hawthorne, these particular French vessels might be exceptions to this, as at least one—and very likely both—had been raiding British commerce for some months, and doing it regularly.

For a few moments he stood at the rail, watching the chasing enemy, looking for signs of poor seamanship—poorly trimmed sails, an indecisive hand upon the helm, tardiness in the sail handlers, but he saw none of these things.

"She appears crack, does she not, sir?" Archer had reappeared at the moment after passing along the orders to Barthe and Franks. Clearly, he was thinking along the same lines as his captain.

"I am afraid she does, Mr Archer." Hayden turned in a slow revolution, examining the brightening circle of sea within which his ship sailed.

"Mr Archer," Hayden began after a moment's contemplation, "I do believe I have made a mistake."

"Sir?"

"Order Mr Barthe to belay setting top-gallants."

Archer stood a moment; Hayden could feel him hesitating. "Aye, sir." He went off at a run, calling out to Mr Barthe and to the men aloft at once.

Although Barthe complied immediately, he did not order the men down off the yards. He hastened aft to Hayden, who remained at the taffrail, his eye fixed on the French frigates.

For a moment Barthe did the same, saying nothing, but then could not hold his peace. "They will be upon us in a trice, sir."

"Not if they are upon their beam-ends, Mr Barthe."

Barthe turned his attention to weather. "It is a gamble, Captain Hayden. There have been squalls in quick succession and then long lulls between."

"Let us hope I am not proven wrong. We shall luff through the squalls, Mr Barthe, and bear away the moment we are able. The French coast is too close for us to run off, and I do not wish to take in sail unless we must to save the ship." Hayden turned to eye the coast, which was almost obscured in the low cloud and mist.

"Only the best helmsman shall have the wheel, sir. I will make certain they understand your wishes completely."

"Thank you, Mr Barthe."

The sailing master went off, calling out the names of the men he wished to take the helm.

Hayden could never remember wishing for a squall, but it was his most fervent desire at that moment. For half of an hour he kept watch on the chasing ships and the northern horizon, willing a squall to burst out of the rain and scudding cloud . . . but none did.

Standing at the taffrail watching the chasing ships, Hayden felt chagrined to the point of mortification. He had made an unconscionable mistake. He should have doused his lamps and lain silently in the dark and hoped the French frigate had not seen or slipped off before the French discovered him. Returning Monsieur Benoît's intelligence to Britain had been paramount and he had foolishly let himself be drawn into an action with the French. He even wondered if pride had not been at work in this and he had not wished to appear shy before his crew—had even feared the Lords Commissioners might question his resolve. He cursed himself silently.

A bloom of smoke—quickly swept off to leeward—appeared at the bow of the nearer ship. A hundred yards aft of the *Themis* an iron ball splashed into the sea.

Among the crew there was shifting if not muttering. At sea, Hayden almost invariably made decisions quickly and with confidence, but this day he second-guessed himself at every turn.

Like a corpulent angel of doubt, the sailing master reappeared at his elbow at that moment.

"There is not a great deal of weight in this wind, sir," he observed.

"Did you not tell me it would make and haul aft, Mr Barthe?"

"I fear I might be proven wrong, sir," Barthe replied quietly.

"Let us hope not, Mr Barthe. Let us hope we are both proven right."

But the wind appeared to be defying both Hayden and Barthe; it was neither increasing in strength, altering its direction, nor sending the hoped-for squalls and gusts that Hayden was gambling on. In the normal course of things, Hayden would never order top-gallants carried in such weather, but present circumstances could hardly be termed "normal."

Again the French frigate fired her forward chase gun, the ball wounding the sea a little nearer than previously.

"Do you make it fifty miles to Pointe de Barfleur, Mr Barthe?"

"Nearer sixty, I should think, Captain."

"Nine hours, then? Perhaps ten?"

"Just after dusk, sir, if this wind holds."

"Will we weather it?"

The sailing master turned to look west, as though he could gauge the distance to the invisible point of France. "On this slant, sir? It will be very close run."

This only confirmed Hayden's own reckoning.

"I believe we could tack in this much wind, Captain," Barthe observed, staring fixedly at the chasing ship.

"On deck!" came a call from aloft. "Gust in the offing."

Hayden turned to windward and could see the tops of the waves being torn away in white spray, the sea rippling into fish scales as it did beneath a gust.

"Let us hope this presages our squall," Hayden said quietly to the sailing master.

The helmsman gauged the progress of the gust, measured its moment of arrival to a nicety, and luffed just enough to shake the wind out of the sails, but not so much as to have them thrown aback. Running off, downwind, was the safest way to meet squalls, but with the mizzen sheeted flat and the mainsail set, the ship would not steer off, and it was often necessary to hand those sails, or at least let sheets fly, before such a turn could be made.

The sails shook and tossed their clews about, rattling the rigging. Even so, the gust heeled the ship over to leeward. Hayden turned to see the effect on the French and found them doing the same, though heeled much further down.

The length of the *Themis'* deck, men whose attentions were not taken up by the present evolution stared, with great hope in their faces, at the heeling French ship.

"Carry away," Barthe muttered, apparently placing a curse on the enemy's top-gallant masts.

In a moment the gust withered away, and the helmsmen put their respective ships back on course, hard on the wind, as close as they could come without giving away speed. All along the deck there was a moan from the hands, and they turned away, back to their labours, with shaking heads.

Out of the companionway, the Reverend Mr Smosh appeared, pushing one arm into a woolen coat, then the other, settling the garment around his shoulders with a shrug. The doughy clergyman asked permission to approach the captain's private area of deck and came to the rail beside Hayden and Barthe.

"Have you come to take the air, Mr Smosh?" Barthe asked.

"Indeed I have, and the sights, Mr Barthe. One should never miss the sights." He paused to reflect. "In truth, my reading class has been superseded by the call of all hands. As I have no willing scholars this morning, and the doctor had no further use for me, I thought I might venture forth and see these French frigates I have been hearing much about."

"Well, there they are, sir," Barthe answered him, "as fine a team as you shall ever hope to see, I would venture."

The clergyman stared at the pursuing ships a moment. "Have they not more sails than we carry? Three tiers to our two?"

"Courses, topsails and top-gallants, Mr Smosh, but the captain believes we shall have a squall by and by and then we shall be more evenly matched in sails, for some of theirs shall carry away." Barthe turned to Hayden. "I thought that gust would convince these Frenchies to take in their top-gallants, but I see they have learned nothing from it."

"I had hoped the same," Hayden replied.

"Do they gain on us, then?" Smosh wondered.

"They do, Mr Smosh," Hayden informed him, "though so little in these winds that one can hardly measure it. I have been observing the speed of the vessels, and it seems for a while they get a wind that carries them nearer and then, for a time, the wind will favour us. Only a few moments ago the furthest vessel appeared to be gaining on her sister, but now she seems to have fallen back somewhat. We could go on in this same manner until darkness finds us, or the wind could carry our enemy up to us within the hour. We will see who the winds favour." Hayden had almost said "who the wind gods favour" but was reluctant to display such paganism before the clergyman.

Within the hour, the wind gods appeared to have made their decision in favour of the French, for the nearer ship began to lob shot very near the stern of the *Themis*, and Hayden had his own stern chase guns readied. Occasional gusts heeled the ships far over, though these were not so strong as to require luffing, though ships had a natural tendency to round up when so pressed. Squalls had ceased altogether, but rain and gusts were common, and the horizon never drew away beyond a league and it was commonly much nearer.

Noon saw the first French ball find the *Themis*, passing through the mizzen topsail and then the main topsail in turn. No other damage was reported, unless it was to the spirits of the hands, who became undeniably disconcerted.

The day's full light never seemed to arrive, a dull near-twilight prevailing, the hidden sun's glow never growing or lessening over the hours. Astern, the chasing ships appeared ominous and relentless, bearing down on them with a predatory determination. To Hayden, there seemed to be no human agency involved but only an unswerving, malevolent will. For someone who had commonly been the chaser, this was a feeling both singular and deeply unsettling.

A liquid bloom of grey-black enveloped the chasing ship's bow. The iron ball howled by scant yards to starboard, the report pealing in its wake.

"Mr Archer," Hayden addressed the young lieutenant, who hovered nearby. "Let us return fire."

The watch warned of a gust just then and the ship heeled to the wind, which whipped about them, pressing the ship over and causing the men at the helm to struggle with the wheel on a slanting deck. The sails appeared to stretch, tight as drum skins, pregnant and slick with rain.

"Luff!" Barthe ordered the helmsmen. "Luff! Let run the foresail's leeward sheet!"

The ship heeled, pressed down by the wind. A cracking of timber and shaking of sail alerted Hayden, who turned in time to see the Frenchman's main and fore top-gallant masts go by the lee at almost the same instant.

A squall of wind struck the speeding ships, shaking anything that was loose and whipping the pennants at the masthead so that they curled and cracked. Hayden saw the French cruiser rounding up into the wind, and then she was absorbed into the curtaining rain. Whether she had been caught aback he could not tell.

The clew of the *Themis'* mainsail flailed the air, threatening man and ship, until the wind relented and let the over-pressed and straining ship back onto her feet. She began to race on, the beam-sea lifting and lowering her in a plunging, ponderous rhythm.

The men on deck all cheered, as though they had been responsible for the enemy's ill luck. In that instant, their spirits lifted notably.

Hayden left the taffrail and went with the sailing master and Archer around the ship.

"We are stretching these shrouds, Mr Barthe," Hayden observed as they came to the standing rigging which supported the mainmast, "if we get upon the other tack, have Mr Franks employ his topburton tackle and set them up properly again."

For a moment all three looked up into the rigging at the straining sails, the rain driving to leeward and splattering against sailcloth and wooden deck.

"How much longer do you think we can carry our mainsail, Mr Barthe?" Hayden asked so that only the sailing master and Archer could hear.

Barthe shaded his eyes from the driving rain and gazed up. "I would have it off now if we had no Frenchmen in our wake."

Hayden was of the same opinion, and Archer nodded agreement. "Do you think they were caught aback?"

"The Frenchman?" Barthe contemplated this a moment. "I couldn't rightly say, Captain. The rain and mist closed over just as her masts went by the board. Perhaps not. I could not see her companion at that moment. Certainly, *she* might have all her masts standing yet."

Hayden looked up at the straining sail with some misgiving. "Let us carry the mainsail as long as we dare, then."

Hayden was sorely tempted to tack, trusting to the lack of visibility to hide them from the enemy—and throwing them off his trail entirely—but he was afraid they would pass close enough to one or the other of the chasing ships that they would be seen, and tacking in so much wind carrying all this sail was a dubious endeavour. Keeping on as he was appeared to be the only sensible course of action, for France was still ominously close to leeward. The thought that he bore information that might prove critical to the defence of England weighed upon him. Above all things, he needed to get into an English port, but he dared not let that push him into doing something reckless that might lead to the loss of his ship. He cursed himself now for engaging the enemy and not attempting to slip away. If what Benoît had told him was true, then certainly that knowledge was worth a hundred French frigates. Before he had been concerned that the Lords Commissioners of the Admiralty would think this reported invasion unlikely and judge him shy for not engaging the frigate; now he wondered if they would not think him a fool for not racing back to England with Benoît's information and upbraid him for avarice and prize hunting when clearly the other matter was of critical importance.

"Mr Archer, order the stove lit. Send the men down to breakfast forty at a time. Keep the other men at their stations. We are in French waters yet, and the two frigates chasing us might not be the only enemy vessels we discover this day."

"Aye, sir." Archer touched his hat and hastened away.

Men had been stationed to watch on all quarters of the ship as well as aloft. The coast was distressingly near, and this poor visibility might lead to surprises Hayden would not welcome. Upon the upper deck, the enforced silence only made the subdued spirits of the men seem more unnatural and ominous.

When smoke began to drift up from the cooking-stove, the men's spirits rose a little, and at eight bells, when the first men were sent down to break their fasts, there was a noticeable lightening of the mood.

The French ships had not appeared in their wake in almost two hours, and this, too, had its leavening effect. Mr Barthe ordered the log streamed and recorded their speed as just exceeding six knots. Following a quick consultation with his charts, Barthe calculated that Barfleur would appear two hours after dark. What concerned the sailing master were the unpredictable tidal currents in that area of the Channel, and he clomped about the deck with a notable scowl upon his doughy face. The leadsman was set to work swinging his sounding lead, but no bottom was found at twenty fathoms, which was information that neither granted comfort nor caused undue alarm.

Squalls continued to sweep down upon them at intervals, often materializing out of the blear not a hundred yards to starboard. The men standing watch and the helmsmen were ever upon the alert, but the murk disguised these bursts of weather until they were all but upon them.

Hayden took a quick breakfast in the gunroom; his own cabin remained dismantled. Despite Hayden's having been blessed with excellent and dutiful officers, they were, with the exception of Mr Barthe, relatively inexperienced and new to their responsibilities. Their judgement had not yet been tested in difficult situations. He only hoped his own, impaired as it was by an almost constant anxiety about his own troubles, would not prove lacking.

Over the course of the morning, the seas built and were soon striking the topsides and sending spray high up into the rigging, where it slatted against sails and slashed down upon the deck with such force it almost seemed not to be liquid at all. The bellying mainsail was watched with a particular fascinated horror. If it had not been of fairly recent vintage it would surely have let go by then, but its seams held up, and Hayden continued to carry it, breaking all seagoing conventions to reef the topsail to ease the strain on the ship while keeping the mainsail set.

There was no sun to allow a noon-sight, but this important hour—the beginning of the ship's day—was marked, the glass turned, log streamed. Now that the *Themis* was apparently free of chasing ships, and the crew had been fed, the men's mood lifted and became almost content, despite the disagreeable weather.

This was only temporarily altered when a black-hulled transport appeared almost under their bow and avoided collision only by some intercession of divine nature. Under normal circumstances, Hayden would have chased it down and made it a prize, if possible, but today he watched it slip astern, trying not to think of the money it represented. He was even more concerned that it might encounter the chasing frigates and inform their captains that the *Themis* held upon her course.

The men, too, watched the little coaster disappear astern, engendering much muttering and many an aggrieved look. How dare a prize appear at *that* moment? Had it no consideration at all?

The wind, which had remained remarkably constant throughout the morning, began to shift from north-north-east to north-north-west. Each time the wind went into the north-north-west Barthe would consult the compass and charts, stream the log, and recalculate their position and likelihood of doubling Pointe de Barfleur. On one of these occasions, Hayden went below to look at the chart with the master, who was guarding this valuable paper from rain on a makeshift table at the foot of the aft companionway.

Hayden glanced at the little "cocked hat"—the triangle within which Mr Barthe believed the *Themis* lay at that moment.

"We get a better slant each time the wind backs into the east," the sailing master observed, "but I fear we are being driven below our course more frequently." He placed a blunt finger upon the chart, a small peninsula that shifted over the paper sea as he spoke. "There is a rocky shoal extending out from Barfleur Point to the north-east which we must avoid at all costs."

"Will we pass outside the shoal or not, Mr Barthe?" Hayden asked. "Or will we be forced to wear her around, for we dare not tack in such a wind."

"I am most sorry, Captain Hayden, but the currents in this bay are not entirely predictable . . ." He stared unhappily at his chart a moment. "I cannot say for certain that we shall."

It was not the news Hayden wished to hear, but nor did he want an overly optimistic lie at that moment. "I appreciate your candour, Mr Barthe. Better we know the truth. Pointe de Barfleur is very low and in this foul weather will not be visible until we are upon it. I say we wear ship now while we have room, and hope the French are far enough behind that they cannot take advantage of us."

"I agree, sir." Barthe's shoulders relaxed a little and there was less tension in his tone.

"Then let us begin immediately."

The two men went up the ladder, but before they had emerged onto the deck a cry came from the lookout Hayden had positioned on the mizzen top.

"*On deck!* Ship on our starboard quarter."

Immediately, Hayden and Barthe went to the rail and stood gazing at the vessel, which had top-gallant masts standing yet.

"Can that be one of our Frenchmen?" Barthe wondered aloud. "How could she get so far to windward of us?"

"She might have had more east in her wind than we have received."

Barthe unleashed a string of curses aimed, perhaps, at the French or the fickle wind or both.

Hayden called for a glass and fixed the French frigate in it just as a hoist of signals went up behind the sails of her mainmast.

"Signals, sir," Archer observed as he arrived at the rail.

"Yes, but is there really a second ship or is she trying to make us think she is not alone?"

No one spoke a moment as they stood gazing at the indistinct form of a frigate in the drizzle and mist.

"Shall I give the order to wear ship?" Barthe enquired.

Hayden did not reply but stood weighing all the possibilities, all the scraps of knowledge he possessed about their present position. They did not know precisely where they were, a dangerous point of land and shoal lay somewhere ahead, a single enemy frigate was stationed on his quarter, and a second might not be too distant. If he wore, these ships might trap him in a corner. If he did not wear, his ship might be in danger of going ashore. There was also a slim possibility that they might weather Barfleur and its imposing shoal. Hayden had never felt so paralysed. There seemed to be no course that offered a better possibility of success. The part of him that made these decisions on gut instinct appeared to have abandoned him entirely.

"I think it might be a danger to stand on, Captain," the sailing master observed quietly.

"If we wear, we might end up in a corner fighting two frigates of superior strength, Mr Barthe. Is there any chance that we might double Barfleur? Can you not give me a more certain answer?"

Barthe would not meet his eye. "I regret that I cannot, sir."

Hayden almost sighed. "Then we shall wear ship and prepare to fight if we must. All hands to wear ship, Mr Archer."

"Aye, sir. All hands to wear ship, Mr Franks!"

Although it took hardly a moment for the crew to find their stations, Hayden was barely able to retain his exasperation. The entire

time, he observed the French ship through his glass, attempting to
see if her captain had ordered his own men to make ready to wear.

"Aloft there!" Hayden called to the hand on the main-top, preserving his hat with one hand as he looked up. "Does this Frenchman
make ready to wear?"

The crewman stared a moment through his glass. "I cannot be
certain, sir, but I don't believe she does, Captain."

"Let us hope he is correct," Hayden muttered to Archer.

"Up mainsail and mizzen! Brace in the after-yards!" A brief pause.
"Up helm!"

The ship began to turn to larboard, seas and wind veering aft.

"Lay the headyards square. Shift over the headsheets!"

Yards were braced, tacks and sheets eased and hauled. The stern
of the ship came through the wind and the *Themis* settled upon her
new course, which would take them more or less back to Le Havre
on their present wind.

Hayden noted Barthe and Archer sharing a glance, both unhappy.

The Frenchman had stood on less than a quarter of a mile before
perceiving what his enemy was about, and he brought the wind
across her stern, though not quite so quickly as the English. When
both ships had settled upon their new course, the French were on
the larboard quarter, but not so far to the north as they had been.
Immediately, upon her new course, a bloom of smoke appeared to
leeward of the French frigate, and a moment later the report reached
the officers standing upon the *Themis'* quarterdeck.

Archer turned to Hayden in surprise. "Certainly we are beyond
the range of eighteen-pounders?"

"Indeed we are, Mr Archer, but that gun was not aimed at us.
They are merely trying to alert their sister ship."

Hayden had sent the men back down to the guns and exchanged
the lookout on the end of the jib-boom. If the second frigate ap-

peared out of this murk, Hayden wanted to see it first. He had witnessed the calamitous results of collision at sea and never wanted that particular experience again.

Archer had positioned himself by the binnacle and sighted steadily across the compass at the chasing ship. "Sir," he said after a few moments. "We appear to be holding our own—not pulling away, but neither are we losing."

"I am happy to hear it, Mr Archer." Hayden fixed the enemy in his glass. "Let us hope this wind drops away, for we have our top-gallant masts standing and our top-gallants still bent, while one of the enemy ships has neither."

This observation spread a little cheer around the quarterdeck, but over the next three quarters of an hour the wind only appeared to be making.

"Ship!" one of the forward lookouts called out. "Point an' a 'alf off the starboard bow."

Hayden hurried forward, as a ship appeared to take form out of mist and rain.

"Open starboard gunports!" Hayden called. "Run out the guns!"

The two ships were hard on the wind on opposite tacks and about to pass within a quarter of a mile. The sea running made opening gunports potentially dangerous, but Hayden had been paying close attention to this particular matter and thought they could risk it yet. Almost before they were aware, the ships drew within firing range. The British, though, were a little better prepared and fired their broadside first, tearing through sails and sending splinters whirling up into the wind.

The reply was not quite so effective; Hayden was certain only two-thirds of the guns had fired, the remaining crews not recovering from the *Themis'* broadside in time.

And then the ships were past. Hayden stood at the rail and

watched the frigate absorb into the blear. That ship had no top-gallant masts. At the moment it disappeared—he was not certain, but so it seemed—the ship began a turn to larboard.

"Aloft there!" Hayden called to the man upon the mizzen top. "Do they wear ship? Can you see?"

"I cannot be certain, sir . . . Perhaps."

"Perhaps" was a particularly useless assessment of the situation, Hayden thought.

"Certainly they will wear if they had not begun to do so," Archer observed, as he appeared from below where he had been overseeing the guns.

"I was only hoping to ascertain how distant they might be by the time they were upon our course. It is always good to know where your enemy might be, Mr Archer, especially on days such as this."

Archer nodded. "If I may, sir," he said quietly, "what shall we do now? Assuming the common allowance for leeway, our course will take us into the harbour of Le Havre, or very nearly."

"Yes, we are embayed. Unless the wind goes into the north-west we shall have to wear, but I would rather wait until darkness is complete before I attempt it."

"It is nigh on eight bells, Captain. The sun will set in just more than three hours, and in this murk, darkness shall not be far behind." Archer leaned a little closer to Hayden. "But certainly the French captains will comprehend that we will attempt to elude them—will they not?"

"I expect they shall, but as long as there is only one within sight, I think we might tack or wear and fight that one off if we must."

"We could set adrift a barrel with a lamp, sir."

"Have the cooper make up a barrel, Mr Archer, though I dare say the French have most likely done the same thing themselves at some time or other. It is an old dodge."

The day wore on, the fickle wind making and taking off, originating from various northerly points of the compass. For a time the wind took off sufficiently for Hayden to have the reefs shaken out of his topsails, but an hour later they were all tied in again. Through the late afternoon the one visible frigate gained a little on the British ship, then lost a little, but overall held her position, the *Themis* proving her equal in speed and weatherliness.

Sometime before the shy sun vanished a dreary twilight settled, the sea turning dull as old coffee, wind cooling noticeably. The men were sent down to their meals at intervals, and only the necessary watch kept the deck in the nasty weather. It was one of the advantages of a frigate; the lower deck—the berth-deck—was free of guns and dedicated to housing and feeding the crew. Messes, each with its own table and benches, were neatly arranged to starboard and larboard, and the men slung their hammocks there by night. It was, comparatively, a dry and, if not warm, at least not uncommonly cold place. Here the watch below could yarn or seek whatever diversions the ship would offer, or sing and play upon Irish whistles and fiddles.

Hayden took a turn through the ship just before sunset and found the cooper, standing among three half-made barrels, a perplexed expression on his face.

"I am not heartened by your look, Pike," Hayden said to the man. "Is there some problem?"

"I've made up three barrels—or started to—and they're no great shakes, sir—none of 'em."

Even Hayden could see the staves—what Pike was calling "shakes"—were poorly fitted.

"I don't know who the coopers were who made these up, sir, but they did not know their trade, that is certain." He glanced up at Hayden. "But I'll find one that will answer, sir. Don't you worry."

"I shall refrain from worrying." Hayden did not put much faith in hanging a lantern on a barrel, anyway.

Upon concluding his tour of the ship, Hayden put his head in the door of the gunroom. He found Smosh and Griffiths taking a glass of wine with Mr Hawthorne.

"Will you join us, Captain?" Hawthorne asked, rising more quickly than the others.

"I thank you, Mr Hawthorne, but not at this time. I have decided to wear ship as soon as it is properly dark. The wind has finally decided that it will not back into the north-west, and shows a distinct inclination to do the opposite."

"We were, but a few moments ago, discussing this very matter, Captain," Smosh explained. "I have noted that winds appear to sometimes 'haul' aft and at others 'haul' forward. Winds also have a habit of backing in different directions, making me wonder how one knows which way they are 'backing' or 'hauling.'" The little clergyman was very red-faced, and to any other might appear to be in his cups, but Hayden well knew the man's enormous capacity for drink. His mind would remain quite clear and his physical abilities undiminished when many another would be insensible.

"When speaking of winds relative to the ship, Mr Smosh, they can haul either aft or forward, though when you hear it said that we shall haul our wind it always means that we shall sail as near to the wind as we are able. We say the wind is 'backing' when it alters its course in a manner opposite to what would be common. In most cases, in the Northern Hemisphere, the wind changes from east by south to west and then into the north. When it does the opposite, we say it is backing."

"Is it not . . . confusing to have the wind 'haul' or 'back' in different directions?"

"Not to seamen," Hayden replied.

"Well, I for one wish the wind would only 'haul' in one manner. It is rather like the orders to put one's helm to starboard, which is followed by the helmsman turning his wheel in what appears to be the opposite direction, to my understanding, and the ship turning to larboard."

Hayden pointed at the massive tiller which swung below the deck-beams aft of the table. "When the helmsman is ordered to put his helm to starboard we are referring to the tiller, Mr Smosh, not the wheel, which, as you say, is turned in what would appear to be the opposite direction. Thus, the ship turns to larboard."

"The wheel is turned to larboard. The ship turns to larboard, and yet the order is to put one's helm to starboard. It is rather contradictory, I find. And does one not say, 'port your helm,' which will then turn the ship to starboard? Why does one not say put your helm to larboard?"

"The words 'larboard' and 'starboard' are very easily confused on a stormy night or in the midst of an action, so the term 'port' is substituted for 'larboard.'"

"But when referring to the sides of the ship, you say 'larboard' and not 'port' . . . Why is confusion not as likely there?"

"In truth," admitted Hayden, "it is, and I have seen it myself. There are some very respected officers who have argued that 'larboard' should be replaced by 'port,' but there are many more officers who do not like to see change, no matter how commonsensical it might be."

"I am, myself, a great lover of traditions, Captain, but some do see their day pass and should give way." Smosh took a sip of his wine. "So the wind is 'hauling forward'?"

"So it would appear. If you will forgive me, I must return to the deck."

All present rose and made more or less proper salutes, and Hayden let himself out. As the door closed behind him he heard Smosh saying, "I have come to find lying to in a small gale most restful. Once one has adjusted one's thinking to the idea that a ship will not founder in such circumstances, the motion of the ship I find rather comforting . . ."

Night had settled over the Channel by the time Hayden emerged onto the deck. The French frigate remained in her place, unable to close the gap, but preventing Hayden from tacking if the wind should ever take off sufficiently to allow it. For a time Hayden watched the chasing ship, her lights winking in and out as she lifted, then settled between the seas. Brief squalls of rain would hide her entirely for moments at a time, but then these would pass and the dim little specks of light would appear.

"Pass the word for Mr Archer and Mr Barthe, if you please, Mr Gould."

The young middy touched his hat, the blackness of the night hiding his expression entirely. A few moments later, the first lieutenant and sailing master hurried onto the quarterdeck.

"I have been observing the Frenchman," Hayden informed them, "and she is quite hidden from us during these little squalls of rain that sweep through periodically. It is my intention to wear ship during one of these, and be upon the other tack before the French realise what we are about. Dispose the crew to wear ship, Mr Barthe."

"Aye, sir." The sailing master went off calling for Franks.

"We dare not open our gunports, Mr Archer," Hayden said, "but we might have employment for our upper-deck guns. Man them and have them ready."

"Aye, Captain."

Although Hayden's crew had become accustomed to such evolutions on their recent convoy, in even severer weather, Hayden still did not like to have men out on the yards in so much wind and with such a sea running. The mizzen must be brailed up and the mainsail taken in to allow the ship to turn, and in the wet and dark and cold the mainsail would feel like a sheet of iron, both stiff and weighty.

The hands went to their stations quietly, without any muttering. The import of this manoeuvre was not lost upon them.

And then they waited, the rain pelting down, wind stealing away the warmth of their bodies until hands became numb and fingers obeyed orders but poorly. For the better part of an hour the weather, though it did not abate, would not bring them the squall of rain they required. Hayden was wondering how much longer he could keep the men at their stations and began to think he had made an error, when the lights of the distant ship dissolved in a watery gloom. A moment later a wind, tearing the tops of the seas and tumbling them to leeward, heeled the ship and smothered it in rain.

Hayden gave the word to the sailing master, who called out through his speaking trumpet.

"Up mainsail and mizzen! Brace in the after-yards!"

The order was repeated by the bosun and his mates, who had stationed themselves at intervals along the deck, for on such a windy night orders were very easily blown to leeward. Protecting his face with a hand, Hayden attempted to gaze out into the gale, but beyond thirty yards all was streaming, liquid darkness.

The *Themis*, as though aware of her situation, answered her helm more smartly than usual and brought the wind across her stern with all speed. In a few moments she was shaping her course north-west by west, out into the Channel. Hayden went to the corner made by the taffrail and starboard bulwarks and gazed out into the darkness, but could see nothing, even though the squall was all but past.

"Aloft there," he called up to the mizzen lookout. "Can you see the Frenchman? Do they wear ship?"

There was no answer a moment and Hayden was about to repeat his call, but louder, when a voice came from above. "Sir! I see them, off the starboard quarter. She's not wearing . . . Wait, sir. I believe they have smoked us, Captain. Bloody frogs are wearing, sir."

Being half a "bloody frog," Hayden tried to not take the remark personally.

A call was heard on the forecastle, which was repeated along the deck.

"Ship on the larboard bow!"

"Ship on the larboard bow!"

Hayden dashed forward as quickly as the swaying deck would allow. There, not two pistol shots distant, was the second frigate about to pass to leeward.

"Stand by to fire," Hayden called and the guns were traversed by crowbars and brute strength.

"Fire as she bears, Mr Baldwin," Hayden ordered.

A moment, and then the first gun belched flame and smoke, the report assaulting all of Hayden's senses. The assault was repeated until all the deck guns had been fired, and more than one had been fired twice. And then the sounds of nature prevailed, the wind and driven rain. Almost a silence, Hayden felt.

For the first time in twenty-some hours, Hayden took a breath that did not feel constrained. Their course was by far the most favourable they had managed in many hours—almost for Plymouth, the French had been taken by surprise, and he knew that his ship could keep the distance between them as long as the wind did not betray them. Their escape seemed, if not certain, at least very likely. Let the gale grow as severe as it liked; the blacker the night, the more likely they would shake off the French.

The watch below was released, and even much of the watch on deck was allowed to huddle on the gun-deck at the foot of the companionway—reward for having been left out in the weather so long.

Hayden had kept the deck most of the long day and much of the night before, and felt burdened with fatigue, his thoughts tending to wander and then slide towards emptiness, his limbs thick and stiff and slow to respond to his wishes. Sleep, he knew, was required to keep his mind and body alert and decisive, but he could not afford it now. Not in this ever-changing situation where a mere shift in the wind might see two French frigates upon them in a trice. He called for coffee again and took it in the warmth of the gunroom with Lieutenant Archer, who had the good sense to leave him unmolested for a quarter of the hour.

Too soon he returned to the deck, the night seeming both colder and darker, the wind more penetrating. Rain slatted down upon the ship in hard-driven squalls, and the wind sang an unholy choir in the rigging.

Ransome was the officer of the watch, and he huddled in the lee of a carronade, his back to the wind.

"Where is our Frenchman?" Hayden asked him.

The young lieutenant straightened up at the sight of Hayden and pointed sharply out into the darkness gathered in the north-east. "There-away, sir. Her position is unchanged. She neither gains nor loses upon this wind, and as far as we know still has her top-gallants, though Mr Wickham swore he saw the Frenchman take them in some time ago. One of the lookouts has reported a second light which appears and disappears, not abeam but forward of our larboard quarter some ways off, sir. We surmise it is the second Frenchman, sir."

This was not welcome news to Hayden, but the darkness allowed him to hide his reaction.

"And our wind?"

"It veers about somewhat, Captain. I cannot be sure of it, but I believe it is hauling into the west, which would be our luck this day."

"Luck is for whist, Mr Ransome." Hayden was about to ask their course but went instead to the binnacle to see for himself. Indeed, the wind was hauling into the west somewhat and already their course was not so favourable. Mr Barthe had retired to take some rest, so Hayden called for his mate, and Dryden was very quickly in attendance.

"What is your belief?" Hayden asked him. "Have we weathered Barfleur or no?"

"Mr Barthe is quite certain we have, sir," Dryden assured him. "But we are no longer sailing for England, Captain, I am sorry to report. This course will take us out into the Atlantic."

Hayden contemplated this information a moment. "Well, it is a large ocean; certainly we can get lost out there."

"So one would hope, sir."

Hayden looked at their position on the chart—not so very far north of the Channel Islands.

"Do you think we might get under the guns at St Peter Port, Captain?" Dryden asked, apparently considering the same options as Hayden.

"It is a risk, that is certain. If this ship to leeward can bring us to or impede us in any way, her consort would be upon us. Although I am sorely tempted, I think I will stand on into the Atlantic. We have frigates watching the entrance to Brest. That is our last hope if we cannot slip away on our own; we would have to elude this ship to leeward to turn south for Brest, but many things can change in a few hours. We shall see what the winds bring us." Hayden did not want to get bottled up in Guernsey when he had such decisive information to carry to the Admiralty in London.

Hayden clambered back up the swaying ladder and took a turn about the deck, speaking to the men quietly, reassuring them with his presence and showing not the least concern for the French or their present position. The truth was, though, he did not like it or feel the least reassured by it. There were two frigates nearby, one somewhat to windward and on his quarter, the other preventing him from turning south. Come daylight they would, if they were able, bring his ship to battle—something Hayden knew he must avoid at any cost less than his ship. Escape by darkness was his best hope, but wearing ship would send him back towards Le Havre and there was nothing to be gained on that tack. The north wind had him pinned up against the coast of Normandy and made Hayden feel a little too much like a sheep being herded along by a pair of collies, each waiting to bite at his heels should he tarry.

At that moment the windward ship fired three guns in slow succession, the muzzle flash illuminating the rain with garish reds and coppery yellows. A moment later, this signal was answered by her sister with two guns, a pause of five seconds, and then a third.

Hayden returned to the quarterdeck.

"What are they saying, I wonder?" Ransome speculated aloud.

"Very likely that the chase is still in sight. I do not think they are planning to attack by night with this sea running and gusts sinking our gunports every quarter of the hour. They are waiting for daylight and a moderating wind. At least one of which we shall certainly have by and by."

"If we cannot slip away this night, they shall have us, then, on the morrow?"

"We have some luck on our side. One of the Frenchmen lost her top-gallant masts and will probably not send up new ones until the weather moderates. We can keep ourselves ahead of her. The other frigate will not attack us alone."

"But could she not attack us and either bring us to or hinder us enough for her consort to catch us up? Then we should have two frigates to fight and only a miracle might save us."

"An English sea officer might chance that, for we commonly come out ahead when broadsides are of equal strength. But this captain is most likely well aware that our gunnery at close range might disable him and then we would escape altogether. No, I believe he will wait until both ships can be brought into action at the same time, or nearly so. After all, we have nowhere to escape to at the moment. We cannot reach England on this slant, and with the wind hauling into the west and perhaps west-north-west we will in all likelihood be driven towards France. Help might materialize." Hayden turned and peered out into the darkness, just able to perceive a faint point of light that appeared and winked out. "I am of a mind, however, that this plan— if it is indeed what they are thinking—might, in the end, favour us, for there will almost certainly be British frigates lying off Brest, and if we are forced out into the Atlantic and have a wind that will allow it, we will shape our course towards that port and hope we can turn the tables on these Frenchmen."

And so the night went, wind and rain coming from the north, the wind backing and then veering, toying with the *Themis* and her crew. Deciding that dawn should be the time when he must be most alert, Hayden had a partial wall of his cabin re-erected and his cot slung there. Sleep eluded him for most of this time, for his mind was overburdened with troubles both present and domestic. Brief reveries that verged on sleep would creep over him, but then he would be startled awake by the news that Henrietta married or by boarding Frenchmen forcing their way into his cabin, and then he would lie catching his breath a moment only to fall back into a state of near sleep, or torpor, perhaps, nightmares lying in wait just beyond sleep's border.

Three

The library was her sanctuary. It was not that the members of Henrietta's family did not read—they read ceaselessly, in truth—but each member of the Carthew clan had their own favoured hideaway where they indulged this cherished pastime. Her father read in his study, half reclining—and sometimes fully asleep—upon an ancient divan. Her mother preferred the morning room for its light, though she read at a small table, her book flat, ankles daintily crossed. Her sister, Penelope, read on a window seat upon the main staircase landing where she could note all the comings and goings of servants, guests, and family. Anne read always in her own chamber, propped upon pillows on her bed—a practise much disapproved of by their mother, who thought it implied laziness if it was not downright slovenly. The inglenook by the fire was Cassandra's preferred place, and then only in the evenings. Like everyone else in the family, she detested cards and games in general; conversation was the main entertainment of the Carthew family. During the daylight hours Cassandra was invariably to be found out of doors, even in the most inclement weather. If she was not upon her horse—and commonly she was—then collecting birds with one of the huntsmen, her poor maid for chaperon, would be her next choice. The Carthew family birdskin collection was said to be second to none and no one thought anything of setting off for some distant corner of England to seek a rare species. Their only regret was that the present war made collecting journeys abroad so difficult.

The library, therefore, was left to Henrietta. Here she read, kept up with her extensive correspondence, and worked away on her secret novel—which everyone in the family knew about.

If Henrietta had a second sanctuary it was within the novel itself, for she travelled there often, her imagination, both rich and fertile, fashioning a place almost as real as her own home. Her world within a world. At least in that world there was hope that things might work out to someone's advantage. Heartache was followed by redemption, the virtuous were rewarded for constancy and nobility of action. The untrustworthy and the weak of will, if not punished, did not prosper in the long run—not within the length of the novel, at any rate. The world of the novel had order. Beyond the library, or at least beyond Box Hill, lay chaos. A world not under the control of one Miss Henrietta Carthew. In such a place some undeserving French refugee might steal away the affection of a man she had believed constant and noble above all other men.

She looked down at the page she had been writing and realised that tears had dribbled down upon the words and spoiled them here and there, running the ink into tiny pools. Snatching up a hanky she kept to hand for just such emergencies, she dabbed at her eyes, sat back in her chair to assess the damage to her page, and released something that was half a laugh, half a sob.

"You are absurd," she scolded herself in a whisper. "Weeping upon your precious book and ruining the pages. It is something your heroine might do." She took up a sheaf of paper and began fanning the spoiled page, attempting to dry the little pools in which minute veins of ink roiled slowly.

There was, at that moment, an unholy clatter beyond the door and then it burst open, revealing the red face of her youngest sister, Penelope, who had apparently run from some distant part of the house.

"She is here!" Penelope announced much more loudly than Henrietta thought necessary.

"And who might 'she' be, pray?" Henrietta responded.

"Elizabeth, of course; who else have we been awaiting these three days past? She's speaking with Mama."

Henrietta began to rise. "Well, I must come, then, mustn't I."

Penelope glanced over her shoulder and then backed up against the doorframe. "Here she is! Here she is!" she literally sang out, then gave a little quiver of excitement.

Elizabeth swept through the door at that moment.

"You will not stay shut up here all day with Henri, will you, Lizzie?" Penelope pleaded. "She is terribly morose, you know . . . on account of . . . well, we are not allowed to say his name. But she is awfully dreary and not good company at all."

"You may rest assured, my dear Penelope, I will visit with everyone who can tolerate my company."

"Promise?"

"With all my heart."

Pen gave another little shiver of anticipation, glanced at her sister, curtsied, and went out as quickly as she had entered.

Elizabeth Hertle drew the door closed behind her. The two women embraced. In truth, they nearly threw themselves into each other's arms, and Henrietta found her tears flowing again and bit her lip in an attempt to staunch them.

"How do you fare, my dear?" Elizabeth enquired as they pulled themselves apart.

"Poorly, if I am to be honest."

They sat down upon the sofa, turned towards each other, Elizabeth gazing into her cousin's face. "You do not look well. I am sure you have not been out of doors in a week. We will go for a long walk this very afternoon. I insist upon it."

"I suppose I should take the air . . ." Henrietta closed her eyes. "I still cannot believe it of him . . ." she whispered, barely able to force the words out. And then she gave way and sobbed, Elizabeth giving her a shoulder.

"There, there, my dear. It pains me to see you so disconsolate. Clearly, Charles' actions have made him unworthy of your sorrow."

"I cannot help it . . ." Henrietta managed.

"No. I do not suppose you can. Heartbreak is akin to an illness; time is required to effect a cure. In the meantime, we have no choice but to endure all the pain and suffering. But we must do everything within our power to shorten the duration of this malady. Therefore, we shall walk and take the air and speak of other things besides the perfidious Charles Hayden, may he be turned before the mast."

"I do not wish him ill," Henrietta said in a small voice. "I cannot. He made me no promise, I keep telling myself. Even so . . ." She pulled away and wiped her red-rimmed eyes yet again.

"Indeed, he did make you a promise in both word and deed and in his letters as well. And he has betrayed that promise in the most contemptible manner possible."

"She must be very beautiful," Henrietta blurted out, unable to stop herself. "Everyone says she is. Do you think in the end he was simply more French than English and required a French wife?"

"I shall waste no time fashioning excuses for him. He acted in the most cruel manner towards you and I will never forgive him. Charles Hayden will never be welcome in my house again, despite being Captain Hertle's dearest friend. I do not care. He is banished. All of his vanities about wine and food may be displayed elsewhere."

Henrietta could not help but remember it was Robert and Eliza-beth who insisted Charles display this particular knowledge—not

Charles, who was invariably modest about his own accomplishments.

"I do have something I need to tell you, Henri," Elizabeth announced, taking her cousin's hands in both of her own. "Captain Hayden came to my house a few days ago. I did not receive him, of course, nor would I accept even a note. But he is in London . . . or was."

"Oh . . ." Henrietta heard herself say, and she slumped back against the cushion. "I see . . . Come to join his bride, no doubt. Was he alone?"

"He was, or so I was told."

"Well, it is his country—or one of them—he may come and go as he pleases." She thought a moment. "He could have written me. It would have broken my heart, no doubt, but better that than learning of his marriage in the manner that I did and adding humiliation atop disappointed hopes."

"It was the least he could have done, but he was too cowardly. Brave as he might be at sea . . ." She let the sentence hang.

Neither spoke for a moment, and then Henrietta ventured, "How long does it take the heart to heal, do you think?"

Elizabeth seemed to believe this a serious question rather than rhetorical. "In my experience and from observation, six months, though I have known recovery to take a year or more, depending upon the heart and how cruelly it was broken."

"A year," Henrietta repeated dully. "It is a long time . . . I do wish there were some physic that would put me to sleep for a twelve-month and allow me to wake recovered, all my troubles behind me."

"Yes, that would be the answer for many a broken heart, but instead we must endure. It is the English way, I fear." She was about to say more, but the door opened quietly and a young man appeared and then pretended to be surprised in a manner that convinced no one.

"Miss Henrietta, Mrs Hertle!" A pleasant smile overspread his face. "I do apologise. I thought the library empty."

"Mr Beacher." Elizabeth smiled, clearly pleased. "What an unlooked-for pleasure. Have you recently arrived as well?"

"No, I have taken up residence here, at least temporarily, to bring some order to Mr Carthew's collections. A more daunting task than originally I had anticipated."

"And how fare your labours, Frank?" Henrietta asked. They had known each other since childhood and had been upon Christian names since the age of six.

"I have had to recruit some aid to tackle the insects—a friend from school."

"They must be formidable insects if you require aid to 'tackle' them." Elizabeth smiled sweetly.

"You know those scarab beetles, snap a man in half if he is not wary."

"Well, do not let your guard down, by all means," Elizabeth responded. "Then we shall have the pleasure of your company at dinner?"

"Indeed." Beacher realised he was being politely dismissed—that he was, in fact, intruding. "I shall look forward to it with great anticipation. Until dinner, then."

And he backed out, closing the door behind him.

"You have never mentioned in your letters that Frank Beacher was lodging here."

"These last years, whenever he is not at school, he is lurking about Box Hill somewhere. Pen is rather mad for him, I think."

"And who is he 'mad for,' pray?" Elizabeth asked, paying particular attention to the answer.

"Pen, I assume."

"That would be something of a drastic change in his feelings, given that he has been in love with you since he was a boy."

"Oh, Lizzie, do not be absurd!" Henrietta actually laughed, something she had not done in some time. "Frank is like a brother to me. There is as much romantic feeling between us two as you would commonly find between a horse and . . . and a dove. In truth, we hardly pay each other any mind. He is off with my father's collections and I . . . well, I have been taken up with other matters of late."

"My dear Henri, you are so modest in your opinion of your own qualities that you interpret any man's interest in you as merely platonic. But Frank's interest in you is of an entirely different nature; he has been your ardent admirer for more than a decade, to which end he has ingratiated himself with your parents and all of your sisters, gaining everyone's good opinion so that they might aid him in his pursuit of the only sister he truly cares for. *You*, my dear."

"Elizabeth, you are not being sensible. Frank has never shown the least preference for my society over that of my sisters, Pen in particular. He has certainly never spoken or said a word that would indicate the least attachment to me other than of a familial nature. No, he is the brother I never had." She laughed again. "My sisters call him 'the hound,' forever trotting along after us, ever amiable, always willing to fetch whatever a lady might want. No, you are certainly wrong about Frank . . ." Her look changed to something like anxiety. "Do you not agree?"

"Of course I do not agree, because I am not wrong. Frank has hidden his preference for you because he is by nature shy and because he is afraid that you will rebuff him. Poor Mr Beacher is waiting for you to take notice of him or show some sign that you return his feelings. He will never speak for fear that you will dash his hopes entirely, for he simply cannot give up; he is hopelessly in love."

Henrietta was now genuinely distressed. "Oh, my . . . Elizabeth, this is awful. I have never felt anything for Frank but brotherly affection. Poor Frank. Are you certain of this?"

"Most certain."

"Oh dear . . ." Henrietta intoned. "Have I been torturing poor Frank, then, without meaning to?"

"'Torturing' might not be the word I would choose, but certainly you have not been making his life more pleasant."

"I . . . I do not know what to say. Or do. Certainly, I should dissuade him of any hopes he might hold for me . . ."

"As kindly as you are able, for I fear it will be a terrible blow to him. Since the day Charles Hayden became an object of your attention Mr Beacher has been very dejected, I should imagine, but now his hopes are rekindled, the flame growing. Snuffing it out, as you must . . . unless you do harbour feelings for Frank that you have never really examined—"

"Really, Lizzie," Henrietta interrupted, oddly uncomfortable with the subject, "now you *are* talking nonsense. I am not that insensible of my own feelings."

But Henrietta did feel rather foolish and obtuse. How could she have been unaware of Frank's attachment? Perceptiveness about such matters was a small vanity of hers, and here, beneath her very nose, she had failed to take notice of Frank Beacher and his feelings. Was it possible that Elizabeth was mistaken? She glanced over at her self-possessed cousin. No, Elizabeth was seldom, perhaps never, wrong regarding matters of the heart. Such things were an open book to her.

An even more distressing thought came into Henrietta's mind at that moment; did everyone know but she? Was it possible she had been that obtuse? She felt her face grow warm with embarrassment.

"Are you well, Henrietta?" Elizabeth asked. "Your colour is very high."

"Quite well . . . other than this illness that time, I am told, will heal."

Elizabeth squeezed her hand. "I should not have told you about Frank. You have enough concerns at the moment. Foolish of me."

"I am the one who has been foolish, apparently, and not only in the matter of Mr Frank Beacher. But knowledge so painfully gained is said to be most invaluable. Imagine how wise I shall be when this year is done. I am all a-shiver with the anticipation of it."

Henrietta could hardly meet Frank Beacher's eyes, though he glanced her way often, and rather hopefully too, she imagined. Although he had been occupying the same chair at table for some weeks, Henrietta had never considered that it afforded an excellent view of herself without being exactly opposite.

Now that Elizabeth had opened her eyes she did see that he hung upon her every word, declared all of her expressed opinions most sensible, and agreed with her almost without exception. How could she have never noted these things before? Each time he most heartily endorsed one of her observations, no matter how banal, Elizabeth would glance her way, an eyebrow rising almost imperceptibly.

Worse than this was Penelope's obvious jealousy and poorly hidden antagonism towards her. This she had long explained away as mere youthful frowardness, but now she viewed it through a clearer lens. Pen was vexed and cross with her because she thought Henrietta her rival for the affections of Mr Beacher. The fact that Henrietta did not appear to care for Frank in the least only provoked her younger sister further. How could Frank prefer Henrietta when clearly she did not return his feelings? And Pen, who could barely take her eyes from him and laughed at his poorest jest, was indulged as though she were a little sister. Poor Pen!

"Anne?" Mr Carthew said. "Have you completed the painting of the view from Cardoff Hill? I thought it was progressing splendidly."

"I have given it up, Father." Anne paid attention to her plate.

"Given it up? But it was . . . *perfect*. Was it not, Henrietta?"

"Very nearly so, I should say."

Henry Wallace Carthew turned his attention upon his second-youngest daughter, clearly distressed. "Carrying endeavours through to their completion is one of the most important qualities one can cultivate, Anne. Is it not, Mr Beacher?"

"Certainly one can never accomplish anything of value any other way. Perhaps you will go back to it, Anne, at some later time?"

"This conversation seems dreadfully familiar," Anne responded. "Has anyone heard it before?"

Mr Carthew set down his glass. "I should certainly leave off scolding you about this matter if you would but take what I am saying to heart."

"There are landscape artists aplenty in this country, Father, and what hope have I of competing with them? I have found a new passion, anyway. I am now entering Henri's field and writing a novel. At least a woman might find some recognition there."

"Is it romantic?" Penelope asked. "Henri's book is terribly romantic—all about love and pining to be married and—"

"Penelope!" Mrs Carthew said sharply. "I do not think Henrietta is in need of your literary insights at this time, thank you very much."

Immediately, Penelope's eyes were shining and she blinked back tears, bending over her food so that no one might notice. "One mustn't whisper a word against poor, precious Henrietta," she muttered.

There was silence a moment.

"Are you really writing a book, Anne?" Cassandra asked.

Anne shrugged, concentrating on her food.

"I should like to write books of my travels," Cassandra announced.

"What travels are these?" Anne enquired. "Your journeys to Hayfield?"

Everyone laughed in spite of themselves. The village of Hayfield was but three miles distant.

"When I *begin* my travels. I should like to see all of the world, amass a collection to be envied, and write volume upon volume about my adventures. See if I don't."

"I cannot bear to wait," declared Anne. "'Romantic Adventures among the Dung Beetles' by Miss Cassandra Carthew."

"'Frolicking with Pygmies' by a Lady of No Distinction," Penelope enjoined.

"'Touring Byzantium: It Won't Take But a Minaret,'" Frank offered rather lamely; only Penelope laughed.

"You have forgotten 'Escaping the Eccentrics,' by a Woman of Reason," Cassandra replied, hardly bothered at all by her family's teasing.

"Eccentric?" countered Penelope. "Eccentric? The Carthew family? Why, I believe you are the most eccentric of us all—with the exception of Father, of course."

"I most certainly am not." She waved a fork in Henrietta's direction. "Henri is the most eccentric, but she is at pains to hide it."

"True eccentrics never make the least effort to hide their foibles," Mr Carthew informed one and all. "It is characteristic of such people that they never make the slightest effort to gain the good opinions of others."

"Actually, in our family Mama is the most eccentric," Anne said slyly. "She is practical, sensible, has no hobby-horses to ride, and has not a single peculiar belief. No, she is rather odd among us."

"Are you certain you are a Carthew, Mama?" Penelope asked.

"By marriage only, my dear." Mrs Carthew smiled out over her brood with a look of charmed benevolence. No Carthew eccentricity was too great for the obvious adoration she felt for her family. Everyone at the table returned her smile, her affection, but then Henrietta noticed Mr Beacher looked not at Mrs Carthew but at her and with much the same expression.

Penelope, too, noted this and her own smile turned bitterly down.

Henrietta wanted nothing more at that moment than to dash from the room; conflicting emotions seemed about to overwhelm her. Instead she returned her attention to her meal, certain she could feel the worshipful gaze of Mr Beacher upon her—as though she did not have enough troubles. She resolved at that moment to speak to him that very evening and put an end to all his hopes. Cruel it might seem, but far better Mr Beacher understood his situation so that he might consider his future in the light of knowledge rather than a future constructed of equal parts longing and fancy. It must be done, for Mr Beacher's sake. Perhaps he might then regard Penelope's devotion differently. And Pen could give up this resentment of her. Immediately, Henrietta felt better, although she did experience a slight tremor or quivering of the nerves at the thought of speaking so directly to Mr Beacher, but she was determined to overcome this. There was the matter of what to actually say . . . but she did trust that she would think of something before the evening was out.

"Henrietta?" Mr Carthew began, bringing her mind abruptly back from other matters. "How comes your novel?"

"It does not, Father. All forward motion has ceased. The author has written herself into a corner and cannot find a way out."

"What is the difficulty, my dear?"

Henri sensed the same lecture so recently delivered to Anne about to be recapitulated. "I do wish I knew."

"She cannot decide the outcome of her two characters," Elizabeth informed the gathering.

"Ah, and why is that?" Mr Carthew wondered.

"It is all rather simple," Penelope offered. "The intellectual one should be thrown beneath a carriage, while the tiresome one should marry an equally tiresome lord and live tediously ever after. The end. There is no other possibility."

"The question is more profound than that," Frank Beacher instructed the youngest sister. "Does knowledge make a person happy, or is a certain degree of ignorance more conducive to contentment? Can one know what goes on in the larger world and still be happy? That is a serious question and not easily managed."

"And one must also ask the question," Elizabeth interjected, "if our contentment shrank in equal degree to each increase in knowledge would we choose to seek more knowledge or retreat from it? But what is the cost of ignorance? And what the cost of knowledge?"

"What choice would each of us make? I wonder. Cassandra?" Mr Carthew wondered aloud. "Happiness or knowledge?"

"I am of the opinion that one might have both. But if that were not the case, I would choose knowledge."

"Anne?"

"Knowledge, no matter the cost."

"Mr Beacher?"

Frank glanced Henrietta's way a bit uncertainly. "If it were a choice between the two . . . I should choose knowledge by day and happiness by night."

"Whatever do you mean?" Cassandra asked, sitting up and looking at him as though he jested.

"I mean simply that at night all of our worries descend upon us and steal away our contentment. When one awakes in the wee hours, the world can seem a very threatening and loathsome place, so it would be best to choose happiness by night. By day, however, these concerns that so try us by night seem less disturbing, so we might choose knowledge."

"If you can find a way to arrange things thus, Beacher," his friend observed, "I do hope you will instruct the rest of us."

"Indeed," Mr Carthew sniffed. "Pen, what of you, then?"

"Contentment. Only a blockhead would *choose* to be unhappy."

"That is not the choice presented in my book," Henrietta objected. "It is much closer to Elizabeth's interpretation; what is the cost of ignorance? What the cost of knowledge?"

"Ignorance," Wilder informed them, "generally costs three shillings a hundredweight . . . except in the environs immediately surrounding Whitehall. Knowledge is four shillings. The economically minded commonly go for ignorance."

Everyone laughed.

Rather too quickly, dinner was over and the women all retired to the withdrawing room to partake of coffee and tea. No one in the family but Mrs Carthew did any manner of fancy work, so needles and hooks were not in evidence. That particular evening Penelope, who had been industriously scribbling away, proposed they compose a poem about Cassandra's future travels, to which end she offered the first stanza.

> *"Young Miss Carthew in her bonnet*
> *Found a ship and stepped upon it*
> *Undaunted by storm and gale*
> *To captain said, 'Oh do set the sail.'"*

This met with everyone's approval, and soon all heads were bent over pieces of paper, quills in hand.

Cassandra, rather than taking offence at this teasing—or perhaps in self-defence—offered the next stanza.

"Here we are," she said, lifting her page and turning it to the light.

> *"She waved to all her timid sisters*
> *Who stayed ashore in hope that misters,*
> *Wealthy lords and handsome swells,*
> *Might dream of Carthew wedding bells."*

Verse after verse followed, to much laughter and teasing, but finally the poetic wells began to run dry. An end was needed and Pen, who had started it all, offered a stanza that seemed to demand an ending:

> *"By and by she missed her home*
> *Her sisters and her little roan.*
> *She said good-bye to all she met*
> *And so took ship and sailed for Kent."*

A final stanza, though, stymied everyone until Henrietta offered:

> *"Then one day from out the west*
> *Came a stranger in exotic dress*
> *Swathed in jewels and foreign baubles*
> *'I'm back,' she said, 'I missed the squabbles.'"*

A little round of applause—completely spontaneous—followed and Penelope set about writing it all out from memory.

"What was it rhymed with 'oasis'?" she asked, bending over her page.

"'Became the most common places,' or something like."

Hearing the familiar footstep of her father passing by beyond the door, Henrietta excused herself and went out, her heart suddenly all up in her chest and beating frantically.

As she expected, she found Frank Beacher in the dining room yet. Hearing the door, he turned and then looked suddenly embarrassed.

"You have caught me smoking," he said, quickly extinguishing his smoke. "I know you said it was a foul habit."

"You have no need to conform your habits to my opinions," Henrietta answered. Though she had been composing a speech all through dinner, it now seemed suddenly foolish and she had no idea what to say.

"Were you looking for Mr Carthew?" Frank asked, glancing at her, perhaps hoping she was looking for him, as unlikely as that might seem.

Henrietta could hardly speak, of a sudden. "No . . ." she managed rather breathlessly. "Not at all. I had something I wanted to say to you, in truth."

"And what is it, pray?" Frank said quickly, hope overspreading his face like light from the rising sun.

Henrietta felt her own face colour and the yearning that flickered in Frank's eyes swept off all of her resolve.

"I . . . I had been meaning to ask you about Father," she said, desperately grasping at anything to fill the silence. "Does he seem rather enervated to you? I confess, I am a bit concerned."

"Well, he is not as young as once he was, but otherwise I should say he is remarkably vigorous given his years."

"Then you do not think his health suffers at all?"

Frank almost looked confused. "I   No, not in the least. His appetite is the same as it has always been. He walks several miles each morning—and at a pace to be envied, I might add. His reason and memory are prodigious, if one discounts the common, everyday things which he retains not at all—such as what hour we might dine, or any small thing he has promised Mrs Carthew he will attend to. No, Henrietta, I am certain your fears are groundless." He smiled.

"I am relieved to hear it," Henrietta said while inwardly berating herself for a coward. "Then I shall return to my guest, Mr Beacher. Thank you for putting my mind at ease on this matter."

"Not at all," Frank replied, again appearing confused.

Henrietta retreated awkwardly, calling herself the worst names as she did so.

An hour later, she and Elizabeth retreated to the library.

"You spoke with Frank . . ." Elizabeth began, arranging her skirts as she sat.

Henrietta finished lighting a candle and all but threw herself down upon a sofa. "I spoke with him," she admitted, "but I could not say what I meant to and instead enquired after my father's health. I believe Frank thought the entire conversation . . . rather peculiar."

"Oh dear." Elizabeth looked genuinely distressed.

"I could not bear to cause him pain," Henrietta said, sensing the next question. "He looked at me with such hope in his eyes and . . . I could not say a word that might injure him. I am such a coward!"

"Do not berate yourself so, Henrietta. It is no easy thing to dash the hopes of another, especially if you care for them at all. Frank is such a good, kind person. I can see why you would not wish to injure him." She looked pointedly at her cousin. "You are certain that was the reason, are you not, Henri?"

"Whatever do you mean?" Henrietta asked sharply. "You cannot think that I am nurturing some secret flame for Frank Beacher, can you?" And then, "You *do,* don't you?"

"It is one possible explanation for why you could not dash his hopes. I have known such cases before where one's true feelings were never comprehended until such time as the object of this unrecognised affection was about to leave for some distant place or became attached to another. And then, too late . . ."

"Well, that is not the case with me," Henrietta interrupted. "Indeed, I do have an attachment to Frank Beacher—after all, I have known him most of my life and he is, as you have said, good and kind. But my affection is that of a sister for a brother. No more. If Frank's feelings for me are not of a similar variety . . . well, I have never encouraged him to hold such hopes. I am just too cowardly and soft-hearted to injure him, that is all. Having been so recently injured myself, I know how painful such matters can be and have no wish to inflict this upon another, especially anyone so undeserving of pain as Frank Beacher."

"I have one last thing to say on this matter, Henri, and then I shall speak no more. Be certain of your own heart. Frank Beacher is a handsome man of good family and prospects, intelligent and amiable. Some young woman will attach his affections one day and then you might discover that your feelings were of a completely different nature to how you always supposed. But it will be too late."

"When such a day comes, I shall be overjoyed for Mr Beacher and not have the least regret . . . well, perhaps I might harbour the smallest of small regrets, but then that is human, is it not?"

"I suppose it is," Elizabeth replied, looked frightfully thoughtful a moment, and then spoke again. "I was happy to see your mood improved materially by our abysmal poetry."

Henrietta gave a little laugh. "Yes, there is nothing quite so healing to the soul as poetry, ill conceived and badly composed. Unfortunately, the curative powers of this physic are short-lived. Melancholy is greater even than rhymes as dubious as 'pachyderm' and 'parasol held firm.'"

"Yes, it is a dark and tireless gravity that draws one down. I feel it when Captain Hertle is away upon his ship in who knows what dangers. One must never let one's imagination take charge, or one is lost to all manner of horrors."

"A vivid imagination is not always the gift it is so often claimed."

The two fell silent, and Henrietta took her friend's hands in hers. She had been so possessed by her own troubles that she had failed to even notice that Elizabeth was weighed down with worries of her own.

"Do not let anxiety overcome your natural gift for happiness, my dear. As we both know, worry accomplishes nothing but vexation, even torment, to the worrier."

"Yes," Elizabeth said sadly, "but it is so difficult to draw back from this particular abyss. Always the mind wants to step near and peer down into the darkness." A tear escaped the corner of one eye and streaked down her lovely cheek. Without thinking, Henrietta dabbed it away with her hanky.

Elizabeth drew back and looked at her. "Your hanky is sodden!" she said.

Henrietta laughed—she could not help it. "I am afraid it is."

Elizabeth produced her own, limp with moisture.

"We could wring them out and have water enough for a bath," Henrietta said, and they both laughed.

"Are not we a pair?" Elizabeth managed.

"If I am ever, even in the slightest degree, interested in a Navy man again you must shake me, Lizzie, until I come to my senses. I am not made for constant worry."

"Nor am I, yet I have no choice in the matter."

"Nor had I," Henrietta said sadly, and fought back tears yet again.

"What time more advantageous might there be than the present?" Henry Wilder asked.

Frank Beacher and his friend sat among Mr Carthew's collection, spread over tables and shelves and upon the floor all around. It looked as though the "collection" had been housed here by the simple expedient of opening the door and tossing in whatever had most recently been acquired without the least care for where it might

land. Insects pinned to boards leaned against tables piled with preserving jars containing foetuses. Bones and fossils were scattered
here and there in a jumble, making the construction of a complete
skeleton—even if all the parts were present—a near impossibility.
A stuffed wolverine snarled down upon the two men from a high
shelf, and tusks of elephants and narwhals leaned precariously against
a wall.

"Poor Henrietta has just had her heart broken and is distressed to
near distraction. I do not think a proposal from me would be looked
upon in the best possible light under the circumstances."

"I am not suggesting you ask for her hand, Beacher. I am merely
suggesting that you confess your profound feelings for her. You did
let her slip away once before—out of timidity, I might add—do not
let this second chance pass by. You may never get another."

"It does not seem . . . proper, somehow, given her recent disappointment . . ."

"Oh, hang what is proper! We are talking about your happiness."
Wilder fixed his friend with a look of complete exasperation. "And
the happiness of Miss Henrietta as well, if I might be so bold as to
say it, for I believe you will make her happy. How can you not when
you have been her most devoted lover all of your days?" Wilder
displayed a dead beetle in the palm of his hand. "Look at the colour
of this buprestid! Have you ever seen its like?"

Beacher shook his head distractedly. "But—"

"You are afraid that she will rebuff you," Wilder interrupted
firmly. "Admit it. It is completely understandable, Beacher. You
would rather have some hope, no matter how slim, than know there
was no reason to hope at all. But I believe some other man, less fear-
ful of rejection, will win her while you dither. Simply inform her of
your great regard for her and of your true feelings. You might even
say she need not reply but that you simply could keep this secret
no longer. She will go away and contemplate what you have said.

Certainly, she knows all of your fine qualities—who could know them better? She might find that her attachment to you is greater than she realised. And if she does not . . . well, Miss Penelope is your most devoted admirer and is by far the most handsome of the Carthew sisters, and that is saying a great deal, for they are none of them plain. She is also lively and charming, and although not your intellectual equal at this time I believe that could change, for she will become less girlish and more serious in a few short years. After all, Miss Henrietta is but four and twenty, so Miss Penelope has at least seven years to devote to improving her mind."

"Henri has always been of serious disposition and studious to the point of being scholarly. Pen will never be her equal in this for, as you say, she is of completely different temperament."

"A lively, charming wife would not be the worst thing in the world, Beacher."

"No, it would not, but such would never suit me."

"Yes, you would not want a woman to carry you away from your beetles and off to a ball. How horrible!"

"I am perfectly happy to attend a ball, now and again, as you well know, but my interests are . . ."

"More weighty, yes, so you have told me . . . more times than I care to remember."

"Perhaps Pen would make *you* a wife, Wilder. As you say, she does not lack beauty."

"She is too besotted by your charms to consider another. Besides, if I were to lose my heart to a Carthew it would be Miss Cassandra. She is the only one who piques my interest."

"Sandra? Are you serious?"

"Indeed, I am."

"You have always had a partiality for girls with yellow hair and blue eyes, I suppose."

"It is a little more than that, I think. Sandra, as you call her, is not about to make a nest. She is a little more adventurous, which would suit me to perfection, do not you think?"

This made Frank Beacher smile. "Oh, so that is it. You see yourself sailing off to distant lands with your wife by your side, collecting in the South Pacific Isles or Borneo, perhaps. Most men would not subject their wives to such discomfort, not to mention the perceivable dangers. But then, we are allowed any type of marriage in our fancies, are we not? Have you expressed these thoughts to Miss Cassandra, pray? Or are you simply prone to suggesting boldness to your friends but do not follow such advice yourself?"

"I have only but met Miss Cassandra; you have been in love with your lovely Henri since you were weaned. I will say, if I were to decide Miss Cassandra was the woman I wished to marry I would speak—while you would still be debating if such a course were 'proper.'"

"So you say, Mr Wilder, but we will see if you are as good as your word."

"I will wager that I will express my feelings for Miss Cassandra before you have done so to your dear Henri, upon the condition, of course, that I grow such feelings."

"I do not think such wagers proper."

Wilder laughed, and after a moment so did Beacher—at himself.

"Well, then let me propose something even you cannot protest is improper. Let us ask the Misses Cassandra and Henrietta to take the air with us on the morrow." He thought a moment. "I suppose we shall have to invite Mrs Hertle as well, as she is visiting Miss Henrietta."

"She will make the perfect chaperon. I will pass along our invitation first thing in the morning." Beacher looked pleased a moment, but then his gaze became distant and a look of confusion settled over his features.

"What is it, Beacher? Have you thought of some reason for this to be improper?"

"Not at all. I had the most peculiar encounter with Henrietta, just after dinner. She found me alone in the dining room; indeed, I believe she knew there was no other present. She said she had something to say to me and looked terribly nervous, but then, just as she was about to speak, I swear she lost her nerve and rather than saying whatever it was she first intended, she instead enquired after her father's health, even though his well-being and vigour are constantly remarked upon by all of his daughters." He shook his head.

"What do you imagine Henrietta meant to say?"

"I truly do not know. I . . . Well, I cannot say."

"I will tell you one thing, Beacher, do not for a moment imagine that she was suddenly going to confess her feelings for you. Even were she mad for you, Miss Henrietta Carthew would never . . . *never* speak first. It is out of the question."

"Of course, you are right. But I do wonder what she intended."

"You must ask her."

"And how would one do that, pray?"

"It is not so impossible as you seem to think. Were I you, and thank God I am not, I would simply say, 'My dear Henri, last night, when we spoke of your father's health, I imagined that you had intended to say something other. Is that true, and if so, what was it you wished to say to me?' "

"I might make her feel most uncomfortable!"

"She is a woman in the bloom of youth, Beacher; such discomfort will not be fatal, I am quite certain." He threw up his hands. "I do not know why I even take the time to speak to you on such matters. Would not you be better off knowing that Miss Henrietta does not share your feelings?"

"You do not understand, Wilder. Young women have very ro-

mantic notions of love and marriage. They are all of them waiting
for some handsome stranger to come along and sweep them away,
like a leaf falling into a fast-flowing river, the current irresistible.
The idea of love with someone as familiar as I am to Henrietta is
simply not romantic. But falling in love with a stranger leads to the
kind of heartache Henri is feeling now—all because she believed she
was in love with this Navy man who cannot even make his post
and was clearly a bounder from the very beginning! I should like to
meet the man and demand satisfaction for what he has done!"

"Have you ever been in a duel, Beacher?"

"You know I have not."

"Then I should not be in a hurry to walk out with a man who has
been in many an action and has actually aimed a pistol at a man's
heart before and knows whether he is capable of firing or no."

"Well, I did not actually mean I would challenge the blackguard."
He looked very sad suddenly. "It takes some time for women to
grow beyond this idea of the handsome stranger and realise that love
can flourish with the familiar. Henrietta and I are perfectly suited
to one another, always content in each other's company, never a
moment of awkwardness or searching about for something of which
we might speak. We find amusement in the same things, enjoy the
same books and make almost identical observations about the people
around us. These things will outlast the foolish romantic notions
common to young women."

"Did you not tell me that Miss Henrietta's aunt expressed this
exact same opinion?"

"Well, perhaps not *exact*."

"So you are of one mind with a ninety-year-old dowager on the
matter of romance?" He raised an eyebrow, but Beacher did not
know how to answer this. "Unfortunate you are not courting Henrietta's ageing aunt, you seem to have much in common."

"You do see my problem, Wilder, do you not? I am too familiar, to Henri. But I believe she will feel differently about this in time. Once she has recovered from her recent disappointment, she might very well see how foolish her ideas were."

"All the more reason for you to confess your own feelings. Then she may weigh up the handsome rogue against the faithful confidant and decide where to entrust her heart. But if you do not speak, she might never suspect that your feelings are anything but brotherly. Only the brave deserve the fair."

"'*None* but the brave . . .'"

"Sorry . . . ?"

"'None but the brave deserve the fair.' Dryden."

"Was it Dryden? I thought it was Shakespeare."

"Perhaps. Everyone seems to have said it at one time or another. I think the Lord said it to Adam."

"Well, there you have it. If the Lord said it to Adam and Shakespeare said it, or very likely so, it is undeniable—perhaps even *Gospel*—truth. Miss Henrietta is fair, so you must be brave. If it were the other way round and you were fair, then she would have to be brave—but I can assure you, Beacher, you are not fair, therefore the part of being brave falls upon you."

"Thank you, Wilder. It is the kindest thing you have ever said about me."

"You are most welcome. Did I also say that you are timid, shy, fainthearted, and without a spine? No? Well, so you are. If you cannot work up your courage to tell Miss Henrietta Carthew how you feel, then she will most likely marry some handsome stranger and live unhappily ever after. And it will be your fault, too."

Beacher stood and paced across the room, lighting a pipe from a candle. "Any such declaration I might make must be timed to perfection. Too soon and she will rebuff my suit, because she is still awaiting her handsome stranger, too late and . . . well, it will be too late, clearly. But how to know when the exact moment has arrived . . . ?"

"Aye, there's the rub."

"Shakespeare."

"Not God?"

Four

He was wakened, by his own order, two hours before dawn, breakfasted sparsely, washed and dressed himself with his usual care but a lack of conscious attention. He cut himself shaving and could not staunch the bleeding for some half an hour, which did nothing to improve his mood.

As Hayden donned his coat, a peal of thunder penetrated dully through the wooden hull followed immediately by a crashing in the rigging. He ran for the ladder that led up to the main deck. His marine sentry, standing more or less where the door would have been had his cabin been assembled, looked at him with alarm.

"Are we being fired upon, sir?" he said, almost all the air sucked out of his words.

"We are." Hayden went up the ladder two steps to a time and made the deck just as the mizzen top-gallant mast carried away, toppling to leeward, an array of shrouds, stays, and halliards stopping it from going into the sea.

"Cut that away!" Hayden called. "It will take the mizzen with it."

It was a long moment while axes were produced. Both Barthe and Franks appeared and began calling instructions of where to cut. Chettle, the carpenter, and his mates climbed up to the mizzen top and began cutting away the rigging, the ship swaying and rain teeming down and pouring off the sails like rain off a roof. Under any other circumstances, Hayden would have long since ordered the upper yards sent down and the top-gallant masts housed, but they had carried them instead, knowing they might be the difference between escaping and being brought to.

Before his own crew could man their guns, the French ship to weather had fired her own guns several times. Bar and chain whirred up into the *Themis'* rigging, tearing away shrouds and ripping gaping holes in sails.

The British guns spoke back, and in a moment their enemy withdrew into the darkness, her guns falling silent. Only the sound of the gale persisted, the dull chopping of the men aloft cutting away the fallen top-gallant mast and yard. These spars tumbled into the sea, suddenly, and were swept astern into the darkness.

Everyone strained to peer through the night and driving rain, trying to find their adversary, but nothing could be seen.

"I dare say that Frenchman is not shy," Hawthorne announced, appearing at Hayden's elbow.

"Nor is he a poor seaman—just to find us on this night and catch us sleeping was not easily accomplished." Hayden turned to Archer and asked, "How is it, Mr Archer, that this Frenchman could come upon us and catch us unawares? What, pray, were our lookouts about?"

Archer appeared abashed in the poor light. "We had so often lost sight of them this night that we thought nothing of it when it happened again. Never for a moment did we imagine they would come at us before daylight. I-I apologise, Captain. I was officer of the watch; it is my failing."

"I would never have believed they would try such a thing myself, but perhaps I should have. These ships have been raiding our commerce by night for several months. They are well used to such manoeuvres, apparently, though it is difficult to imagine they are commonly this daring in such foul weather."

Hayden went to the rail and stared out into the night, trying, with one hand, to shield his eyes from the driving rain. His servant carried up his oilskins and a sou-wester, which Hayden donned over his already soaking uniform.

"I dare say, that was rather enterprising of this Frenchman, was it not, Captain?" Hawthorne was attempting to part the darkness to Hayden's left.

"More than enterprising. I do hate to be outwitted, but I have been this night. We will see what the damage is soon enough—less than the French captain hoped, I suspect. I admire his audacity all the same. If he could have disabled us or caused enough damage to our rig—for that was his sole intention—then he might have produced a tangible advantage come daylight."

"Is he finished for now, do you think?"

"So I believe. He will not have the element of surprise again so will wait for morning and see what profit his gunnery might have gained him." Hayden turned away and looked up into the rigging—the sails curving apparitions in the blackness.

A very long half of the hour brought Barthe to the quarterdeck.

"How have we fared, Mr Barthe?" Hayden asked.

"Better than I hoped, Captain. The mizzen top-gallant was the worst of it. Oh, that Frenchman shot away some stays and shrouds forward and tore some holes in our sails. We'll have all the rigging put to rights in an hour. The mainsail received the worst injuries, sir. I am not sure it will stand this night—not if the wind keeps making."

The main should have been taken in hours ago, Hayden knew.

"We shall have to hand it and send it down, Mr Barthe. No easy thing in this wind. But it must be done. Our old main shall have to go in its place, for we may be in need of it come daylight."

"Aye, sir. McGowan patched and resewed our old main, sir, but even so, I would rather take my chances on the new one, even damaged as it is."

Barthe knew his trade thoroughly, and Hayden trusted his judgement in such matters. "Then hand the main, Mr Barthe, and we will set it reefed if needed."

The sailing master waddled forward quickly, leaving Hayden to wallow in chagrin. He had been taken unawares by this French captain. The man was clearly more formidable than Hayden had imagined. Or was it merely that Hayden's own mind was so clouded by his difficulties he had made poor decisions? He vowed silently to bear down and push all thoughts of Henrietta and his recent troubles from his mind. To let this Frenchman outwit him once was embarrassing, to let him do so a second time might prove their undoing.

The single hour remaining until daylight seemed to have quadrupled in length, but then light, when it finally arrived, could barely penetrate the low, dense cloud. The wind was making yet and the seas were steeper and more threatening, sweeping down on the frigate and tossing her about like a jolly boat.

Hayden, however, was not unhappy to see the weather worsening. It would be a great risk to open gunports in such a sea, and deck guns would be unwieldy if not dangerous. The chances of hitting any target smaller than a first-rate at more than a hundred yards would be very small. The French would not bring him to battle this morning despite their superiority in numbers. He prayed the weather would not moderate.

Standing by the leeward rail clutching the mizzen shrouds, Hayden called for the sailing master, who quickly appeared.

"Captain?" he called over the sound of wind and sea.

"Mr Barthe, what would our course be back to the Isle of Guernsey?"

"Let me give it to you exact, sir. A moment, if I may." He hurried off to consult his chart.

Hayden stood watching the seas roll away towards France, their crests blowing off into long, white streaks upon the gunmetal water. If he wore ship at that moment and stood in towards Guernsey, he did not think there would be much the French could do about it. Certainly, they would attempt to close with him and bring him to battle, but under these conditions he thought he might risk it. Gunports could not be opened and he was willing to gamble that he could inflict as much damage on the French as they would manage on his ship. Boarding under such circumstances would be impossible. The Channel Isles were under threat, as the Admiralty well knew, and Hayden hoped there would be ships of war there that could aid him in his return to England or by driving off the French frigates.

"East-south-east, sir," Barthe announced as he reappeared.

Hayden nodded. "Well, Mr Barthe, previously I spoke against it, but I now believe a sojourn on the fair Isle of Guernsey should do us all a world of good. We might find entertainment and acquire some French wines of excellent vintage. Would you concur?"

"Indeed, sir. I believe it is a risk well worth taking. We have already seen that our rate of fire is double that of these Frenchmen, and as there are but two of them that should answer."

"Then we will wear ship, Mr Barthe, before the men are called to breakfast." Hayden turned and waved towards his first lieutenant. "Mr Archer. We shall wear ship and shape our course towards Guernsey."

"Aye, sir. Mr Barthe . . ."

Barthe and Archer went hurrying off, calling out orders as they went.

Hayden gazed towards the enemy ships, wondering if he was making the right decision. If luck turned against him, his ship might be disabled and lost . . .

"On deck!" came a call from above. "Sail, dead astern, sir."

Hayden started immediately along the sloping deck towards the stern rail, finding his way around the carronades. "Can you make it out?" he shouted to the lookout.

"I cannot, sir. It isn't a chase mary, sir. . . . Maybe a coaster, Captain. Two-master, I think . . . No, three, sir."

Hayden cursed under his breath. "Where is Mr Wickham? Hobson! Find Mr Wickham and send him aloft with a glass."

"Here, Captain." Wickham shot out of the companionway, almost lost his balance on the slanting deck, rescued his hat as the wind took it. Under one arm was tucked a glass, and his coat luffed like a sail without a sheet. In a trice he was climbing the mizzen shrouds, his unbuttoned coat flailing around him like the wings of a bat.

Hayden waited until he reached the tops, watching as he lodged himself in a secure place and fixed his glass upon the sea astern. The silence among the crew was profound, every soul awaiting Mr Wickham's verdict.

"A ship, Captain," Wickham called down. "Maybe a frigate, and making good speed, I should say, sir."

"Is she one of ours, Wickham?"

"I cannot tell, Captain."

Hayden took his eyes away from the midshipman and found Archer and Barthe staring at him, the same unspoken question in their eyes.

"We dare not wear now, Mr Archer. Not until we know the nationality of this ship. Where is my glass?"

The two officers saluted and began calling out orders, bringing men down from aloft. Hayden's glass was carried up from below and he fixed it on the distant sail, just visible in their wake. The hull of the ship appeared and disappeared upon the swell, making it all but impossible to learn anything about her. They would have to wait . . . and hope it was a British ship.

Archer cleared his throat. "Shall I send the men to their breakfast, sir?"

Hayden nodded. "I believe you should, Mr Archer."

"Aye, sir." But Archer did not turn to go. "What does she look like, sir?"

Hayden offered the glass to the lieutenant, who came and braced himself against the rail. After a moment of intense scrutiny, made difficult by the pitching and rolling ship, he lowered the glass and shook his head. "I could not even say with certainty that it is a frigate, Captain Hayden."

"She is a mystery for the time being."

His servant appeared then. "You have been invited to breakfast in the gunroom, Captain."

"An invitation I shall accept with gratitude. You have the deck, Mr Archer. Send for me if any of these ships do anything the least unexpected."

"I shall, sir—immediately."

Hayden went down to the gunroom, where he found the officers not required on deck during this watch. Ransome was there, as were the doctor, Hawthorne, Smosh. Hayden took the place set for him—the place of honour—and everyone took their seats.

"I am told a third ship has joined our little squadron," Smosh offered, allowing a servant to serve him a generous portion of "eggs Themis," with onions and pease. He glanced over at Hayden.

"Yes, Reverend, but as of yet we do not know if she will join our side or the enemy's. Noon shall bring an answer to this question."

Though the gunroom was situated in one of the more comfortable parts of the ship when in a seaway—aft and on the lower deck—the motion of the ship was such that there was no truly comfortable place. A quick hand was often required to preserve a plate or piece of cutlery from sliding off to leeward. Great care was taken of glasses and their contents. Hawthorne commented that these were of less value now that Guernsey—and smuggled French wine—seemed unlikely.

"Is it not the oddest thing that our government does everything within its power to prevent the smuggling," Smosh said, "yet I doubt there is a Member of Parliament or a government official in possession of the means who does not drink smuggled French wine and perhaps garb his wife in smuggled lace."

"It is but part of human nature, Reverend Smosh," Hawthorne assured him. "I am familiar myself with many a man who mouths pieties at every opportunity yet when out of sight of his wife and family lives as debauched a life as any rogue. Why, I would not doubt some of these men are the said same government officials and Members of Parliament, too. We are not an admirable race, I do not think . . . present company excepted, of course."

"We are just at sea too much of our lives," the doctor observed dryly. "Debauchery takes time and study to be properly accomplished, like any other endeavour."

"I dare say, Dr Griffiths, there are some men upon the lower deck who are fairly depraved when opportunity presents itself."

"So there are, but these are but the common depravities, Reverend. For the truly refined variety, I believe, one must dedicate one's self, body and soul—not that I am any authority, I should add."

"I am greatly relieved to hear it," Smosh said. "Hypocrisy, though, if I may return to our earlier subject, is as common as Mr Hawthorne says, though I do not know why."

"We know the doctor is free of this sin," Hawthorne enjoined. "He has taken the Hypocritic Oath."

This engendered much laughter—more than the jest deserved—

but the tension aboard ship was very great and any relief offered was not to be missed.

The meal was quickly disposed of, and officers excused themselves to be about their business. Hayden and the surgeon were left alone over coffee. Once Hayden had enquired after the sick and hurt, and the doctor's own health, the conversation, uncharacteristically for these two, withered away to an uncomfortable silence. Hayden had his own problems to consider, and the doctor . . . well, Hayden was not sure what might be on his mind.

After a moment, Griffiths seemed about to speak but then perhaps thought better of it or was not sure how to begin. Finally, he said, "You may have heard a rumour, Captain, that I have sent for my charge from Gibraltar—Miss Brentwood?"

"I did not realise she was your charge or that you were in any way responsible for her."

The doctor sat back in his chair, looking embarrassed though trying not to. "I suppose I have taken on that responsibility, Captain. We have exchanged letters, Miss Brentwood and I, and I am convinced that she would choose death over dishonour, which I simply cannot allow."

Hayden considered a moment before speaking, preferring to tread lightly where the subject was so delicate. "I do know, Doctor Griffiths, that you bear a burden of guilt—unwarranted, I might add—at the death of a young woman in similar circumstances. That does not make you the protector of every young woman who has lost the use of a hand and who has run afoul of luck."

The doctor met his eyes. "If not me, then who?"

"Pardon me . . . ?"

"I am not being entirely facetious. Who would rescue Miss Brentwood if I did not? She would probably be dead or wishing she were dead. I simply cannot allow this poor girl to suffer. I cannot, Captain."

"It is very noble of you," Hayden said quickly. "But do you not worry that she might misconstrue your interest in her? She might apprehend your concern for her as something more than charity. There might, in her mind, be a promise of some nature in such kindness to a woman to whom you are no blood relation nor even a family friend."

The doctor did not answer this but only looked somewhat distressed. "I do worry that such a thing might occur." He was silent a moment, contemplating the empty table before him. "Or has occurred."

Hayden shifted a little, sitting back, not wanting to prompt the surgeon to speak, but only to listen if Griffiths so desired.

Hesitation was quickly overcome, apparently, for the doctor went on, looking up at his friend and captain. "In her last letter . . ." He took a quick breath and let it out in something like a sigh. "In her last letter Miss Brentwood did write in a manner . . . so unguarded and familiar as to cause me the greatest possible alarm." The doctor's misery seemed to almost overwhelm him. "I have hardly spent three hours in this young lady's company; is it possible that I have attached her feelings in so short a time? I will tell you, I have failed in similar endeavours when the number of hours I had to perform this miracle was almost without number. Do you think this possible? Could she be so easily won? Not that I determined to win her. Nothing could have been further from my intentions."

Griffiths looked up at him appealingly. Hayden had seen drowning men look less desperate.

"She is a young woman in difficult circumstances, as we have noted. Along comes a gallant Navy surgeon who has prize money in the offing. This gentleman is clearly kindness personified and rescues her from her plight. How could she not be affected? Even if it is really gratitude confused for true attachment, it is no less strong."

Griffiths shook his head. "I did not foresee this, I can tell you. I always imagined myself with a woman . . . of greater learning."

Hayden thought of the woman Hawthorne had met in Bath; the woman upon whom all Griffiths' hopes had depended, he had been told, though those hopes had been dashed. She was apparently very learned.

"Have you pledged yourself to this lady . . . in word or deed?"

"Not in word, certainly. In deed . . . it would appear she believes so."

"Well, Dr Griffiths, though it will bruise her feelings, I am sure, you must be entirely forthright about your intentions. There must be no misunderstanding."

"Yes, of course. I must." He bit his lip. "Certainly I must."

Hayden did not feel he could linger. There were two French frigates and an unknown ship within sight. He was needed on deck.

"If you will excuse me, Doctor."

"Certainly," Griffiths said, standing. "And thank you for your counsel in this matter."

"Not at all."

Leaving the gunroom, Hayden could see Chettle and his mates at work, finishing a new top-gallant mast with smoothing planes. They had this laid out between the rows of tables and were receiving some abuse from the men nearby, who thought their mess should not be turned into a shop for the shipwrights. Hayden stopped a moment to approve the carpenters' work.

"We shall have a new yard ready in two hours, sir," the carpenter reported.

"Well done, Mr Chettle."

A dull and distant thud brought a sudden silence. A gun had been fired.

Hayden climbed quickly up to the main deck, attempting to appear calm the whole while. Here he found his officers gathered at the taffrail, quizzing their newly acquired escort, barely visible through the sheets of rain slatting down into the sea and upon His Majesty's ship *Themis*.

"There you are, sir," Archer said as Hayden approached. "We just sent Hobson to find you. It seems the Frenchman to leeward has reason to believe this new ship is also French. He just sent up his colours and a hoist of signals behind his sails. A gun was fired as well, sir."

"And has the other ship answered?"

"We cannot be certain, Captain." Archer handed Hayden his glass.

Archer's glass was partly fogged inside—not an uncommon occurrence—and the distant ship was doubly obscured. He called for his own glass to be carried up from his cabin, and fixed it upon the distant ship, still small, even in the circle of his glass. She was under storm canvas—but was that a hoist of signal flags behind the topsails?

He lowered his glass. "Where is Mr Wickham?"

"Aloft, sir."

Hayden craned his neck to look up, a hand preserving his hat. "Mr Wickham! Can you make out a flag upon that ship?"

Wickham leaned over from the tops to call down. "I cannot, sir, but she appears to be answering signals from the other ship, Captain. She is most assuredly French."

Hayden turned back and found the ship in his glass again. "She has not come up as fast as Wickham predicted," he observed.

"No, sir," Archer replied. "We believe she tore out her mainsail clews, sir. We saw it suddenly begin to flog, and then they had the devil of a time to hand it. That has slowed them somewhat."

Although this was good news, it brought to mind the precarious state of Hayden's own main. He prayed they would not need to set it that day.

"If you were one of these French captains, Archer, what would you do?"

"Me, sir? I would close with us and open fire, Captain. There are British cruisers in these waters. I would want to take my prize before she could be rescued. Damn the weather. Deck guns can be fired. I would be making every effort to bring us to battle."

"That is what I would do as well. And now that there appear to be three of them, I believe they will do the same."

"And we, sir? What shall we do?"

"We shall attempt to hold them off until dark. By then we shall have enough sea room to manoeuvre. Let us pray this gale lasts and even freshens."

"I shall speak to Mr Smosh about freshening the gale, sir. He has influence in high places, I am given to understand."

"Very enterprising of you, Archer."

"Thank you, sir. I do try."

Half an hour later Wickham appeared on the deck, his oilskins dripping, a glass half protected by a coat.

"You still believe her a corvette, Mr Wickham?"

"I do, sir."

"Can they catch us before darkness, do you think?"

"The windward ship might, sir. She will have a better slant if she comes after us. The ships to leeward . . . They will not catch us unless the windward ship can slow us."

"My thoughts exactly. Find Mr Barthe and Archer. I wish to have all your thoughts on a particular matter."

"Aye, sir."

Wickham, near frozen as he was, went stiffly off. Hayden crossed to the windward rail and, taking hold of the mizzen shrouds, leaned out over the writhing sea and gazed down at the topsides. His officers gathered a moment later.

"If this windward ship bears down on us, I am wondering if we can luff—not near enough to the wind to chance backing our sails—but as near as we dare, open our gunports as the crest passes and fire a broadside the length of the Frenchman's deck. If this can be timed to the moment he is bow down and his deck exposed, and we load half our guns with grape and the rest with shot, we will cause a great calamity among his crew, and much damage to his ship. Can it be risked, do you think?"

The two young men and the master all stared out over the high-running sea. Barthe spoke first; indeed, Archer and Wickham appeared to be waiting for him.

"The wind has not held steady to even one point of the compass, Captain," Barthe began. "It has veered about as much as a point, and even two at times. Should we get a shift to the west as we luff, we might well be caught aback and then . . ." He did not need to finish—they might lose masts, which would leave them at the mercy of the French.

"I am forced to agree, Mr Barthe. The wind is not fixed in direction. Do we dare open ports, do you think?"

"We will certainly roll to starboard when we luff, sir," Wickham replied smartly. "And then back to larboard. It would have to be timed to a nicety—the ports opened at the exact instant, guns run out and fired. If the Frenchman is bow-up at that exact moment . . . well, we shall put some holes beneath the water with a bit of luck, but his deck will be largely unharmed."

"I agree. We shall only have one opportunity, and wind and sea might not favour us."

"I for one think it is worth the chance, Captain," Archer stated firmly. "If we luff and it is clearly not possible to open the gunports then, although we will have allowed the Frenchman nearer, he will not be able to open his ports either, so it will profit him little. The only danger is being caught aback. Put Dryden on the wheel or Mr Barthe or yourself, sir. But if we can damage this Frenchman the others will not come up with us before darkness, I do not believe. It is our best chance."

Hayden could see the sailing master listening to this and gazing down at his boots on the streaming deck, a look of disapproval and concern upon his wind-reddened face.

"Mr Barthe, I do not think you are in agreement with Mr Archer?"

"With all respect, sir, I am not. I think we can drive this French-man off or keep up a running battle with him until dark. It is a daring plan, Captain, but I fear the wind will betray us at the wrong moment."

"I share your reservations, Mr Barthe, but sometimes in war it is important to do the unexpected. I do not believe our Frenchman will imagine for a moment that we would luff and rake him. I am determined to attempt it. If gunports cannot be opened safely when we have luffed, we will fire our deck guns and fall back onto our course. If we wait until the precise moment to luff, we may drive our Frenchman down to leeward of us. I would rather have him there than with the weather gauge."

Archer and Wickham both nodded. Barthe, Hayden was certain, would co-operate completely, no matter how much he objected to doing so. Hayden would have preferred to have Barthe's enthusiastic support, but it was not required.

"Shall I send Dryden to the wheel, sir?" the master asked quietly.

"If you please, Mr Barthe." Hayden turned back to quiz the windward ship with his glass. "Now let us see if this Frenchman will co-operate. He was not shy by night. Let us discover if he is so brave by day when he cannot come upon us by stealth."

Hayden put Archer in charge of the gun-deck. They would have only one opportunity to fire a broadside. Opening gunports, run-ning out the guns, firing, and closing the ports would all have to be done in a blink. There could be no hesitation, no misunderstanding of his intentions. All must happen in one smooth motion, like the throwing of a javelin.

"Mr Wickham, I shall have you stand in the aft companionway, upon the ladder. When I give the order, you must pass it immediately to Mr Archer." Hayden turned to his first lieutenant. "You comprehend, Mr Archer, that it all must happen upon the instant; ports opened and guns run out all but simultaneously. We will fire our broadside upon your order, whether the Frenchman's deck is exposed or no, for the ports must be shut the instant the guns are fired. We do not dare to leave them open for a more advantageous shot. Have you any questions at all? Do not hesitate to ask, we can have no confusion."

Both young men assured him their comprehension was complete. The ship beat to quarters and Hayden toured the gun-deck to assure himself that all was ready. The gun crews listened gravely to his explanation of what was planned, and all nodded their apparent understanding. They were steady men, Hayden knew, and he did not doubt for a moment that they would fulfil their part. Whether he could time the turn and catch the enemy unawares was another matter.

Upon the main deck he found Wickham with a glass fixed on the windward ship.

"I believe she is bearing down on us, sir. It is hardly perceptible in these conditions, but see if you do not think the same."

Hayden watched the ship for some time and then lowered his glass. "I agree with you, Wickham. An hour will see her near enough for us to put our helm down. When I am ready to luff, we shall give the gun crews warning so they are standing ready. We can have no mistakes."

"There will be none, sir." Wickham said this with such youthful confidence that Hayden almost smiled. Innocence that complete was to be wished for, he thought.

The morning wore on. Necessary conversations were reduced to terse whispers with many a quick glance towards the French frigate. On the quarterdeck, the gun crews hunched down behind the barricade so as not to alert the enemy to Hayden's intentions. Even so, these men popped a head up on occasion and monitored the approaching enemy vessel with a dread-filled fascination. All of them comprehended the risks involved.

The telltale at the masthead was scrutinized by all the experienced sailors, and every time the wind shifted into the west without warning, these men glanced at one another, their anxieties unspoken but almost clearer for it.

After the wind hauled forward it would settle back to blowing from the north, steady for a time, and then, without warning, haul either forward or aft, sometimes as much as two points, just as the master had claimed.

It was unsettling, but Hayden intended to stay with his plan unless the wind began veering about without any periods of settling into the north. He was glad that the howling of the wind hid the sounds of his stomach, which was nervously announcing its reservations about his plan. It was embarrassing that his own body should betray him so, but there was nothing to be done for it.

For a long time the French ship hardly seemed to be gaining at all, but then it began to grow until there was no doubt the distance between them was closing. A chase piece was fired from the Frenchman's foredeck but was well wide and short of its mark.

"Shall we return fire, sir?" Ransome stood near Hayden, eyes fixed on the chasing ship.

"No. They will not damage us in this sea. Nor are we likely to cause hurt to them."

A nervous-looking Rosseau appeared on deck, looked over the three chasing ships, and turned very pale. Capture by his own people and execution for siding with the enemy were his greatest fears. "There you are, Rosseau," Hayden said. "I have instructed the sergeant-at-arms to lock you in leg irons in the event that we should be forced to surrender, though I should not worry; I doubt it will come to such a pass."

"*Merci*, Capitaine. I hope the same." He glanced at the ships again, reached up to touch his face, and Hayden thought he saw the man's hand trembling.

The gale gave no indication of taking off, and the sky remained heavy and deep with cloud. Rain squalls swept down on them at intervals, obscuring the chasing ships. Out of this blear seas came sliding and hissing to roll the ship to leeward. Wind in the rigging howled up and down a haunted scale.

The chasing ship continued to lob shot at them, and finally, as she came within seventy-five yards, she struck home, sending a shot through the transom and into the empty gunroom, the stern having been thrown high as the bow pitched down into the trough.

Hawthorne went below to assess the damage and returned a moment later. "This Frenchman did not approve of our table wine, apparently," he reported to Hayden. "Blasted it all over the gun-room."

A quarter-keg of claret had been shattered, the marine informed him, its contents sprayed crimson over the white-painted walls and deck-head.

"The tiller and tiller ropes were unharmed?"

"Yes, sir, just the wine and the bulkhead before it. The servants are cleaning up and Chettle is seeing to the damage to the hull."

"Well, the French do tend to be snobs about wine, Mr Haw-thorne."

"That is because they have never tried English wine, sir."

Hayden laughed despite the situation.

He had not taken his eyes off the pursuing ship the entire time they spoke. "Mr Dryden," Hayden said to the man at the helm.

"Our design remains the same. When I give the order, I want you to port your helm and luff up as close to the wind as you dare. We will open ports, fire a broadside, and fall back on our course immediately. Is that understood?"

"Yes, sir."

"Mr Wickham, station yourself in the companionway now and have Mr Archer warn his crews to be ready to act with all speed upon my order."

"Aye, Captain." Wickham jogged over to the companionway and positioned himself several steps down, passing Hayden's warning to Archer.

Hayden kept his eye fixed upon the chasing ship. A bloom of white smoke at her bow was immediately swept off by the wind and the screech of an iron ball passed narrowly by. There was no room now for error. No place for panic. He pressed all doubts down and fixed his eye on the heaving French frigate. It was Hayden's desire to begin his turn as a wave reached them so they were turning into the crest, complete it as they passed over, open ports as the second crest passed, fire, close ports, and bear off. The waves were steep and close together, as they tended to be in the Channel. There would be little time between them.

"Mr Hawthorne . . ." Hayden said, still watching the French ship.

"Aye, sir."

"Fix your eye to windward. If a rain squall appears, alert me immediately."

"I will, sir."

The Frenchman was sixty yards off, then fifty. Hayden could sense the men around him shifting, wondering when he would give the order.

"Mr Dryden?"

"Sir?"

"Begin your turn upon my order. Not before." Hayden turned

his attention away from the Frenchman and began watching the seas, a quick look up at the telltale—wind holding in the north, a little east perhaps. He timed the passing of the sea beneath his hull.

"Port your helm, Mr Dryden."

He glanced over at Wickham, who stood poised upon the ladder as though ready to leap down to the gun-deck upon the slightest twitch from Hayden. The ship began to turn, heeling to larboard as she rose to the sea. Dryden and another turned the wheel as quickly as they were able, but every inch was a struggle. The frigate rounded up, slowly, her bow rising, up and up then over the crest. Still the ship turned, rolling now to starboard as the sea passed beneath them. Sails began to shake and crack in the heavy winds.

The second crest surged towards them and the *Themis* began to climb again, her head pushed off a little more than Hayden would have wanted.

The ship was almost upon the crest and seemed to hang there an instant, and then, as the wave passed beneath she rose, freeing her gunports, beginning at the bow.

In that instant, Hayden called out over the winds, "Mr Wickham! Open gunports!"

"Squall coming," Hawthorne reported, no more than a little apprehension in his voice.

"How distant?"

"Not a hundred yards, sir."

Even over the wind Hayden heard the squeal of hinges as the gunports opened. He turned towards the French ship, which had been caught completely unawares, just as it began to plunge into the trough.

Overhead, sails went mad, vibrating the *Themis* in their frenzy.

"Fire!" Hayden called over the chaos.

The carronades hissed back on their slides and a deafening blast tore open the air. All was lost in a cloud of acrid smoke, and then that was swept away to leeward. The sound of gunports thudding closed came to him. Just before the bow of the French ship rose on the next sea, Hayden had a vision of her deck. Guns dismounted, men strewn about like shattered dolls. Hardly a soul standing. She was so near, Hayden thought she might ram his ship, but she turned to leeward, stunned Frenchmen picking themselves up. Hayden saw an officer, face bloody and one arm hanging limp, staring at him grimly as the ship passed. It was not a look of reproach so much as a look of terrible understanding. And then the French ship was gone.

"Put us back on our course, Mr Dryden," Hayden said, just loud enough to be heard.

The men at the wheel began fighting for every spoke, but Hawthorne's squall reached them at that moment and the ship would not answer.

"Let the mizzen sheet run!" Hayden shouted. Immediately, he went to the wheel, but Wickham and Hawthorne were quicker. All eyes turned aloft to the flailing canvas, rain slatting down like grapeshot. The thrashing canvas went still, pressed back against the masts and rigging, pinned there.

"God-damned . . ." Hayden heard the sailing master say. "Back the fore staysail!" He went running then, stumbling forward, calling out, "Haul the fore staysail sheet to starboard!"

"Mr Dryden," Hayden said, coming to the wheel. "Port your helm."

"Sir."

"She will not fall back onto her course, nor will she come through the wind. Port your helm. The masts will stand or fall. We cannot change that."

All way was lost, and for a moment the ship wallowed. Hayden looked up at the foremast, which would certainly be the first to go. The ship plunged down into the trough, throwing the sails aback with even greater force. Hayden was certain the masts would go at the instant. And then the ship was forced back, the rudder drawing her stern slowly to starboard. She seemed to hang there a moment as if undecided, in the grip of the howling wind, and then her head fell off to larboard and a moment later the sails filled with a boom. For a moment she did not answer her helm and continued to turn, but then she gathered way and the men at the helm brought her up, near to the wind, then a little nearer.

Hayden felt himself take a breath, the first in several minutes apparently, and the hands cheered. The French ships came back to mind and he made his way aft to the taffrail, where he could see the damaged frigate rolling downwind, officers trying to bring order to her ruined decks. And then she rolled to starboard and Hayden saw a gun slide back from the larboard rail, pick up speed quickly, and then slam into the bulwark opposite, sending splinters flying.

"Was that a cannon?" Hawthorne asked.

"Yes, one of their stern-chasers, I think. It has damaged the wheel, or perhaps that was our gunnery. We shall not need to worry about them for some time, I should think."

"Luck chose to side with the British that time," Hawthorne agreed.

"In every possible way. I don't know how our masts are still standing. It is a miracle, really."

"I shall inform Mr Smosh; he will be sorry to have missed it."

The second frigate and the chasing corvette had drawn nearer—nearer than Hayden had hoped, but he had not counted on being caught aback. The squall passed over and the wind reduced a little—it was not buffeting Hayden around so—though the gale was not showing any signs of dwindling.

For a long while Hayden stood at the rail until he was more or less satisfied that the chasing ships were not gaining. Archer and Wickham approached, standing two yards off until he noticed and motioned them to come aft.

"Well done, Mr Archer, Mr Wickham."

"Thank you, sir," Archer answered. "We took the top of a sea over the sills but managed to get the ports closed before it became a deluge."

"I was afraid we might."

"We will have everything put to rights before long."

"Very well. I will send word down to my steward. Let us repair below and share a meal. In half an hour?"

"Why, thank you, sir," the lieutenant said, clearly pleased.

"Do not be too grateful; I plan to offer my hospitality in your gunroom."

They all laughed, largely from relief at having survived the brief action unharmed.

Hayden took a tour of the gun-deck, which certainly had taken a soaking, and then the main deck, where he found Mr Barthe worriedly examining the larboard foremast shrouds.

"Your fears were well founded, Mr Barthe," Hayden said quietly. "We were caught aback . . . but we survived it."

"We did, sir, but our rig has paid a price. He reached out and shook one of the shrouds with both hands. I shall have them all set up taut again, for we stretched stays and shrouds terribly." He paused and met Hayden's eye. "It was well done, Captain."

"Thank you, Mr Barthe."

Hayden went down to the gunroom, where a meal was soon served. Hayden could not remember breaking his fast, though it was now past noon. His stomach, which had been overcome by nerves earlier, now cried out for sustenance and he ate as though he had not seen food in days.

"We certainly caught that Frenchman by surprise," Wickham observed rather smugly.

"Yes, and he caught us by surprise last night." Hayden thought of the carnage aboard the French frigate and the bleeding officer who had stared at him as he passed. His fork stopped en route to his mouth. "There is not a Frenchman aboard that ship that does not hate us with all of his heart and soul at this moment . . . and all of the British nation with us."

Perhaps the gravity of his tone spoke to them, for the two young officers hid away their smug smiles for a moment.

"What shall we do now, sir?" Wickham asked.

It was the very question Hayden had been asking himself. "We will see what the weather gods bring us, Mr Wickham. If the wind would take off enough for us to tack, I would do it in a trice. Both the undamaged ships are to leeward of us and we could make a board towards the English coast. I do not want to wear, as we shall lose ground to them. If the wind forces us all south, I should hope to round Ushant and find a pair of our frigates cruising off Brest. How we will do that with our chasing ships to leeward I cannot say." He eyed Wickham. "The weather is making our decisions, Mr Wickham, and we are but a cockle boat blown this way and that awaiting the wind's pleasure."

The relative warmth and sanctuary offered by the gunroom could not be long enjoyed on such a day—not by the captain—so Hayden very soon excused himself to return to the deck. His timing, however, could hardly have been worse; a squall swept down on the ship out of the north just as he emerged from the companionway and rain drummed madly upon his oilskins, soaking through almost without pause. Cold knifed through his clothing and the warmth and companionship of the gunroom were leached out of his body and soul in an instant.

The sea was a massive acreage of confused and surging hills, murky and dark, but streaked here and there with startling white. Crests broke and tumbled all around. Hayden thought the sea in such a state might be a home for whales but men did not belong there and the sea suffered them grudgingly.

Ransome, who stood with his shoulders hunched and back to the wind, spotted his captain and straightened.

"How fare our escorts, Mr Ransome?" Hayden asked him, almost shouting over the gale.

"I believed they gained upon us for a time, but now they appear to have fallen back, sir." He waved a hand towards the larboard quarter. "In the squalls they disappear entirely. But they are always there again when the squalls pass."

"They are not going to give us up on account of a little foul weather. What of the ship we raked; is she still in sight?"

"We lost all sight of her, Captain, but one can hardly see two miles and often fewer in this weather. She might not be so far off."

"Yes, we cannot count her out. Where is Mr Barthe?"

"He went down to see the doctor, sir. He slipped on the deck and twisted his ankle. Can hardly stand now, Captain Hayden."

"That is the worst news!" Hayden said, stifling a curse and genuinely alarmed. In such poor visibility and with the coast of France not very distant to leeward, he wanted his sailing master upon the deck, not lying below in a cot.

"Dryden believes we are due south of Start Point, sir. About fifty-five miles off the French coast. He does think we are being driven south, sir, and the winds have a little more west in them, if I am not mistaken."

"And the weather glass, Mr Ransome?"

"Steady, sir, or very nearly so."

Hayden nodded and crossed to the transom and wedged himself against the rail in the corner. His glass was carried to him by a seaman and Hayden steadied himself, fixed his eye upon the French ships, and raised the glass to his eye. Even in calm conditions it was not easy to find an object so small at such a distance in the lens of a long glass. Hayden had seen new midshipmen who could sweep the entire ocean and never find the object they wished. Many years at sea and familiarity with the instrument had taught him all the tricks. It was very rare that he would raise a glass to his eye and not have his object in view.

The two enemy ships were hard on the wind, climbing the seas and sending white water shooting from their bows each time they plunged into a trough. Their position relative to the *Themis* was largely unchanged; still the same distance to leeward and on the larboard quarter. Hayden scanned the sea in every direction, crossing the deck to sweep his glass to windward. Despite its being perhaps the most traversed area of sea in the world, he could find no other sails. The weather had chased everyone who did not need to be at sea into shelter.

His situation did not seem so terribly bad at this moment. Driving off the ship to windward made reaching England possible if the gale would moderate enough that he dared tack. His decision to attack the frigate off Le Havre did not seem quite so foolish now, given that he believed he could be in an English port in two days or fewer. This engendered a greater sense of relief than he would have imagined.

Ransome came and stood nearby, staring at the chasing ships.

"We must do everything within our power, Mr Ransome, to keep these Frenchmen distant until dark. We will separate ourselves from them this night." Hayden turned to the young lieutenant. "Has anyone seen to Mr Barthe? Is he still in the sick-berth?"

"He is, sir. Hobson went down to see him but has not yet returned."

"Then I shall look in on him myself, Mr Ransome."

Ransome saluted quickly, and Hayden crossed to the companion-way, going carefully down the heaving ladder—a stair, really—for tumbling down onto the gun-deck could mean a broken limb.

Upon the lower deck, opposite the midshipmen's berth, Hayden found Barthe in the surgeon's domain, seated upon a chair, his foot immersed in a bucket.

"Seawater," the doctor said from across the enclosed room, where he bent, looking in a seaman's ear.

"Seawater . . ." Hayden repeated.

"To bring down the swelling. It is cold as snow, or very nearly, and should do nicely."

"Ah." Hayden looked over at Mr Barthe, who appeared both sheepish and miserable.

"After all my years at sea, Captain Hayden, I cannot believe I would slip and turn my ankle in nothing more than a gale."

"It should have taken a tempest, at least," Hayden agreed, then turned to the doctor. "Is it broken, do you think, Dr Griffiths?"

Griffiths crossed over to a man hidden by the sides of a cot. "I cannot be certain," the physician replied, "until the swelling has been reduced. Mr Barthe cannot bear weight, which I hope means nothing in this case." Griffiths completed whatever he had been doing with his patient and turned to Hayden—his patient, Hale, sat up, took one look at Hayden, and collapsed back down into his berth.

"With all respect to the doctor, I am quite certain it is no more than a sprain," Barthe assured him. "Turned it over clumsily. Damned stupid thing to have done. I'll be back on my feet in a day, Captain. Until then, the doctor has a cane he is no longer in need of, I think."

"You will do no such thing," Griffiths said, standing erect between the beams and fixing an angry look upon the sailing master. "If it is broken, you will make matters worse—perhaps much worse. You will stay off your feet entirely for several days."

"But, Doctor," Barthe protested, his face going red, "we are being chased by French cruisers; the captain has need of me."

"Any assistance you may offer from a chair, Mr Barthe," the doctor said firmly. "But your usual cruising of the deck cannot be done, or I shall confine you to a cot."

"Sir . . ." Barthe appealed to Hayden.

"You may provide a great service, Mr Barthe, by overseeing Dryden's navigation . . . which you may do from a seated position. All of your duties on deck Mr Dryden can perform, and when he cannot be on the deck, Mr Franks and my lieutenants will manage nicely. Do not walk before you are able. I have a hobbled bosun; I shall not have a hobbled sailing master as well. For the moment we have sea room and are very certain of our position, so I think you should remain here under the doctor's care until we cannot do without you or the doctor has seen fit to have you carried up to your navigation table. That is an order, Mr Barthe, not a request."

"Aye, sir. But I should be there when Franks sets up the shrouds. He has a great inclination to set them up too tightly, sir."

"I shall see to it myself that he does not, Mr Barthe. You may rely upon it."

Hayden spoke briefly with the few men in the sick-berth and then nodded to the doctor, who followed him out. They walked off a few paces where they might speak in private.

"Is it broken, do you think?" Hayden asked.

"I cannot say. Mr Barthe is a large man and yet has rather delicate ankles and small feet. It is not impossible that he has a broken bone, though I am inclined to think that it is a sprain only. I shall know better once the swelling goes down. You must see to it that he is kept off his feet for a few days. If his foot is broken he might bring complications upon himself that he does not want. Some bones in the area of the foot do not readily knit back together—for reasons poorly understood—but I believe walking on an unhealed break can bring that about." The surgeon paused and regarded Hayden, his look measuring and shrewd. "You have need of him?"

"Dryden is very competent, but we may be forced to go very near some islands or even between the islands and the French coast. It is very demanding navigation, and a mistake might cost all our lives. Yes, I have need of him. Not at this very moment, but soon."

"I will give him all my attention and send him up the minute I deem him ready."

"Thank you, Doctor. I am master and commander, so I may have to assume both duties, I suppose."

"For which you are well trained, I am certain."

"Well enough, though I will say that Mr Barthe is a better navigator than I shall ever be. When his future as a lieutenant was blasted, the Navy gained an excellent sailing master."

"I fear Mr Barthe does not see it in quite the same way."

"I am certain you are correct. I shall look in on Mr Barthe later, if I am able."

Hayden climbed slowly back to the upper deck, fatigue suddenly washing over him and hindering every movement. As he mounted the ladder to the upper deck, a cry reached him.

"*On deck!*" the watch called from above. "Sail . . . off our larboard quarter. A league, sir, perhaps half a mile more."

Hayden bounded up the last few rungs and went immediately to the rail. There was an abrupt lightening off to leeward and aft, the sun piercing down through a hole in the cloud, illuminating the breaking seas so that they stood out against the dark ocean in stark relief. In this irregular patch of light, a sail appeared, reddish brown against a black sky.

Wickham and Archer both stood there with glasses up to their eyes.

"Is it a fourth ship?" Hayden asked.

Archer handed his commander his glass, which Hayden fixed on the distant vessel. A moment of careful contemplation.

"That will be the frigate we raked," Hayden informed Archer and Wickham and saw them relax visibly. He handed the glass back to Archer. "She has returned much more quickly than I hoped. The damage to her rig must have been less than it first appeared."

At that moment, the hole in the cloud shut and the distant ship appeared to wink out like a snuffed candle.

"She is some way off, sir," Wickham said, lowering his glass. "Four miles, I should think. She will not close with us this day unless the winds decide to favour the French much more than us."

Hayden looked around at the sky. The hole in the cloud made him wonder if the gale was blowing through, but there was no other sign of it, the cloud remaining dense and heavy in every direction.

Hayden felt the men around him on the deck waiting. Waiting for him to find a way out of their present predicament, for every man aboard realised that if the French ships ever closed with them they would all be prisoners.

Wickham was looking at him oddly.

"Mr Wickham . . . ?"

"Excuse me, sir, but you appear to be bleeding." The young man made a motion towards Hayden's neck.

Hayden reached up a hand and brought his fingers away crimson. The wound he had inflicted upon himself earlier refused to heal.

Five

His love walked upon the ground. Or so Frank Beacher kept repeating to himself. He did not inflate her accomplishments to near genius, nor did he consider her beauty to be above that of all other women. Her wit, though admired by all who knew her, was not greater than several others of his acquaintance. Erudition she possessed, certainly, and an excellent comprehension of various subjects. No one was ever heard to deny her charm, which perhaps was more irresistible than that of most women. But then, he believed he was allowed to inflate at least one of her many gifts—he was in love, after all, and was not that a lover's prerogative?

Their taking of the air with Henrietta and Cassandra was not proceeding entirely to plan. He and his friend Wilder were walking ahead—though now waiting upon a rise—while the objects of their attention idled along behind, chatting with great animation with Mrs Hertle and Penelope (who had invited herself along), as though unaware that two gentlemen awaited them.

The effect upon the two gentlemen was to make them feel extraneous to, if not unwanted by, the two women with whom they hoped to find some few moments alone.

Elizabeth Hertle looked up, spotted them upon the rise, and waved a gloved hand before returning her attention to her companions.

"Had I realised we would be left to our own company, Beacher, our time would have been better spent in shooting."

"At least we might have got something for the pot, gaining us acknowledgement from Mrs Carthew."

The two were silent a moment.

"I have it," Wilder said suddenly. "You fall down in a dead faint and I will kneel over you and chafe your wrists and fan you with my hat. If neither Miss Cassandra nor Miss Henrietta shows any alarm at this, we will quit this damned house and the Carthew family for ever. What say you?"

"An admirable plan, but I have always been a failure at play-acting. Perhaps you should collapse and I will fan."

Wilder began a swoon, and Beacher shot out a hand to steady him. "I said it in jest!"

His friend laughed. "So did I!"

"What is it that amuses you gentlemen so?" Elizabeth asked as they approached. They were, all four, pink-cheeked from the sun and exertion of walking up the long hill.

"We were just surmising, Mrs Hertle," Wilder answered, "that if one of us lay down and pretended to have swooned you would all walk by without taking the least notice."

The women laughed. "Why, that is utterly unfair to us, Mr Wilder," Henrietta declared. "If we found one of you lying upon the ground we would assume you had thrown yourself down in a puddle so that we should not soil our hems and we would, one by one, use you as a stepping-stone to cross over. That is how noble we believe you to be."

"Indeed, Miss Cassandra, we are excessively noble, but as we have not found a single puddle into which we might throw ourselves we are rather desolate. Are we not, Beacher?"

"Inconsolable, really."

"There is a small stream ahead," Cassandra offered innocently. "If the bridge is out, you might throw yourselves into it . . ."

"Well, then, let us pray the bridge has been washed away," Wilder enjoined.

"And the stream is in flood," added Beacher. "It is not worth doing if our lives are not in danger. That is the thing about puddles, one is only in mortal danger in the very deep ones."

"In the very deep ones we should have to heap you up, gentlemen, for one of you is not thick enough to keep our hems dry."

"Then we must eat more, Miss Cassandra, so as to become thicker. We must not risk your hems."

There continued much teasing and jesting on the matter of hems and puddles as they walked along beneath the overhanging trees. The April day was excessively fair and unseasonably warm, and, as Wilder had observed, the rains had been few, so the ground was dryer than any expected. Bees hummed among the spring flowers and the trees were all in their coats of soft, new green. Nary a cloud ventured forth that day, and a vault of deep azure spread from horizon to horizon almost without interruption. The walking party turned onto a path that branched from the lane and wound up through the trees. This way was so steep that the gentlemen must here or there offer a hand or an arm to one lady or another so that they all might proceed in safety. Wherever possible Beacher tried to offer such assistance to Henrietta, as Wilder did to Cassandra, though the latter was often heard to say, "Why, thank you, Mr Wilder, but your assistance is not required here where it is not so very steep. I intend to climb mountains one day, you know."

Penelope seemed to require the assistance of Beacher at every turn, until her sisters began to tease her, saying things such as, "Why, Pen, I believe you require Mr Beacher's hand almost constantly. What could have made you so feeble of a sudden, I wonder?"

In less than half an hour, they reached the top and laid blankets upon the greening grass with a view to the distant south. A picnic was spread out and enjoyed, with many jests about the thickening of the men present and many an insistence that they eat more as the stream might be in flood and the bridge gone.

As they ate, the conversation turned to other matters, such as the doings of the neighbours. When it was mentioned that one young woman of their acquaintance was soon to be married, Wilder ventured to ask a question of all the ladies.

"How long an acquaintance must a young couple require before the man should speak?"

"Most men should never speak, as they have so little to say," Cassandra replied.

"You have a very low opinion of men," Wilder said.

"Not at all. Women are far worse. Most have nothing to say at all. Present company excepted, of course."

"We Carthews all have too much to say," Henrietta observed.

"My question was asked in earnest," Wilder insisted.

"Seven years," Henrietta replied quickly. "Not a moment sooner."

"Mrs Hertle, you must have a considered answer to my question, though everyone else seems to think it in jest?"

"It depends upon the couple, Mr Wilder. It would be rather foolish for a gentleman to speak before he had attached a woman's feelings. But if, once that has been accomplished, he hesitates too long, then the poor girl doubts his attachment and may withdraw her own affection."

"You are saying neither too soon nor too late?"

"Yes, I suppose I am."

"But how is a gentleman to know when the moment is right?" Beacher asked rather anxiously. "I have known many instances where the man assumed that the woman returned his feelings only to have his suit rebuffed when he did speak, much to his pain and mortification."

"Any gentleman of an age to be married—and I do not speak of years—will know the right moment," Cassandra declared. "What would you have a woman do? Wear a white ribbon in her hair when the moment is perfect?"

"That would be much appreciated," Wilder said. "If you would please do so, all of the male sex would be for ever grateful."

"We will do no such thing," Henrietta said firmly. "It is not seemly for young women to go about signalling their readiness like . . . like . . . mares!"

"Hear, Henrietta," Elizabeth agreed. "I am of one mind with Cassandra; a man who is not able to read a woman's heart is not ready for marriage, as marriage much depends upon one's ability to penetrate the heart and mind of one's husband or wife. A man who cannot recognise when a woman's feelings have turned towards him is far too young for the gales and calms of marriage."

"But what if a man never knows?" Beacher lamented. "Are such men doomed to remain always alone?"

"They should never marry," Elizabeth asserted. "Unfortunately, there are interfering busybodies about who will steer them or give them a shove at the right moment, and they will speak and the poor girl in question is herself too young to realise that the boy is unsuited to the long, demanding years of marriage. We have all seen such unhappy unions. I dare say spinsterhood is preferable." She shuddered visibly.

"Then you are all in agreement that sensing the right moment is a test of a man's suitability for marriage?"

"In a way, yes, though it is certainly not the only thing that makes a man suitable."

"What are the others, pray, Mrs Hertle?"

"I do not know if I will say more, sir. To what purpose do you ask these questions?"

"With only honourable intentions, madam. Mr Beacher and myself hope one day to marry and therefore need to understand what will make us suitable prospects and then what aspects of our character we must nurture to be exemplary husbands and fathers. We have no intention but that, and would never dream of using anything you might say to take the least advantage of any young woman. And though I am a near stranger to you, Mr Beacher you have known all your lives and you must therefore have the highest opinion of his character. I hope he will vouch the same for me."

"What say you, Mr Beacher?" Cassandra asked.

"Wilder is an untrustworthy rogue. The young women of London cast themselves at his feet and he but walks upon their hearts like so many stepping-stones."

"Beacher!" Wilder said, pretending to be offended.

"I jest. He is as good-hearted as a girl of six, and I say this as a compliment. He is as honest and considerate and amiable as a man of four and twenty might be. There is many a mother out there scheming to have him for her own daughter, but Wilder is a romantic and waiting for the mate of his soul."

"Well then, Mr Wilder, as Frank has given you such a good character, and Frank is our dearest confidant and brother, I will answer your question. First, he must be a man, not a boy. He must know his own mind, have the respect of others, be charitable when it is appropriate and decisive when needed. Confident but never arrogant. He must listen to the opinions of others, even if the final decision falls upon him. Amiable, of course, lively, of good humour, and he must laugh readily and not become downhearted when things turn against him, for life will test everyone sooner or later." Mrs Hertle stopped then, considering, perhaps, other qualities to add to her catalogue, but Cassandra took it up.

"No young woman wants a man who is a despot in his own home and believes everyone must bend to his will and can never make the least accommodation for others."

"I could never marry a man who did not love music," Penelope declared passionately. "Such a man must be dead to all finer feelings."

"Well said," Cassandra agreed. "Never marry a man who is dead."

"I did not say 'dead'!" Pen protested. "'Dead to all finer feelings.'"

"And that as well. A man dead in any way at all is to be avoided."

"Miss Henrietta," Wilder addressed her, "have you nothing to add to this growing catalogue?"

"Honesty, Mr Wilder. Above all things, honesty."

"And loyalty," Beacher added.

"I am not soliciting your opinion, Beacher. We are enquiring into the female mind on such matters."

"Yes, the male mind is too well known. 'Beauty,'" Cassandra announced. "Men desire beauty and little more."

"I do think that is somewhat unfair," Wilder addressed her. "I for one am seeking a woman who does not fit into the common mould, who does not desire only a house and children and a comfortable income. Someone with a sense of adventure."

"Sandra intends to climb mountains and see every corner of the world, Mr Wilder. Perhaps we should arrange a marriage for you."

"I am perfectly capable of arranging my own affairs, thank you," Cassandra told them firmly. "And I am certain that Mr Wilder does not desire a woman as headstrong as I am. Leave the poor man in peace."

"Every woman—but Cassandra, of course—desires a home and a secure life in which to raise her children. It is part of the female character, I think." Elizabeth looked around at her cousins to see if they did not agree.

"So we might add a house and a comfortable income to the inventory of merits a man must have?"

"By all means, add whatever merits to this list that you wish," Henrietta agreed, "but we will lose our hearts to whom we lose our hearts. Some might choose not to marry for love, but for those who do . . ." She lifted her hands and shrugged helplessly. "We may only pray that the man who steals our heart is good and kind. Beyond that, wish for anything you desire, but do not put too much store in it."

"You are saying the heart will make its own decision and not consult the head?"

"I fear so, Mr Wilder. And all of our fancies and hopes shall be set aside and we shall have to make the best of the situation we find ourselves in."

"The heart shows little wisdom in these matters, Miss Henrietta," Wilder said. "At least, that is what I have observed."

"Can one not fall in love with another because of the qualities we have listed?" Mrs Hertle proposed. "That is to say, those are the very things that draw our own feelings?"

"Such as a house and a comfortable income?"

"Those are material things, Mr Wilder. I was speaking of human traits."

"That seems rather mature, Mrs Hertle. Is anyone's heart formed of such seasoned wood?"

"Elizabeth's is," Henrietta informed the others. "It has never been swayed by a handsome face or a thin veneer of charm. No, she fell in love with Captain Hertle because he was like her, dependable no matter what the situation."

"I am rather more romantic than that, Henri!" her cousin protested.

"Are you, my dear? Then only you and Captain Hertle know of it."

"Which is as it should be," Elizabeth replied.

When the men had been sufficiently "thickened" and the women had attempted to eat as to achieve the opposite, the group broke up, Elizabeth taking Pen off somewhat against her will to appreciate the views towards the north. Cassandra and Wilder walked to the hill's very crest to enjoy both the views and to see the locally famous oak that was said to have been planted there on the birth day of Queen Elizabeth, though no one quite believed it. It was, however, very suitably gnarled and excessively broad across the bole.

Henrietta and Beacher were left alone on the blanket, enjoying the new warmth of the April sun. It took Beacher a moment to work up his nerve, but then he said:

"Henri?"

She was tilting her face to the sun, eyes closed, a tiny smile upon her lips.

"Hmm?"

"Last night, when you enquired after your father's health—I mean after dinner . . ."

"Yes?"

"Well, I did imagine that you meant to say something else but had a change of heart . . ."

"Oh, that." Henrietta gave a little laugh. "Elizabeth had this absurd idea—I am almost embarrassed to say it. Please promise not to laugh?"

"I do promise."

"She had this idea that your feelings for me were . . . rather more romantic than brotherly, and I had come to put my mind to rest on that matter. But then I realised it could not be so. We have been sister and brother all our lives. It would be almost . . . indecent for either of us to feel any other way." She smiled as though to say, "See how foolish I was."

"But I do, Henrietta," Beacher forced out, almost a whisper.

Henrietta's eyes came fully open now, and she stared at him in the greatest possible surprise.

"You do what?"

"Have feelings for you . . . I have had for . . . for ever, it seems."

"Frank, do not make a jest of such things."

"I am utterly sincere."

"Oh, Frank"—she put a hand to her mouth—"this will never do. We are destined to be siblings. That is what I have always believed— that we would be brother and sister into our old age."

"But I . . . I have thought otherwise. That your feelings for me, in time, would change. That you would see I am devoted to you in both heart and soul and have been since we were very young."

"I can hardly think what to say," Henrietta stammered.

"You need not reply or say anything at all. I simply could not go on without telling you. Earlier you said that you valued honesty above all other virtues—I have been honest." Frank rose up. "I shall go and see how the views look to the north this day. Will you accompany me?"

"I . . . if you do not mind, I will remain here and ponder what you have said."

"As you wish."

Beacher wandered off, but not to the north as he had told Henrietta. Instead he skirted the hill until he found a west-facing outcropping of stone and sat down, staring off towards the distant horizon. "Well," he said softly to himself. "For good or ill I have confessed my feelings. Now we shall see." Sitting there, he vacillated between hope and despair, one moment thinking that Henrietta might look within and discover that she shared his feelings, the next certain that she would dash all his hopes for ever and he did not know what he would do.

Henrietta almost desperately wanted to take Elizabeth aside to tell
her what had occurred, but no such opportunity presented itself and
so the walking party meandered, at a pace so slow as to be torture,
back at last to Box Hill.

They returned pink-cheeked from the sun and exercise, doffed
their outer garments, and went off to their various pursuits, there
being more than an hour remaining until dinner.

Henrietta whispered to Elizabeth to meet her in the library, and
a quarter of an hour later she made her way there, fending off well-
meaning enquiries from her mother as to the pleasures of their
outing.

Elizabeth perched upon a sofa with a book open upon her lap. She
looked up, her brows pressed together, and said, "I am quite certain
my French was much better than it is now when we were young. Do
you remember how well I spoke and could read everything? I am
making very heavy sledding of this book, I must tell you."

"Your French was of the very first order, I am sure, but never
mind that now. I must tell you of my conversation with Frank. It is
positively awful."

The book snapped closed and was quickly deposited on a small
table as Henrietta sat down beside her cousin. Elizabeth immediately took both her hands.

"Do tell me. Do not make me wait. Here is my hanky. Try not
to weep, my dear. It cannot be so very bad, can it?"

"You were absolutely correct," Henri finally managed to press
out. "Frank . . ." For a moment she pressed her eyes closed and made
herself breathe—a measured in and out. "Frank confessed his feelings to me this very afternoon. How could I have been unaware of
them these many years?"

"And what did you say to him in return?"

"He begged me say nothing at all but stated that he could not
keep his feelings secret any longer and that he must tell me. And

then he went off and left me in such a state of confusion as I have hardly ever known. Good, dear Frank! I feel utterly wretched to think that he has known a single moment of heartache on my account."

Elizabeth's lovely brows pressed together in confusion. "So he asked your hand but bid you not reply?"

"No such thing occurred. He merely told me of his profound attachment. And then went off." She drew back a little, as though some understanding had come over her suddenly. "If he feels thus, then why did he not ask for my hand?"

"It is rather . . . odd." Elizabeth looked down at her cousin's hands held in her own. "But, Henri, what of your own heart? What is it that you feel?"

"I feel . . . I feel as though I am spinning, round and round, until I cannot keep my feet beneath me and everyone . . . everyone who reaches out to me only does so to spin me faster."

Six

Upon returning to the deck, Hayden found the sea and weather unchanged but for a noticeable hauling of the wind into the north-west. He welcomed the lengthening days of spring with a daily growing joy and sense of hopefulness, but on this date the long day was as much an enemy as the French. His only hope of escape was darkness. An almost irresistible urge to constantly scan the horizon had to be opposed. He could not count on rescue by British ships, though the fear of a fourth French ship appearing had to be constantly pressed down. To show confidence in such a situation was the captain's duty, but Hayden had never understood how difficult this would prove. There was little to be confident about. If this miserable gale moderated, the French ships might be carried up to him on a more favourable wind or his ship left wallowing. At that moment, the gale was his ally.

There were so many possibilities of weather and ill luck that his head swam with them. And occasionally, unbidden, his troubles with Henrietta would surface and it was only with difficulty that he turned his mind away. It was a measure of how much this estrangement distressed him that even in his present danger his mind ever returned to Henrietta.

The ship's bell sounded. Five and one half hours of daylight re-

mained. If the heavy cloud persisted, twilight would be blessedly
brief and neither starlight nor moonlight would penetrate down to
the sea. They might be able to effect an escape under cover of darkness. Hayden turned back to the chasing ships, gauging their speed.
For now he must keep the distance between them. If they closed to
within a few hundred yards, he might have no chance of escape.

Hayden spoke with the master's mate, Dryden, and explained Mr
Barthe's condition and their present predicament in detail.

"I have kept up Mr Barthe's dead-reckoning, sir, taking into account tidal currents and leeway. I do not think I can be too far off
our present position, though a landmark would be most welcome."

"There will be little chance of sighting land for some hours, depending upon what we do this night. If the wind continues to back
we shall be forced south; rounding the corner of Brittany will then
become a matter of the gravest concern. Seldom can we see beyond
a league in this weather, and we dare not come upon a lee shore
with so little offing. It would be the end of us."

Hayden went below with the master's mate and looked over his
chart, scrutinizing all his calculations, which appeared to have been
done meticulously. The "cocked hat"—the triangle within which
Dryden placed the *Themis*—was larger than Hayden would have
liked, but he did not think their position could be calculated more
narrowly. The important thing to remember was that their ship
could be anywhere within that triangle and was probably not at the
precise centre.

Upon the deck again, Hayden found himself gravitating to the
stern rail, where the sight of the chasing ships was like a sore that
one could not leave alone; one was drawn back to it again and again.
A throat was cleared three paces off.

"Ah, Mr Hawthorne," Hayden said, waving the marine lieutenant forward. "Is there some matter upon which you require my assistance?"

"Not at all, sir, I was merely hoping for a better view of the French. Their uniforms are so stylish, do you not find?"

"No more than your own, Mr Hawthorne."

The marine came and stood beside his captain. Ransome approached at that moment and reported progress on several matters upon which Hayden had given him orders. He touched his hat with great respect and went off at a near trot.

"Is it my imagination, Mr Hawthorne," Hayden wondered aloud, "or is Mr Ransome suddenly the most dutiful officer aboard my ship?"

"So it would appear, sir. He has also been going to great lengths to cultivate Acting Lieutenant Wickham. And how better to impress young Wickham than by becoming as dutiful and conscientious as our young lord?"

"I see, and impressing Mr Wickham will gain him what exactly?"

"A cynical man might think it has somewhat to do with Mr Wickham's two unmarried sisters, both reportedly handsome and amiable and certain to have sizeable sums settled upon them, I should think."

"Have we cynical men aboard this ship?"

"I have been told there might be one or two."

"Do you think Mr Wickham is cognizant of Ransome's design?"

"He is a trusting young lad, sir, for all of his natural abilities as a sea officer."

"Yes, I am afraid you are right." Hayden considered this a moment. "Let us wait and see if Wickham does not work this out on his own."

"I agree, sir."

"You have heard about Mr Barthe, no doubt?"

"I have been receiving hourly reports from Mr Wickham, who has been slipping down to look in on the sailing master whenever he is able."

"Now, that is dutiful. The doctor believes it is only a sprain. Nothing life-threatening."

"If I were one of the cynical men rumoured aboard our ship, I might think Mr Wickham's concern for the sailing master had somewhat to do with Mr Barthe's lovely daughters, or one in particular."

Hayden looked sharply at Hawthorne, who stared out to sea. "I do hope you jest. The Marquis would never allow such a match."

"I am quite certain you are right, but a young man's heart—not to mention his imagination—is very adept at sweeping aside any possible impediments to his suit."

"Well, that is a situation doomed to heartbreak and disappointed hopes. Is Mr Barthe aware of this attachment?"

"I do not know if it is an attachment. Perhaps more of an infatuation, I should think. And as to Mr Barthe, I cannot say if he is cognizant of it. But could he even dream of a more advantageous match for one of his daughters? Even if Wickham were not from the family he is, certainly he would be a captain and very likely an admiral one day. His future is almost assured. For the daughter of a sailing master there could hardly be a better match."

"Mr Barthe should contemplate this matter a little more reasonably. He would realise that it can never be."

"In such matters, Captain, an old man's heart—not to mention his fancy—is very adept at sweeping away any possible impediments to an advantageous match for his daughter." Hawthorne turned to look more directly at his captain. "Would you not wish Mr Wickham to be the suitor of your own daughter, should you have one?"

"Indeed, I could think of no one better. How is it, Mr Hawthorne, that you are aware of all these goings-on when the captain is not?"

"The captain has greater matters requiring his attention—the safety of the ship and two hundred souls, foremost. You mind the souls, I shall see to the hearts."

"I believe we shall leave the souls to Mr Smosh. Now, there is a man likely to grow an infatuation for one of Mr Barthe's daughters. Has he met them?"

"I do not believe so. And with all my great respect for our good priest, I do not believe he should make as excellent a husband as he does a ship's parson."

"Between us, I fear I must agree. I do not believe that Mr Smosh is cut out for the constancy of marriage." Hayden could not help but smile to hear the marine make such a statement. Hayden thought much the same of Hawthorne—a much better marine officer than husband and father.

"I rather think we should keep him clear of Mr Barthe's daughters, for the good of all concerned."

"Why, Mr Hawthorne, do I detect a note of protectiveness in your voice? Can it be that these young ladies have drawn out some noble instinct within you?"

"The relations between the men aboard this ship are complicated enough. Allow romantic attachments to inflict themselves upon some of these gentlemen and . . . well, disappointed hopes, fortune seeking, not to mention more ignoble behaviour, and you shall have such resentment and anger between your officers as no captain can heal."

"Mr Hawthorne, you never cease to surprise me."

"Thank you, sir. I take pride in it."

"And well you should."

The two stood at the rail in companionable silence for a few moments.

"How certain are we of finding our own cruisers lying off Brest?" Hawthorne asked after a while.

"They are there, or should be."

"Like the frigate that was supposed to be lying off Toulon warning British ships that the port was in French hands? Driven off by a gale not so very different from this, if I remember correctly?"

"Not impossible, as you suggest, but this gale at least is not making the coast around Brest a lee shore. Any frigate under command of a determined officer should be able to stay on station."

"Then let us pray for determined officers. Captain." Hawthorne touched his hat respectfully and went off, leaving Hayden alone at the rail. He raised his glass and quizzed the French ships again—was it his imagination or could he see them gaining measurably on his own ship?

The afternoon wore on, ships gaining then losing, wind hauling forward a point or two and then aft. All in all, the weather almost seemed to be forcing the ship to round the point of Brittany and the not-so-distant island of Ushant. Although this would take him further from England, the idea that the *Themis* might join forces with British frigates watching the harbour of Brest and turn the tables on the ships chasing him was some compensation. The idea of new prize money seemed a balm to all his trouble, especially since his prize agent would no doubt attempt to tie up any previous monies the prize court saw fit to finally award him.

Hayden did, at that moment, wonder if he was becoming one of the avaricious sea officers he had so long despised, putting prize money before duty, but then decided that his orders had been to destroy the frigate sailing from Le Havre and the most likely course to accomplish that would be to join up with the frigates on station outside the roads at Brest. Once the French frigates had been taken, he would sail with all speed for Plymouth and send his report to the Admiralty.

Immediately, he felt better.

The wind finally decided to do as the sailing master had earlier predicted and went into the north-east. Although this might allow Hayden to shape his course for the Irish station, he chose instead to use this wind to take him around Ushant and into Brest roads.

Late in the night, with the wind taking off and the sea going down, Hayden, Barthe, his mate Dryden, and Lieutenant Archer all huddled over a chart showing the coast of Brittany and the waters through which they sailed. Where their ship lay upon this chart, however, was a matter of distressing uncertainty.

They had seen neither land nor sun for the last few days, and the Channel was beset by tidal currents that could not be predicted with perfect reliability. They had also been set south to some unknown degree by the winds so that the distance to the coast of France was uncertain. When all the lines representing these factors had been pencilled upon the chart and allowances made for the possibility of error, not to mention the unknown, the area in which the *Themis* might be found was distressingly large. In fact, it included the north coast of the island of Ushant itself.

"Well, Mr Barthe," Hayden observed, "as we are not upon the rocks I would assume we are not here." Hayden placed his finger upon the aforementioned outpost of France.

From above, the men heaving the lead and calling the depths could be heard through the deck planks.

"If we are so near to Ushant," Archer offered thoughtfully, "then the French ships would be very foolish to try to pass inboard of us."

"If they believe they are in the same position we do," Hayden replied. "If they are certain we are more distant from the island— and these are *their* waters—then they might well sail inside us and try to prevent us from reaching Brest roads. I have no doubt that they have penetrated our plan."

Wickham appeared at that moment, emerging from his watch below looking not the least refreshed. He joined the others gathered about the chart in the small circle of light offered by a swaying lantern. A glance at the chart was all he needed to understand the nature of the debate.

"One would think this bloody island would have the decency to remain fixed in one place," Wickham said, "but I have known it to be several miles further out to sea than it had any right to be."

"They are a froward lot . . . islands," Dryden agreed.

Hayden looked around the circle of faces and found certainty nowhere. "Well, I see nothing for it. We must give Ushant a wide berth unless we catch sight of it as the weather lifts. If the French slip inboard of us, then we will have no choice but to shape our course accordingly. I will not risk my ship and two hundred souls."

It was an answer that pleased no one, for it placed them in an awkward position if the French could sail in between the *Themis* and the coast of France, but no one was willing to assert that they knew, unequivocally, the position of their ship.

"We will hold this course until daylight, at which point, if we have not caught sight of Ushant, we will turn south, wind allowing."

Heads nodded in agreement, and both Archer and Barthe acknowledged the order by repeating it. The little gathering broke up and Hayden went up onto the deck with Wickham, who was about to begin his watch.

"Daylight will find us soon enough," Wickham observed as they emerged into weather that had moderated a great deal in the past few hours.

"Where are the Frenchmen?" Hayden asked Ransome, who met them at the ladder head.

The young lieutenant pointed to lights some distance astern. "They show no signs of gaining or of altering their course to larboard, Captain."

"I suspect they are no more certain of their position than we," Hayden declared, undecided if he should take comfort from that idea or not.

"The wind has taken off considerable, sir, and the sea is not so angry as it was. No bottom at fifty fathoms. Our course remains west by south." Ransome waved a hand at the sea. "I fear we might have a sea mist forming to the south, sir."

Hayden almost brightened at this observation. "So we might hope, Mr Ransome."

The sun's rising was drowned in a blur of silvery fog and the wind died away to a whisper. The sea, which had diminished through the night with the dying wind, fell to a low, oily swell.

The pursuing ships were lost in the obscuring mists, yet there was no wind upon which the *Themis* could make good her escape. They were becalmed . . . somewhere.

Seven

Y ou burned it . . . before reading it?" Henrietta gazed at her cousin, Elizabeth Hertle, who made a small shrugging motion and opened her hands, which rested in her lap.

Elizabeth had admitted to having burned a letter received by her from Charles Hayden before she had set out from London.

"What could Mr Hayden possibly write that would change my opinion of him? That he did not mean to cause you pain? That he was overcome with remorse and guilt?—though not enough, apparently, to have him act honourably. No, there was not a single thing he could say that I was willing to hear. Mr Hayden is not welcome in my home; nor are his badly contrived excuses. He is a rogue, and I do not suffer rogues . . . nor do I apologise for it."

Henrietta noted that Elizabeth was no longer using "Charles," which formerly she had when she was speaking of him with affection, or even "Captain Hayden," which she commonly had to express her high regard. It was now "Mr Hayden" or even "that man."

"I should not like to earn your bad opinion, Cousin."

"I am quite certain you never shall, Henri. Never could you act dishonourably—it is not in your nature."

A soft knock on the door curtailed Henrietta's answer, and this was followed by the appearance of Frank Beacher, a hat in hand and dressed for the outdoors.

"It would seem I have not arrived at the best possible moment. Shall I return later?"

Henrietta stood. "That will not be necessary; I am quite ready to take the air."

"Would you care to join us, Mrs Hertle?" Beacher asked.

"Very kind of you to enquire, Mr Beacher, but I have promised Penelope that I would visit with her. Enjoy your walk, my dears," she said, and smiled upon the two benevolently.

Penelope, Elizabeth noted, looked more like her mother. The sisters Carthew were either slightly round-faced, with beautiful complexions, blue eyes, and corn-silk yellow hair, or they were oval-faced and dark-haired with eyes almost difficult to describe, for they could be either brown, flecked with amber, or, in the right light, deeply green. They were all of them lovely, she thought. All themselves. Henri was the most dutiful and possessed the purest intellect, while Anne had the most independent mind or perhaps "spirit." Unlike Henri, she chafed at all the bonds of family and even of her sex. Not that she did not adore the Carthew clan—Elizabeth was quite certain she did—but the expectations of family she had little time for. More than anything, Anne wished to make her own life on her own terms.

Penelope was clay not yet formed. She had aspects of all her sisters—but these things she was merely trying on, Elizabeth thought, like dresses to see if they might fit. Being the youngest, she dwelt in the shade cast by her accomplished sisters, and struggled mightily even to be noticed. But she was, Elizabeth could not help but see, growing into the most beautiful of the Carthews, and notice was being taken of this—by a good number of young men. And like all girls her age, this notice did not escape her. She rather enjoyed it, in truth. But her heart belonged to only one young man—and he, as these things often went, was mad for another: Henrietta.

Pen might have been young, but she was no more a fool than anyone in her family and she was busy remaking herself to win the regard of Frank Beacher. She was not fashioning herself into a little Henrietta—she was too bright for that, and by temperament too dissimilar—but she was becoming more serious of mind, more gracious rather than girlish. She worked to acquire wit and charm—and where better to learn these traits than in a household where they flourished?

Despite these newly serious aims, she knelt upon a rug on the floor and played with a puppy, displaying all of the abandon of a girl one third her age. She even giggled.

In the manner of all puppies, he suddenly jumped up and wandered clumsily off, sniffing along the floor, his soft, yellowish coat all but aglow in the firelight.

Pen watched him a moment and then said, "Do you know what all the whispering is about, Lizzie?"

"Whispering?"

"Yes. I have come upon Cassandra and Anne whispering together, and immediately they saw me and went silent and looked as though they had been caught engaged in some enterprise that was terribly forbidden."

"Well, if they have some secret, they have not seen fit to include me. Might it have something to do with the two handsome young men dwelling beneath this roof?"

"So one would assume." She considered a moment. "They never include me in their secrets." This she said with the smallest indication of petulance—a little slip in the new persona she was crafting. She made that peculiar noise with tongue and teeth that people did when they called to animals, and the puppy came dutifully lumbering back to throw himself half in her lap, then rolled over to be patted. As casually as she could, Pen asked, "Do you think that Henri has . . . had a change of heart towards Frank Beacher?"

"I suppose it is possible. He is very amiable, is he not? Possessed of an excellent mind and temperament. There is much to recommend him."

"Oh, yes . . . a very great deal," Penelope gushed. She stopped petting her little charge. "He is rather mad for her, is he not?"

Elizabeth did not want to injure her young cousin, but she wondered if the truth might not prepare her a little for what Elizabeth was beginning to think was inevitable. "It would seem that he is, Pen."

Nothing was said for a moment, though Pen's face darkened noticeably, and a veil of unhappiness appeared to spread over her as she absorbed this.

"Too bad about the Navy man . . ." she said after a moment. "Everyone was of the opinion that they would marry, though no one approved, of course."

"No one approved?"

"No, everyone thought it a poor match. Henri is not so strong as you, Lizzie; if her husband were at sea and in danger most of each year, she should pine away and most likely grow ill. Or so everyone said, but I thought—if he made her happy—well, she would learn to live with his absences."

"They are difficult," Elizabeth almost whispered.

"But he turned out to be a bounder, sadly." Pen glanced up. "Sorry, Lizzie, what did you say?"

Elizabeth shook her head and waved a hand as though to say, "Nothing at all," though she felt suddenly like weeping.

Pen began to gently scratch the pup behind the ears, and he closed his eyes as though transported. "I do not really believe Henri has feelings for Frank—except of the fraternal variety, of course. She is just confused and heartbroken, and sees Frank as the devoted friend and someone who would never cause her pain or behave dishonourably. She has been knocked over by her captain's betrayal and Frank has caught her. That is all. I do hope one of them sees this before it is too late." She glanced up at her cousin. "Do you not agree?"

"I . . . I am not so sure. Aunt Hertle is of the opinion that it is better to discover yourself in love with someone with whom you have had an acquaintance of some years than some stranger who sweeps in and snatches away your heart. Henri and Frank have known each other almost all their lives."

"Perhaps, when one is as old as Lady Hertle, such an opinion seems sensical. I am in agreement with the sentiment Henri expressed at our picnic recently—our hearts make choices our minds might not approve. 'Choosing' to fall in love with someone, or not to fall in love with them . . . well, that is not love at all. That is merely 'selecting' as one might a gown or jewellery or a carriage."

"You are romantic, Pen."

"I am!" she said a bit curtly. "And I am not ashamed of it."

"Good for you."

A silence that extended beyond ten minutes ensued and then, without looking up from slowly petting her dog, who was now asleep and breathing softly, Pen said, "Mr Wilder has been paying much attention to Cassandra, has he not?"

"I suppose he has," Elizabeth answered, thankful to have the subject changed. "What do you think of him, Penelope? I cannot claim to know him at all."

"Nor I, really. Frank likes him overly, and father is developing a very high opinion of him."

"I sense that you do not share this entirely?"

"Certainly, I have not formed a poor opinion of him . . ." She stopped here to reflect, a look of mild confusion creasing her brow.

"But you are not certain?" prompted Elizabeth.

"I suppose I feel I must know him better. Then perhaps he shall gain my greatest approbation . . . or so I hope." She tried to smooth the pup's curly hair, though it sprang back at each attempt. "Is it not peculiar how some people we feel immediate affection for—as though we have known them for years when it can sometimes be only a few hours. And others we never feel that for, even when they give us no reason to think or feel otherwise."

"Do you think that Mr Wilder is of this latter category?"

"I cannot say. Certainly he is not of the former. And I do not mean to suggest that I mislike him or have any reason to feel other than kindly towards him. He has been a perfect gentleman—is very pleasant company at table. Mr Beacher and he can be very ironical when together. My, they have made me laugh!"

"Mr Wilder seems . . . to lack a certain seriousness. He still dreams that he will sail off to some distant land and make discoveries and win great fame and reward."

"He and Cassandra are of one mind in this . . . of course, people do sail off and make discoveries and gain the regard of the great and learned. Father's elephant tusks did not come from Sussex, after all."

"People do, but I suspect the hardships are much greater than either Sandra or Mr Wilder comprehend. I believe these people who go off to distant places are of a different breed to most of us. We think some small inconvenience a hardship—when we are shut up in the house by rain for more than three days together. They must walk miles in mud and heat being devoured by insects, always wary of snakes and wild animals. The most alarming illnesses descend upon them, and they are without the comforts of civilisation for months—sometimes years—on end. Do you really think that Cassandra would delight in such a situation? Would Mr Wilder?"

"I should wager my money on Cassandra before Mr Wilder, to be sure."

They both laughed at this.

"Do not breathe a word to Mr Wilder, but I do agree. Therefore, he is not suited to her. He would be back in London inside of a month—classifying her collection."

"For our Cassandra," Penelope observed, "we require someone wilder."

"My dear, you have stooped very low for that terrible pun."

"One must always stoop low for puns—they are of no value otherwise."

"Hmm." Neither spoke a word for a moment.

Then, to break the silence, Elizabeth said, "Perhaps I should have a tête-à-tête with Anne or Cassandra and endeavour to discover the cause of all this 'whispering.'"

"Ask if it has anything at all to do with a letter. I thought I heard them whisper 'letter' but could not be certain."

"I shall certainly bring up the subject of letters. Has one of them received a letter recently?"

"Several. They are both great letter writers, as you well know. Which letter they might be referring to I cannot say."

Anne and Cassandra had to be gathered together, since they were commonly involved in wholly different endeavours, as their very distinct personalities dictated. The former had been diligently at work upon her newest pursuit—a novel—and the latter only just returned from riding with Mr Wilder and Mr Carthew. They were soon herded into the library, where a fire was kindled, and they sat near the hearth, each a picture of good health and surprising contentment, given their relative youth.

The truth was that Elizabeth was not very much concerned about Anne and Sandra's secrets or even a letter. She was much more concerned with the fragility of poor Pen's heart at that moment, as the man she adored clearly courted her older sister. Being excluded by her siblings, though a common enough occurrence, was only lowering her mood even more. Elizabeth's sole intent was to appeal for greater understanding of their poor sister, who was having her heart broken for the first time. She hoped to remind them of their own first heartbreak.

To begin, Elizabeth heard about their days, which were filled with activity both physical and mental. She then slowly worked around to the real purpose of this gathering.

"Penelope and I had a lovely visit this morning . . . and I must tell you she is very distressed that Mr Beacher is showing so much preference for Henrietta. You both know Pen's feeling for Mr Beacher?"

They both did and said so, though neither seemed to take her point. Clearly, they thought Pen's devotion to Frank Beacher merely a childish attachment that she should grow out of, and the sooner the better.

"Pen is not a child any longer," Elizabeth insisted, "and has grown a woman's heart—not unlike your own. Perhaps you have not had the misfortune of having your heart broken, but I can assure you it is an affliction as severe as the worst fever. I do think we should make an effort to be a little solicitous and kind to poor Penelope as she finds her way through this. A woman's heart she may have, but it is a young woman's heart and not yet proof against the pains and disappointments she will encounter."

Cassandra and Anne looked suitably chastised and prepared to treat their sister as an emotional invalid for the time being.

"She especially dislikes being excluded from your confidence and said you have been whispering about something or other of late . . ."

Elizabeth was not prepared for the reaction to this. She had known these young women all their lives and was very familiar with their range of expression. They both coloured noticeably and glanced at each other in something like panic.

In less than a moment, they both had excused themselves on some thin pretext and nearly fled the room. Lizzie was left alone in both confusion and alarm.

"What in the world are these girls up to?" she wondered.

Clearly, this letter—assuming it was a letter—had somewhat to do with Pen, or her sisters would not have kept her in the dark. Whatever could it be? she wondered.

The door opened at that instant and Henrietta came quickly in, her cheeks all aglow from the fresh air and spring sun.

"Why, Henri, you are positively glowing with youth and health. What young man would not have his head turned were he to see you now?"

From the look on Henrietta's face you would have thought there were no words that could cause her greater distress.

"Frank Beacher has just asked for my hand," Henri announced, threw herself down on a chair, covered her face, and began to silently weep.

It took many a moment for Henrietta to master herself, with several setbacks along the path. Tears were wiped away, began to flow afresh, were erased, returned, and were stoppered more or less, though Elizabeth did not doubt that they lurked very near the surface. In truth, they pooled and glistened at the edges of Henrietta's eyes, threatening always to spill over.

Perhaps the most alarming aspect of this display of feeling—to the perception of Elizabeth—was that it did not seem an outpouring of overwrought emotion or overwhelming joy. Henrietta was genuinely distressed . . . and Elizabeth had been promoting this attachment, had almost been acting as matchmaker, and yet now that Frank Beacher had finally spoken, Henrietta seemed disconsolate. It was not at all what she had hoped for or ever expected.

"Henri, Henri," she said softly, almost cooing. "What is wrong, my darling? You are under no obligation to marry Frank Beacher, and if you do decline I dare say he is young and hearty—he will survive."

"I cannot tell you why I have responded . . ." For a moment she appeared to be at a loss, and then she merely gestured to herself: ". . . in this manner. I really cannot. I am just . . ." But she could not finish, for tears began to flow again and did for several more minutes. "I am just so . . . unhappy. I can hardly bear it, Lizzie . . . And I do not know why."

The two cousins sat upon the sofa, one overcome by sorrow and the other feeling alternately confusion then consternation and embarrassment that she had promoted this match. Clearly, she should have listened to her own words when she spoke against interfering busybodies pushing young people together. It was one thing to ignore the advice of well-meaning friends and relations, but to utterly ignore your own, hard-won wisdom was simply folly . . . and she did not like to feel foolish.

Eight

They floated on a sea of mercury, drowned in a milky haze. The air, cool and deathly still, was aglow with glistening droplets. Every surface of the ship was overlain and dripping with water condensed out of the haze. The creaking of cordage, men moving about, muttered conversation from below, and then the plaintive cry of a gull somewhere out in the fog—but where Hayden could not say. The sound could have come from aft, or from out to sea, or from any point of the compass at all.

The hands went about their duties on tiptoe, their bare feet padding, almost silently, over the sopping deck. Every ear aboard strained to hear, and every hand aboard feared the sudden explosion of a broadside from an unseen ship.

"Mr Wickham?" Hayden whispered.

"Sir?"

"Did you hear that? A voice, I think."

Wickham stood by the rail two yards off, a glass, all but useless in this fog, in hand. He turned his head slowly to the right and then left. "I did not, sir."

"Pray you, listen . . ."

The two stood as still as hills, holding their breath, straining.

"Yes," Wickham said, "I heard . . . *something.*"

"What did it sound like?"

"I cannot say, Captain. Voices. It sounded like voices."

"Were they speaking French?"

"I do not know, sir. I could not even say with certainty that it was men at all. Birds, perhaps." The boy shrugged.

As if he had spoken words to conjure, a gull came gliding out of the fog, mewling its sorrows to an uncaring sea. It veered to avoid the *Themis'* sails, which hung sodden and limp. Its cry was answered out of the mist, and then again from elsewhere.

A dull thud, distant and muffled, reached them.

"There, sir!" Wickham intoned. "There they are."

"But where away?"

Wickham raised a hand and indicated the west, more or less.

In such dense fog, sound seemed to come from everywhere at once—and from nowhere. Standing on the quarterdeck, as Hayden did, the bow of the ship was sometimes obscured by veils of mist that drifted ever so slowly over the deck. Even when these wafted off it was impossible to say how far into the mist his vision could penetrate, for there was no object visible to judge by. Hayden guessed that they could seldom see more than two hundred feet, and often less.

Blind as they were, they listened intently. Constantly, heads turned, fearing the dark mass of a ship would drift out of the blear.

"What was that, sir? Did it sound like an oar thumping against a hull?"

It was Hayden's turn to shrug. Wood against wood—he could be no more certain than that. There was at least one ship out there . . . somewhere. "Samson bar, mayhap," he ventured.

The sails wafted overhead, a slow snaking movement, and then fell still again. It was as though the ocean had sighed once and then gone back to sleep. The ship lifted on the low swell—lifted and settled, hardly rolling at all. Sails hung slack, dripping onto the deck and the men gathered at the guns below.

A muffled laugh came from the foredeck and Hayden saw Franks hurrying towards the source, flexing his rattan. Hayden was glad to learn the bosun had the common sense not to beat the man—the sound would carry a mile, perhaps further.

The sails wafted again, filled halfheartedly, and drew the ship forward. Hayden would have ordered the yards braced to take the greatest advantage of this little zephyr, but he dared not allow the men to make the least sound. No, they would have to make what use of the wind they could.

He crossed to the man at the wheel—the quartermaster.

"A spoke to larboard, Harvey. Let us fill the sails if we can."

The sound of the wheel turning even so little and the wheel rope thrumming through its blocks, the creak of the rudder, all seemed to echo about the ship and then ripple out into the mist. The quarter-master grimaced as though the sounds caused him physical pain.

A moment later, as if in answer, voices came back to them.

"What do they say?" Barthe asked in an anxious whisper. The sailing master was seated on a little bench built into the taffrail, having hobbled there with a cane, against the doctor's orders.

"I do not know, Mr Barthe," Wickham answered.

"But is it French, Mr Wickham? Can you not tell?"

"I canno—" But he stopped mid-word as more voices reached them, these seeming to come from some point aft.

Barthe went to speak again, but Hayden made a motion for him to stay silent, and with some difficulty the master swallowed his words.

"That sounded like English, sir," Wickham whispered, a look of utter surprise on his face. "Did you not think so?"

Hayden could not be certain and said as much. He motioned to another of the midshipmen who emerged from below at that moment. "You have good ears, Mr Gould. Come listen."

Gould stood, still as the air, for some minutes, and just when Hayden thought they would not hear any such sounds again, voices carried to them on a small breeze. The words seemed shattered into syllables, all echoey and distorted, as though they floated up out of a deep, deep well.

"Was that English?" Hayden asked softly. "Or was it French?"

Gould shook his head. "I do not know, sir, but it sounded like someone shouting orders—did it no—"

The fog lit orange to starboard, and the thunderclap of a gun swept over the *Themis*, silencing everyone utterly. Two more guns fired in quick succession.

"Have the French smoked us, sir?" Wickham whispered.

"I cannot imagine how they could . . ."

"Fog signal," Barthe whispered. "I've heard it before. It's how the French signal in a fog. A single shot, then two close together. Listen."

The signal was returned, from somewhere out in the fog, and then a third time.

"All of our Frenchmen accounted for," Wickham said with some satisfaction.

But then a fourth ship answered from somewhere forward, and another off their larboard bow. Then yet another from astern, or so it seemed.

"My God, sir," Gould whispered, "I thought we were to find British frigates here."

"Can those be echoes from cliffs?" Hayden glanced over at the sailing master, who appeared very pale.

Barthe shook his head of greying red hair. "I'm quite certain we are too distant from shore. Six ships, sir. Very likely all Frenchmen— unless our own frigates are returning their signal to confuse the enemy."

For a moment Hayden was tempted to do the same, though he could think of no practical purpose in doing so. He looked up at the sails, which fell limp at that moment.

"Mr Barthe . . ." Hayden turned towards the sailing master. "I believe this fog will burn off shortly. Are you of the same opinion?"

"Most assuredly, sir."

"Then let us break out our French uniforms and ensign. If there are French ships all around, we must appear to be one of them. Mr Gould, go down to my steward and tell him we must have the French clothing—for all the officers."

Hayden was glad he had preserved the French uniforms they had employed aboard the prize frigate *Dragoon*, when he had been forced to masquerade as a French captain chasing an English ship. It seemed like half a lifetime ago. But now these uniforms might be the only thing that could preserve his ship.

He looked up at the sails, hanging limp and sodden. Even the pennant at the masthead stuck to the dripping mast and showed no sign of wind. He almost wanted to pray. A bit of wind, enough to put a little distance between these ships and their own—and hope that the French did not proceed in the same direction. A zephyr. A sigh. Anything . . .

Two seamen, accompanied by Hayden's steward, bore a chest up onto the deck. It was quickly unlocked and uniforms distributed according to size rather than rank.

"I am sorry, Mr Archer, but Mr Barthe shall have to impersonate my second-in-command. You would never fit this jacket."

"Not to mention the shoes . . ." It was Hawthorne, smiling wickedly. He had arrived on the quarterdeck at that instant, clearly intent on joining the French Navy—never wanting to be left out of any enterprise. But Hayden could not even manage a smile. Their situation was beyond desperate. If there were actually six French ships all in close proximity, it would be something of a miracle if they survived.

"Gould? Jump down to the sailmaker and have him send up a sail we might hang over the stern to hide our transom. It will give us away, sure. Quick as you can. Tell him to waste no time in deliberation. Better too large than too small."

"Aye, sir." Gould went down the ladder at such speed, Hayden was certain he must fall and break a bone, but he survived it.

"Where is the French ensign? Let us have it aloft this moment."

The ensign was spread out on the deck aft of the wheel and then run aloft, where it hung limp and all but unrecognizable.

Hayden shrugged off his coat and waistcoat, sliding easily into the French captain's uniform. In a moment his officers were all clothed like Frenchmen, standing uncomfortably around the quarterdeck in their unfamiliar uniforms. But Hayden slipped out of his English skin and into his French one so easily he hardly noticed. People thought of him as being half French and half English, but what no one understood was that he was *entirely* English and *entirely* French at one and the same time. It seemed an impossible contradiction but was, nevertheless, the truth. He was not a half-breed but a dual-breed—a man of two nations and nationalities, two cultures and entirely opposing sensibilities, all housed within the same frame.

"There you are, my French brothers," Hayden said, smiling. *"I have missed you."*

A bell rang out in the mist, sounding so close it might have been their own. At that moment, the French flag wafted once to larboard, then a little breeze unfurled it and, at the same instant, filled their sails. The frigate gathered way, ever so slowly, then answered her helm; it was as though she had come back to life, resurrected by the sea god's breath.

An apparition loomed out of the murk, a featureless shadow. And then Hayden could make out rigging and sails. A ship—sailing in the opposite direction.

"What ship?" a man called out to them in French.

All of Hayden's officers looked to him, but it was a question he had not considered. For a moment his mind seemed to go blank as he groped for the name of a French frigate of similar size. *"Résolue,"* he called out.

Aboard the French ship he could hear the officers in hushed conversation, but he could not make out what they said. And then the ship was gone, dissolving into the white not seventy-five feet astern. Gone as though it had been a ghost ship, the ghosts muttering among themselves. And then he heard a French voice call out orders, and the sounds of men running and ropes being coiled down and yards shifting carried to them on the cool, translucent air.

"They are wearing, sir," Wickham whispered in French.

"Yes." The words chilled Hayden right to his heart. He could hardly catch his breath. "Mr Wickham, climb the mainmast as high as you dare. Take another man with you—a steady man with good eyes. And order him not, for God's sake, to call out in English!"

"Aye, sir."

"Mr Archer. Sail handlers to their stations."

"Will we stand in towards the coast, sir?" Archer asked.

"Only if we must."

"I shall muster the men silent as a prayer, sir." Archer hurried forward, sending runners off with his orders.

"Harvey," Hayden whispered to the man at the wheel. "Bring her up as close to the wind as you dare. We must keep the sails full at all costs. Do not let them luff."

"Aye, sir. You won't see a shiver, Captain. I promise you."

Barthe had got to his feet and leaned heavily upon his cane, agitated but unable to pace as he was accustomed. Even so hobbled, he made his way close to Hayden.

"That was a three-decker, Captain," he whispered. "Ninety-eight guns . . ." The sailing master said this with such alarm it made the hair stand up on Hayden's neck.

"There is very little chance that they will find us again in this fog, Mr Barthe."

Barthe bent back awkwardly and cast his gaze up. "They will if our masts are above the fog, sir."

That was precisely why Hayden had sent Wickham aloft to the highest point he might reach. "Let us pray this fog can withstand the sun a little longer."

"There will be many a man praying for precisely that, sir, I will wager."

"Mr Ransome? I want men spaced at no more than a dozen feet all the way up to Mr Wickham aloft. He may send his messages to the deck one man at a time as quiet as may be." He turned to Hobson. "Who is our lookout on the jib-boom?"

"I cannot say, sir."

"I will have you out there, Hobson. Send whoever is there back to his post."

"Aye, sir."

Gould appeared at that moment with the sailmaker and several hands in tow lugging a heavy sail. Quickly, it was hung over the stern as if drying, though whom it would confuse on such a day Hayden did not know, as everything was dripping wet.

Wickham had reached the uppermost yard and sat astride it, hardly visible from the deck. The hands sent aloft to convey his sightings went scampering up after, and in a moment a message came down—*"No ships in sight. Not a mast to be seen."*

Hayden was more relieved than he could say. There was still some chance that they might slip away before the fog burned off. If only he might have a little wind—not enough to sweep the fog away, just enough to allow them to carry on. A few leagues and he would escape the French at last.

He went to the stern rail and looked down past the sail draped there at the wake his ship left—barely a little eddy line astern. Hardly a wave. It was enough to make a man weep.

Guns fired somewhere out in the distance. Answers again seemed to come from all around—muffled reports. No muzzle flash to be seen. Hayden put a hand on the rail and looked up to find Wickham, who had a glass to his eye and was slowly sweeping it in a long arc. The acting lieutenant stopped a moment and swung his glass back, seeking at one point of the compass. For a moment Hayden held his breath, but then Wickham went back to his slow quizzing of the void.

Hayden returned his attention to the deck, where it seemed every hand stared at him, and then looked quickly away.

"Sir?" One of the men stationed at a carronade pointed into the fog astern.

Hayden turned, but there was nothing. He looked back to the man who had spoken in time to see the gun captain punch the man urgently in the shoulder—he should never have spoken and knew it.

"What did you see?" Hayden demanded.

"A . . . shadow, sir. Something . . . there, sir!" His hand shot up.

Hayden spun about in time to see something dark and ghostly passing through the mist. It did resemble a shadow, though very faint, featureless and dusky. And then it, too, was gone.

"Was it a frigate?" Barthe asked. The pain in his foot had sent him back to his bench, where he twisted round to get a view of this apparition.

"So it seemed—perhaps," Hayden whispered.

Voices were heard then, calling out in French.

"What ship?"

A brief interchange in which Hayden clearly heard someone say, ". . . *le comte*" twice.

The voices fell silent, and then the wind died, the sails swooning all around.

Barthe muttered an oath and then all was silent. Not even the call of a gull.

Gould put a hand to his ear and tilted his head. "Do you hear that, Captain? Is it the sound of sweeps?"

For a long moment Hayden listened. The restive sails hissing forth and back, rippling then falling still. And then, so faintly he might have imagined it, the measured wash of sweeps dipping, then again. For a moment, the rustle of sails overcame it, but then they fell still and he located the sound again.

"They have launched boats," Hayden whispered.

"Where away?" Barthe came to his feet, both hands on the rail and his cane, leaning against the bench, rolled loudly sideways, and crashed to the deck. Hayden put his foot on it instantly and one of the hands then took it up, returning it to the chagrined sailing master.

Hayden raised a hand to interrupt Barthe's apology. He wanted silence so that he might listen.

"Where away" was indeed the question. Somewhere in the blear, but where, Hayden could not say. He turned his head from this side to that, but the sound emanated from everywhere and nowhere.

A sound that might have been wind or voices whispering. And then, dead astern, a pistol shot. Hayden saw the muzzle flash but could make out nothing more.

"Pass the word for Mr Hawthorne," Hayden said quietly. "Drag this sail clear of the chase pieces. We shall load one with grape and the other with cannister shot."

Hayden turned to gaze up at the masthead. Wickham was turned aft, staring into the fog. Then he noticed his captain and raised both hands and shrugged.

Hawthorne came hurrying aft at that instant.

"There you are," Hayden said to him. "Position your best marksmen—three here at the taffrail but clear of the gun crews.

And four in the mizzen top. Tell them to fire at any ship's boats they see, but not a single shot at a ship. This boat is planning to stay close to us and signal our presence."

"But will we not be alerting the French to our position by firing guns, sir?"

"Indeed we will, but if we can drive this boat off we will alter course and fall silent again. If we fail to drive it off . . . we are lost." Hayden turned to his midshipman. "Mr Gould. Find Mr Archer and have him order a boat launched—as quietly as can be managed."

"Aye, sir."

Hawthorne touched his hat and went off with Gould. A moment later, Hawthorne was back with three marines in his wake, all stripped of their red coats.

"If you send a boat, may I go with it, Captain?" Hawthorne asked.

"Yes. I will send a few marines as well as the hands to man the oars, and put Mr Ransome in command."

"That will answer, sir."

Hayden turned in time to see the boat swing aloft. For a moment he stopped to admire the skill of the men who, with barely a whispered order or a nod from the officers, launched the boat as smoothly as could be done. They had become a good, steady crew in the few months since Hart had departed. For a moment Hayden felt a glow of pride in them, as though they were all his sons.

He sent the word for Ransome, who appeared out of the mist that drifted over the deck. "Sir?" The lieutenant touched his hat.

Hayden carefully explained what he wanted done.

"Do not lose sight of the *Themis*, Mr Ransome, or you might not find your way back again. Do you understand?"

"I shall have one man keep the ship in sight at all times, sir." Ransome went off to gather his crew and arms.

Without so much as a splash, the cutter touched the Atlantic's surface and settled, bobbing gently. Hayden nodded to Hawthorne, who hurried off to collect his own men.

Sailors and marines went over the side, stealthily as they could, and then without even an "Away boat" the cutter appeared astern and then faded into the murk, the oarsmen rowing in a slow, quiet rhythm.

"Can you make out the French boat?" Barthe asked, staring astern.

"I cannot—" But Hayden was interrupted by a flash and then the report of a pistol.

Immediately, his own cutter altered course towards the enemy boat. With every stroke the boat became less defined, the colours duller—then it was grey, dissolving into the murk. Hayden could see Hawthorne in the bow, a musket to his shoulder. They were almost out of sight when several flashes appeared at one time, the reports reaching him almost at the same instant. The French quickly gathered themselves and returned the British fire, but then all was lost in the blear and only the sharp crack of musket and pistol remained. And then silence.

"Can anyone see them?" Hayden asked. But all the men at the guns shook their heads. Not even the sound of oars could be discerned.

For a long moment nothing could be heard but the breathing of the gunners, none of whom shifted or moved in the least degree.

The mist astern of them swirled and a little breeze touched Hayden's face, the sodden sails half filled. At a word from Barthe seamen ran to tend the mizzen, which threatened to back and gybe. The mizzen sheet running through its block, unnoticed under most circumstances, made the most unholy squeal.

Every eye was fixed astern. "If this wind carries us a hundred paces . . ." Barthe whispered to Hayden. "Ransome may never find us."

"We can hardly anchor," Hayden said.

"No, sir, and we will accomplish little by letting sheets fly, they are near slack as it is."

Although that was true, the ship was moving.

"I told Ransome to keep the ship in sight . . ." Hayden wanted to pound a fist on the rail. If he waited for the lieutenant to find him, he might lose his ship. He turned to the seaman who was running messages. "Pass the word up to Mr Wickham: Can he see our cutter?"

"Aye, sir." The man went off at a silent run, and in a moment the word reached the midshipman aloft.

Staring up, Hayden saw the boy look down at him and shake his head. The cutter had sunk into the fog.

"Do you think the French might have taken them?" Barthe asked.

"Unlikely, unless there was more than one boat out there in the fog. Not impossible." Hayden's indecision passed. "We cannot wait for them, Mr Barthe. I will not send every man aboard into a French prison to save a dozen men from the same fate. Let us make the most of this wind. Mr Ransome will have to look to himself."

But there was little they could do but let the wind press them on. Hayden dared not send men aloft to loose sail, for silence was more important than speed. There appeared to be French ships all around. Their only hope lay in stealth, in slipping away under cover of fog. If only they could hear the French ships approach so that they might slip off before they were discovered.

The explosion of guns firing rent the air, the angry flashes visible in the fog not so far off. And then Hayden heard men crying out.

"Is there a British ship out there?" Barthe asked, almost breathless.

"Perhaps, Mr Barthe, but I believe a Frenchman just mistook one of his own frigates for the *Themis*."

This appeared to sober Barthe considerably.

"Have we gunports open, Captain?" Barthe asked.

"And guns manned to larboard and starboard," Hayden replied.

A stain appeared in the fog aft. For a moment Hayden thought it was smoke from the guns, but then he saw movement.

"There they are, sir!" Gould whispered, and the word passed back through the ship, a muffled susurration that went all the way out to Hobson on the jib-boom.

Hayden shrugged his shoulders to work the knots out of them. "Yes, bring the men aboard and stream the cutter."

The cutter caught them up and was brought alongside, the men tumbling over the rail, several wounded. Ransome and Hawthorne came immediately aft.

"We drove the boat off, sir, but there is a ship in our wake—a first-rate, it appears, sir."

"In this small wind we shall leave any three-decker behind," Hayden assured them. "You had some wounded?"

"Yes, sir. And they did for Greenfield, Captain. I ordered him put over the side. I am sorry, sir."

Hayden nodded. "I am sorry as well." Seamen preferred to be buried at sea with words said over them, preferably by a parson. To be slipped over the side in the midst of an action was one of the men's nightmares. There were numerous stories, most if not all apocryphal, of men found floating, alive, who had been put over the side because their mates believed them dead. Each story more horrifying than the last.

Ransome was powder-stained and looked shaken, as though something had happened of which he did not wish to speak.

"You may repair below a moment if you wish, Mr Ransome."

"Thank you, sir."

"And Ransome?"

"Sir?"

"Well done."

"Thank you, sir."

Ransome made his way, swaying, across the deck and disappeared below.

"Is he injured, Mr Hawthorne?" Hayden asked the marine.

"No, sir." Hawthorne looked almost as out of sorts as Ransome, giving Hayden the impression that he might weep. "Greenfield was crying out and moaning, sir—from the pain of his wound, you see. The lieutenant ordered his mates keep him quiet . . . lest we be discovered." Hawthorne worked his jaw, but no words came. "I believe they may have—without meaning to in the least—suffocated him, sir."

"Good God. Are you certain it was accidental?"

"I was in the bow, sir, watching for the French. I cannot answer that with certainty."

"Who were the men?"

"Again, Captain. I was removed from it . . . Ransome would know."

"Well, I cannot leave the deck to speak with him now. Why do you think they may have done for him?"

"I believe they tried to muffle Greenfield's cries with a shirt, sir, but they smothered him instead."

"You do not think he died of his wounds?"

"Perhaps the doctor could say, Captain, but I do not possess such knowledge."

"We will never know now," Hayden said softly. "You may go, Mr Hawthorne."

"Thank you, sir," but the marine stood a moment more.

"Mr Hawthorne?"

Hawthorne nodded, groping for words. "They were all good men, sir. Not a blackguard among them."

"I have no doubt of it, Mr Hawthorne. I am certain it could never have been done a-purpose, but . . ." Hayden looked up at his lieutenant. "But murder without intent is . . . murder under the law . . . God save them, if that is the case."

The marine lieutenant retreated and left Hayden standing at the rail alone. Despite the near-flat sea, he reached out and took hold of the rail. He swore under his breath. There had been a murder aboard this very ship before Philip Stephens had sent him aboard. Maybe she was a bad-luck ship, as many said. Hayden muttered another curse. He would have to enquire into this matter most carefully— there would almost certainly be a court-martial. And Ransome . . . he should have spoken up. Hayden should not have heard it first from Hawthorne. He found this possibility of murder more distressing even than their present situation. Certainly it must have been an accident—certainly it must.

Hayden tried to turn his mind from this matter. It would be dealt with in its own time. There was far more pressing business before them.

Again guns were heard out in the fog. A series of three evenly spaced shots, a pause, and then two more.

He glanced at Barthe, who twisted about on his bench every few moments, first looking this way, then that.

"What are they saying, I wonder?"

Barthe shrugged. "I wish I knew, sir. That is a different signal to what we heard before."

From all points of the compass, the signal was answered.

"Six ships," Barthe counted. "And all of them too near, sir . . . wherever they are."

The *Themis* sailed, ever so slowly, into a thick bank of fog, the air seeming to cool all around. At almost the same instant, the sails fell limp and barely rippled as the ship rolled ever so slightly, forth and back.

"Can this little wind not hold for half of the hour!" Barthe muttered.

The bow of his ship was devoured by the fog until Hayden could not make out his foremast. They could have been floating through the sky, the world far below them, for even the sea immediately aft was lost in fog.

"I've never seen fog so thick, sir," Barthe whispered.

"Nor I, Mr Barthe."

A few moments they drifted, unable to tell if they made way or lay becalmed or even made stern way. And then, in the depth of silence, a muffled running of bare feet, and one of the hands shot out of the fog, running like he was pursued by devils.

"Ship off the starboard bow, Captain!" the man said, trying to pitch his voice low.

"Helm to starboard," Hayden ordered the helmsman, and then cupped his hands to his mouth and shouted, in French, up into the rigging. "Ship on the starboard bow!"

Wickham took up the call and repeated it as loudly as he was able. Hayden grabbed the pull and rang the ship's bell madly. All the while he stared into the fog, thinking for a moment that Hobson had made a mistake, there was no ship, or it was not so near as he'd thought.

But then a jib-boom thrust through the cloud, not ten yards to starboard, drawing in train the bow of a ship. The bow seemed to be moving so slowly that it was minutes until the rest of the ship was revealed—a two-decker, not thirty feet distant, two rows of gun-ports open. And there she lost all way, her crew and officers staring down at the British frigate from their higher deck.

"*Praise to God,*" Hayden called out in French. "*We did not col-lide . . . even going so slowly . . .*"

The French captain came and leaned over the rail, looking down at Hayden. "*Capitaine,*" he said, "*we know you are an English ship. Do not attempt to claim otherwise. Surrender or I shall fire into you. At this short range, I don't think even your gunnery will preserve you, Capitaine.*"

Hayden was looking directly down the barrel of a French gun. All around he could feel his men holding their breath. He was about to claim his innocence again and argue that he was French, but he fixed his eyes upon the French captain standing at the rail and realised that the man was not going to be bluffed—he knew the truth.

"I regret, Capitaine," Hayden answered in French, *"that I cannot, with honour, surrender without firing a shot."*

The French captain—a man of middle years—nodded. *"Fire your larboard battery and strike your . . . our colours, Capitaine. And then, please, prepare to surrender. I will send my lieutenant aboard."*

Hayden turned to find Archer standing in the companionway, a look of utter shock upon his face.

"Mr Archer. Fire the larboard battery, if you please."

Archer nodded dumbly, touched his hat, and went below. A moment later the larboard battery fired as one, a horrible explosion, and then the smoke blossomed up, covering the deck. The silence that followed seemed so utterly profound and complete, as though the entire world had lost its voice.

"Strike the French colours," Hayden ordered into that terrible void.

Seamen hurried to do as he bid.

At that instant, Hayden heard the sound of a gallery window opening and then a splash—the British signal book in its lead covers had gone into the sea. Perse had performed this last duty flawlessly, as always.

A strange numbness had crept over Hayden, as though he had breathed in the cold fog and it had frozen his heart. His mind seemed very clear and uncluttered, with no extraneous thoughts creeping in.

He had lost his ship . . . *He had lost his ship!*

Turning, he gazed along the deck at all the men mustered at their guns or waiting to handle sail. They stared back, pale-faced, their thoughts impenetrable. No doubt they had all heard stories of French prisons. There were no illusions on that score.

The French flag came down to the deck—though Hayden was not sure why. It would be raised again in a moment.

Hayden ordered the starboard guns run in and secured and the gunports closed, and then he mustered the men on the foredeck and along the larboard gangway.

"Offer no resistance," Hayden said to them. "I believe we shall not be treated unkindly. It is no dishonour to surrender here, to a much superior ship, becalmed and unable to effect an escape. You have all performed your duties in a manner that would make any captain proud. Not once have you shied or failed out of fear. It has been an honour to be your captain." Hayden saluted them and the men all returned that salute.

A boat from the French ship came alongside and a young lieutenant clambered quickly up the side, looking both apprehensive and excited at the same moment, though the former he tried to hide. Hayden met him at the rail. The young man—hardly more than twenty—saluted and Hayden returned it. He had never expected to do what next he must do. He offered up his sword.

"My captain has instructed me to inform you that you may keep your sword, Capitaine. My boat will carry you over. Do not be concerned, your crew will be fairly treated." The young man gestured, and with a single look back at the anxious faces of his men, Hayden climbed down into the waiting boat.

The boat pushed off, and someone on the deck called out, "Three cheers for Captain Hayden!"

And the men *huzzah*ed three times with such energy that it must have carried for miles—and though Hayden was more moved than he could say, he thought it was also a shout of defiance. His crew had lost their ship but would not so easily give up their pride.

Ropes were being carried from the French ship to the *Themis,* and armed men ferried across by boat. His ship, lifting and falling on the swell and adrift in curling mist, appeared utterly forlorn to him. A prize of the enemy. A symbol of his failure. It even occurred to him to curse Stephens, who had informed him that there was but a single French frigate sailing from Le Havre. He knew, however, that the failure had been his. Bad luck might have played a part, but he had made poor decisions. He could see a few men watching him go. Upon their faces looks of utter hopelessness. Hayden had always pulled them through before, no matter what the circumstances, but this time there was nothing he could do. They were prisoners of the French and the French were killing each other by the thousands— how would friendless British sailors fare in such a world?

Some of the hands were stirred away from the rail and sent aloft— to take in sail, no doubt.

That was all the time Hayden was allowed to gaze at his ship or even worry about the fate of his crew, for he was alongside the French seventy-four and climbing up the side. As he came over the rail he was met by the same officer who had demanded his surrender. The man saluted him, and Hayden returned the gesture.

"So," the captain said in cultivated French, "at last I am allowed the honour of meeting le comte."

Hayden could not have been more surprised. "I must disappoint you, Capitaine," Hayden protested, "for I am no count, nor a nobleman of any kind. Charles Hayden, a mere master and commander. Not even a post captain."

"Raymondde Lacrosse, capitaine of Les Droits de l'Homme."

"'The Rights of Man,'" Hayden repeated.

"Oui, Capitaine. Exactly so."

"I offered my sword to your lieutenant."

"I require only your word that you will not use it against my people while you remain our guest."

"You have my word."

"Come, there is a meal awaiting in my cabin."

As they passed along the gangway, Hayden realised he was the object of the greatest fascination to the hands and officers alike, as though they had never seen an Englishman before. Certainly, they had not seen many who had just surrendered their ships.

Down they went to the gun-deck below. Hayden could not help but notice that there appeared to be no shortage of men aboard this ship, unlike British ships, which commonly sailed short of their proper complement. Here each gun had its proper number.

He was led into the captain's cabin, which had not been disassembled as would be the case on a British ship. Here a table was spread with simple serving dishes and servants stood silently by.

"Forgive my table, Capitaine," Lacrosse said. "Since the revolution it is no longer acceptable to display too much silver."

Hayden was shown to a chair, which a servant pushed in behind him.

"Pardon me, Capitaine Lacrosse, but I must ask what will be done with my crew and officers."

"They will all be fairly treated, you need not trouble yourself in the least in that regard. As long as they cause no trouble, that is. But once they are ashore, they will be sent who knows where and I will have no influence over their treatment, I am sorry to say. I doubt they will be treated worse than the French sailors you have locked up in your hulks. Of course, your officers will be exchanged, and quickly, I should think."

"Thank you, Capitaine," Hayden said. "Why did you call me the count?"

Lacrosse smiled charmingly. "It is said, because of your command of our language, that you are a Frenchman. An émigré captain from the French Navy, in fact, a nobleman and a royalist."

Hayden felt a little shudder of apprehension and realization, as though he had been cast into the winter sea. Unwilling to admit his heritage for fear of reprisals against his mother's family, Hayden responded. "When I was a small child, my nursemaid was a lovely French woman. You see, my mother was an invalid and had very little to do with raising me. She died when I was a boy. As a result, I spoke French before I learned English, or so I am told. My father was a post captain in the Royal Navy—Captain William Saunders Hayden."

"I am very sorry to hear of your mother's misfortune, Capitaine. My condolences. You are aware, Capitaine Hayden, that certain factions within France are causing . . . a hysteria within our borders?"

"I am, yes."

"You might be accused of being a Frenchman and a royalist. In short, a traitor."

"But I am neither."

Lacrosse shrugged, pressing his ample lips into an inverted U. "That may be so, but you might have need to prove this, and rather quickly, too. The Committee of Public Safety does not require a great deal of evidence to send a man to the guillotine. Have you anyone in France who might identify you? Preferably someone of influence . . ."

"No—no one," Hayden said, hardly able to draw breath. Was it not enough that he had lost his ship? Now he would be accused of being a traitor . . . to France! "You must know, Capitaine Lacrosse, that we have so many British officers awaiting promotion. We have no need of French sea officers at this time." Hayden did not want to say that British sailors would be shot before they would take orders from a Frenchman, but thought better of it.

"May I trust you not to repeat what I am about to say, Capitaine?" Lacrosse enquired, very quietly and speaking perfectly acceptable English. "I cannot stress enough that private conversations, such as the one we are now engaged in, have been all the evidence required to see a man guillotined."

"You have my word as an officer."

Lacrosse nodded. "I am aware that French officers seldom serve in your service, but the Committee of Public Safety, well, I caution you again, Capitaine, all they would require is a single citizen to point a finger at you and say, 'Yes, I know him. He is *le comte de Periger,*' or any such name, and that would be adequate. Men have been executed on less evidence. Far less."

"But I am an Englishman . . ." Hayden protested, sitting back in his chair, stunned by what this man was suggesting.

"Not if Robespierre decides otherwise."

Servants brought in the first course, but Hayden felt so ill at that moment he was afraid to eat. Then he decided he must lest he offer insult to Lacrosse, who would have the treatment of Hayden's crew under his control until France was reached.

"The Admiralty would certainly vouch for my nationality. Admiral Hood knew my father. Philip Stephens, the First Secretary, knows all the details of my parentage and service. I could write to him . . ." Certainly Stephens would have the common sense not to reveal the identity of his mother? The man was brilliant; he would never make such a blunder.

There was a knock upon the door and a whispered conversation between an officer and Lacrosse's steward.

"Excuse me, Capitaine Hayden." Lacrosse rose and went out of the door. Hayden could hear his voice beyond but pitched too low for him to comprehend the words.

A moment later he returned and, to Hayden's horror, set a wooden box upon the table. The box that held Hayden's letters.

"It would appear, Capitaine Hayden, that there are letters here, addressed to you, that begin, 'My Darling Son.' These letters are all written in French."

"It was a scandal at the time," Hayden said quickly. "After my mother died, my father married my nursemaid. She was much younger than he, and her family in reduced circumstances. My father was lost at sea. My stepmother removed to Boston, where she married again—a shipowner. An American."

Lacrosse stared at the open box, the letters so neatly folded and arranged. "These letters represent a very grave danger to you, Capitaine Hayden. A very grave danger."

Nine

The lockup had been arranged just aft of what Hayden thought might be the sail room. A few low tables with benches, crudely built of poorly dressed planks, were arranged against one bulkhead. How many others might be locked up here with him Hayden could not say. Not that it mattered. On a fair wind, the harbour of Brest was but a few hours distant.

Unable to sit, Hayden rose and tried to pace, but the beams overhead were too low to allow it, so he returned to the hard bench. Sitting still, however, proved difficult. Hayden was now well aware that he would almost certainly be intensely questioned as to his origins once he was on French soil. The letters from his mother—letters that had slipped from his mind in the moment—would be scrutinized for any incriminating evidence.

To an Englishman the idea of a French officer serving as a captain in the British Navy was absurd. If nothing else, English pride would not allow it. From his conversation with Lacrosse, however, he had been made to realise that the French did not perceive this as an impossibility.

There was rattling outside the door, and then Archer was thrust in and the door closed behind him. Hayden heard a bar set in place and a key rasping in a lock.

"Mr Archer. Have you been hurt?"

The lieutenant shook his head, though he did look over his clothing—unlike Hayden, he had changed back to his British uniform—as though he expected to find damage. "No, sir."

"Please, sit, Lieutenant. What is being done with our crew—can you say?"

Archer braced himself on an overhead beam. His face was ashen and he swayed where he stood. "All of the officers were carried aboard this ship, Captain. The hands were kept aboard the *Themis*, which I believe from what I overheard is being sailed to Brest." Archer slumped down on the bench opposite Hayden, put his elbows on the table and a hand to either side of his narrow face. He appeared about to weep but mastered himself almost immediately. *"We have lost our ship, sir."* These words, so final and distressing, he whispered from a dry throat so they sounded like a pronouncement from some distant underworld.

"Yes. I have turned it over and over and do not know what else I could have done."

"It was just the worst luck, Captain. Nothing more. The Admiralty will certainly agree. It is a pity, though, that it befell us."

Archer did not know what Benoît had told Hayden—his failure to carry this vital information to England would be enough to blast his career. There could be no excuse for this, especially as he had fired first into the French frigate off Le Havre. His enemies, whoever they were, would say he should have let the frigate pass. They might even question his waiting for Ransome to return in the cutter.

Archer appeared not to notice his commander's distress. "I suppose we have had our share of good fortune, sir," the lieutenant observed. "Escaping Toulon Harbour on so little wind was nothing short of a miracle. We might have known ill luck would balance this out."

Hayden made no comment on this and instead asked, "Where are the rest of my officers? You said they were brought aboard?"

"I believe they are being questioned by the captain, one by one. Captain Lacrosse asked me about your parentage, sir, and how you came to speak the French so well. I told him your father was a sea captain, and beyond that I claimed ignorance." He leaned closer and spoke in a whisper. "I thought your mother's nationality should not be mentioned, sir."

"Thank you, Archer. That was very astute. Do you think the others will comprehend that my mother's family might be in significant danger if the connection became known?"

"I do not know, sir. Certainly, Wickham and Hawthorne would never say a word of it. Mr Barthe . . . well, he speaks before he thinks, on occasion." Archer's gaze turned up a moment. "The other reefers . . . I fear they have little comprehension of the situation in France. Ransome . . . I cannot say. The doctor, of course, would never be duped into saying anything; he is private to the point of being secretive with us. He will claim ignorance of anything beyond his own name."

Despite the circumstances, Hayden almost smiled at this assessment of Griffiths—which he agreed with in every way.

"How long do you think it will take to arrange an exchange, sir?"

"I wish I knew, Mr Archer. Sometimes it is weeks, at other times months. The good news is that we have an abundance of French officers imprisoned in England, so finding officers of equivalent rank to exchange will present no difficulties. The greatest impediment will be the French government—it is in utter disarray, if not chaos. The French Navy, though we dare not say it aloud, is little better."

The ship creaked audibly at that moment, heeled a little to starboard, and then the unmistakeable burbling of water moving past the planking came to them.

"Wind . . ." Archer said.

"Yes, but from where?"

"I am not certain. Maybe one of our own men will be able to tell us when he is sent down."

As if on cue, the door was opened noisily and Ransome was let in.

"Mr Ransome," Hayden greeted him. "They did not mistreat you, I hope?"

"Not in the least, sir, though I was closely questioned. I told them we were cruising and no more."

Ransome came and took a seat beside Archer—he appeared utterly exhausted in the dim light of the single lamp.

"Did they quiz you about my parentage?" Hayden asked quietly.

Ransome looked startled. "They did, sir, to my surprise. I told them your father was an English sea captain and your mother French."

Hayden closed his eyes.

"That was a damned fool thing to say!" Archer informed him testily.

Ransome was clearly offended. "Captain Hayden's French mother is hardly a secret, Mr Archer. And why does it matter? I should think they would be disposed to treat Captain Hayden more kindly on account of his being half French."

"It might not matter in the least," Hayden interrupted, "but I have relations in France and they may be . . . in some danger because of their connection to me."

"How so, sir?"

"They could be accused of being spies or of lacking revolutionary zeal, which will get you an appointment with the guillotine in these times."

Ransome sat back on the bench. "I am most heartily sorry, Captain. Never for a moment did I comprehend that I was betraying your mother's family."

"I should have warned everyone to say nothing. I confess, I never expected us to become prisoners. The captain has my mother's letters, anyway. I told him she had been my nursemaid and taught me the French language, and then she married my father when my English mother died. That is my story. If they press me for her maiden name, I will tell them it is Mercier—a common enough name. Mercier."

"They asked your mother's maiden name, Captain," Ransome admitted. "Thank God I did not know it. I do apologise for not thinking first."

"You more than likely will not be the only one to tell them about my French mother, Mr Ransome. Do not let it trouble you."

"Very kind of you, sir." Ransome did look as though he felt the fool.

Wickham was let in next—the French captain was questioning the British sailors according to rank, it seemed. He, too, had been asked about Hayden's parents, but beyond the sea officer father Wickham had claimed ignorance. Like the others, he told Lacrosse only that they had been cruising and happened upon the frigates outside Le Havre, to which place they had gone hoping to intercept some coastal transports.

"I have some other news for you, Captain, and I do not believe it shall prove to be propitious . . ." Wickham informed his captain. "They carried Rosseau aboard and he was closely questioned by the captain, but at too great a distance for me to comprehend what was said. He was led away in manacles."

"That is not good news. I shall tell Lacrosse that he was a prisoner . . . escaped from a hulk and caught rowing in the Channel." Even to Hayden's ear this sounded implausible, but what was he to tell Lacrosse? Rosseau had been serving in the Navy and had been captured. The only explanation for him now being aboard Hayden's ship was escape and recapture.

One by one the officers and warrant officers were sent down. Barthe, Griffiths, the midshipmen, Hawthorne. Even Franks was taken aboard *Les Droits de l'Homme*.

They all sat in the faint, orange light that flickered off the deckhead and the bulkheads. They were a melancholy-looking group, that was certain.

"Even with our swords," Hawthorne observed, "we are too few—by perhaps half a dozen—to take the ship by main force."

"Three men per deck should prove adequate," Griffiths replied. "They are only Frenchmen, after all."

These two were attempting to raise the spirits of their fellows, Hayden could see. It was a duty he should be performing, but he was so devastated by the loss of his ship and by worry over the fate of his crew that he could think of not a single word to say.

Some of the French hands, under the direction of an armed officer—hardly more than a child—carried in bread and wine.

When they had retreated and the door was locked, Hawthorne asked, "Was that one of the ship's boys? He was rather well turned out."

"That was a midshipman, Mr Hawthorne. An *aspirant* he is called in the French Navy."

"And what is it, pray, that he aspires to," the marine enquired, "long trousers?"

Despite this being one of Hawthorne's more common sallies, the others laughed.

The sound of the lock being turned took their attention, and as the door opened they found the butt of their jokes returning.

"Capitaine 'ayden?" the young man said. "Capitaine Lacrosse asks that you attend him?"

Hayden's officers stood as he did. Leaving Archer in command, against the possibility that he did not return, Hayden followed the young officer out. Two armed men trailed behind. Up through the ship they climbed to the quarterdeck. There he found Lacrosse standing by the larboard rail. Hayden tried to catch a glimpse of the compass as he passed near the binnacle but could not. By the position of the sun—late afternoon—he judged the wind to be nor'west by north and their course to be nor'east by north—perhaps half a point east of that. The *Themis* was not in view, nor could he see any other ship.

Lacrosse acknowledged him kindly.

"It would appear, Capitaine Hayden, that you have not been entirely truthful with me. Your mother—your birth mother—is French. Her letters would seem to bear this out."

This was not unexpected, so Hayden had the benefit of some time to consider his answer. "I apologise, Capitaine Lacrosse, for telling you this lie. As you no doubt have learned, I have relations in France. I fear for their safety should the connection between us become known."

Lacrosse continued to stare out over the ocean towards the western horizon. For some minutes he said nothing. "I have always believed the French to be cultured and humane, but I have been forced to realise that we are a savage people. At the outbreak of the revolution I was a thirty-six-year-old lieutenant, and though I was of a noble family—well, in France there were noble families and there were noble families, if you take my meaning. I did not expect rapid advancement. Now, but five years later, I am a *capitaine de vaisseau*. Most of our naval officers—a great many of noble birth—were released or fled. I am still here because of friends in Paris and because I have long held eccentric views on government—I thought it should be elected." He paused but a second. "Can you hear the sound of the guillotine, Capitaine Hayden? No? That is because you are not French—just as you have claimed. I hear it, though it performs its terrible duty many leagues away. Every French *citoyen* can hear it. In France, even on a French ship, one can never know who might be an informant—who might send you towards the maelstrom that is the guillotine. It is known that I have a box of your correspondence, but no one is aware of its contents but me and a lieutenant I trust utterly. The letters from your mother I shall destroy personally. I regret this, but any other course could put us both in danger. Do you understand?"

"I do, Capitaine Lacrosse. And I am in your debt."

"So many innocent people have died, Capitaine Hayden, and more every day. It is a stain upon my country that will never be washed away." He met Hayden's gaze. "Take a turn around the deck, Capitaine. The day has become most pleasant."

Hayden was about to thank the Frenchman, for certainly he was now deeply in his debt, but a lookout aloft cried out, *"Sail!"*

And there it was, just barely visible to the naked eye, emerging from the retreating fog bank, a three-master, Hayden thought. All about there was a buzz of French as the officers went to the rail to see. Lacrosse's glass was delivered to him and he fixed it on the distant sail. Quietly he spoke to his lieutenants, who all gazed through their own glasses. A shaking of heads.

Lacrosse summoned Hayden, who had removed to a few paces to give the French privacy—he owed Lacrosse every possible consideration.

The Frenchman held out his glass. "We cannot identify this ship, Capitaine Hayden. Perhaps you know it?"

Hayden took the glass, uncertain of how far his gratitude might extend. He fixed the lens upon the distant vessel, trying to hold it in the centre. The ship yawed a little to larboard, perhaps, and the light struck it clearly upon the starboard side. Gunports were unmistakeable, but only a single row. He lowered the glass.

"I cannot be certain," Hayden said in reply to Lacrosse's inquisitive gaze. "It appears too small to be a seventy-four-gun ship."

"British?"

"I cannot say, Capitaine."

"Of course. Well, we shall see how fast a ship it might be. It is shaping its course to meet us, but I believe we will prove to have the heavier broadside, should it prove to be British."

"Capitaine . . ." One of the lieutenants gestured towards the ship. "We believe there is a second ship hidden behind the sails of the first."

Lacrosse raised his glass, stared a moment, and cursed.

"*Sail!*" the lookout called again. "Astern of the first."

With his naked eye Hayden could not make this ship out immediately, but then it sailed into the open and the golden light of the late afternoon.

"*Deux frégates,*" Hayden heard one of the lieutenants pronounce quietly.

Hayden was of the opinion that the first looked too large to be a frigate, yet only a single row of gunports had been visible to his eye. Certainly, Pellew was cruising these waters with *Indefatigable*. This caused a marked increase in his pulse. *Indefatigable* was a razee—a larger ship cut down to make a single-decker—in this case, a sixty-four-gun ship turned into a vessel with a single deck of twenty-four-pounders. He tried to hide his reaction. A little luck and he might not be a prisoner when the day ended. He glanced at the westering sun—two hours of sunlight. And then at the converging ships—not five miles distant. The wind could hardly be called a breeze. and though it was fair for Brest, at that moment there was a dark cloud above the horizon in the north. If the wind veered north it would almost certainly strengthen and carry these ships with it.

Hayden could hardly contain his excitement and fought to master himself. He did not want to reveal the truth to Lacrosse or his officers, but he thought it more than possible that these ships were indeed British—the very frigates he had hoped to find lying off Brest. His own officers would have their spirits lifted by such news, but Hayden resolved to remain on deck as long as he was allowed, in hope of knowing beyond a doubt under which flag these ships sailed. How long he might keep the deck before he was escorted below or had imposed too long upon Lacrosse's goodwill Hayden did not know, but he would find out.

That Lacrosse would destroy his mother's letters was something of a risk for the Frenchman. Were any of his crew aware of these letters—or the lieutenant who apparently found them to prove untrustworthy—and their existence reported to the authorities, Lacrosse might be sent spinning towards the maelstrom of which he spoke. In the present climate of France it was not good to run afoul of the authorities, especially if you were of noble birth. The immigrants fleeing France brought stories hardly to be believed. A sixteen-year-old boy of very limited understanding was guillotined for shouting, *"Vive le Roi!"* A woman, though able to prove beyond a doubt that she was not the woman wanted by the authorities, even if she did bear the same name, was guillotined anyway so that they might cross the name off their list.

Hayden thought of the melancholy Sanson who had come aboard his ship as a French prisoner. He had been trying to escape his family—which had been executioners for several generations. In the end, he had escaped by taking his own life. Had he known what would take place in France but a few months later, he might have counted himself fortunate.

Lacrosse, Hayden thought, was an honourable man of the old school. Hayden might be the enemy, but he was also a brother officer, and to see him murdered for no reason was something Lacrosse would not allow if it were within his power to prevent it. Hayden hoped that, were he in a similar position, he would act in the same way, but given the perceivable risks he was not utterly certain that he would.

Taking Lacrosse at his word, Hayden, with his two guards in train, walked the deck. He wanted to stand and stare at the converging ships, for the second, hidden behind the first seen, was now clearly visible, but thought this might prove insulting to his captors, so he managed only a glance in that direction every few moments. There was nothing to distinguish the ships as being from either nation that could be seen with the naked eye.

Perhaps three quarters of an hour later, though, Hayden arrived on the quarterdeck, where he found Lacrosse and his officers in muted conversation. They appeared to reach some agreement, and suddenly the lieutenants began shouting orders. The course was altered and yards shifted. *Les Droits de l'Homme* was put before the wind. She was flying from the approaching ships.

For a moment Hayden stood transfixed by the nearing vessels as they were brought astern. Without a glass he could not tell that they were British, but clearly the French were more certain.

"Capitaine Hayden," Lacrosse said, and beckoned him near.

Immediately, Hayden went to the stern rail where the Frenchman stood.

"We believe these are English cruisers—two frigates—though one seems much larger than the other . . . perhaps a razee." He fixed his glass upon the ships. "Some ships that have been cut down are said to be poor sailers. Others are thought quite swift." He passed the glass to Hayden.

Hayden stared for some moments to give himself time to consider. As an officer, he was sworn to give no aid to the enemy. Yet this man had his mother's letters, still intact as far as Hayden knew— though somehow Hayden did not think he would now go back on his promise to destroy them. The question was, could he give any information to Lacrosse that would not compromise the safety or ability of the British cruisers?

Hayden lowered the glass and returned it to its owner. "I regret to say these ships are unknown to me, but they do appear to be sailing quite swiftly, Capitaine, do you not agree?"

Lacrosse nodded, disappointed in the response. "Perhaps you should go below, Capitaine Hayden . . . for your own safety."

Hayden gave a slight bow in the man's direction, looked again at the chasing ships attempting to gauge their speed and the speed of *Les Droits de l'Homme*. He was escorted below, and the two guards at the door of the lockup let him in.

"Have we gone about, Capitaine?" Wickham asked. "The motion of the ship has altered."

"We are running," Hayden informed them, "and not just before the wind but from British cruisers, too! A frigate and a razee less than a league and a half in our wake."

The reaction of the men was almost a cheer, and they were all on their feet in an instant, their looks of dejection and melancholy replaced by grins and glowing faces.

"What ships, sir, do you know?"

"I believe one might be *Indefatigable*."

"She should not tire of chasing us, then," Hawthorne quipped.

"You do realise, Mr Hawthorne," Barthe said, clearly offended by his light spirits, "that we are on our way to a French prison?"

"I believe we will shortly be freed when this cursed ship is taken, Mr Barthe." He waved a hand at the surrounding bulkheads. "This is all the French prison we shall ever see."

Barthe shifted on his bench. "Well, I do hope your prescience proves correct, sir, but do not count your chicks before the cockerel has *fucked the damned hen*!"

This caused a good deal more laughter than Mr Hawthorne's observation; even the marine laughed.

"I have been guilty of that a few times in my life," Hawthorne admitted when he finished laughing.

"Of what," enquired Wickham, "fucking the damned hen?"

"Gentlemen," Hayden cautioned, "we are yet prisoners of the French, and I do not think this laughter will endear us to them. There will be time enough for levity if this ship is taken by our cruisers. Until then, we both live and eat at the sufferance of our gaolers. Let us not antagonize them unduly."

This brought about a semblance of decorum and many a suppressed smile. The material change in the men's demeanour was unmistakeable—they were animated, smiling, their eyes were no longer dead and staring off into some vague distance. It was as though they had been informed of the death of a loved one and then told it was all a mistake—the person lived yet unharmed.

Hayden beckoned Ransome and the two retired to a table set apart and screened off from the rest by a scrap of sail—a private "cabin" built for Hayden's use. There was a small table with two benches here and a cot leaning in the corner.

"Mr Ransome, it is my duty to enquire into the death of Mr Greenfield. I understand that one or more men were attempting to make silent his cries of pain by covering his mouth with a shirt or cloth of some kind. Is it possible that he was smothered by this action—even by accident?"

Ransome put two fingers up to the bridge of his nose, closing his eyes for a moment as though collecting his thoughts. "I cannot answer your question with any certainty, Captain. He was grievously wounded—shot through the back." He touched his breast with a hand and then gestured over his shoulder. "About this level. His breath was bubbling, sir, and he was choking on blood as well. We did not know for certain that there was only a single French boat out in the fog and Greenfield was making a terrible racket, sir. I ordered Braithwaite and Carlson to keep him quiet as best they were able." Ransome's gaze became darker by the second and his skin actually appeared to grow blue-grey and dull. "One of them—I disremember which—removed his jacket and tried to silence Greenfield by putting it over his face. He had collapsed, and I couldn't see what happened clearly even if I had been inclined to look, and I must tell you my attention was engaged elsewhere."

"How close was Greenfield to you, Mr Ransome?"

"Amidships . . . and I was in the stern-sheets. Mr Hawthorne and his marines were forward."

"So Braithwaite and Carlson were attempting to muffle Greenfield's cries with a jacket—and then what happened?"

"We were fired on again—muskets and pistols—and we returned fire. And then Carlson informed me that he believed Greenfield had departed this life." Ransome touched a hand to his forehead, his gaze far away. "Immediately, I went forward and found Greenfield limp. There was a great deal of blood soaking through his shirt and jacket where he was wounded and also around his mouth and face . . . and about his neck as well. He was not breathing and I could detect no pulse—at either his neck or wrist. As every breath had previously been accompanied by bubbles and gurgling at the wound in his back and now there was none, I ordered him slipped over the side, my reason being that it would be very disturbing to the men to have a corpse there so close by and I had want of their entire attention at that time."

"Did Braithwaite and Carlson look distressed or guilty in any way?"

"They both appeared very distressed and out of sorts, sir, but one of their comrades had just died. Braithwaite and Greenfield were in the same mess, Captain."

"So there was no enmity between these two and Greenfield?"

"I do not believe there was, sir. Certainly not of which I was aware."

"The first opportunity, I will ask Lacrosse for ink and quill so that you might commit your account to paper."

"Will there be a court-martial, sir?"

"I do not know, Mr Ransome. If I deem Greenfield's death accidental, I do not believe the Admiralty will pursue the matter. Even so, I must report the possibility that Greenfield's death was accidental and not necessarily caused by the enemy. I will at this time ask the doctor's opinion on the matter. He might have questions for you. I must also speak with the others involved, although but for you and Hawthorne all the others are aboard the *Themis*."

Ransome nodded. Hayden asked Griffiths to join them and he came and took a seat alongside Ransome.

Hayden explained what transpired and what Ransome had told him, asking the lieutenant to verify that what he said fairly represented his own report.

"Tell me where the wound was," Griffiths instructed Ransome, turning away from him. "You may touch my back where you believe the ball entered."

"Here, Doctor," Ransome said, touching to the left of Griffiths' spine just below the scapula.

"Was it musket or pistol?"

"I cannot say, as I believe both were fired in our direction."

"You told Captain Hayden the wound gurgled when he breathed?"

"Yes, sir."

"Was there a great deal of blood or little?"

"A profusion, Doctor Griffiths. The wound bled terribly and could not be stopped."

"And how was he lying? On his back or his chest?"

"On his side, Doctor—or so he was when I went to be certain he was not still alive. He was in a pool of blood."

"Were his lips blue when you went to see him?"

Ransome pursed his own lips together. "I cannot say, Doctor. His mouth was so bloody . . . I do not know."

"The blood emitting from his wound—did it come in a regular rhythm or did it simply flow in an even stream?"

"I am sorry, Doctor, but I could not see, as Greenfield was down among the men amidships and I was in the stern. Carlson or Braithwaite might be more able to answer that question, sir."

Griffiths could think of nothing more to ask, and Hayden released Ransome to go back to the others.

"What think you?" he asked Griffiths very quietly.

"I do not know what to think. Mr Ransome could not answer the most relevant questions because he could not see the man, or so he claims. If the blood was pulsing from the wound, then it is likely the aorta artery was damaged or even severed and would have led to death within a few moments. If Greenfield's lips were blue, then he died from suffocation."

"Then you cannot say for certain what caused his death?"

"If I could see the body . . . which was rather conveniently disposed of."

"Let us question Mr Hawthorne."

Hawthorne took Ransome's place. At that moment, a distant gun was heard.

All conversation ceased a moment and then a second shot came.

"Not so near yet," Hayden informed the others. "Let us continue. Mr Hawthorne, you brought this matter to my attention. What made you do so, if I may ask?"

"It appeared to me that Greenfield put up something of a fight, to begin, when Braithwaite and Carlson were asked to keep him quiet. They had him down in the bottom of the boat, sir, one holding him, the other pressing the shirt over his face. Greenfield struggled mightily against them."

"That is your entire reason, then?"

"Well, no, sir. Greenfield was not well liked, sir. And Braithwaite . . . well, he is a rum bastard, if I may say so."

"I thought Greenfield and Braithwaite messed together?"

"That may be, sir, but there was no love between them. Wickham might be able to tell you more, sir."

"What order did Lieutenant Ransome give Braithwaite and Carlson, do you remember?"

Guns sounded again, muffled by the hull and decks above. A gun aboard the French ship spoke in return, the report echoing down through the ship like a great hammer blow.

"He ordered them to keep him quiet if they could. I must say, Captain, Greenfield was crying out and moaning terribly. Certainly, the French could not have been in doubt of our whereabouts, or at least how near we might have been."

"So Greenfield's struggle led you to suspect he might not have died of his wounds?"

"Well, he was kicking the planks very hard and flailing. It was all they could do to hold him. I thought he had a good deal of fight in him for a man so close to death."

"Did you see Greenfield's wound, Mr Hawthorne?" Griffiths had been listening, his countenance growing more and more grave.

"I did. He had been shot in the back."

"Where?"

Hawthorne reached over his own shoulder and patted his back. "Just here, sir."

"Are you certain, Mr Hawthorne?"

"Most certain. One of the men called out that Greenfield had been shot, and as I was reloading my musket I turned and saw him slumped over his oar. There was blood soaking through his jacket up here, high on his back on the left side."

Griffiths and Hayden exchanged a glance.

"From the moment he was struck by the ball until he died, how much time passed?" Griffiths asked.

Hawthorne paused to consider this, as though he were running over the sequence of events in his mind. "Not very long, Doctor. Five minutes . . . Certainly not so much as ten."

Hayden looked to the surgeon, raising his eyebrows, but Griffiths signalled that he had no more questions to ask.

"That will be all, Mr Hawthorne. Thank you."

Hawthorne, who was taller than Hayden, rose to a stooped position, touched his imaginary hat, and crouched off to join the others.

"There appears to be a notable discrepancy between the two accounts," Hayden observed.

"Indeed, and it is notable in several ways. It seems very unlikely to me that Greenfield would die so quickly of a wound inflicted so high on his back. If he was not smothered, then I would guess the likely cause of death would be loss of blood. But a wound here . . ." He reached over his shoulder and touched his back . . . but then he frowned. "Unless it was nearer the aorta than Hawthorne indicated . . ."

"But you cannot state with certainty that Greenfield did not die of loss of blood?"

"I cannot state with certainty anything at all. I was not there. The wound was in his back, but where I do not know. A major artery might have been severed, but that is not certain. Did Greenfield die because he was smothered? A man cannot last very long without air, but he can take a damned long time to die of blood loss. If he died in five minutes, he was either smothered or a major artery was severed."

"Both men stated that there was a great deal of blood in evidence."

"That is true, but a small amount of blood spread about can appear far greater than it truly is. I should not take that too seriously."

Both men were silent for a moment, turning over what had been said. *Les Droits de l'Homme*'s gun fired again.

"It does seem an odd time to be enquiring into the matter of Greenfield's death," Griffiths observed.

"The human memory is very fallible. The sooner such matters are brought to light, the better."

"I am sure you are right. And it does give the men something to contemplate on . . . other than French prisons."

"There is that as well. I do wish Braithwaite and Carlson were here that I might enquire further into this matter."

"Certainly, if they are guilty—and not fools—they will contrive to agree upon a single story. One in which Greenfield bled his poor life away while they cradled him in their arms and undertook, in the most gentle manner, to discourage him from crying out."

"Which is why I wish I could speak to them now before they have had time to compose such a story." Hayden paused a moment. "I cannot quite comprehend why Ransome would misrepresent what occurred . . . It would be more in his character, as I have come to know it, for him to cast all of the blame on Carlson and Braithwaite."

"He did give the order to silence Greenfield. Others heard him say it. Certainly, he must apprehend that some of the blame might be attached to him."

"Yes, I suppose that is true."

Griffiths pitched his voice so low that Hayden could barely make out his words.

"Lacrosse questioned me—quite intently—about your parentage. Specifically, your mother. Of course, I told him I knew only that your father was a post captain in the His Majesty's Navy. Nothing more."

"He knows of my mother's origins. Others were not as circumspect as you. And he has my mother's letters—all written to me in

French, of course. Do you know the French believe I am some roy-alist sea officer who has enlisted in the Royal Navy! I believe I have convinced Lacrosse that this is not the case."

"He has your mother's letters . . ." Griffiths looked even more grave than common. "Does this put her family in danger?"

"Under the present circumstances in France? Yes, certainly. La-crosse has promised to burn the letters. Did you know he was a baron before the revolution?"

"It is a wonder he still has a command. It is a wonder he is alive."

"Precisely. I believe he is an honourable man who does not want to see my mother's family persecuted without cause."

"He should beware of aiding you. Were it to come to the atten-tion of the Committee of Public Safety—well, who knows how they would interpret it."

"Indeed. The man has put himself at great risk on my behalf."

The doctor fixed his gaze on Hayden a moment. "What will he ask in return, I wonder?"

"If he is truly honourable, nothing."

"It is his duty to keep his men safe and his ship out of enemy hands. If either of these comes into doubt, I believe he will consider it more honourable to perform his duty than to aid a family he knows not at all."

"Yes. I wish I could know if he had destroyed the letters, as he said he would. I do, however, think there is a good chance *Les Droits de l'Homme* will be a British prize before the night is out. And then the letters will be mine again . . . if they have not been burned."

"Let us hope. I for one do not relish the idea of a French gaol. Officers they will quickly exchange . . . Surgeons? I am not so certain."

"Do not be concerned, Dr Griffiths. There are French surgeons aplenty among our prisoners. You shall be exchanged along with the rest of us." Hayden almost patted the doctor on the shoulder but stopped himself. "I believe we should rejoin the others."

The two men went out to take their place among the other *Themises*, and for a moment this caused an awkward silence, but Hawthorne soon swept that away and speculation began about the British ships whose guns could be heard firing now at regular intervals.

"Were there but two British ships, Captain?" Wickham asked.

"When I was on the deck that was the case. We might hope others have joined them, but if not I think two can manage perfectly well, do you not?"

"Certainly, sir, but I am worried that this ship might make Brest before she can be taken. Mr Barthe was just speculating that we might not be so far off the coast."

"Do you think so, Mr Barthe?" Hayden asked.

"I cannot say for certain, sir. We had seen neither land nor the sun these three days past. My dead-reckoning put our position south of Brest and about four leagues distant from the French coast, but I would not bet a farthing on it, sir, nor even a ha'penny."

"Where are we steering, then?" Smosh asked.

"We were steering west by north-west, more or less," Hayden told him, "though I could see neither sun nor compass, so I cannot be certain. Since then, Lacrosse has put the ship before the wind and we are flying east by south."

The sound of a ball finding wood crashed through the ship above, causing a moment of silence.

"Banish every thought of a huzzah, Mr Hobson," Hayden ordered the midshipman, who seemed about to jump up and cheer. "If our own cruisers free us, you may cheer as much as you wish. Until then, we shall cheer only in the quiet of our own minds."

The men all nodded, clearly requiring no more explanation than that.

"Mr Wickham, do the French realise that you speak their tongue?"

"I do not believe so, sir. Lacrosse spoke to me in quite acceptable English."

"In that case, I should not give it away if I were you. It is quite well known that I speak their tongue, but they might feel free to speak French out of my hearing if they believed no one else understood. This might give us some small information we do not have. The same applies to you, Mr Archer, or anyone else who has a smattering of French. Keep it to yourselves; you might hear something of value."

The men ate in near silence, the sounds of firing guns, both on *Les Droits de l'Homme* and from the distant ships, chiming like slightly irregular clocks. It was too early to sling hammocks, and the men sat about after their meal talking quietly. A few fell asleep leaning against a bulkhead. Hayden's watch had not been taken, and he consulted it after a while, wondering how long until dark—half an hour, more or less.

Voices were heard outside the door and the lock turned. A dull thud of a wooden bar being removed and then the door slowly opened, a face appearing in the dim lamplight, peering in to be certain there was no ambush.

"Capitaine Hayden? Capitaine Lacrosse requests your presence."

"Mr Archer," Hayden said to his senior lieutenant. "In the event that I do not return. You are in command."

"Aye, sir."

Hayden followed the Frenchman out and two seamen armed with muskets fell in behind. In a moment they were upon the lower gun-deck. The gunports were closed here and the gun crews had not been mustered, though in every other way the deck appeared to have been cleared for action. The upper gun-deck had all the gun crews mustered—both the larboard battery and starboard—though they stood idle at that moment and the ports were yet closed. The firing came from the upper deck and Hayden went quickly up into a late afternoon, wind making and seas quickly mounting. Darkness appeared to be gathering its forces just beyond the limited horizon and streams of rain could be seen all around. The two British ships were not distant, and the larger, Hayden could now see, was undoubtedly a razee. Pellew was the most determined captain in the Royal Navy, Hayden thought, and he did not expect him to give up this chase until the French ship had hauled down her colours. *Indefatigable* was certainly the right weapon for the job, and in the right hands, too. Both British ships were firing their chase guns, and Lacrosse's crews on the quarterdeck were engaged in this same exercise.

Hayden was quite certain that the French seventy-four would be neither as handy nor as swift as the smaller British ships, and though Lacrosse might have some advantage in weight of broadside, one English ship could engage him while the other manoeuvred to rake his ship. The sea was already running so that *Les Droits de l'Homme* did not dare open her lower gunports, meaning that the weight of broadside would favour the British. At least that was Hayden's assessment of the situation in the first moment he was on deck.

Lacrosse noticed him and motioned for Hayden to be brought forward.

"Capitaine Hayden." He gave a slight bow. "If I may have a word with you . . ."

Despite the guns being fired but a few yards away and the sound of British shot tearing into the air, the two officers retreated to an empty patch of deck to converse. Hayden admired Lacrosse's composure. He might have been out enjoying his garden, for all the fear evident in the man's demeanour. For his part, Hayden thought it would be ironic if he were killed by a British gun.

"There is a disagreement among my officers, Capitaine Hayden,"

Lacrosse began, "regarding our exact position. Many sections of the coast in this region are very dangerous. The disagreement is over how close to the coast we might be."

Clearly, Lacrosse wanted the greatest possible value for the favour he had promised Hayden, and given the situation of his mother's family, Hayden wondered how he could refuse.

"You do realise, Capitaine Lacrosse, that giving you such information would be seen as aiding the enemy, for which I could be court-martialled and executed?"

"I assure you, Capitaine, that no one beyond myself would ever know that you offered any aid to me at all. I might also say that if we were to go ashore your men would be in as much danger as my own. Certainly, you consider it your duty to preserve the lives of your own men?"

"Indeed. Unfortunately, we had seen neither land nor sun for three days running and my sailing master was uncertain of our own position when we surrendered our ship. That is God's truth."

Hayden could not read Lacrosse's response to this. For a moment he said nothing. "Unfortunate," he said at last and, excusing himself, rejoined his officers. Hayden was left standing on the quarterdeck, sharing the danger with the French officers. He even wondered if Lacrosse had done it a-purpose to demonstrate his own indifference to danger and death and to put the *Anglais* at risk. Hayden leaned his hip against the rail, crossed his arms, and fixed his attention on the chasing ships. Although the sea was getting up, they maintained a regular fire, perhaps every fourth shot finding *Les Droits de l'Homme*, though usually passing through the sails and doing little more harm. The scream of the iron ball parting the air was something felt in the chest. It demanded fear—like putting your hand on a viper in the dark. For Hayden, there was no possibility of not feeling apprehension, it was simply a matter of keeping it locked up. The pounding heart, the knife of fear awakening every nerve, the growling stomach where the fear went to prowl.

But he had become something of a master at this. And a fatalist as well. He truly believed that when one's time came there was nowhere one could hide. Better to die standing than grovelling— that was his belief. Die with the deck beneath one's feet, not one's knees.

So he stood, staring down the British guns, damned if he would show the least sign of fear before these Frenchmen. And it appeared they were equally determined to demonstrate their *sang-froid* before the *Anglais*.

The running sea raised the stern and then rolled along beneath until finally the stern sank into the trough and the bow was cast up—the motion of a seventy-four-gun ship so different from his own frigate. This thought of the *Themis* reminded him that she was now in enemy hands—a prize of war. He might not have been the first British captain to lose his ship, but, even so, the thought of it caused both distress and humiliation. For some reason, he imagined the *Themis'* former captain—the notoriously shy Hart—gloating and spreading it about that Hayden was a reckless pup who knew neither ships, nor men, nor war.

Lacrosse and his two senior officers huddled by the binnacle in whispered but heated debate. Clearly, they were not of one opinion, and Hayden was quite certain it was their present position that was the subject of this dispute. Perhaps it was not even their position that was debated but the uncertainty of their whereabouts.

Les Droits de l'Homme was sailing more or less east, Hayden thought, with the wind now behind them. If the coast was near and no bay or harbour offered shelter and the protection of shore batteries . . . they could be trapped against the French coast or worse. Visibility was very poor even by daylight, and darkness would reduce it to a musket shot or little more. Had he been Lacrosse, he would be more than concerned.

Lacrosse suddenly drew himself up and declared to his officers, *"I shall not surrender my ship to any two frigates. The English will have to board my ship and tear down the flag with their own hands!"*

A ball crashed into the stern just beneath the level of the quarter-deck. Hayden was glad his own men were being held forward and below the water line. The French gunners fired back, their own shots striking even less frequently than the British, though it must be admitted that a seventy-four-gun ship did offer the larger target.

After only the briefest period of observation, it was apparent to Hayden that the British ships were gaining, ranging up on either quarter. He could very clearly make out the gun crews, bent over their guns, swabbing and ramming home powder. Of course, Hayden had been aboard a French ship fighting a British ship before—although the French ship was a prize and the British vessel crewed by mutineers. Even so, he had fought the English and risked being killed by them. Standing on the quarterdeck in his French captain's coat, the present situation felt oddly familiar—as though he actually *had* once been a French officer just as the French believed.

An eruption of fire and smoke at the bow of the chasing razee sent an iron ball screaming overhead. It tore a hole in the mizzen but did no other damage. Hayden estimated that the ball had missed him by fewer than a dozen feet.

Upon the nearer British ship—the razee—Hayden could see marines climbing up to the foremast tops, muskets slung over their backs, red coats standing out against the dark sky. The quarterdeck of the French ship was about to become an even more dangerous place to be. Lacrosse responded by sending his own sharp-shooters up the mizzen.

Another ball found the stern of the French ship with a crash that

Hayden felt through the soles of his boots. There was a part of him that felt a great deal of pride in this display of British gunnery—and a part of him that wished they could be a good deal less accurate.

The hands began to carry up weapons—pikes and cutlasses, pistols and tomahawks—and these were distributed to men who were ordered to sit upon the deck amidships hidden from the view of the enemy. Two young officers were put in command of the boarding party and the ropes for the grappling hooks coiled down and ready to throw.

Hayden thought that boarding with such a sea running would be difficult if not impossible. The British snipers began firing at that moment, and at least one thing was not in doubt—they had smoked the French boarding party because the British marines were shooting as often at them as at the men upon the quarterdeck.

Lacrosse appeared to have forgotten about Hayden and went about his business very coolly. It was clear to Hayden, however, that the spirit of *liberté* had spread among the crew and they did not take orders from those above them readily. Although he saw little open defiance, compliance was grudging and dilatory, and the execution of orders would certainly have been unacceptable aboard his own ship.

French sailors were not in open mutiny, but very clearly they, like Lacrosse, could hear the sound of the guillotine, though for them the sound was the heads of their oppressors tumbling into the basket. Lacrosse, they knew, could be disposed of in the blink of an eye. They neither feared nor respected him. He was an officer's coat stuffed with straw.

Hayden had been in command of an untrustworthy crew and he felt some pity for Lacrosse—but not too much, as he knew this situation would make it easier for the British ships chasing. Musket balls began smacking into the wooden deck and one of the men at the wheel fell in a swoon, a ball in the back of his skull. A young *aspirant*—a boy whose voice had not yet begun to change—was shot through the leg, and then, as he fell, through the bowels.

He dug his fingers into the shoulder of another *aspirant* who bent over him. *"Les Anglais,"* he said, *"they have killed me . . ."* His eyes, so innocent but an instant ago, filled with a terrible knowledge. *"They have killed me."* And then he released his friend, closed his eyes, and fainted away, his limbs thrown out like a sleeping child's.

A grumbling began among the boarding party crouching in the waist, with many a dark look cast back towards Lacrosse and his officers. Then, to Hayden's utter and complete surprise, these men rose as a mass and, in open defiance of shouting lieutenants, streamed below out of the gunfire.

Hayden turned back to find Lacrosse standing motionless beside the helmsmen. He called no orders, nor did he protest in any way. Everything about him, his face, his posture, revealed that he knew there was nothing he could do. At that moment, Hayden realised that if Lacrosse could not get his ship into a French port or under the protection of shore guns, it was lost, and despite his declared defiance, Lacrosse knew this full well.

The French officer turned away, back to the chasing enemy.

Well, Hayden thought, one hardly need look further for an explanation of why the war at sea is being largely won by the British.

The Royal Navy ships ranged nearer, and Hayden thought they might soon be in a position to bring their broadsides to bear. At that point, Hayden thought he would volunteer to go below. Facing enemy guns was one thing; being killed by British guns to prove his aplomb was just bloody foolish.

A squall overtook all of the ships, pressing them on, stretching the canvas so that it looked about to tear out its clews. The seventy-four appeared to surge ahead, picked up and carried by a wave. At the same moment, *Indefatigable* tore her mainsail to ribbons, and she fell back almost immediately.

Hayden wondered if *Les Droits de l'Homme*'s sails would hold, given that many had been holed several times, but a glance showed them all bearing up to the gust so far. For perhaps ten minutes the gust held, and Hayden wondered if it was a gust at all or a general increase in the wind, when suddenly it fell away and the ship began to slow.

From the forecastle the cry *"Land! Land ahead!"* came with such a tone of panic that everyone turned towards the bow. Out of the grey, cliffs loomed, and before the bow breakers foamed white.

Lacrosse jumped to the wheel and wrenched it to starboard.

Not heeding the danger, Hayden leapt up onto the rail, grasping the mizzen shrouds, and screamed at the top of his lungs in English, *"Land! Land dead ahead!"*

He could not know if his voice was heard, but the razee began turning to starboard and the frigate to larboard. Before *Les Droits de l'Homme* had turned a point, Hayden was thrown down onto the deck, landing on one foot and then sprawling. One of the chase guns thundered by on its carriage, barely missing him. A rending and splintering came from forward and the foremast went over the bow. The ship was hard aground.

Hayden staggered up to see *Indefatigable* making her turn, barely out of the breakers, and bear off south. The frigate also managed to turn, but then she too went aground and was thrown immediately upon her beam ends. Hayden saw the first wave break over her side and exposed copper.

A wave lifted the stern of *Les Droits de l'Homme* and threw it to larboard. Hayden stood up to find water sloughing down the gun-deck below, no doubt washing in through the shattered stern gallery.

Lacrosse screamed orders to his officers, but even they looked about to panic. The men were jumping to the shrouds and clambering aloft, but as they did so the mainmast went by the board, throwing the men down hard upon the planks below. Hayden hurried over the sloping deck to Lacrosse.

"Capitaine!" he shouted above the sound of men calling and crying out. "My officers . . . they are locked up below."

Lacrosse grabbed the shoulder of a frightened *aspirant. "Go with Capitaine Hayden,"* he ordered, *"and release his men."*

The boy, for he could not have been more than fifteen, ordered Hayden's two guards to accompany them, but by the time they were on the upper gun-deck the two men retreated with the stream of men coming up from below.

"We must hurry!" Hayden urged.

But panicked men climbing out of the bowels of the ship would not let them pass, and they were forced to stand aside until what seemed like all six hundred souls had passed. The boy looked so terrified that Hayden thought he might bolt with his frightened countrymen. Water was pouring down the next ladder, which was leaning at a precarious angle as *Les Droits de l'Homme* began to heel to larboard.

As each wave struck, the ship was driven further up the rocks upon which she had impaled herself, and Hayden and his companion were hurled almost off their feet into the knee-deep water. The lower deck was half awash, the larboard side almost filled to the deck-head. Any lanterns that had been hung here were out or gone, and almost no light made its way down through the streaming scuttles. Above the grinding of the hull on rocks and the general hubbub of wind and frightened men, Hayden could hear the muffled shouts of his crew, crying out, and pounding upon the door. But the two sentries who had been standing guard were gone, the door still barred and locked.

"I have no key," the *aspirant* said, looking around in terrible distress, as though he might find a key hanging upon a hook.

The hammering on the bulkhead became more desperate by the second. Hayden called out but could not be heard over the banging. Finally, he hammered on the boards with his fist and heard Archer and Hawthorne urging the others to silence.

"Mr Archer!" Hayden yelled at the top of his voice. "The guards have run off with the key to the lockup, but I shall find a way to have you out in a moment. Compose yourselves and remain quiet so that I might give orders for you to aid me."

"Aye, sir," Archer called back, his throat already hoarse from shouting. "But the water is rising in here, sir. I don't know how long we shall remain above it."

"I will have you out of there, Mr Archer, if I must break all of my bones to do it. You have my word."

"Bless you, sir."

Even in the quick light Hayden could see that the lockup had been built in such a way that it would be easier to break in than out. The fastenings were driven from the inside through substantial, horizontal planks and into temporary posts.

"What is your name?" Hayden asked the *aspirant*.

"Pierre, Capitaine."

"We must have an axe, Pierre, or even a capstan bar."

The boy, who was shivering from the cold water that washed about their belts, shook his head. "An axe . . ." He shrugged.

"Then let us hasten up to the capstan."

Reaching the ladder on the half-flooded, sloping deck was no easy feat, and Hayden knew that getting a bar and returning would take more time than he wished. But there was nothing for it. He needed something to batten down the planks. His fists would not answer, even if he broke them as he promised.

Hayden pushed the boy up the streaming ladder and clambered up hand over hand behind. They went as quickly as they could to the capstan and took down one of the ash bars. These were both long and heavy upon a seventy-four-gun ship, and two of them were required to bear it under those conditions.

It took a moment to slide it down the ladder, brace it from getting away, and then both clamber down onto a deck even more filled with water than when they had left but a moment before. Bracing themselves on the uphill side of the lockup so that gravity might aid them, Hayden and the *aspirant* used the bar as a battering ram and soon drove one plank loose.

Hands took hold of it from inside and they quickly wrenched it free so that Hayden could now see the faces of all his captive men, staring out at him from inside, panic barely held in check.

The next plank was more stubborn, but with the men all pulling and Hayden and Pierre driving their bar as hard as they were able, it finally gave way and was pulled free. The midshipmen clambered out through this hole, but the others were all too large. With the aid of Wickham, Hobson, and Madison, the battering ram became more effective, though they once lost their footing and took Hayden sliding into the bulkhead in a pile, the deck was so slick. As each wave drove the ship up the reef, Hayden and his helpers had to wait a moment for the ship to settle, then quickly smash their ram into wood.

The third plank was torn from its ports, and the rest of the *Themises* struggled out, Mr Barthe needing Hawthorne and Franks to pull his substantial bulk by the arms through the too-narrow opening.

"All of you with me," Hayden called over the noise. "And bring along that French boy. When all the others lost their nerve and fled, he kept his head. I should never have managed it without him."

The boy got such a pounding upon the back as they went, one would never have thought him an officer but merely a mascot, much caressed by all the crew. He hardly knew what to make of it.

Hayden led the way up to the next deck. As he put his feet upon the wet planking at the ladder head, the mizzen went by the board. There was no mistaking the rending and breaking of timber, the snapping of rigging. He felt it all through the deck. Hawthorne brought up the rear, and here, in better light, Hayden could see that all of the men, including the marine lieutenant, were shaken and blue-pale.

"Is anyone injured?" Hayden asked, noting that Archer's hand was bleeding.

Everyone denied any such thing, even Archer.

"Doctor, will you see to Mr Archer's hand when we are upon the upper deck?"

"I will, sir," Griffiths responded. Hayden took a count of heads and led them on—twelve Englishmen, including himself. Hawthorne, Griffiths, Archer, Ransome, Wickham, Hobson, Madison, Gould, Barthe, Franks, and the Reverend Smosh.

The upper gun-deck was reached in a moment, and just as they were all accounted for, two guns broke free from the starboard battery and slid down the deck, one toppling from its carriage and rolling and bouncing until it thundered into a gun opposite, shattering its carriage. The other gun tumbled down the ladder opening forward and crashed upon the deck below.

"This is a dangerous place to be," Hayden said to Barthe. "Follow me."

In a moment they were upon the upper deck in the face of the storm. And what a scene it was. Men clung to the high side of the ship and to one another as though to let go would begin a slide to hell. All around the seas broke, sending heavy spray crashing over the weather side. The ship lay, listing terribly to larboard, her bulwarks all but in the water. With each sea the ship heaved a little and then settled with a rending of planks and timbers. The shore was distant some half a mile or more, and in between stretched a thousand yards of churning, running ocean, April-cold and murky grey.

If that was not enough, the wind drove rain upon them without mercy. The drops slashed down upon Hayden's face as though they were beads of glass. His hat had been lost, and he held up an arm to protect himself.

"God have mercy," Hayden heard Barthe intone.

The crew members of the *Themis* all looked around as though they had just woken to find themselves in some level of Hades, unexpected and undeserved.

"Good Lord, Captain," Hobson cried out, "are we lost?"

"No, Mr Hobson, we are not lost," Hayden said, firmly if not testily. "Nor will we be if we master ourselves and do not give way to panic and fear. I do not think boats can be launched and taken safely ashore in such a sea, but this gale will take off shortly, I hope, and until then we will remain patient, follow my orders and those of Captain Lacrosse, and we will all survive. This ship will not break up for some days, and I do not think our gale will last so long. Have patience and good faith. God will preserve us."

When Hayden had spoken Barthe, who sat with his good foot wedged up against a scuttle, addressed his crew mates. "I would venture I am the only man here unfortunate enough to have been wrecked before, and I will tell you that panic is a greater enemy than the sea. If we do not give way to it and follow the captain's orders with a will, we shall stand a very good chance of passing through this with our lives. Give in to the fear that we all wrestle with and you will surely die." The old sailing master fixed each of the midshipmen with a dark glare, as though to be certain they understood the gravity of his words. Hayden thought that if they were not frightened near to death before, they certainly were now.

"Captain," Smosh said, "if I may . . . ?"

"Yes, Mr Smosh, certainly."

And Smosh led them all in prayer. Hayden had not heard an appeal so heartfelt aboard the *Themis* since he had first come aboard, not even when Smosh had held service in the midst of a pestilence that had killed over twenty of the *Themis'* crew and laid low double that number for some weeks with a grave illness.

Every man there bowed his head penitently—even the papist French sailors nearby, so in fear were they for their own lives. The French, however, crossed themselves thrice when Smosh completed his prayer.

Hayden took hold of the bulwark and stood, holding on lest he slide down the deck. Not far to the north he could see the British frigate in much the same position, beam on to the sea, laid over on her beam ends, hard aground yet still quite distant from the shore. Her masts, too, were gone. The other British ship had disappeared into the rain and growing twilight. Darkness was all but upon them. Shore, backed by cliffs, was already a dim line of white where the seas broke heavily upon the beach.

Hawthorne dragged himself up beside Hayden and cast his own gaze upon the distant shore. "Could you swim it, Captain?" he asked quietly.

Hayden shook his head. "No. The sea is too great, and it is common in such places for there to be an undertow that will drag a swimmer out to sea. We have the ship's boats and, come daylight, we shall build rafts. That is our best hope. We shall not have rescue unless this gale moderates a good deal, and I see little sign of that."

Hawthorne, for once, did not look the least jocular but, like all the others, ashen and blue-lipped, his hair plastered over his forehead from the pelting rain. "There are some six hundred French sailors," Hawthorne said so low that Hayden could hardly make out his words over the wind, "will they be the least concerned for English prisoners or will we be left here to our own devices?"

"Lacrosse is an honourable man—an officer and nobleman,

though *citoyen* now. He would give up his place in the boats to one of us, I am sure . . . but his crew . . . I saw the officers openly defied by a boarding party but a few hours ago. If the French sailors refuse to take orders, we shall be in a great deal of trouble. We are but a dozen, but much may fall to us, for I do not believe our men will forget their duty or shy from danger."

"Sir . . ." Hawthorne said, nodding his head towards the stern, "Captain Lacrosse in the offing."

The French officer was making his way along the sloping deck. Here and there a sailor would give him a hand, for they lined the bulwark, clinging to it as the point furthest from the terrifying sea. Many a man, however, turned his face away and Lacrosse was forced to get by as best he could.

Hawthorne made room for him at the rail. It appeared to Hayden that Lacrosse had aged several decades; he looked gaunt and thin and bent. As he pulled himself to the rail beside Hayden, Lacrosse was racked by a prolonged fit of coughing.

When he straightened, red-faced, he asked Hayden, "Are all your men present and unharmed?"

"Yes. My first lieutenant has injured his hand," Hayden gestured towards Archer, whose wound Griffiths had already dressed with a strip of cloth, probably torn from a shirt hem. "I would never have got my crew free without your *aspirant*, Pierre."

Lacrosse brightened slightly at this news. "He has the body of a boy but the heart of a man, that one." Lacrosse leaned closer to Hayden and in heavily accented English said, "You must know, Capitaine Hayden, that discipline has broken down in the French Navy. *Liberté* and *fraternité* mean that no man is obliged to take orders from another but is free to do as he pleases. Our very lives depend upon all of the men here taking the correct measures at the right time . . . Though I am ashamed to say it, I am less than certain my crew will accept this."

"You may rely upon my own men, Capitaine," Hayden informed the Frenchman, trying to allow no sense of pride to enter his voice. "They are very steady and have proven themselves again and again. They will attempt whatever is asked of them. But we are only twelve."

"I may be forced to ask your aid, Capitaine Hayden, and the assistance of your men. We are in a very dire situation. This gale will draw the heat from men who are wet to the skin. We have no food and no water. But a short time ago the weather glass was seen to be still falling. This gale will last at least a day more, and I have seen spring gales last much longer." Lacrosse looked off at the distant shore, now almost dark. "Is it possible, do you think, to row ashore through this surf?"

"Perhaps, but a boat could never return against this sea. Launching boats safely will be near impossible."

Hayden could see Lacrosse nod agreement; apparently, Hayden had confirmed his own belief.

"If there is no sign of the storm abating by first light, Capitaine Hayden, I will order a boat put over the side. I might be sending men to their deaths, I don't know, but we must try. As frightened as the men are to be stranded on the ship, they will be more frightened to go into a boat until they know it can be managed."

"I have men I could send," Hayden offered.

"I might accept this offer, Capitaine, if you are certain."

Hayden assured him that his offer was in earnest.

"Thank you, Capitaine. There is little I can do for you in this situation, but do not hesitate to ask my help if you require it."

Hayden found he was touched by this, for both men knew there was little either could offer, but even so Hayden was certain Lacrosse would do whatever was within his power.

"Thank you, sir," Hayden replied.

"Bonne chance."

The deck was sloping to the degree that men could just sit upon it and not slide down, though walking upon it with wet leather soles was treacherous. Everyone was huddled in the shelter of the starboard bulwarks or behind the netting where hammocks were stowed. Although this offered some little protection from the wind, it offered next to none from the pelting rain.

Hayden had begun to shiver, and he could see many others in much the same state. It was going to be a night of great misery, and he could see the men gathering into knots in largely vain attempts to gain warmth. His own men did the same, but Hayden feared it would make little difference.

Darkness settled about them, but the gale did not abate or even falter. The wind continued to howl up and down an eerie scale, and the seas crashed against the hull with numbing regularity, some sending icy salt spray over the already shivering men. The noise and bitter wind overwhelmed the senses and drove men inward in an attempt to escape into some kind of silence and calm.

Hayden's hands and feet began to ache, and he stuffed his hands into his armpits as best he could. Exhaustion leached away all his strength, or so it seemed, for he had been awake for much of the previous three days. He lay down and curled onto his side on the hard deck, closed his eyes and felt the rain clatter down upon his face and the wind push at him like a hand trying to rouse him from his slumber. For moments at a time he would slip away into unconsciousness, but then he would be roused back into a kind of torpor where lethargy overwhelmed him, cold racked his limbs, and his mind was blank and despairing.

And so the endless night crept on. There was no bell or even a moon to measure out the hours, but Hayden began to think that dawn would not come to this place. Men would now and then sit up and beat their arms against their sides in an attempt to restore some warmth, but it profited them little. Sometime, deep into the night, Hayden heard men shouting from a distance and then realised the sound was coming up through the planking from the half-flooded gun-deck. He was certain he heard cursing in French and the sounds of a struggle, but then it came to an end. Were *Les Droits de l'Homme* his own ship he would have forced himself up to investigate, but this was Lacrosse's vessel and Hayden did not think French sailors would obey orders from an English prisoner when they openly defied their own officers.

He slipped back into his torpor, listening to the menacing voices of the gale, occasionally doused by heavy, salt spray from the icy Atlantic. Upon one of these rude awakenings, Hayden opened his eyes and caught sight of something. Immediately, he sat up and realised there were flames burning some distance off—upon the shore, no doubt.

"Bonfires," came Griffiths' voice over the wind. "They were lit some time ago." The doctor was sitting up, his hands thrust in the front of his jacket. "Have they come to rescue us?" Griffiths asked, struggling to speak; he was shivering as badly as Hayden.

"Perhaps—or they are keeping vigil, waiting for the ship to break up to see what manner of flotsam the sea might carry ashore." That appeared to give Griffiths pause to think. "How fare you, Doctor?" Hayden asked.

"My very soul is frozen, I think. I have been passing the hours by making mental notes on the process by which the human body is overwhelmed by cold. If I live, it shall make a fascinating study. I might write a pamphlet."

"I am pleased to see that you have turned this night to profit. Very enterprising of you. I have been lying here in a state of utter numbness of both body and mind. It is a strange kind of delirium, I find, which can be described as neither dream nor wakefulness."

Barthe sat up at that moment, perhaps wakened by the others. "I can no longer feel my cock, Doctor," he said. "If I live, I shall never have use of it again."

"You shall find your manhood as useful as ever, Mr Barthe," Griffiths assured the sailing master, "once your body's furnace has begun to burn again."

"So I pray."

"As d-do we all," Griffiths replied.

Hayden lay down but turned a little that he might catch a glimpse of the distant fires now and again. The presence of people on the shore gave him hope somehow.

Sometime before dawn Hayden could bear it no more and stood on the sloping deck and began to stiffly work his arms, certain that if he lay still a moment longer his blood would freeze. There was yet no sign of daylight, but he could feel the approaching morning. The gale blew unappeased, and the sea, steel-cold, ran just as high, although the tide had ebbed and was near low water now. Hayden wondered if the rocks *Les Droits de l'Homme* was wrecked upon would be visible. Certainly, a boat could not be launched if that was the case. A thought that the tide might ebb so far that all might walk ashore came to him—there were places along this coast where that would be possible—but not near here, he knew.

Around him a whispering blended with the sounds of the gale. The French sailors began to stir. Many began to mutter prayers and cross themselves. Then, like Hayden, a few rose up and tried to restore some warmth through movement. The British sailors forced themselves up as well.

Sunrise did not occur that day, but only a dull, growing illumination that had no discernible source; a kind of twilight that Hayden knew would persist through the day. There were no victuals and no water—nothing to sustain the men but a slim hope of reaching shore.

Hayden made his way aft and soon found Lacrosse speaking with his lieutenants—*pleading,* actually, was what it appeared to be. But whatever it was, the lieutenants were not giving way, and finally Lacrosse noticed Hayden and took his leave of his officers, making his way awkwardly along the sloping deck.

"How fare your men, Capitaine?" Lacrosse enquired in English. There was no place for the two captains to have a private conversation, so the best they could do was not to speak French.

"They have all lived through the night, but I do not think any man will survive long without water and victuals and shelter."

Lacrosse shook his head sadly. "Several men perished this night, two by foul play, I fear."

"Sir?"

"We found a pair, stabbed to death on the gun-deck, apparently over some small scrap of food."

Hayden could not sit in judgement—there had been a murder on his own ship when he was her first lieutenant, and now this matter of Greenfield. "I do not think this gale will blow itself out this day, nor even on the morrow. Will you still launch a boat?"

"That is my desire, but all of my lieutenants, they do not want it. I have no one but an *aspirant* to put in command of such a boat."

"Can you not order one of your lieutenants to take this command?"

"It shames me to say this, Capitaine Hayden, but I believe they would all refuse. If I lose the support of my officers, how are the men to be governed?"

For a moment Hayden hesitated to speak. Clearly, Lacrosse hoped Hayden would offer to take charge of the boat, or perhaps put one of his own officers in command, but Hayden was uncertain. It would take great seamanship and a measure of luck to get a boat ashore in the sea that was running. Hayden was willing to attempt it, but he would not leave his own men. He was also reticent to leave Lacrosse on his own. The man had done him a great favour destroying his mother's letters. Hayden was loath to leave him now. There was also the possibility—and not a remote one—that a boat would not make it through the surf. Hayden might drown his entire crew on such an enterprise. And there was one other significant problem—no one wanted to be first.

"I would put one of my officers in charge, if that will meet with your approval," Hayden said at last.

"I see little other choice, Capitaine," Lacrosse replied, both relieved and shamed.

"Then let me speak with them. We will send the small boat?"

"Yes. I will find reliable men to man the sweeps."

Hayden went back to his own crew.

"Shall we send a boat, then, sir?" Archer asked as Hayden approached.

"That is Lacrosse's wish. He has asked that one of us take command of it. As he will supply the men to man the sweeps, it must be someone who speaks French."

"I will do it, sir," Archer said immediately.

"I commend you, Mr Archer, but as the officer in charge must take the helm, and you have an injured hand, I shall have to ask another."

"Then it must be me, sir," Wickham said before Archer could protest. "No one else speaks their tongue well enough, and I have taken command of many a boat, as you well know."

"I do, Mr Wickham, but I want you to understand, nothing you have ever done will have prepared you adequately. In truth, I am far from certain that a boat can be got ashore safely."

"If you please, Captain," Barthe interjected, "with no disrespect to any man present, to pilot a boat through such waters is not a matter to be taken lightly. I would venture that only yourself, sir, Mr Franks, and I have long enough wakes to even attempt it." He gave a little bow to Wickham. "No disrespect to you, Mr Wickham, but you have never been in such a sea before in an open boat."

"I take your point, Mr Barthe," Wickham replied, "truly I do, but you do not speak French and Captain Hayden requested someone who has command of that tongue."

"That cannot be denied," Barthe agreed, "but I would put forward that I should take command of the boat and you should come as my second and translate all my orders upon the instant I call them out. That is the only way we have any hope of success—or so I believe." Barthe turned to Hayden. "Do you not agree, Captain?"

Hayden did not like any solution, that was the truth of it. Barthe was certainly correct—Wickham had never taken a boat through such a surf and the chances that he would succeed were slim. For that reason, Barthe was certainly the better choice to take command, but the possibility of the oarsmen misunderstanding his translated order, or of the instant it took to make that translation, might be enough to see them all put under. Hayden knew that he was the right man for this endeavour, but Hayden was also certain that Lacrosse would need his assistance if he was to preserve lives.

"Mr Barthe, we shall have to have a perfect understanding between yourself and Mr Wickham, and Wickham and the oarsmen, so that there can be no delay in translating your orders and no delay in their execution. There can be no hesitation on the part of the oarsmen lest it lead to disaster."

"I agree, sir," Barthe said.

Lacrosse chose older seamen for boat duty, and Hayden thought, though they all looked apprehensive, they appeared to be steady men. After asking Lacrosse's permission, he gathered these men together with Wickham and Barthe and made certain that all of the French commands were clearly comprehended by all and that Wickham knew the proper translation for each. He even ran them through a pantomime drill, to be certain that there would be no

misunderstanding. Even so, Hayden feared he had forgotten some
order that Barthe would call out and Wickham would not know the
correct French for it.

Launching the boat was not an easy feat in such a sea. There were
no masts standing and no yards to be used to swing the boat out, so
it had to be manhandled by the crew, all of the Englishmen involved, including the doctor. Hayden would have liked to have seen
the boat manned and oars in place and then slid, bow first, into the
sea, but it simply could not be managed with such a weight under
these circumstances. The boat would have to go into the sea and be
held alongside until the crew was aboard. There was, Hayden knew,
a good possibility of the boat capsizing right there next to the ship.

With many a bruise and barked knuckle, the boat was launched,
the oarsmen clambering aboard even as the boat lifted wildly then
dropped with the surf, banging hard against the ship again and
again.

Hayden and Hawthorne steadied the hobbled Mr Barthe and
helped him aboard as the cutter surged up, whereupon the master's
ankle gave way and he tumbled down awkwardly into the boat.
Hawthorne turned to Hayden in horror, but it was too late to bring
the master back now. He pulled himself up painfully and took hold
of the tiller, not meeting his captain's gaze.

"Luck to you, Mr Barthe," Hayden said, and the sailing master
gave a curt nod. Hayden had never seen the old seaman look so
grave. Until that instant, Hayden had not realised how little hope
Barthe had of the enterprise's success.

All the men settled in their places, took up their oars, and in a
moment Barthe, through Wickham, ordered the boat away, both
the Englishmen forcing confidence into their voices that Hayden
now knew neither felt.

"Do you think they will manage it?" Hawthorne asked as they
watched the French crew ship their oars.

"I am not sure Barthe is confident."

"You know he cannot swim a stroke?"

"It would not make the least difference, Mr Hawthorne. No swimmer is a match for this sea."

"God preserve them," Hawthorne intoned.

"That and good seamanship."

"I would rather the oars were manned by Englishmen," Hawthorne said quietly.

"Lacrosse chose steady men. I have no doubt of that."

"Then you are more confident than Captain Lacrosse." Hawthorne nodded in the direction of the French captain, who stood with one hand over his mouth, appearing to hold his breath. If his own son had been aboard the boat he could not have looked more distressed, or less confident of the outcome.

Every eye aboard watched with hope and dread. If the boat could be taken ashore safely, then that would mean another boat could do the same. The problem then would be that there was only one other boat and it would bear but thirty souls in this foul sea.

Each wave lifted the little boat up and swept it on, Barthe and Wickham fighting the helm and calling out orders to the oarsmen. A sea broke over the stern and the boat was lost to sight for a moment as it slid into the trough. Hayden fully expected their next view of it would be the boat overturned and all of the hands thrown into the sea, but it lumbered up to the top of the crest, clearly burdened with water and with more than one man bailing to preserve his life.

Again the boat went down into the trough and all the men aboard *Les Droits de l'Homme* strained to catch sight of it. And yet again the stern was thrown up, caught by the wave, slewed to starboard, and disappeared.

A long, anxious moment was endured aboard the wreck, and then the boat came up again, the helmsmen fighting to keep the stern square to the seas. Again the boat was seen to yaw as the wave took hold of the stern and threw it to starboard. This time Hayden was certain the boat had broached and been swamped or overturned.

If the boat lifted above the sea on the next wave, Hayden could not see, for a larger wave interposed itself. There was a groan from all the men aboard. Some covered their faces, and Hayden thought that not a few wept, for here was their single hope lost.

Hawthorne cursed under his breath.

But then the boat lifted into view. It was deep in the water now, and Hayden feared that if it rolled even a little the water it had shipped would wash to one side and the weight would overturn the boat. The men were pulling for their very lives, Hayden could see, even at this distance, Barthe and Wickham standing in the stern fighting the tiller.

Down again the boat went, and it was lost from view for some moments.

"They were not so far from the beach," Hawthorne whispered to Hayden. "Do you think they might cling to the boat and be washed ashore?"

"I do not know," Hayden replied softly. "They might be more distant than we comprehend."

"I do hope we have not lost our shipmates, sir."

"God preserve them both," Smosh said quietly, sidling over to where Hawthorne and Hayden stood, braced against the sloping deck. "Cannot Mr Wickham swim so short a distance?"

"The surf is very great, Mr Smosh, and the sea yet very cold. Twenty minutes in this water and all of a man's vital energy will have been sapped away. If the boat overturns, I hold little hope for any man to survive."

"I have prayed to God to preserve their lives—even the papists—but God has his own plans for us and is little influenced by Smosh, I fear."

A cheer went up around them at that moment, and Hayden could see men from the shore wading into the surf, and then the boat appeared, almost up to its gunwales, the oarsmen all tumbling out. They were helped ashore, staggering through the surf, bracing themselves as it ebbed and then thrown forward onto their knees when a sea swept over them. But they were ashore.

Around Hayden men jumped to their feet and pounded one another on the backs as though somehow they had been responsible for this miracle.

The storm, however, was not so pleased and howled all around as though angered anew. Hayden was nearly pushed off his feet and could lean against the wind with all his weight. Around him men slumped down onto the deck, clinging to one another as the wind screamed and rippled their sodden clothing.

There was no choice but to lie flat on the deck so that the heeled ship provided some small protection. Within moments the sea mounted and began to crash against the hull, shoving the massive ship each time. A splintering and rending of timbers was heard aft and a moment later two shattered sections of the transom floated off into the foaming waters.

"She is breaking up!" Griffiths looked over at Hayden like a man about to be cast into this cold, fearsome sea.

"The stern is the most vulnerable part of a ship, Doctor, and it was much damaged by British gunfire. We have many hours yet before we need worry about her breaking up."

But even so, all the men aboard stared in horror as the sections of the transom drifted off. Lacrosse scuttled across the deck to Hayden, his wet hair whipped back by the wind.

"We dare not launch a boat in this, Capitaine Hayden," he called over the wind, his voice hoarse from thirst.

"I agree, Capitaine Lacrosse. We must wait for the sea to moderate and this wind to take off."

A wave boomed against the hull and shot spray high into the air before it slatted down heavily upon the deck. Hayden and Lacrosse both wiped salt water from their eyes and faces, but Hayden thought the look they shared said all that was needed—getting a twentieth of the men safely off this ship would be the most they could hope for.

All through the morning and then the afternoon the shipwrecked men lay on the deck, their stomachs boiling with hunger, mouths and throats gummy from thirst. As one had no choice but to shout over the wind, conversation was difficult and men soon gave it up. Each lay with his own thoughts, and Hayden believed that there was no more fertile soil for fears and doubts than inactivity. Had he been in command he would have employed the men in making rafts or in some other enterprise.

Waving the doctor near, Hayden leaned near and asked as quietly as the wind would allow, "How long can men go without food and water, Doctor?"

"Commonly, one would say without food, many days, although in this matter every man is different. Water, however, one cannot do without for more than four days, and under these circumstances perhaps as few as three and one half. It is singularly cold for April, Captain, and as we are all wet to our very skins the wind will draw away our reserves more quickly than we realise. I, for one, am shivering without pause." For a moment Griffiths appeared to consider his answer. "Although this might disgust everyone, Captain, it is possible to drink urine, as it is aseptic and can be imbibed without detriment."

"Let us hope it does not come to that."

Griffiths clearly had more to say, so Hayden remained propped up a little on one elbow.

"Sir, there is but one boat remaining and near to six hundred souls aboard this ship. How many might be carried safely ashore?"

"Thirty, more or less," Hayden said.

"And can it then return to take away more?"

"Not while the storm persists."

"Then some five hundred seventy shall remain aboard?"

"Yes, but we will make rafts and attempt to reach the shore upon those."

This proposal did not seem to raise the doctor's hopes in the least—if anything, he looked more despondent.

"Doctor, if we are able to launch the boat this day, will you go with it?"

Griffiths shook his head. "I believe my knowledge will be required here, Captain. Ashore there are surgeons enough."

Through all of the meagre morning the wind battered man and ship, wailing up and down a discordant scale. There was little anyone could do but lie on the hard planks and shiver miserably. Hayden's mind was given over to something like dream, and he thought often of Henrietta and imagined a warm meeting where all of their misunderstandings had been swept aside and their affections were all but impossible to keep in check.

This waking dream was interrupted often by Hayden wondering whether the penetrating cold caused more misery than the hunger and thirst. His muscles ached. His very bones were in agony. Spasms of shivering would overwhelm him and he would lie hugging himself and rocking on the hard planks. Around him men moaned and muttered and cursed their ill luck. Prayers were offered up in both French and English, and not a few in the language of Bretagne.

Hayden was uncertain how much time passed, for his watch had ceased to work, water having penetrated its case, no doubt, and there was no way to find the sun. Forcing himself up, he went in search of Lacrosse, whom he found on the slowly disintegrating quarterdeck.

"Capitaine Lacrosse, I would like to put my men to work building rafts. To lie here doing nothing, I believe, will only make them more despondent, and when this weather takes off we might be able to use rafts to get ashore."

Lacrosse nodded, and vigorously. "That is wise, Capitaine Hayden. I will set some of my own men to do the same. The carpenter's tools were not saved, however, so we have little but our hands and some cordage that tore away when we lost our masts."

"Did I not see a boarding party go below to the gun-deck before we struck the reef?"

This brought an unhappy look to the French officer's face, but he nodded.

"Perhaps some of their tomahawks might still be on the gun-deck. I will collect some of my men and search."

Hayden made his way back along the sloping deck and explained his plan to his crew. Immediately, they were making their way stiffly down the remaining ladder forward to the gun-deck below. But for a thin ribbon upon the seaward side, the deck was entirely awash. The opening torn in the transom allowed the sea to wash fully in, and with each wave the water level rose to the point where even amidships the men were fighting to keep their heads above water. Worse, however, was the flotsam that washed back and forth, caved-in barrels, strakes of heavy timber, capstan bars, and gun carriages that would crush a man were they to pin him against the hull.

The silence of profound apprehension settled among Hayden's men, who watched the deadly flotsam as though it were about to pounce. Waves thundering against the hull were immediately followed by the water level rising and the flotsam being washed from the stern towards the bow, battering along the hull and thudding dully together.

Hayden ordered the doctor and the other nonswimmers to remain on the upper deck. "You can be no help here," he told them, "and we cannot spend our energies rescuing any man."

There were still half a dozen guns lashed to the starboard side, but the rest had rolled or tumbled down into the water, doing who knew what damage to the ruined hull. Wisely, no one wanted to be downhill of these guns, so Hayden picked a spot where there was no gun poised to come sliding down on them and turned to Hobson and Gould. "We will not last twenty minutes in this water. Best we get on with it. Be wary. There is much dangerous flotsam here, and if you are pinned against the hull there will be little any man can do."

The midshipmen nodded quickly.

Hayden let himself go and swam a few strokes to the leeward side of the wrecked ship, keeping clear of a half-submerged gun carriage. The iciness of the sea scythed into his muscles and he felt the strength torn away. A sea washed in at that moment, filling all the air space, and he felt himself swept towards the bow. The sea washed out and Hayden madly grabbed for anything that would hold him in place, trying desperately to see if dangerous flotsam bore down upon him. When he surfaced, he called out for the midshipmen and found them both clinging to a cleat not too distant and cursing like Mr Barthe. As the water reached a brief equilibrium, they all put their heads under and groped about with hands and feet.

Hobson surfaced as Hayden did, they both took a breath as a sea washed in and then held on for their lives. Something heavy lumbered into Hayden and broke him free. But he dived under it and managed to find purchase. Again the sea washed out the stern and Hayden found Gould and Hobson both coughing madly. He swam a few strokes and caught hold of Hobson.

"I have an axe, sir," the midshipman said, and held the weapon up. "There is another just here," he said, nodding downwards.

"I will find it," Hayden replied. "Both of you get up onto the deck."

He watched them go, gauged the position of all dangerous flotsam, and then forced himself down into the frigid cold one last time. If he could not lay his hand on the axe, he would have to give it up. He could not bear it longer.

An iron ball he found, and cannister shot, and just when he was about to give it up, he laid his hand on the axe and shot up, cracking his head cruelly on a carline. There was no air to breathe, and Hayden found a streaming line used to run out a gun and clung to that while the water tried to sweep him towards the stern and out into the storm. A broken barrel struck him a glancing blow on the shoulder and he near dropped his precious axe. A moment later, he was crawling up onto the thin ribbon of planks not submerged and then onto the ladder and up into the wind, his treasure in hand.

Hawthorne and Franks had wrapped the two midshipmen in their own coats, which though not dry were certainly better than the sopping garments the boys wore. Franks took Hayden's coat and with massive hands wrung from it all the water he could and then beat it on the deck to dry it more. Hayden was shivering so severely that he could not manage speech and allowed Hawthorne to take his waistcoat and shirt and twist the water from them. By the time he had donned his still-wet clothes, Hayden thought he would depart this life on the spot, the cold had knifed so deeply into his heart. The doctor chafed his wrists and one of the French lieutenants came aft and produced a flask, giving all three of the swimmers a precious mouthful of brandy. This emptied the flask, and the Englishmen stammered their thanks through blue lips. The man shrugged and tossed the flask into the sea, to prove it empty to the crew, Hayden suspected.

Mr Franks took charge of the raft building. Lumber was needed, and being sensible of the state of the ship, the bosun went about prising it loose from places where it would not weaken the structure.

Hayden and the two midshipmen huddled as best they could out of the wind and trembled like men with the palsy. Three French sailors who had been bunched beneath a hammock came and wrapped the midshipmen in it and then sat close around Hayden, bearing the brunt of the wind and sparing what little heat they could from their own frames.

Lacrosse approached to find out how Hayden fared and looked very concerned. Hayden motioned him near with a shaking hand.

"C-Captain La-c-crosse," Hayden whispered in English, "this ship will not l-last long. The sea is w-washing in and out and w-will break it apart from the i-i-i-inside out."

"Save us," Lacrosse said, crossing himself. "I will put some of my own crew to work building rafts . . . but rafts will never pass through this . . ." He waved a hand at the sea breaking all around and streaked with white. The French captain went off awkwardly along the slippery deck and called together his lieutenants.

Griffiths, who hovered nearby, came nearer. "How long do we have, do you think?"

"Until m-morning," Hayden replied.

The doctor said nothing but went crabwise along the deck towards the men building the raft. Best they knew how little time remained.

The construction of rafts proceeded so slowly that Hayden worried they would not be able to carry a quarter of the crew even if the sea would allow them to be launched. For the first time, doubt began to invade his thoughts—like hands reaching up out of the sea and pulling him downwards. It occurred to him that he might not escape this wreck with his life. If the storm did not begin to abate by morning, they might be forced to launch the one remaining boat before the ship began to break up. He felt a fool for not taking Wickham or Barthe into his confidence before they set out for shore—someone needed to survive to pass on Monsieur Benoît's warning of the French massing at Cancale. If Hayden died here, that knowledge would die with him.

Hayden lay down upon the deck, where he hugged himself and shivered in the midst of his French protectors. When he was lucid he thanked them, or perhaps he dreamed he did.

He opened his eyes at some point, surfacing from his torpor and half-dream, and found the night had settled around them. The sounds of the storm still raged, but new tones had been added, the creaking and working of timbers as the ship was wrenched apart from inside. Even in his reduced state and with his mind half taken by fancy, Hayden realised their danger was great and the destruction of the ship imminent.

The night crept by, moonless and chill, the secret sea running high and the wind shrilling over the deck. Hayden never became warm, but the frigid numbness and palsied shaking did pass, even though it took some hours. Before first light men rose and set to the building of rafts; no doubt it had become apparent to all that the ship could not hold together much longer. When light did come, Hayden was met by the gruesome sight of men lying utterly still upon the deck, their comrades unable to stir them. Griffiths, the French surgeon, and his mates went about the deck seeing to these men, and to the dismay of all more than a few were slipped over the leeward side, where the sea carried them off. Three dozen, the doctor reported when this gruesome task was completed.

By the time light began to grey the sky, the deck commenced to move and was clearly going to buckle. Once that occurred, the ship would swiftly break up. Lacrosse found him and, after enquiring after his well-being, led him as far away from others as the sloping deck would allow. The Frenchman looked about to collapse, Hayden thought—unshaven, ashen, his eyes appearing to be sunken back into their sockets as though he retreated from the sight of this horrible day.

"The ship will not remain as it is for much longer," Lacrosse began, speaking quietly, his voice a croak from lack of water. He bent over then and grimaced, hands upon his knees—hunger pains, Hayden knew, for they had doubled him over several times during the night. Lacrosse forced himself upright. "I do not believe we can wait for the sea to become less. We might wait too long. I will put my strongest men to the oars, but the sick and the weak must go into the boat. They have not the strength to take to the rafts and have no chance of survival if left on the ship."

"I agree," Hayden said. "All of my men are hale and have been employed in the making of rafts; they shall not take up any space in the boat."

Lacrosse tilted his head to one side. "I had hoped that you might have a man to take the command and helm the boat, Capitaine. I have no one I trust to do this."

"Only Mr Franks or myself has the experience, and Franks speaks not a word of French and I will not abandon men on the ship."

"I have a man—a good seaman—who speaks English *très bon*. I would send him like your young Lieutenant Wick—"

"Wickham."

"Yes. He will call out the commands of your Mr Franks, just as young Wickham did."

Hayden looked out over the breaking sea. Certainly, the conditions were worse than the previous morning when they had launched the smaller boat, but to remain aboard the wreck was very likely a more certain death, he believed.

"I will speak with Mr Franks," he said.

Stiffly, he went forward to find Franks overseeing the construction of yet another raft. Hayden looked quickly at the rafts that were more or less ready to be launched, and those in build, and could see immediately that barely half the men would find a place on these makeshift vessels. The remainder would be left to the wreck, hoping that whatever pieces they might cling to would be washed ashore.

"Mr Franks . . ." Hayden beckoned the bosun. "If you please."

"Sir?" Franks limped quickly towards his captain.

"Mr Franks, Captain Lacrosse is seeking a man to take the helm and command of his barge as soon as it can be launched. It is his hope to convey ashore the sick and those too weak to fend for themselves. He has asked if such a man might be found among our crew, and I believe only you have the experience to manage it."

Franks did not hesitate. "I would do it, sir, though I speak not a word of their tongue."

"Lacrosse assures me that he has a man who speaks both languages very well and will act as Wickham did, conveying your orders."

"If that is the case, then certainly, sir. I shall endeavour to con the boat through the surf, sir, and bring everyone safely ashore, may God help me."

Hayden had never heard Franks invoke the aid of a deity before, but he had little doubt that many had found renewed faith these last hours.

"I shall inform Captain Lacrosse," Hayden replied. "And Mr Franks . . . good luck and God's speed."

"Thank you, sir."

Hayden went back to Lacrosse, who was then gathering together a crew to man the oars. The sick and men deemed too weak to save themselves were being chosen by the surgeons and then brought to one place convenient to boarding the boat. The boat itself was larger than a British barge, and proportionately heavy. There was but one method of launching: It had to be manhandled into the sea. Lacrosse called out orders, and to Hayden's surprise the French sailors appeared to willingly comply that day, perhaps realizing that too much independent action might lead to their own deaths. With each passing sea the water would rise up and bury the leeward barricade, washing up the deck, which could be felt moving beneath the feet of the men.

In their weakened state, moving the boat into the water took as many men as could find purchase upon the hull. Even then it was not managed quickly or without a few small injuries, but at length the boat finally slid into the Atlantic, where men attempted to hold it close alongside and tended painters attached fore and aft. Franks clambered in first, showing it to be no easy task as the boat rose and fell, wanting to smash itself to kindling against the hull. To be caught between boat and wreck would mean injury or even death, so the men all but threw themselves aboard, where they crouched down looking even more frightened than they had aboard the wreck.

The oarsmen went aboard two or three at a time, and then the sick were handed across, and then the weak, many of whom looked near to death. All of the ship's boys were then ordered aboard, which they managed with the nimbleness common to their years. Hayden's own midshipmen requested to be allowed to stay with the wreck and take their chances on the rafts, which Hayden allowed, as he believed the odds of survival in the boat were little better given the power of the sea.

There was a muttering among the seamen gathered by the boat then, and a sailor jumped from the wreck, tumbling into the bottom of the barge. Angrily, Lacrosse ordered the man out, but as he was seized upon by the oarsmen three more men leapt in, all but atop him. Pushing and cursing began all around, and Hayden himself would have been knocked to the deck in the press, but some unknown hand bore him up. At that instant, a great sea passed and the deck was felt to bow up beneath the men's feet with a terrible rending sound, and then suddenly men were shouldering one another aside and trampling over the fallen to throw themselves into the boat. Men distant from the boat were forced into the sea by the men behind pushing themselves forward, and Hayden was pressed from all sides, thrown first this way and then that. The calls of officers were lost in the melee.

Franks was screaming to *"push off, push off!"* but the men pouring into the boat—some by contrivance, but many merely pushed by the men behind—made escape impossible. Of an instant the boat was overburdened and heeled heavily to leeward, throwing all the men aboard to one side, and then to the horror of everyone, the boat rolled slowly over, casting all aboard her into the roiling sea.

"Hold fast to the ropes!" Hayden shouted in French, taking hold of the stern line himself, but the boat was pulled away by the overwhelming force of the sea and the men were powerless to stop it. All let the rope go before they, too, were dragged into the water.

In the water men were trying to take hold of the capsized boat, which now lay between them and the wreck. Frantically, they attempted to crawl over one another, many a face pushed or pulled under by a frightened comrade. A few managed to make the wreck and were pulled from the sea by their fellows, but most were swept away, the last sight of them a terrified countenance going under.

"Mr Franks!" Hayden called. *"Franks!"*

The only reply was the cries of the drowning men, all of whom were quickly swept beneath the sea, the boat—their only hope of survival—washing away, its bottom barely visible in the foam and spume.

The men on the wreck looked on in horror, not only because they had just witnessed a hundred men go to their deaths but because they had clearly seen the fate that awaited them, and soon, too.

Lacrosse's voice could be heard in the ensuing silence ordering the men back—an order obeyed but barely, and with many a resentful and sullen look towards the *capitaine*. The British sailors found each other among the retreating Frenchmen, all present but their bosun.

Archer looked more distressed than Hayden had ever seen him. The young man looked as though he would fall down on the deck and sob—as though he had lost a brother.

"Mr Franks, sir . . ." he said, and then fought to master himself. "Mr Franks . . ." he said again, and put his hands over his face.

Gould stood a few paces distant, not nearly as distraught as Archer, but silent and awed. "Is he . . . lost, sir? Without question?"

"I lost sight of him, Mr Gould, but certainly it would be a miracle if he survived. And I sent him . . ." Hayden drew a quick, involuntary breath, "though I knew he did not wish to go . . ."

The British sailors all collapsed upon the deck. Hayden was grateful no others had been forced into the sea by the press and that only one had been lost. Surely a hundred French sailors had died— probably more.

For a long while no one spoke, and then Smosh offered to lead them in prayer, which he did, speaking so plainly about Mr Franks and in a manner so heartfelt that all were affected. Hayden felt that if the quality of prayer spoken upon a man's passing was heaven's measure, then certainly Franks would walk among the angels. He had been a less-than-accomplished bosun, but he had been a good and loyal crewman and had made every effort to learn the trade in which he knew full well he was deficient. Poor Franks had no family, for his wife had borne him no children and she had grown sickly and finally passed on, leaving Franks a near pauper to the debts owed the many physicians and surgeons who had ministered to his unlucky spouse. Hayden did not know how to take the measure of a man's life, but Franks' existence had been hard, that was certain, though many could say the same. But, even so, Franks' life had no leisure, little comfort, no recognition, and more heartache than deserved. In the great sea of British life, Franks' passing had made barely a ripple. That was the truth, hard and cruel as it was to say. And it was the fate of most, Hayden knew, and there was no reason to believe that he would be an exception. The anonymity of death was complete. Once the few souls acquainted with a man had passed, he was a name on a stone—and a very great many could not even hope for that.

With these melancholy thoughts bringing him very low, Hayden looked out at the distant beach where so many had gathered to watch what transpired. He doubled over a moment in pain from hunger and thirst, as everyone did at intervals. And when this spasm passed he felt the loss of Franks and the absence of Mr Barthe. There was, among his remaining crew, no one with more experience than himself. All decisions must be made without any hope of drawing upon the experience of another. And the decision that must be made was when to launch the rafts.

The wind had not abated since sunset the previous day and the sea remained high, breaking in many places from the wreck almost into the shore. Hayden did not believe a raft would go far without overturning. Watching the progress of the capsized boat, he could see that it was borne more south than shoreward and would in all likelihood take hours to drift ashore . . . if it did not find an under-tow that carried it back out to sea. How long would a man last clinging to a raft that might be thrown over by every breaking sea? Not long enough to reach shore was the conclusion that Hayden came to. Again he wondered if these might be his last few hours.

Lacrosse sought him out then. The Frenchman looked done for, haggard and pale, as though he had been hungry for a year, not a few days.

"I have come to beg your forgiveness, Capitaine Hayden," La-crosse began. "I requested your officer take charge . . ." He tried to swallow. "The unforgivable actions of my own crew caused his death . . . and the deaths of many others. I am sorrowful and I am ashamed."

Hayden did not quite know what to say. "Your situation—your

command—is all but impossible, Capitaine Lacrosse. To govern men who will not consent to be governed without the common means of discipline . . ." Hayden shrugged. "It cannot be done. The failing is not yours."

"*Vous êtes très gentil, Capitaine Hayden.*" Lacrosse tried to work some moisture into his mouth. "Some of my crew have petitioned me to allow them to launch a raft. I have given my consent, though I spoke against this, as I believe it is very unlikely they will succeed. They are determined to make the attempt, even so. What is your opinion, Capitaine? Will you launch the rafts you have built?"

Hayden shook his head. "I am of the opinion that we must wait until the very last instant, for, like you, I do not think a raft can pass through the seas without being capsized." Hayden pointed. "I watched the boat drift south. I believe it will take some hours to go ashore. Men upon a raft will be thrown into the sea, and I do not believe they can cling to the raft long enough to make it ashore. It is beyond human endurance. I would choose to stay with the ship until it begins to break up. We can only hope it will hold together until the gale moderates."

Lacrosse nodded, his look pained and grim. "I fear you are right, but these men are determined and I have chosen to allow it. If they reach shore . . . we will know that it can be managed. If they do not . . . may God preserve all of our souls."

"Yes," Hayden said softly. "Amen."

Lacrosse gathered together the men who wished to launch the raft—seven men—and, exhorting the others to keep their distance, found a few more men to help with the launch. It was not easily managed nor efficiently done, but the raft finally half slid and half tumbled into the sea. The seven crew, holding barrel staves as paddles, clambered aboard the swaying platform. The sea took them as they settled to their knees, throwing them at the side of the heeling ship with a crash that nearly tumbled them all into the water, and then swept them away. Although they paddled madly, their efforts appeared to be wholly ignored by the high-running sea. It tossed them up, then sent them spinning down the wave face, catching them up and passing beneath. The men gave up paddling and instead clung to the raft, lying facedown, instinctively keeping their weight low. Hayden could see the fear on their faces.

Like the capsized boat, the raft was carried more south than east. Every man aboard clung to that raft with their gaze, all of their hopes riding with the terrified occupants. Not a dozen waves had passed beneath the clumsy vessel before one broke upon it, and Hayden watched as the men were hurled into the sea and the raft capsized. Perhaps three managed to scramble back aboard the overturned raft. They could be seen looking about for their companions, but they were already lost.

The raft was barely three hundred yards away when it was thrown over again, and this time only a single man could be seen, clinging to the wreckage, as it crested the next sea. The others were gone. That man remained aboard as the raft drifted slowly south, and was soon too distant for anyone aboard the wrecked ship to distinguish the slight form of a man. Whether he remained aboard or not, no one could say.

Archer looked over at Hayden. "Well, sir, I doubt British seamanship can make a raft seaworthy or that our own crew would fare better."

"I am afraid I agree, Mr Archer."

"Then we are to risk our luck on the wreck and hope this gale takes off enough for us to launch rafts and bring them safely to shore."

"Yes," Hayden admitted. "It is the only course of action open to us, though I have tortured my mind in an attempt to discover anything else we might do."

"As have we all, Captain."

A desperate silence descended upon the shipwrecked men, all of whom were racked with spasms of pain from hunger and thirst and most of whom shivered with cold and controlled their limbs but poorly. Although knots of men sat, backs to the wind, heads bowed, most lay upon the deck, curled up against the wind, trying to preserve the smallest spark of warmth. Many were now insensible, or nearly so, and unable to perform the smallest act that might preserve their lives. When the ship broke up, Hayden knew most of these men would be washed into the sea.

The screech of working timbers as the ship was prised apart by each passing sea had grown dreadfully loud. Some men covered their ears against it. The deck worked as the seas passed into the hull and then out again. Hayden could see it almost ripple from stern to stem with each sea. He found this more fascinating than frightening, which said much for his state of both mind and body. Like most, he was exhausted to the point of collapse and comprehended that his judgement was much reduced.

Sometime in the early afternoon, a series of massive seas broke upon *Les Droits de l'Homme* and the upper deck began to tear free. A violent wrenching and rending was heard, and the timbers began to snap like kindling. In less than five minutes a section of the bow broke away and was driven over the reef and broken into two pieces. Upon these, swept by the seas, Hayden could see men clinging one to another, and scrambling as the section rolled to its natural trim.

"Stay together!" Hayden ordered his men. "Where is the doctor?"

"He's assisting the French surgeon," Archer informed. "They were aft, sir."

Hayden forced himself up to his feet. "Dr Griffiths!" he called over the sounds of the gale, the rending of timbers.

He spotted Griffiths, hurrying aft as best he could among all the men and over a sloping, slick deck.

"Shall we launch the rafts, sir?" Ransome asked.

"No, Mr Ransome. The rafts will take us to our deaths without question. We must cling to a section of the wreck. It is a slim hope, but the only one we have. Link arms. Let no man be torn away. Take hold of that French boy, Mr Hawthorne. He is the lad who helped me free all of you."

Hawthorne found Pierre and bodily moved the boy into the centre of the British sailors, where the midshipmen had been sent as well.

"Well, young Pierre," Hawthorne declared above the noise, "as a reward for saving us from drowning we are going to allow you to drown among Englishmen—a singular honour for a Frenchman. We do hope you are properly grateful."

Despite the desperateness of the situation the British sailors laughed, earning them the oddest looks from the French sailors.

There was a rush to the rafts by the French sailors, and near battle broke out to launch these ungainly craft and clamber aboard. Men were struck down by their mates and shoved into the sea. Several rafts were overset by men leaping aboard them without thought to the crafts' stability. A large section of the stern broke away then— perhaps half the quarterdeck. Some men aft elected to stay with the larger centre of the wreck and leapt over the growing gap. Half of an hour was needed to rip the stern section loose, all the while the men aboard crying out and calling for God to preserve them. Finally, it tore away entire and immediately commenced breaking into smaller sections. Hayden could see Lacrosse and his officers upon one of these, lying upon their bellies and clinging to whatever purchase could be found.

All about the ship flotsam floated up, some of it sections of the deck below. A large section of lower deck appeared aft and was pushed into the lee of the wreck. With only an instant to decide, Hayden leapt to his feet. "Onto that section of deck!" he called to his men, and pointed. "All at once, now."

He began dragging up the nearest man to him, and then another, pushing them towards the submerged rail. In a moment, Hawthorne had taken ahold of this raft—perhaps twenty feet by a dozen. He could not hold it, though, and for a moment Hayden thought it would be swept away, but instead it washed back towards the wreck and in that instant the British sailors all tumbled aboard, as did a few Frenchmen, as well as their mascot, Pierre.

"On your bellies!" Hayden ordered. "Link arms and take hold of the edge." The men did as he said and linked legs wherever they could as well.

In a moment they were fifty feet from the wreck, which was breaking apart rapidly, the men aboard being cast into the sea or leaping for anything that might float and grasping hold with cramping hands.

Smosh lay near to Hayden and he was praying calmly, asking God to deliver them though they were unworthy sinners. For some reason this reference to their sins made Hayden want to laugh. "Grasp on, Mr Smosh!" Hayden implored the priest. "Let no man slip away!" A sea broke over them, almost tearing Hayden free. His hands were weak from cold and seemed like claws, stiff and unwieldy. The raft was awash half the time, the men's faces in the water as often as not.

Hayden could hear the men's breath coming in short, terrified gasps. Looking up, he could see the last section of the ship collapsing down into the water and then surging up in pieces, men being spilled into the frigid sea. Even over the howling gale he could hear their cries. This piece of deck might not make it ashore, but he was certain that it afforded them a better chance than staying with the wreck. He had ordered everyone to jump aboard because it was larger and heavier than any of the rafts that had been built. There was a slim possibility that it was too heavy to be thrown over in the breaking seas. That would be seen soon enough.

Seas began to mount up as soon as they reached soundings, but here along the relatively shallow coast they quickly became very steep, piled upon each other, and broke violently and often. Each sea lifted the heavy section of deck and drove it both south and east towards shore. From Hayden's vantage, staring out to sea, he had time to contemplate the long, irregular rows of waves rolling towards them. Some of these were low swells that merely lifted their raft and set it down into the trough, but successions of high seas would come—four or five at a time—that would angle the raft up so that it was all the men could do to stay aboard. Too often a sea would mount up too steeply and the top would topple off, breaking heavily upon the raft and its occupants, pressing them down so that they must hold their breath and cling to the edge of their vessel with all the strength that remained to them. When it seemed to Hayden that he could hold his breath no longer, the raft would stagger up so that it was only half in flood, and a chorus of coughing and gasping would be heard all around.

"Hold fast!" someone would shout then, and another sea would throw itself upon them.

Sailors were strong men who did hard labour every day, Hayden well knew. Their hands were especially strong from regularly hauling ropes, and this was the only reason they had lasted even this long. To Hayden's right lay Dr Griffiths, and to his left the French aspirant, Pierre. The boy looked frightened and was shivering uncontrollably.

"*Link your arm with mine,*" he instructed the boy in French, and this was awkwardly done, as the boy's limbs would hardly obey. "Dr Griffiths, do the same."

The surgeon linked elbows with Hayden. His face was blue-white and his lips bloodless. In their year of sailing together Hayden had never seen him look so frightened.

"Another few waves like that last," the doctor said, "and I shall be gone."

"We will not let you go, Doctor." And then, to the man upon Griffiths' right, "Mr Hawthorne, hold fast to the doctor."

"I shall not release my hold upon you, Doctor, until we are standing upon the shore."

Griffiths nodded his thanks.

"Hold fast!" came the call.

The raft began its vertiginous climb over a steep wall of grey-green water. It seemed to Hayden that it rose to a point of being almost vertical, though surely this was imagined. Even so, he was certain this time it would be thrown over—gravity would not be denied. The crest broke upon them, but it was largely foam and comparatively harmless. The wave passed beneath then, and he tilted now the other way, though not so steeply—a wave's back was never so steep as its face.

Two seas passed then, neither steep enough to cause alarm. Hayden could hear the men muttering *"Thank God"* and gathering their reserves to face the next onslaught. It came soon enough in a sea so steep that Hayden was certain it would throw them all into the ocean, but somehow their platform remained upright, though it had turned about so that Hayden now looked towards the shore, which was closer than he had dared hope.

He hadn't realised how much more difficult it was to be on the downhill side of the raft as it lifted to the seas, looking down into the trough. If he hadn't been able to link legs with the man behind him Hayden was certain he would never have kept his hold of the raft.

Another sea threw itself upon them, slanting the raft impossibly up, then casting a deluge upon them. Up the raft went until it was nearly vertical, Hayden holding on with every bit of reserve he could manage, feeling his numb fingers beginning to slip—and then the raft dug its edge in so that Hayden was submerged to his waist, and then went over, so that he was entirely under green water.

The raft was torn from his hand, and Hayden was plunged into the cold Atlantic. His hold on the raft had been lost, but he had grabbed the man to either side and now he kicked and struggled to find the surface. In a moment he pushed his face above the heaving surface, pulling Griffiths up as he did so. The young *aspirant* could swim, and he surfaced as Hayden did, looked about wildly, and then struck out for the raft, which floated not a dozen feet away.

"Do not struggle, Doctor," Hayden called, turning the surgeon on his back. "Kick your feet, but stay upon your back."

A wave fell upon them, its massive weight driving them under. It took a moment for Hayden to get them to the surface again, but he could feel Griffiths kicking and waving his arms rather ineffectually. The raft, by some act of providence, was nearer and in three strokes Hayden had hold of it. Pierre was already aboard, looking like a drowned pup, but he grabbed the doctor by the shoulders of his coat and pulled him awkwardly aboard and then gave Hayden a hand.

Around the raft, men were struggling to get back aboard; some appeared to be flailing about merely trying to stay afloat, and Hayden, realizing that Ransome could not make it on his own, rolled back into the water and went clumsily after the lieutenant. It took longer than he thought and exhausted all his reserves to accomplish, but Hayden brought Ransome alongside the overturned raft, though he had no energy left to drag himself aboard and would not have made it had not hands reached out and pulled him up onto the planks.

Too exhausted to take hold, Hayden waited for the next wave to wash him back into the sea. "Sir!" It was Gould, shouting almost in his ear. "You must turn about and grasp on, sir, or you will be lost."

With the help of Gould and Archer, Hayden managed to get himself around and tried to grip the planks with hands that more closely worked like claws and felt much the same.

"How many did we lose?" Hayden asked.

"We are all here, sir, but for a Frenchman or two. I don't know how, Captain, but we all got back aboard." He paused a moment, a look like pain crossing his face. "But we will not manage it again, God preserve us."

Hayden tried to twist about and saw Smosh bleeding profusely from his scalp. "Mr Smosh, you are hurt, sir."

The man nodded dumbly, clearly dazed and uncertain. The men either side had hold of him, for he was unable to fend for himself.

"Raft landed on him, Captain," Griffiths called. "But I'll see him put to rights as soon as we have made shore."

Shore, however, was no nearer. The raft was being driven slowly south but never seemed to draw nearer the beach, as though the waves drove it shoreward but some invisible current drew it with equal force out to sea.

"Captain?" Archer called. "I believe we have passed through the worst of the surf, sir."

Hayden looked about and after a moment began to think Archer was not wrong. The waves now were smaller, and though they broke often it was not with the violence of the seas they had just come through. Yet the raft remained too far from shore for any to swim; many no longer had the reserves to keep hold but lay near to senseless, the motion of the raft half rolling them one way, then another.

We shall all perish from exposure to the elements if we cannot get ashore soon, Hayden thought, but even so, his spirits lifted noticeably. Maybe they *could* survive!

"What are these men about, then?" someone asked.

Hayden twisted around and on the beach south of them he could see a knot of men, perhaps a dozen of them, bearing something down to the surf line.

"Is it a boat? Do they carry a boat?" one of the midshipmen asked.

"I do believe it is exactly that, Mr Hobson," Hayden replied.

"But can they launch it?"

Hayden looked around. "I believe we have drifted inside a reef or perhaps a bar. The seas are breaking further out." The seas the raft climbed now were not nearly so high, and though they did mount up and break almost as often as they had previously, they were less threatening. "I think we could bring a boat through such a surf," he announced. "And if these men are fishermen, I am sure they will manage it."

"I hope they are smugglers, sir," Hawthorne said.

"Are smugglers notably better boatmen than are fishermen, Mr Hawthorne?"

"No, sir, but they might carry some brandy aboard."

A few men managed a truncated laugh and a few more shook their heads. Many lay still as the dead, and Hayden feared they were exactly that.

The boat was soon skidding into the water, where men held it against the seas while the oarsmen clambered aboard. The men in the surf steadied the boat with difficulty against a series of waves and then, as one, gave it a great shove, the oarsmen setting to work that same instant. Quickly the boat gathered way and then met the first sea, which flung it up until it was lost to Hayden's view behind a wall of water. A moment later it appeared again, waterspidering over the high-running sea. Across the long trough it would gather way, the men leaning back into their oars. And then they would meet the onrushing sea, and the boat's way would be all but lost, so that when the sea finally rolled on beneath them, the boat would be dead in the water. The men would set to work again. In the stern of the squat little craft two men fed out rope, attached now and then to a small cask to buoy it up. These casks were swept off downwind and driven southwards by the seas. Hayden worried that they would make the boat impossible to steer in time, pulling her stern south, but the men appeared to know their business.

A high sea broke upon the raft, but there was little weight in the crest—all foam and little green water. Looking around at the faces of the men stretched out upon the planks, he thought that few would not live another hour. One by one they would be washed away by the seas. If this boat did not reach them, Hayden believed that he would die there, so close to his mother's country—a British sea officer washed up on the shores of Bretagne in a French captain's coat.

He could not hold himself twisted around for very long, and he lay back down, exhausted, gathering his reserves. When he felt the muscles in his back begin to unknot he forced himself up again. For a moment he could not find the boat, and then it rode up over a sea, its bow cast high. The men still bent to their work, driving the little craft over the hostile waters.

"Will they reach us, sir?" Gould asked, his voice dry and weak.

"I-I think they might. They are certainly not holding back, I can tell you."

"They must not know we are English."

"Perhaps . . . but you might be surprised at how men will work to save their fellows in such circumstances—even their enemies. It is as though our misfortune has reduced us to the same state—men in grave danger and not Frenchmen or Englishmen—just men who all want the same thing, to live through this day."

Hayden lay back down again, too exhausted to move. His hands would no longer answer, and he could do no more than hook his wrists over the edge of the plank. His left hand was cut, and a thin trickle of blood, diluted by seawater, washed down his fingers, though he felt no hurt at all.

Gould took a turn twisting about to look for their would-be rescuers and then collapsed back upon the raft. The boy pressed his eyelids together, and though it was impossible to distinguish tears from rain or spray, Hayden could see the boy's shoulders shaking.

"Are you injured, Gould?" Hayden whispered.

The boy shook his head. "No, sir. The boat . . . it will never reach us, we are being swept past."

Forcing himself up, Hayden turned as best he could. In a moment he found the boat, larger than it had been, but Gould was not wrong—the raft was being driven south more rapidly than the boat was making its way seaward. The two would not meet as the rowers had foreseen. Even as Hayden watched, the boat altered its course and began working its way south.

He remained in that position as long as he could, until a wave broke over him and drove him almost across the raft, where he fetched up between two French sailors, who took hold of his legs lest he slide into the sea.

Hayden muttered his thanks, but the French sailors were concentrating on the men in the boat and shouting encouragement and pleading with the men to row. At that distance Hayden doubted the men's entreaties could be heard, but they did not seem aware of this.

Hayden was almost too thirsty to speak, his mouth so parched it stuck together and his tongue seeming swollen and drunken. Gathering himself, Hayden crawled on his belly back to his place between Gould and Archer.

"Sorry, sir," Archer rasped, almost unable to speak. "We will take better hold of you."

"It is impossible, Mr Archer, to hold fast to anything when your fingers will not close and you have no feeling in your hands at all. Do not blame yourself."

Archer only nodded gratefully.

"Will the boat not reach us, sir?" he asked then.

"I cannot say. They might yet. We are drifting slowly and they are under oars. But they cannot turn directly south for fear of being rolled over and must quarter the seas, and are therefore coming after us crabwise. It will slow them considerably. We will soon know how great are their hearts, how strong their desire."

"Very great and immensely strong, I hope, sir."

Hayden passed again into a timeless torpor, a confused reverie where dream and reality mixed in ways he did not understand. The rough plank beneath his cheek was cold and slick, but he hardly took notice. He could be lying upon a bed of boulders and he would hardly have cared.

A distant shout penetrated this strange state, but Hayden thought it only fancy. Then he heard it again, calling out in French.

"Sir?" Gould nudged his arm gently. "Sir? Did you hear that?"

Hayden roused himself, confused. The day was wearing on—late afternoon, he thought. And the wind seemed to be taking off—now that the gale had done its job and destroyed *Les Droits de l'Homme*. Perhaps thirty yards away, he saw the French boat crest a wave, the men at the sweeps pulling hard, though their cadence had slowed noticeably since they began.

Hayden forced himself up to his knees, looking seaward to spot any large waves about to sweep down on them. But the sea was definitely going down, and though large waves remained they were not nearly so steep. It took all of his strength to remain there, upon his knees, helplessly watching the boat chasing after them. For a while it appeared to gain, and then he was not certain it was not falling behind. He dropped onto one thigh and buttock, bracing himself with his hands.

How utterly empty he felt, drained of desire, of strength and emotion. His thoughts were so spare—as though the noise of the mind had been drained away, leaving only a single, clear voice, though tired and confused. He watched the battling boat with utter detachment, as if it were not him whose life was dependent upon these Frenchmen reaching the raft. As though he were not upon the raft at all. As though he had drifted free of it, free of all the bonds that held him to this world, to this life.

Ten

J ust before the dinner hour the entire family and houseguests all made their way to the withdrawing room upon hearing the pianoforte being exercised by Mrs Carthew. She was not as accomplished upon this instrument as at least two of her daughters, but she played with great feeling and chose her music to flatter those skills she did possess. The first piece was followed by a round of applause, and then, just as she was about to perform an encore, she stopped.

"If my memory grows worse I shall forget all your names, and my own as well," she declared, and began to search her pockets hurriedly until finally a letter was produced. "Ah! I do apologise, my dear Lizzie; this arrived with the post, and I have been carrying it about all afternoon meaning to give it you. It is from Captain Hertle, which makes my lapse even more unforgivable."

Penelope retrieved the letter before any could rise and carried it straight to Mrs Hertle, who received it with both joy and trepidation. A small blade was produced by Mr Carthew, and the seal broken. Elizabeth held the letter up to the light, clearly hungry for every word, turned pale as milk, and could not catch her breath. Everyone thought she would topple from her chair.

"Elizabeth," Henrietta cried, "what is it, my dear? What does it say?"

Elizabeth was unable to answer, tears streamed down her cheeks, unable to utter a word, and waved the letter towards Mr Carthew that he might read it himself.

"'My Darling Lizzie,'" he read, taking the sheets of paper, "'I have this hour received the worst possible news, and I must ask you to sit down and prepare yourself for it. Charles lost his ship to a French squadron a few days past. He and his officers were taken as prisoners aboard a French seventy-four, *Les Droits de l'Homme*. Not long after, this ship was chased by a pair of Royal Navy cruisers and *Les Droits de L'Homme* was driven ashore in a full gale, with great loss of life. We were informed by the captain of a lugger we captured this very day that only two Englishmen survived—a boy and an older officer with red hair—almost certainly Charles' sailing master, Barthe. I am, as you can imagine, utterly desolate. I have lost my oldest, dearest friend and brother. This terrible, terrible news will come as a shock to you and I do hate to send it, but certainly Henrietta must be informed at the earliest possible moment. Poor Henri, and you too, my dear, for I know what high regard and warmth of feeling you held for my friend—'" But the reading was cut short. Henrietta stood up from the sofa, covered her mouth with a hand, and would have collapsed had not Wilder been standing so near that he caught her and lowered her back to the cushions.

Eleven

A song, long and languid as a river murmuring among stones. Rippling through the leaves, a susurration, as the breeze ebbed and flowed. Night, Hayden thought, and a nightingale. Warm, dry air drifted in the window bearing the fragrance of a garden. *Land.* He was ashore . . . Somewhere.

When next he woke it was to the sorrowful cooing of doves, echoing from the far reaches of the afternoon.

Well, I am alive, Hayden thought. But he could not bring himself to move, as though enervation had overwhelmed the part of his mind that commanded his limbs. He did breathe—in and slowly out. And he was warm! Luxuriously so! For a few moments he lay, basking like a cat in the sun, feeling the warmth in all of his limbs. He had thought that no matter what the outcome he would never feel warm again.

Finally, and with great effort, he raised his eyelids. He was in a small, plain chamber, furnished with an ancient armoire, a battered trunk, a rush-bottom chair, and a chest of four drawers. Upon the chair perched a girl of perhaps seven years, her legs swinging back and forth, her gaze fixed upon him. When Hayden opened his eyes, the legs stopped swinging, she leaned forward, half in alarm, half surprise, and then she leapt down to the floor and went running out.

"Mama!" she called. "Mama. The gentleman has awakened! He is not dead!"

The sound of hurrying footsteps—heavier than the girl's, but not heavy—and then a woman of perhaps thirty appeared in the door-frame, the girl clutching her skirts and peering out from behind.

"It is a miracle," the woman muttered, and then spun and hastened off. "Jean!" she called. "Jean! You must bring the doctor."

And then she swept back into the room and crouched by Hayden's bed in a rustling of skirts.

"Monsieur? Monsieur? Can you hear me?"

"Perfectly, madame, *merci vous.*"

"I cannot believe he has lived," she muttered as if he were not there. "God must love you, monsieur." She stood up and then leaned over, speaking to him as though she thought him half deaf. *"I will bring you broth, monsieur. Broth . . ."*

Hayden lay, listening to the bird sounds outside the open window, smelling newly mown grass. Cattle lowed off in the distance, and then he heard feet pounding on the ground—running as though someone's life depended upon swiftness.

He felt no desire to move and remained still, half upon his side, his chest turned down upon the mattress. Several times, he noted, his eyes blinked. Someone entered the room, but Hayden was slipping away—back into the all-enveloping darkness and the song of the nightingale.

A distant bell rang the hour, but Hayden did not tally it. His eyes opened once again, only to find the same small girl, swinging her legs upon the chair and singing almost silently to herself.

"Mademoiselle," Hayden croaked, his mouth so dry he could hardly prise it open.

The girl was off the chair and running from the room, calling as she went, "Mama! He spoke! Mama!"

Footsteps returned, grew louder, but instead of Mama, a gentleman strode in. He settled a pair of spectacles upon his nose, pulled the chair over near to the bed, seated himself heavily, and took up Hayden's arm by the wrist. Fishing a watch from a pocket by its chain, he thumbed it open and very studiously took Hayden's pulse.

"Do I live?" Hayden enquired in French.

"So it seems, though I do not know how. You were ice water when you came ashore, and could barely draw a breath. Many thought you dead on the beach. You were lucky I was present, for I found you were alive and ordered you carried here, to the house of Charles Adair. For three days you have hovered in that dark place between death and life. In truth, you were so close to death I wonder if you saw the gates of heaven? Some do, you know."

Hayden shook his head—the smallest motion, but all he could manage. "I have been wandering in a dark wood, full of mist and shadow . . . following the call of a nightingale. I awoke here with a small girl watching over me. Perhaps she is an angel."

"So she would wish, but not yet."

The doctor let go of his wrist and sat back, hands on his ample knees. "Your pulse is not yet strong, but I believe you will live. Capitaine?"

But Hayden had slipped away, and wandered again among the shadowy trees, shafts of faint moonlight illuminating a low mist. The nightingale began to sing.

When Hayden woke again it was to warm sunlight playing over his face. He rolled onto his side and covered his eyes with a forearm. Where was he? Had there really been a doctor or had he dreamt that

as well? There had been so many dreams, all run together into nonsense.

Hayden glanced towards the chair pushed up against the wall.
His little guardian angel was not there. With effort he sat up, but
immediately became so dizzy that he slumped down again. He must
have made some noise, for a woman appeared at the door, paused,
then came in.

"Are you finally awake, Capitaine?"

"Yes. How many survived the wreck, madame? Can you tell me?"

"Very few, I am sorry to tell you. I have heard one hundred to
one hundred twenty, more or less. And a few *Anglais*—prisoners."

"Five hundred dead . . ." Hayden said hoarsely. "May I have
water?"

"Yes, and some broth and bread at least. You have hardly eaten in
more than three days, nor have you taken much drink."

"I ate?" Hayden was surprised. "I do not remember."

"You have been wandering along the borders of the land of the
dead, Capitaine." She smiled. "I think you have only now returned."

Hayden noticed a French captain's coat hanging on a hook.

"I washed it, Capitaine," she said, noting where his gaze had
gone. "It was filthy and needed mending. You will not have reason
to criticize my work, you will see."

Hayden tried not to show his reaction to this. "I am certain you
are right, madame. *Merci*."

She curtsied and slipped out.

They believe I am a French officer, Hayden thought. A captain!

In his present reduced state he could not decide if there was any
advantage to this or if it was a terrible gamble—a danger to him.
Certainly, if he were delivered to the French Navy he would be
found out in a moment—and more than likely deemed a spy! But if
he could have a few days to recover . . . He and Wickham and Hawthorne had stolen a boat and sailed from here before. It was not

impossible. His exhausted brain took hold of this idea. Perhaps there was still a chance he could carry Benoît's warning to the Admiralty. They were not far from Brest when *Les Droits de l'Homme* went ashore. The British frigates he had so desperately hoped to find must be there. A small boat would be all he required to reach them.

Better that than spending months in a French gaol waiting to be exchanged, wondering all the while if the French had crossed the Channel to England. How infamous he would be if it ever came out that he had been the man who had failed to carry the warning to Britain.

That slim hope made his decision. Going into a French gaol was out of the question. If he were found out in the next few days he would claim he did not realise they thought him French—confusion caused by his excellent command of the language, no doubt. It was not without risk, but while he was still deemed very ill—and certainly he was too weak to effect an escape—he could feign ignorance. Once he was recovered, he would have to decide if there was any possibility of escape—in which case he would claim to be French until it was proven otherwise.

Broth and bread were carried to him by a servant. Hayden ate this with surprisingly little appetite and then forced himself up onto wobbling legs and shuffled to the window. The house was larger than he had expected, his window on the first floor looking over a garden. Beyond were fields, rolling off into the distance—hill beyond hill—all separated one from the other by hedgerows of trees and underwood that ran every which way utterly without pattern.

It was all very familiar to Charles Hayden, who had spent much of his youth not too distant from here—or so he assumed. His legs, however, would not bear him long and he tottered back to bed, dizzy, nauseated, and sweating.

"*Merde,*" he whispered.

"You should not say that, monsieur."

Hayden turned his head and found the little girl who had watched over him earlier. "Excuse me. I thought I was alone."

"You are never alone, monsieur. God is always listening."

"Certainly he has better things to do?"

"No, monsieur, He has not. God hears every word, no matter how quietly you whisper." She regarded Hayden a moment with the seriousness of a child. "I prayed for you," she informed him.

"Thank you, mademoiselle, it was very kind of you."

"It was excellent practise. I will be a sister one day."

"No doubt that is why God granted your request and saved my miserable life."

She gave a little nod, as though to say, "Perhaps." "Who is Henry?" she asked. She said it in the French way—'Enree.

"I do not know. Who is Henry?"

She shrugged. "You kept saying it when you were fevered. Is he your brother?"

"I have no brothers—and no sisters, either. What else did I say?"

She shrugged. "It was all raving and made no sense. Mother said you must never put any store in what a person says when they are fevered."

"In this I believe your mother is very wise."

For a moment she looked surprisingly thoughtful, as though this idea were novel. "Did you see the gates of heaven? The doctor said you did. Were they really made of pearl?"

Hayden was of half a mind to tell her he had and make up some fantastic story, but there was something about the earnest way she listened for his answer that stopped him. "I did not see the gates of heaven, I am sorry to say."

"Oh." She looked terribly disappointed. "I thought he might be teasing. Grown-ups do."

"They do, sometimes, but I am telling the truth."

She nodded, not looking at him. "If you had seen them there would not be the least doubt, would there? That heaven existed, I mean."

"Yes, and it would be comforting."

"There is a man who lives in the village who tells everyone that he was pronounced dead and floated up to the gates of heaven. They opened to receive him, but then an angel sent him back to complete his life. He says that he has something great to accomplish, though he does not yet know what. It is strange—no one believes anything else he says, but that story no one doubts." She looked up at Hayden. "Is that not odd? Why would he tell the truth about that one thing and nothing else?"

"Maybe one does not tell lies about heaven."

"Yes, perhaps that is it. Though he said King Louis was still alive and travelling about France disguised as a tinker. Do you believe that?"

Hayden laughed softly. "Do you?"

She shook her head. "It would be very difficult to travel around the country without a head. Everyone would notice."

"Exactly what I was going to say. The village you spoke of . . . what is it called?"

"You do not know?"

"I do not know where I am or how I got here."

"The village of Quimper is not so far away. I have been there many times."

"Ah, you look like a traveller."

"Do you think so?"

"Very much."

"One day I hope to travel to Domrémy-la-Pucelle, where Joan of Arc was born. Have you been there?"

"No, but I wish I had. I have not seen your father? Is he away?"

She looked around as though to be certain they were alone. "My father has fled, monsieur. They were coming for him." Then she said quickly, "But you must say nothing."

"You need not worry, I am very accomplished at keeping secrets."

"So am I, monsieur. And so is Mama." She looked suddenly worried that she had spoken of this. "My father would beat me if he knew I spoke of this to you."

"He will never hear of it from me. You are safe."

This appeared to reassure her. "I do not believe he will ever return, anyway. I hope not. He was always very cruel to me and to Mama."

"I am sorry to hear it."

This curtailed the conversation for a moment. When Hayden was looking for something to say, surprised at how poorly his mind worked, the girl's mother appeared.

"Charlotte, the captain is far from recovered. You must not bother him."

"She is no bother, madame. She is very charming."

"So everyone says. Capitaine, you will excuse me, I hope, but I do not know your name."

It was a question Hayden had been dreading. If he gave a French name, he was setting his foot upon a terribly dangerous road.

"Does the Navy not know I am here?"

"There were so many, Capitaine, spread among the families in the village and all around. Some have now gone to the naval hospital in Brest, a few have gone to their own families. Many are too ill to travel."

"And the *Anglais*? What of them?"

"I do not know, Capitaine. Perhaps they have been taken off to the prison in Quimper or to Portanzeau." She tilted her head to one side and regarded him. She was a pretty woman, Hayden thought. A little careworn, perhaps, an air of disappointment in her manner and movement. Across the bridge of her nose a little spray of freck-les gave a suggestion of youth, and then full lips that never seemed to smile. "Your name, Capitaine . . . ?"

"Mercier. Gil Mercier."

"You were the captain of the ship that was wrecked? *Les Droits de l'Homme?*"

"No. I was merely returning to Brest with my friend Capitaine Lacrosse when we were chased by two British ships and driven ashore."

She shook her head. "The English," she said with a little shiver, "they are without mercy. So many lives . . ."

Hayden was about to explain that it was their own fault—they did not know their position—but decided this would be unwise. "They are mad dogs, madame," he said gravely. "Mad dogs."

Hayden was served both dinner and supper in his room that day, but on the next he shakily joined the family for dinner at table. It was a small household, reduced by the absence of Monsieur Adair and an older son who was away at the military academy—as safe a haven as one could find should the Jacobins come after his family. A Girondiste family lived in constant fear and danger—the distant sound of the guillotine, as Lacrosse had told him, could be heard both day and night. Madame did everything to keep up a pretence of normal life—for the sake of her daughter, Charlotte, Hayden was certain. He learned that a cousin—a girl of twelve—had lived with them for some years but had been sent away to live with other rela-tives, much to Charlotte's distress; she did not understand why the girl had gone.

"Her auntie missed her so," her mother explained, "and had no children left, as they had all grown up and moved away."

"That is all very well, Mama, but Audrey had lived with us for so very long. She was like a sister to me, and I do not think it was fair that she should be sent off when she did not want to go herself."

Madame Adair glanced at Hayden—all unsaid.

"Mayhap, I will send you to visit with Auntie and Audrey awhile."

"I should like it much better if they came to stay with us—as they used."

"It is difficult for them to travel now; that happens when you get older. Would you not dearly love to see Audrey and your auntie, too?"

"I would. But I should miss you, Mother, and Madame Lucy too."

Madame Lucy, Hayden had learned, was Charlotte's doll.

"Madame Lucy could travel with you if you liked."

"She is afraid to travel, Mama," she replied softly. "The Jacobins . . ."

After dinner, Hayden walked out into the garden. Even mild exertion left him shaking and sweating, but he was determined to get his strength back as soon as he was able. Once he had named himself Capitaine Mercier he knew his time in France must be very short. He might be found out in only a few days. If he had known he would be weak this long, he would not have been so quick to claim himself French.

A servant appeared bearing a tray with a coffee service upon it. Two cups, Hayden noted, when it was deposited on the small table. A moment later Madame Adair appeared, arranging a shawl upon her shoulders.

"May I join you, Capitaine?"

"My pleasure." Hayden rose, stiffly, and held a chair for her.

She poured coffee for both of them, holding back her shawl in a gesture that was both somehow elegant and charming.

The sun had travelled far into the west, drawing out the shadows of trees and fences, casting a soft, honeyed light over that little part of Brittany. Throughout the day a north-east wind had blown, but it had died away to a sighing breeze, and then to a calm. Neither spoke for a time and Hayden did not feel speech necessary—unlike many, Madame Adair was not made uncomfortable by silence.

She sipped her coffee, admired the view, and, Hayden sensed, rested from the labours of the day. An estate of such size required a great deal of looking after, and she had shouldered that burden as well as running the household and raising her daughter and now-absent son.

"The doctor told me you would be able to travel within a week," she offered into the evening's silence.

"Yes, and I shall be a burden to you no more."

"You have not been a burden. It has been a pleasure. Charlotte could not be more delighted to have you here. She would pester you from morning until night if I allowed it."

"Charlotte may 'pester' me all she likes. She is a treasure."

"She has not had a father for some time . . ." She hesitated and then said, quietly, "A very long time."

"She told me her father had fled the Jacobins."

"I have ordered her never to say such a thing . . ." She looked at Hayden quickly, clearly alarmed.

"You need not be the least concerned. What goes on in Paris is the greatest crime in the history of our nation. All of my family are dead . . . and I do not sleep well, myself."

"My condolences, monsieur," she whispered, meeting his eye for a fleeting second.

"Will you send her away? Must you?"

"It would be better . . . Safer."

"Surely even Robespierre would not hurt a child . . . ?"

She shrugged, pressing her lips together just a little. "I fear she might see her mother being taken away. No child should bear witness to that."

The horror of the statement almost took his breath away, not least because it contained not a shred of melodrama. Mothers found themselves upon the guillotine every day, many of them for no greater crime than being insufficiently zealous revolutionaries. This reminded Hayden, cruelly, that he was not immune to the madness. Lacrosse had warned him that some believed him a Royalist sea officer in the British Navy. And now he was claiming to be a French captain. Whatever had possessed him, he did not know. Clearly, his mind had not been working properly or he would never have been so foolish.

"No," he replied, "no child should."

"Do you have children, Capitaine Mercier?"

"No, madame, I am not yet married."

"I am very surprised to hear it. A man of good family, I should guess, and excellent manners and temperament. I expect many a mother harbours hopes that you might become her son-in-law someday."

"If so, they hide their hopes well."

"Come, do not be coy, Capitaine. Is there not a young woman whom you will soon make very happy?"

This brought up a subject that, even in his present circumstances, was not far from his thoughts, and he felt a little sag of despair. "I believed there was, but instead she made me unhappy—at least for a time."

"Ah. Love is never an easy journey, Capitaine. Not for the faint of heart, that is certain. But there will be other young women . . . of greater understanding, I am quite certain. Do you know what my mother told me? Beauty quickly fades and charm wears very poorly, but a good house and an adequate income can last a lifetime."

"She was a romantic, I see."

"Indeed she was—that is why she gave me such advice. Being a romantic had brought her much heartache." She gave a sad shrug, and thoughtfully pushed her lower lip into the upper. "But being practical can turn out much the same. In love there are so many ways to go wrong and only so very few, I think, to have it turn out well."

They were silent a moment, the late-evening light casting their angular shadows across the grass and into the trees opposite. The evening insects took over from their brethren of the day. A cricket began to creak away, and then frogs in the nearby pond sent forth their throaty declarations.

"What is it like to have an aspiring saint for a daughter?" Hayden asked, changing the course of the conversation.

This did elicit a small laugh, many years evaporating from Madame Adair's face in that instant. "It is difficult to live up to her expectations, Capitaine, I will admit. But I have told her that saints are very forgiving of others' shortcomings." Her smile disappeared.

"I'd better not tarry too long, then," Hayden said, "I am certain to disappoint her."

"Are you in the habit of disappointing the female sex, Capitaine Mercier?" she asked playfully.

"Never by intent, madame. Never by intent."

Since he had woken in the home of Madame Adair—he did not think of it as the home of Charles Adair—he had fallen into bed each night so utterly drained that he wondered if his heart would continue beating. Even so, he would surface late in the night and lie awake, sometimes colder than a winter wind. Nightmares plagued him, of drowning in the wreck, sucked down into the hold by an irresistible current, or swimming endlessly through her darkened hull, among menacing flotsam, unable to escape. He dreamed also that the French landed in England and caught the nation unawares, driving the British armies before them.

He would then lie awake, his mouth dry, a dull headache and general malaise and weakness overwhelming him. After he had taken his coffee in the garden with Madame Adair, Hayden's night followed this same general course of events, and he lay awake, feeling very low and anxious, wishing the nightingale would sing again.

Instead a dull pounding on the front door, and a hushed voice imploring that someone open up—in all haste!

Hayden lay very still, listening. A second voice could be heard inside—a servant, he believed, summoning Madame Adair. As quickly as he was able, he dressed and stumbled down the stairs, unsteady on his feet and light-headed. As Madame Adair, candle in hand, unbolted the door, a clearly frightened woman pressed in through the narrow opening, not waiting for the door to be properly opened. Immediately, a servant closed the door and threw the bolts.

"They have taken madame!" the woman muttered.

"Mon dieu!" Madame Adair exhaled, and appeared about to collapse. "Spare us!" she muttered. "Spare us . . . Do they come this way? Tell me!"

"I do not know . . . I-I do not believe they do."

"But you are not certain?"

The woman—a servant by her dress—shook her head, looking down at the floor.

Madame Adair put a hand to her heart, hardly able to catch a breath. She saw Hayden at that moment.

"The Jacobins, Capitaine Mercier—they have taken my neighbour, Madame Genot. Her husband fled with Monsieur Adair."

"You must fly!" Hayden said.

"Fly? Where? No one would dare hide us—nor could I ask them

to. No, I am done for. If they come for me . . . I will die," she said, and began to weep.

Servants were roused and all the windows were shuttered and locked, all the doors barred, to what purpose Hayden did not know. If the Jacobins came for her, this would only anger them and make it more likely that servants or other innocents would be taken as well—even recovering sea officers.

Snuffing out all the candles, the household huddled in the drawing room—all but Charlotte, who had not been wakened and remained in her bed watched over by her nursemaid. In the darkness they waited, a single window open so that they might hear the approaching Jacobins. A shaft of thin light from the waning moon crept slowly across the floor, and a small breeze wafted in, carrying the perfume of spring mixed with the faint odours from the distant farmyard. No one spoke. Some held hands, others sat alone, but no one dozed or appeared to be called by sleep, though they all looked haggard and exhausted. In the darkest corner, two women prayed, whispering their fears to God and Mary and their Son, begging deliverance.

"I should have sent her away," Madame Adair whispered to herself, unaware that she spoke aloud.

The floor clock in the entrance hall measured the endless night—a strict, metronomic clicking that somehow brought to Hayden's mind that other machine that measured human lives—and brought them to an end. So far apart were the chimes that cried each hour and each half that Hayden wondered if the mechanism had ceased to function.

Many days into the night, footsteps pulsed up the lane from the distant road, the pace frightening. The footsteps slid to a stop in the gravel and approached the door followed by a palm dully thudding on wood.

"*Madame,*" came a breathless whisper. "*It is me—Prévost.*"

Madame Adair rushed to the window. "Prévost," she said, "what is it?"

"They have the doctor. And they come this way."

"Do they go to Brest, Prévost? Or do they come here?"

"I cannot say, madame. Let us hope it is Brest. I must go. Good luck, madame. May God be with you."

"And you, Prévost."

"Merci, madame." And the footsteps stole away, hushed now, not madly running. Perhaps across the fields, Hayden thought, in the shadows of the hedgerows, as he had done once not so very far away nor so long ago.

Madame Adair stayed by the window, her hands upon the sill, leaning out, listening. Hayden crossed the room and stood vigil beside her, one hand upon the sill and one upon the frame. He could hear Madame Adair breathing—sharp little gasps as though her lungs were already full and she could take in nothing more.

A susurration through the willow leaves as the breeze sighed, and then, faintly, a hollow clatter—horses.

Madame Adair glanced at Hayden, such fear and appeal in her eyes that he felt a compulsion to take her in his arms, to protect her. But what could be done against the Jacobin madness?

At the foot of the lane voices could now be heard—arguing, Hayden thought, but he could not be sure. This went on a moment, and then the sound of horses making their way up the path of beaten earth. Again a voice raised in protest.

"It is the doctor!" one of the servants said. She had risen from her chair and stood a few paces behind Hayden. "Madame, it is the doctor!"

The horses stopped and another heated exchange occurred. Hayden could pick out the doctor's voice now. "Everyone knows she hated him," the man declared. "Everything about him. To kill such a woman because of the beliefs of a man she despised . . ."

Several voices rose and a little breeze through the leaves obscured the words. Hayden and Madame Adair both leaned as far out as they dared, desperate to hear what was said. Ten minutes this lasted, Hayden was sure. The clock in the hall chimed, and this seemed to silence the men in the lane. The breeze, too, fell still.

"It grows late," one complained. "Can we not decide? Either we take her now or we go home!"

What was said then was too quiet to be heard. And then the horses moved again.

"God save us," Madame Adair said, unable to stay silent. "They are coming."

"Listen . . ." Hayden hissed. "Are they not turning around?"

Every soul in the room held their breath. The hooves clattered dully on the ground; the breeze whispered among the branches. And then the little zephyr sighed and fell away. The sound of the hooves had grown fainter. They were upon the road, travelling to-wards the nearby village.

Madame Adair turned away and collapsed back against the win-dow opening. A servant came forward just as Hayden reached out and took her arm. They guided her to a chair and she slumped down in it, muttering thanks to God and weeping almost silently.

"Oh God," she choked out. "Oh dear God. They were coming for me . . . and then they went away."

"It was the doctor, madame," one of the servants said. "He con-vinced them to leave you . . . But he is lost."

This caused many a sob and prayers for the poor doctor.

"We are spared this night," Madame Adair declared at last, and rose to her feet, wiping away tears. "Let us go to bed. Sleep is the best defence against the trials of tomorrow."

Everyone filed out, and Hayden returned to his chamber. Instead of bed, though, he pulled up the chair and opened his window and shutters. Dawn was three hours distant. He knew that he must slip

S. THOMAS RUSSELL

out of this house before any officials came again, but the chances of him making his way to the coast and stealing a fishing vessel in his present state—and alone—were very slim. It was unlikely he could walk as far as the village. There was no way to send word to England of what he had learned from Mr Stephens' spy.

A Royalist family might hide him—but since the uprisings had been put down such families were keeping their loyalties utterly secret. Even if he thought Madame Adair might hide him he would not ask it of her—and there was no reason to believe she would. Her husband might have been a Girondist, but that made them supporters of the revolution—not opponents of it. Even so, she was now in as much trouble as he.

The latch on his door turned, a narrow crack appearing as the door pushed in. He thought it was the breeze, but then the crack widened a little more until whoever was outside could see him sitting in the spare moonlight. Before Hayden could speak Madame Adair let herself in, closing the door silently behind. Hayden rose from his chair and was about to speak, but she put a finger to her lips and crossed the room to where he stood.

"Are you well, madame?" he whispered.

She shook her head, and even in the feeble light Hayden could see the glimmer of tears pooling in her eyes. "They will be back," she whispered. "Whoever sent them will be angry that they did not do as they were ordered and they will be sent again—or some others."

"You must get away. Is there no one you trust who will hide you?"

"I would not ask that of anyone . . ." She looked down at the floor, a hand to her forehead. Then she took the hand away and raised her face so that she looked up at Hayden. "There is one chance, Capitaine Mercier . . ." But her voice or perhaps her nerve failed her.

"What? What is it?"

She took a deep but ragged breath. "They will not put me upon the guillotine, monsieur . . ." Another difficult breath, and then in a whisper so soft he barely heard, ". . . if I am with child."

She could hold his gaze no longer and hung her head, a little sob escaping, but she stifled it. Reaching up, she put a small hand lightly upon his breast and met his eyes again. "There is no one else who might help me. I can hardly ask . . . a servant. Discretion is imperative." She closed her eyes a second. "The Jacobins will come back for me. Tomorrow, most likely. There is no recourse. If they come for me I am doomed. I have only this one chance; to be with child. My life would be preserved . . . if only for a few months—but this madness, it cannot last for ever. Do you see? My only chance to live." Tears welled over. "I have a daughter . . ." But she could say no more and began to weep almost silently, hiding her face with her hands.

"Shh." Hayden took her hands away from her face and gently led her towards his bed; it took him only that long to decide. It was not done out of desire, nor for conquest, nor even affection—though he did feel gratitude and great fondness for her. Survival was their motive. The Jacobins would murder her—without cause—and he could not bear the thought of it.

For a second she paused to shed her gown, so that she wore only a light shift. Into the bed they crawled, awkward, embarrassed, both still frightened by what had happened earlier. The fear inhibited them at first, but they pressed close and clung to each other until their desire began to rise, and then she guided him atop her, pulling up her shift. In the waning moonlight, the fine lines of her face disappeared and she appeared less troubled and weary, as though the moon gave back her youth. They were gentle with each other, but she buried her fingers in the hair at the back of his neck and very softly moaned close to his ear, whispering endearments in French.

After, she lay on top of him, her hair tickling his face.

"I can tarry but a moment," she whispered. "Do not let me sleep."

But she did not rise immediately, and Hayden sensed her reluctance. All of life was so uncertain, yet here was this small moment of contentment, if not safety—each of them wanted to cling to it and draw it out even five minutes more. Who knew what the next day would bring?

A zephyr sighed in the open casement and then the nightingale began to sing, clear phrases offered up to the stars, far above human strife and suffering.

Twelve

Mrs Carthew, who had not raised six daughters by being indecisive, ordered everyone but Elizabeth out and called for Nan, a servant who had nursed all of the girls through their childhood illnesses so that everyone had come to think of her as having healing powers. Dinner was forgotten, Henrietta borne up to her room, and the rest of the family scattered to various corners of the house with their nearest confidant, to weep and whisper.

"Thank God it was not Captain Hertle!" was perhaps the sentiment expressed more often than any other.

Some time after the letter had been read, Penelope came rushing into the library to find Elizabeth seated by the fire, the recent missive from her husband laid upon a small table near to hand.

"It is a letter from him!" Penelope blurted out.

"What, pray, is a letter from him?"

"The letter that Sandra and Anne have. It is from him—the one who died." She waved at Elizabeth's letter.

"Captain Hayden?"

"That is the one. Henrietta's Navy man. I heard them whispering. They said they were going to burn it."

"Are you certain, Penelope?"

"Yes. Well, mostly."

This made Elizabeth hesitate. "And where might one find them, pray?"

"In the little sitting room. Where Mama likes to hide."

"I shall go to see them . . . alone."

Penelope's face fell in disappointment. Clearly, she wanted to see her sisters, who had seen fit to exclude her from this plot, get their comeuppance. Elizabeth thought she might say something at this point about the propriety of eavesdropping upon the conversations of others but wanted to reach Anne and Cassandra before any letter might be destroyed.

Cassandra and Anne were indeed in the small sitting room, and Anne settled a pillow hurriedly as Elizabeth entered. The two young women could hardly have looked more guilty.

Elizabeth was not quite certain how to proceed. She would much rather the girls speak up and tell her what had been done—if anything. Confronting them would surely lead to retaliation against the informer—and it would not take them a moment to work out who that might be.

"Is something the matter?" Mrs Hertle enquired innocently. "You both look as though you are to be sent into exile. Do tell me we have not received more bad news . . ."

Neither answered for a few seconds, and then Cassandra spoke. "We have done something that perhaps we should not have . . ." she said very softly.

"Oh dear," Elizabeth replied. "And what terrible deed could this be?"

The two girls glanced at each other. "A letter came a few days ago for Henrietta. It was from Captain Hayden—the late Captain Hayden, though we did not know he was late at the time. We carried it home from town where we had retrieved the post and . . . after lengthy discussion, apprehended it."

"Apprehended it?"

"Yes. We kept it secret and told no one . . ." Cassandra coloured noticeably.

"We knew you had burned Captain Hayden's letter and thought . . . Well, we thought that a letter from a dishonourable rogue could contain nothing that would cheer Henrietta but perhaps a great deal that might cause her distress. And as she was getting on so well with Frank, who we both believe is her true intended—"

"You did not burn it . . . did you?" Elizabeth interrupted.

Cassandra produced the letter from beneath the pillow and passed it into the hands of her older cousin.

"You had said you burned Captain Hayden's letter and would not read it . . ." Anne repeated rather defensively.

"That is true, but the letter I burned was addressed to me. Had it been addressed to Captain Hertle I would have delivered it to its proper recipient."

"Do you think we have done wrong, then?"

"With the best intentions, I have no doubt, but yes, I do. Whatever the effect of the letter might be, it is Henri's to read . . . or not read. Only she can decide."

"Will you take it to her, then?" Anne asked.

"And will you tell her that we . . . held it for a time?"

"Could you not tell her we forgot? She has enough to distress her as it is without being angry with us as well."

"Normally, I should never lie to protect you from the consequences of your own actions. But in this one case I shall not tell, and for the very reason you have just stated. Henrietta has experienced quite enough sorrow this day. I do hope this letter will not bring her more." She hesitated a second. "I will keep this letter and give it to her on the morrow and allow her to think it came with the post. But the two of you must never tell. Not as long as you live."

"Oh, thank you, Lizzie!" Cassandra said. "We shall never breathe a word, shall we, Anne?"

They almost threw themselves at her feet, they were so grateful.

Elizabeth tore herself away, but stopped with her hand on the doorknob. "Mark my words," she said to her cousins, "I shall not lie for you ever again. Next time you get yourself into difficulty, you shall have to get yourselves out. Is that understood?"

Satisfied that she had been suitably strict, and feeling that she had taught the girls a valuable lesson, even if she could not say exactly what it was, she went in search of Penelope. If she was going to tell a lie—even one of omission—she would be certain those who might reveal her duplicity had all sworn a most solemn oath of secrecy.

Henrietta insisted that she would not lie abed the day after they had received the terrible news from Captain Hertle. Instead, she forced herself to go through the motions of a "normal" day and begged a walk with only Elizabeth for company.

"He betrayed my confidence, broke my heart, exposed me to the worst public humiliation, and yet I am as devastated as I would have been had he done none of these things. Some small part of me should be thinking, 'There, Charles Saunders Hayden, you got the come-uppance you so richly deserved!' but I do not feel that in any corner of my being. Had none of this occurred—his betrayal and marriage to that woman—I would hardly be more desolate." Henrietta shook her head.

There had been a distinct and uncharacteristic lack of tears this morning, as though the reservoir had been drained that night, for certainly Henri had hardly slept. She was as pale as flour, her eyes puffy and red-rimmed. Even her beautiful, musical voice sounded thin and worn, and she appeared to stoop a little as she walked.

"You were in love with him, Henri. I believe what has happened is worse than his mere betrayal. Once a woman's feelings have been attached, it takes no small amount of time to sever that attachment. You have both been betrayed by a man you trusted and cared for, and you have lost the man you hoped to marry. It is a blow doubly cruel, and the fact that you have even raised your head from your pillow this day is . . . well, it speaks to your great inner strength, Henri. Few others could do it."

"I do not feel particularly strong, Cousin. Mama never coddled us. We could not lie abed for every little ache and complaint. We must be dizzy with fever and near delirium before we could stay abed. I dare not do as I wish—pull the coverlets over my head and hide from the world for a fortnight, at the very least."

"Well, I suppose the air will do you good."

This caused Henrietta to smile, though quickly it twisted to a wince.

Elizabeth carried the intercepted letter in her pocket, and she was as aware of it, with every step, as though it were made of wood, not paper. Although she did not know its content, she feared terribly that it would be but another blow to her beloved cousin, and she was now as reticent as Cassandra and Anne had been to deliver it into Henri's hand. In truth, one moment she would decide to withhold it until a more propitious time, or until Henri seemed at least a little recovered. But then she would think she had no right to do so and had lectured Anne and Sandra on this very subject. The letter belonged to Henrietta—for good or ill. But then she would glance her cousin's way and one sight of her would have her again thinking that withholding the letter a few days, perhaps a sennight, might be a far kinder course. What harm could be done? Charles Hayden was dead. The letter could cause nothing but more heartache, and clearly Henrietta had all she could bear at that moment.

They came to an overlook, and beneath an ancient hornbeam

found the little bench that was the object of their outing. Elizabeth brushed it clean with a hanky she had brought for this very purpose—as well as two others in case Henrietta had need of them.

A moment they sat, and then Henrietta released a sigh so laden with sadness and confusion that Elizabeth covered her cousin's hand with her own.

"And then there is Frank . . ." Henrietta said softly. "I do not know what I shall do with poor Frank. His offer could hardly have come at a worse moment. It is so unfair to him that he has been almost entirely driven from my thoughts. I feel wretched about it."

"It was the worst timing," Elizabeth agreed. "It does, however, put a question in my mind when his offer of marriage has been entirely lost in your grief for another. What does this say about your feelings for the two gentlemen, one whose hopes depend entirely upon you, and another who dashed your hopes in the cruellest fashion?"

"I should love Frank," Henrietta stated. "I should love him with all my heart. Who is more deserving? Certainly not Charles Hayden, who injured me so."

"And yet . . . ?"

"Just so," Henrietta whispered, pressing down her tears. *"'And yet . . .'"*

Henri dabbed at her eyes with a square of linen, looked at it and declared, "It is sopping."

Elizabeth produced one from her pocket. "I have two others," she informed her cousin.

"Oh, I have several more than that, secreted all about my person."

They both laughed rather bitterly.

"A horse trough might be the answer. I could lean over it and fill it every hour or three. And then . . . I could climb in and literally drown in my own tears."

"There will be no drowning," Elizabeth informed her firmly.

"I was speaking in jest."

"Do not jest about such matters, my dear. It unsettles me."

"I am sorry, Lizzie. I did not mean it in the least. I am overcome with sorrow and many other feelings as well, but I intend to last through it and make a life all the same. And in the next few days I must decide if it will be a life with Frank Beacher. I cannot leave him wondering for too long despite my own situation. Certainly, he deserves better than that."

"Yes, you are right." Elizabeth took a long breath. "Henri? I have something in my pocket that I am loath to give you."

"Whatever do you mean, Lizzie? What is it, pray?"

"It is a letter . . ." She caught her breath. "From Charles Hayden—written and sent before he lost his ship, clearly."

Henrietta held out her hand immediately. "Lizzie, you must give it to me this instant. Whatever does it say?"

"I do not know, my dear. What Charles Hayden could write to you after what he did I cannot imagine."

The letter was produced and passed to Henrietta, who once she had read the address hesitated to open it.

"It might distress you terribly, my dear Henri. Shall I take it back and hold it a few days until you are more recovered and able to bear up to whatever might be written inside?"

"No, thank you, Lizzie. If I might just compose myself but a moment . . ."

It took much longer than "a moment." Henrietta rose and paced back and forth several times before the bench. Began to break the seal (her cousin had carried along a little clasp knife for this purpose), then stopped. Paced again.

After some time spent thus she settled upon the furthest edge of the bench, perched as though she might fly, and broke the seal with hands that trembled visibly. Immediately she read, a hanky pressed to her cheek with one hand, prepared to intercept any overflow.

Elizabeth heard her breath catch and then she leaned back against the bench, a free flow of tears running down her cheeks. "He did not marry," she managed. "It was all a lie." A moment and then she pressed herself to sit back up and raise the letter again, but she could not read it for tears and pressed it on her cousin.

"Oh do read it, Elizabeth. I cannot see for weeping."

Her cousin snatched it up, desperate herself to see what was written there, and with difficulty read:

> *My Dear Henrietta;*
>
> *Before anything else is said, I must inform you, all rumours that I married while parted from you are utterly untrue. No such thing occurred. Two women, French émigrées, mother and daughter, have been making this false claim and using my name to amass a vast quantity of debt, and to acquire substantial sums from my prize agent. Neither Lady Hertle nor Mrs Hertle will speak with me nor read any correspondence I write, so I have been at my wits' end to find some way to send you word of what has occurred. I am also very dismayed to think that the claims of these two women have caused you distress. The worst of all this is that, at the request of Sir Gilbert Elliot, I aided these two women in coming to England and they have repaid my kindness by using my name to defraud any number of merchants and my prize agent and to cause you pain. Seldom has a good deed been so unjustly repaid.*
>
> *I do hope you will read this and understand that I did not betray your trust in any measure and that my heart has not changed in the least these past months except that it is even more your own.*
>
> *Your Very Own,*
> *Charles*

"I should never have known a moment of doubt," Henrietta managed. "Nor judged without having heard his own explanation. And how can I ever make it up now? My poor, darling Charles. I would have been in London and seen him one last time had not all . . . *this* occurred. It is more than a heart can bear, Lizzie. More than a heart can bear."

"To think if I had but opened my door and had a five-minute explanation with him, the entire misunderstanding would have been swept away . . ." But Elizabeth could not finish, she was so distressed.

Mrs Carthew sat at the head of the table, sipping upon a cup of coffee. There were no others present. "We all have a burden of guilt in this unfortunate matter. Each and every one of us spoke most harshly against Captain Hayden . . . and now we learn he was both innocent . . . and dead. Not one of us can now apologise or make amends. We must live knowing we had so little faith in him, even though both Captain Hertle and my own daughter held him in the highest possible regard."

Elizabeth was quite certain that her own guilt was vastly greater, as none of the Carthew family had known Charles but Henri, while she had known him for several years and had previously given him the highest possible character. "Captain Hertle will never say it, of course, but he will be most disappointed in me that I so readily thought the worst of Captain Hayden. I fear he will think me disloyal if not foolish." She thought a moment. "If only I had not seen her with my own eyes . . ."

"Whom, my dear?"

"The French girl—Bourdage, I believe. She would be notable in a room full of the most handsome women. It was that beauty, re-marked upon by all who met her, that made me believe Captain Hayden's betrayal possible. Very few men could have resisted it, I dare say. But apparently he did."

"There is nothing to be done for Captain Hayden now. No apologies to be made but in the silence of our own hearts. It is Henrietta for whom I am concerned. She has been wrenched first in one direction, and then another, and then yet another, poor girl. And that is not even to make mention of Frank Beacher finally speaking after all these years. Why in the world he should do so now after such a prolonged period of hesitation, I cannot imagine."

This sentence, spoken in all innocence, had the effect of increasing Elizabeth's guilt tenfold. If not for her—though she suspected that Mr Wilder played some part in it as well—Henrietta would more than likely never have said or done even the slightest thing that might have encouraged Frank Beacher, in which case he would not have dared speak for risk of having his suit rebuffed.

"As if Henrietta did not have enough to concern her, now she must think of Frank and his feelings as well."

"You do not think she would say 'yes' to Frank, now, do you, Aunt?"

"It is not out of the question. And do not misunderstand me. Other than his propensity to be very timid in matters of the heart, I am more fond of him than I can tell. There is not a thing one can say against him. Why, many a mother has him under consideration for their own daughter. Mr Beacher and Henrietta are not unsuited to one another and would, I think, not be unhappy. But I am not certain that 'not being unhappy' is the same as being happy, nor might it suit a girl of Henrietta's temperament." She refilled her cup from a silver coffeepot. "Frank Beacher, however, is a matter for Henri to decide. Mr Carthew would certainly welcome such a match so there would be no impediment from that quarter. But what to do about

Henri now? That is my concern." She looked up at Elizabeth, considering. "I wonder if you should not take her away, Lizzie, perhaps to visit Lady Hertle. Not immediately, of course, but when she is a little recovered from all of these terrible blows she has been dealt."

"It is not out of the question. I should not take her to London, which I believe would only increase her sorrows. Plymouth, I hate to say, might be little different, even though Aunt Hertle and Henrietta could hardly hold each other in greater affection. But Plymouth is the place where much of her time with Captain Hayden was spent and the memories that city might engender could cause her more heartache. We might consider going to some place she enjoyed as a child—the Lake District would be beautiful in May, and we would be far from the sea, which I believe a good thing.

"It might be the very thing. I think we must get her away. A little time and distance will allow her to see things more clearly, I am quite certain."

As she left the dining room and crossed through the hallway, Elizabeth became aware that someone lingered upon the stair.

"Mrs Hertle?" the lurker asked.

"Mr Beacher. Can you not find a more comfortable seat than a stair tread?"

"Not at the moment. I have been hoping you would pass and that I might claim a moment of your time . . ." Frank Beacher appeared very subdued, as though the loss of Charles Hayden had been a blow to him—when in fact it was a great boon to him and his aspirations. Apparently, his concern for Henrietta and his unanswered question were depriving him of sleep.

"I should be most happy to oblige, Mr Beacher, on the condition that we walk out into this fine day even for a moment."

"I should like nothing better."

The two passed through the house, across the stone terrace and down into the garden, which had been artfully terraced towards the south, providing the house with a magnificent view while allowing the many varieties of trees to grow to their mature heights without any danger of obstruction.

"It is a lovely day," Frank observed, "if one considers only the weather, of course."

"Indeed it is."

They walked on a moment.

"Mrs Hertle, might I enquire after Miss Henrietta? How is she bearing up to these terrible shocks?"

Elizabeth was about to provide one of the common replies—"as well as can be expected" or "far better than hoped"—but then she thought that Mr Beacher's question was not a mere formality but asked out of a concern that was both genuine and deeply felt. He was not losing so much sleep for nothing.

"She is terribly distressed if not distraught, Mr Beacher, I will tell you honestly. Not that it should be unexpected given the nature of recent events. I have never seen her brought so low or melancholy sink its claws so deeply." She turned to Mr Beacher, who took this in with great seriousness. "You have not spoken to her?"

"Not for several days—since you received the news from Captain Hertle."

"If it is any comfort, Mr Beacher, she has spoken of you with both affection and concern these last days."

"I am not the one requiring comfort, Mrs Hertle. Nor have I sought you out to learn Henrietta's inclination on certain matters, though of great import to me, not to be considered in the present circumstances. It is Henrietta's well-being that is my sole concern. If I may in any way be of service to Henrietta, do not hesitate to ask."

It occurred to Elizabeth that she might suggest he visit elsewhere for a fortnight and relieve Henrietta of the burden of giving him a reply—which was weighing heavily upon poor Henri, Elizabeth knew. But any such response would injure Mr Beacher terribly, and she could not bear to do it. Frank was exactly that kind of person— no one wanted to bruise his feelings.

"I do not know what anyone can do for Henrietta at this moment. She must grieve, and grief is rather like a poison in one's soul, Mr Beacher—the only poultice that will draw it is time." Something caught her eye on a nearby hilltop. "Is that Cassandra?" she asked, pointing.

It was without question a woman on horseback, and then, from behind a stand of beech trees, appeared another—though this a gentleman equestrian.

"And Wilder," Beacher replied.

"They both ride very well," Elizabeth observed.

"Well, if you are going to explore distant lands, being able to sit a horse is certainly a necessity."

"Not to mention elephants and dromedaries, though I do not know how one learns to ride those."

"I shall get them each a pair for their birthdays," Frank declared, which made Elizabeth laugh—something she had not done in several days.

Beacher stopped walking suddenly. "You will tell Henrietta, I hope, that I am most concerned for her?" He stopped an instant. "And as to an answer to my question—she need not even consider it until her mind and heart are much recovered."

"Your patience in this matter, Mr Beacher," Elizabeth said with feeling, "is . . . is . . . well, very noble."

"It is the least Henrietta could expect of me." He considered. "I suppose at some point I shall begin to look a fool—though Wilder assures me, when it comes to this matter, I have looked a fool for many years."

"Never for a moment, Mr Beacher," Elizabeth assured him, though of course it was a lie.

"Good riddance to him, I say. Yes, yes," Cassandra went on, "I know we all judged him unfairly, and without question he was a very brave man and served England dutifully, but would he have made my sister a proper husband? I rather doubt he would. Henrietta requires a husband who will be at home with her, to appreciate all of her finest qualities."

"A devoted admirer, then?" Wilder enquired.

They had just cantered up the hill and now walked their horses side by side, allowing the poor beasts to catch their breath—hardly a necessity, as Cassandra and Wilder had spent the morning riding just as they were now so as to further a free flow of conversation.

"Well, something more than just an admirer, but, yes, Henrietta is a creature worthy of great admiration. Do you not agree?"

"Entirely, and so too does my friend Beacher."

"The rather sad end of the Navy man has cleared the way for them. The sooner Henrietta comes to her senses on the matter, the better off she and Mr Beacher will be—and I shall not hesitate to tell her so—when she is somewhat recovered. Perhaps tomorrow."

"I am sure that Mr Beacher would approve of your intentions, though perhaps you might wait a bit longer—a sennight, perhaps."

"Do you think?"

"Mmm."

"I shall wait, then." A small pause. "Do you not think there is a bit too much . . . *melodrama* in Henri's response to all of this?"

"The man she hoped to marry did just die. Before that, she believed he had betrayed her."

"I suppose . . . but even so, she is getting a great deal of attention . . . which is rather like her, actually."

"Sibling jealousy?" Wilder asked, trying not to grin.

"It certainly is not!"

"Not even in the smallest degree?"

"Mr Wilder! I am deeply offended at the mere suggestion! My sister is very dear to me!"

"I have no doubt of it, if only she would stop mooning around over this dead sailor and get on with it."

"I said no such thing!"

"Perhaps not, but it was certainly what you meant."

"Mr Wilder! How could you think me so heartless? I believe you—like Frank Beacher—are in love with my sister." She turned up her nose, gave a heel to her mount, and set off at a canter. Immediately, Mr Wilder was urging on his own horse, and dodging clods thrown up by the hooves of Cassandra's mare as it raced along the crest.

In a moment they were climbing the next hill, and as they reached the top they allowed their horses to walk again. Both Wilder and Cassandra were red-cheeked and laughing.

"I will be completely frank with you, Mr Wilder; your inclination to point out my shortcomings is rather a disagreeable quality."

"Then you prefer flattery?"

"I do. The more extravagant and embellished, the more I like it."

"Then allow me to say your devotion to your sister in her time of need is exemplary, even selfless. I am surprised that she has not sallied forth to thank you, on bended knee, no less, for the sacrifices you have been willing to make on her behalf. Your heartfelt offer to exchange places with the late Captain Hayden was particularly touching, if a bit impractical."

"Now, that is how I prefer to hear a gentleman talk! Do go on,

Mr Wilder, I am certain you cannot have exhausted the catalogue of my virtues in so brief an account as that."

"Why, Miss Cassandra, I have not even begun. Have I yet mentioned your superior understanding?"

"No, but I believe you should."

"I do not know if I have the superlatives to do justice to its superiority."

"I believe if you think deeply upon it, you will acquit yourself in a manner that would make your family very proud."

"I should never wish to let down my family." He pretended to contemplate the matter for a few seconds. "In prudence, discernment, astuteness, perspicacity, wisdom, indeed in genius, I hardly think you have an equal."

"Mr Wilder! I am beginning to think your understanding almost equal to my own."

"And then there is your discernment in weighing such matters as 'attention' and who might be getting more of it. In this, I say with confidence, you have no rival. Indeed, I should say your scale is so perfectly balanced and your mind so attuned that not the slightest attention goes unnoticed but it is weighed to a nicety and recorded in the ledger."

"I am not so enamoured of this line of flattery as I was the last."

"Then have I remarked upon your great beauty, Miss Cassandra?"

"Not with a frequency that would do it justice."

"Of course, a gentleman must approach such a subject with delicacy."

"My beauty is such that simply to behold it banishes all indelicacies—or so I have been told."

"Of course that is so. Where to begin, though . . . I should say, Miss Cassandra, that your nose is the most perfect hillock in the entire south of England."

Cassandra laughed. "Mr Wilder! Surely you exaggerate! It might not even rival the most perfect hillock in Kent!"

"I never exaggerate," he stated firmly, as though mildly offended that she might even suggest such a thing.

"Do forgive me. I cannot think what made me say it."

"As I was saying, your nose is the most perfect hillock in the south of England . . . perhaps beyond."

Cassandra stifled a giggle.

"And your eyes . . . I am quite certain they see much further than any of your sisters'."

"Mr Wilder, if you keep this up you shall turn my head, I am quite certain of it."

"And your feet! Your perfect, delicate, tiny little feet. How rapidly they carry you about; how certain they seem of where they go. I dare say they have never taken you any place you did not intend. How many can make such a claim? I should say not a single soul in all of this sacred isle."

"You would appear to be saying my feet are quite reliable?"

"Reliable!? Faithful, trustworthy, steady, loyal. The English language cannot begin to do them justice."

"Loyal . . . What woman does not all but swoon to hear her feet so described. If I tumble from my saddle, I do hope you will catch me?"

"My dear, I am quite certain your feet will catch you before a mere mortal, such as myself, would be able. And I have not even mentioned your knuckles."

"No. No, Mr Wilder, I must protest. Another word and I fear I shall no longer be the master of my own feelings. If you are indeed a gentleman, you must desist, I beg you."

"Though it is difficult to stop singing your praises, Miss Cassandra, if you insist, I shall give it over . . . for now. But I might have to take it up again at some future time. How could I not?"

"Yes, I dare say, it is a bit overwhelming for mere mortals, such as yourself."

"I do not think you could begin to understand." Something took Wilder's attention from his companion at that moment. "Is that Miss Henrietta and Mr Beacher—there, in the garden?"

Cassandra straightened a little in her saddle. "Is it not, rather, my cousin Elizabeth? Henrietta has no dress with skirts that colour. Surely it is Lizzie. See the way she walks. She does not glide as does Henrietta. I wonder of what they speak?"

"It can be but one thing—or person, I should say."

"Henrietta?"

"So I would assume."

"Will she agree to marry him? Frank, that is?"

"You are her sister, surely you know better than I."

"I believe she will. I do hope so, anyway. Frank will make her very happy. Much happier than she could ever have been with that Navy man . . . no matter how dashing he might have been."

"I never met the captain myself, but Frank has been my friend for several years and I do not hold a higher opinion of anyone in our circle."

"Not even yourself, Mr Wilder?" She let just a hint of a wicked smile show.

He turned his attention to Cassandra, suddenly completely serious. "Most especially myself."

Thirteen

Henrietta felt the spring sun soak into her skin, infusing each layer with warmth and health as it drove out all the cold and dampness of winter. She sat upon the bench with her face turned up to the sun, thinking that when she felt the sun reach her bones and flood them with warmth she would begin to mend from all the misfortune that had befallen her these last weeks. Healing would not be quick, but even to feel that it had begun would be more of a relief than she could say.

Spring spread all around, trees in new leaf, grass so green it appeared to glow from within as though it contained its own fire. Flowers pushed up through the crust of the earth and each day grew an inch until they opened their comely blossoms to bumbling, droning bees. The scent of the weeping willow, a few feet distant, was like a faint perfume of distant China, from which place the tree had once been carried as the tiniest sprout. The earthy aroma of spring welled up from the ground all around, laden with the fragrance of decay and renewal.

When the warmth reaches my bones, Henrietta thought, then I shall join in this renewal and become whole again. Even my torn heart shall be knit back together.

"There you are, my dear. I have searched everywhere. Certainly,

I should have known you would be by the pond. But your face is all pink! Should we not move into the shade?"

Henrietta opened her eyes to find her cousin Lizzie standing over her, a look of concern upon her face.

"I am happy in the sun. I feel the warmth of it seeping into my flesh and mending me in some way I cannot explain."

Lizzie took a seat beside her on the bench. "You are not a plant, you know."

"I believe there is a little plant in all of us but most are unaware of it."

"It is a strange belief." Lizzie glanced at her cousin. "But if it makes you happy to believe it, then you may."

"Mmm." Henrietta closed her eyes and attempted to return to basking. The sun had come so near to her bones, and now Lizzie, whom she was always pleased to see, had come to interrupt, if not the process, at least Henrietta's awareness of it. And the awareness seemed to her to be as important, if not more so, than the outcome.

"I was speaking with Frank Beacher earlier," Lizzie said after a moment. Henri could tell by the studied casualness of the statement that Lizzie was reticent to bring it up.

"I observed the two of you walking." *Though did not join you* was left unsaid but far more significant.

"He did say that if there was anything he might do for you, dear Henri, you had but to ask. And also that you may rest assured, given the series of circumstances that have occurred since he spoke, you need not feel the least obliged to answer until you are much recovered. He said this most emphatically."

"Dear Frank. He is so obliging—and genuinely so. He has been that way since the age of six—and perhaps before."

"He is a very kind young man."

Henrietta closed her eyes and tried to feel the progress of the sun into her being, but she had lost the way of it. "I would be safe with Frank, would I not?"

"It depends, my dear, on what you mean by 'safe.'"

"I mean my heart. As safe as could be. Frank is not about to become adventurous. I should not have constant nightmares of him drowning or dying in some terrible eruption of violence. I have known Frank Beacher all my life and I trust him utterly."

Perhaps Elizabeth felt she must have something to say on this matter, for after a moment she offered, "I believe one might safely say that about Frank Beacher. He is virtuous and trustworthy . . . to a fault."

"I do not think that either of those characteristics could be called 'faults,' Lizzie."

"No, certainly they are not. And his profession will never put him in harm's way. I also understand that he stands to inherit a sizeable estate?"

"Not so large as Box Hill, but adequate."

"And you will have Aunt Hertle's house in Plymouth and some other monies she will bequeath you. You shall never lack comfort."

"I feel there is a good deal to be said for comfort—a homely house, children, if I am so blessed, an income that can be relied upon, and a husband who comes through the door each evening and tells me of his day's activities over a proper dinner."

"It does sound . . . certain," Lizzie whispered.

Henrietta opened her eyes just long enough to find her cousin's hand and squeeze it within her own.

"No more Navy men for me, Lizzie."

Elizabeth swallowed with difficulty. "I understand," she said softly. "Life is uncertain enough."

"I do not approve of gambling at cards—gambling in the truly important things is . . ." She glanced at Lizzie, realizing what she was about to say might appear a judgement. "I will marry Frank Beacher and he will love me until the end of his days. I am quite certain of it."

"So which have you chosen, my dear Henri? Knowledge or contentment?"

"Was that my decision? Or some other's?" She looked over at her cousin, appealing. "What do you think I have chosen, Lizzie?"

Elizabeth shook her head and for a moment said nothing. "I did not understand," she began, a little edge of sorrow in her voice, "when first I married, that I would send my very heart to war . . . and far oftener than I would choose." She took a long breath, but there were no tears. "I now possess the deepest knowledge of what a hollow creature I should be without it. You have made an intelligent choice, my dear. I . . . I would expect nothing less."

"Do you think me a coward?"

Lizzie looked over at her and smiled bitterly. "Because you do not wish to risk your heart? It is a most sensible decision." Tears welled up in her eyes. With difficulty she whispered, "I just do not know if it is truly possible."

Fourteen

Hayden's conscience awoke an hour before the household stirred and left him lying in the early dawn, thinking of Henrietta. He tried to tell himself that they were estranged and therefore what had occurred with Madame Adair was of no concern to Henrietta—but he knew the "estrangement" was due to a mere misunderstanding that could be cleared away by a single conversation. He did not think what he had done was wrong under the circumstances, but certainly it was a betrayal of trust and Henrietta would certainly see it as such. Of course, he had promised Madame Adair on the soul of his mother that he would keep their secret as long as he breathed. Henrietta would never learn of it . . . but *he* knew and it made him feel low and unworthy.

Where did I get this schoolboy sense of honour? he wondered.

It had also occurred to him that Madame Adair's plan had only the smallest chance of success. From his meagre knowledge of these matters, Hayden was aware that when a man and a woman wanted a child they could lie together every night without success. But when a child was not the first desire, a single night together would almost always see the job done. Poor Madame Adair—her ruse would be found out within a month. He knew that she hoped the madness would be over by then, but he feared this was but fancy;

the guillotine would persist in its terrible duty for some time to come.

When he heard stirring in the house, Hayden rose, fatigued from lack of sleep, and anxious about the day.

Madame Adair had already broken her fast by the time Hayden arrived downstairs, and Charlotte was being bundled off to visit neighbours, much to her chagrin.

"But why must I go, Mama? You know how I hate her!"

"Do not torment me with questions, child. You have made excuses several times before, and this time you must go. It is only polite." She held up a hand, anticipating Charlotte's next words. "Argue further and I shall send you again next week."

So Charlotte acquiesced, though frustrated and mystified by the strange logic of adults.

The sun was barely risen when poor Charlotte was taken off by servants. Madame Adair curtsied to Hayden but did not meet his eye or betray any familiarity whatsoever. She excused herself and instructed a maid to serve him his breakfast in the garden.

Settling himself at the table beneath a flourishing chestnut tree, Hayden gazed off at the distant road that wound north towards Brest. From that quarter would come the Jacobins—although if Madame Adair had spoken the truth, they would not come for her by day. There had been an uprising against the revolutionary government in this part of the country already; the Jacobins did not want to provoke another and so did their work under cover of darkness.

Carts and drays did appear from time to time, and now and then a man on horseback, some of whom were Army officers. A sizeable carriage went by apace, a whirl of dust in its wake. But no gangs of Jacobin thugs, he was relieved to see. The aura of fear and anxiety that overlay the farm began to ease a little. The day was shaping up to be exceptionally fine, fleets of benign clouds sailing across the blue surface of the sky. Birds went winging this way and that, bearing straw and string to build their nests with, and, in the branches above, overladen bees trundled from one blossom to the next, humming like contented hobbyists. One could almost imagine that all was well with the world.

After he had eaten, Hayden set out to walk about the fields, trying to regain his strength. A herd dog attached herself to him, perhaps thinking he went to fetch home the cows, but the cows had already come in to be milked and fed, so she was bound for disappointment on that score.

The farm was spread over countryside as rolling as a stormy sea, the fields all slanting this way or that, hardly one level. Within a quarter of a mile, Hayden was forced to rest upon a little section of tumbledown stone wall. He was out of breath, shaking and slippery with sweat. To escape across country he would need to be able to manage several miles in a few short hours. The only way to hasten his recovery, so that he might undertake this ordeal, was to force himself to exercise. Walking to begin, and then he would start helping with the light farmwork. What the farmhands would think about an officer in the French Navy doing farm labour he did not know. He would tell them it was the age of equality or something of that sort.

Forcing himself up, Hayden went on, finding a stick for a cane, his attendant herd dog, rushing ahead, then returning to verify his progress, as though he were her charge and she dare not lose him. After another quarter-mile Hayden stretched out on a dry, south-facing slope and fell asleep in the spring sun. Indeed, he could not remain awake, so exhausted was he by walking a mere half-mile!

He woke sometime later, pink-cheeked, frowzy, and overheated. Going on was out of the question, so he grumpily decided to turn back, disappointed with his recovery.

"Back to the damn farm!" he informed the herd dog in French (certainly, the dog did not understand English, he reasoned). "I feel

I have grown old before my time. I am certain I did not manage half a mile."

And the half-mile back was much longer. He teetered into the farmyard, shaking and thirsty, only to find men sprawled beneath the shade trees in little knots, two servants with buckets plying among them, offering water. A French Army officer of unknown rank sat in the chair Hayden had occupied that very morning, and all around a small company of soldiers stood sentry, muskets at the ready.

Prisoners, Hayden realised, and before his exhausted mind could comprehend what this meant, one of the men jumped up and exclaimed, "Captain Hayden! Praise God! You are alive, sir!" It was Gould, and all about rested the officers of the *Themis*.

Other men broke into grins and began to rise as well, muttering both astonishment and thanks. Too late, Hayden replied in French, gesturing with his hands, expressing polite bewilderment at this odd mistake. Immediately, the French officer rose and approached him. Archer, meanwhile, had jumped up and taken Gould by the arm.

"This is not Captain Hayden," he said to the midshipman. "Whatever are you thinking? Can you not see this is a Frenchman? Your brain must be addled by the sun."

The French officer appeared to look Hayden up and down. "Who are you, sir?" he asked.

"I am Capitaine Gil Mercier," Hayden claimed confidently, showing now some resentment at this foolish mistake. "I was a guest of Capitaine Lacrosse aboard *Les Droits de l'Homme*. These *Anglais* were prisoners aboard. That is why they recognise me, though apparently they do not know my name."

The officer motioned Archer forward and then asked him, "Do you know this man?"

"Yes," Archer answered in bad French. "He sailed with Capitaine

Lacrosse and was wrecked with the rest of us. Capitaine Mercier. He saved many lives, monsieur, and we are much in his debt."

"What did this other man call him?" he motioned to one of his soldiers. "Bring that *Anglais* forward."

Gould was helped to his feet and led forward.

"Ask him what he called Capitaine Mercier," the officer instructed Archer.

Archer complied and then repeated. "'Hayden' is what he said, and he apologises for not knowing the Capitaine's name. He is very chagrined to have made such a mistake."

Madame Adair appeared at that moment and the officer made a small bow to her. "Madame, is this man known to you?" He gestured to Hayden.

"Of course, yes. He was brought here from the wreck almost dead. It is a miracle he is still among us. His name is Capitaine Gil Mercier, sir." She looked at Hayden, suddenly concerned. "Capitaine? Are you well? Bring a chair!" she called to the men bearing water buckets. "Sit, Capitaine. You are not yet recovered enough to go so far. Please . . . sit."

Hayden tumbled down into the chair, dizzy and suddenly hot.

Even the Army officer looked concerned.

"Then you are certain he is Capitaine Mercier?"

"He was brought here by a local doctor who was on the beach when the ship broke up. He wore a captain's uniform—shall I have it brought out for you?"

He shook his head. "That will not be necessary. My apologies, Capitaine. I wish you a speedy recovery." The Frenchman returned to his chair, speaking quietly to one of his men.

Hayden wanted to retreat—into the house or anywhere beyond the gaze of his men. He also did not want to appear to stare but was desperate to know who had survived their ordeal.

Madame Adair called for a servant to bring him water, and this helped a little. Hayden thought his crew all looked as ill as he did, and he was gratified to see them loaded onto a dray when they departed. Prisoners were often marched many miles to gaols—difficult enough for healthy men.

As the dray retreated down the lane, Hayden could see the dull-eyed gazes of his crew as they stared back at him. A strange guilt came over him. He should be with his crew, not making more than likely futile plans to escape. But there was no going back now. To admit he had lied would bring about an immediate and official response. He was going to have to make his escape in his present condition. Waiting until he recovered was no longer possible.

"Why did that man call you ''ayden'?" Madame Adair asked.

He shrugged. "He did not know my name, I suppose."

She tilted her head and gazed at him quizzically. "He seemed very pleased to see you . . ."

"I made it my duty to aid them when the ship was wrecked. I am ashamed to say it, but the crew of *Les Droits de l'Homme* did not respond to their situation with courage, let alone gallantry."

"Well, I am happy you survived, Capitaine," she said, and smiled, the worry disappearing from her face for an instant. "Did you sleep well . . . after our visitors left?"

"I was attended by a nightingale; did you hear it? So beautiful and sorrowful."

She looked suddenly sad. "I do not think it will sing again this night, Capitaine."

"I would be very melancholy if it went away."

"Not so sad as me."

She turned on her toe and sailed off towards the house. Hayden wondered if everyone saw what he did in the way she moved—some little contentment in the midst of madding distress.

Hayden called over one of the servants who had taken water to the prisoners. "Do you know where those *Anglais* were being taken?"

"To Brest, Capitaine."

"Brest? But Quimper Prison is in the opposite direction . . ."

The man shrugged. "That is what they said, Capitaine Mercier."

"Merci."

Hayden moved to a chair beneath the shade of the chestnut and watched the road north. It was not long before the servant was proven right—the dray with its guards went slowly up a hill, the horses straining.

When Hayden had recovered a little of his strength, he stumbled up to his room, resting once upon the stair, and dropped onto his bed like a sack of oats. He woke to a tugging upon the shoulder of his jacket.

"Monsieur Capitaine . . . Monsieur Capitaine?"

"Mademoiselle?"

Charlotte stood over him.

"Will you not eat, Capitaine Mercier? Mama desires that you do."

Hayden swung his feet over the side of his bed, and sat up, bracing himself with an arm to either side. Before him Charlotte stood almost eye to eye. "Mama says that one must eat to grow strong."

"She is very wise, your mother."

The girl nodded as though this was merely understood and beyond question. A tray of food sat upon a small table; the smell of it drifted to Hayden.

"No one woke me for supper?"

"We tried, monsieur, but you would not stir. I have been shaking you now for at least an hour."

"So long? I was very tired." A thought arose from the confusion. "Did you not go off to visit with friends?"

"I did, but they sent me home. Madame Lepic said that Hortense had taken ill, although she did not seem it in the least."

"I am sorry she grew ill. But you do not feel sick, I hope?"

The girl shook her head.

"Tell your mother I will eat now. And thank her for my supper."

"Of course, monsieur." She ran off.

Hayden wondered if she had been sent home because the neighbours did not want to be seen aiding a woman who was most likely about to be taken away. No doubt everyone within several miles knew of what had occurred the previous night.

Hayden ate; the food and the scents wafting in his window reminded him of his boyhood visits to his mother's family. If his friends back in England knew how much love he felt for this country, they would probably be shocked. How he wished this terrible war would end! Suddenly, and overwhelmingly, he felt repelled by it. By a war where his two people fought, where madmen and mobs cried out for the blood of women like Madame Adair. Where children were orphaned by some impersonal strike of a committee member's pen.

When he was finished, Hayden carried his own tray downstairs, wanting to step out for a breath of the evening air. Gravel rattled beneath his boots as he crossed to the grass, the fragrance of the April evening as intoxicating as a woman's perfume.

He stood upon the crest that looked out over the long valley and felt the soft breeze wash over his face. For a moment he closed his eyes, and when he opened them again the darkness appeared to have seeped up from the moist ground to thicken the air.

Madame Adair stood beside him, her arms crossed over her breast, a shawl gathered close. How she had crossed the gravel without him hearing he did not know.

"Madame," he said, giving a little bow.

"Capitaine. I shall miss this view . . . terribly." She fell silent for a time. Nighthawks flitted across the clouds and the few stars waking. "I only hope they do not wake Charlotte. I will make no resistance so there is no noise. Will you sit with me, Capitaine? When they come I will be here, beneath my favourite chestnut."

"Certainly, yes."

She turned and put a hand gently upon his arm. "Thank you, Capitaine Mercier, for what you have done. If there is a child, please know that I will raise him—or her—with all my love."

"Thank you, Madame. I will pray that you are spared."

She nodded her thanks.

They arranged the chairs so that they looked out to the southwest, where the last light of the spring day ebbed away over the horizon.

A servant brought them coffee and a blanket for Madame Adair to wrap herself in. Little was said, though once it was utterly dark Madame Adair reached out and took Hayden's hand and held it with a certain tenderness. The night crept on, the clock in the hall counting each muffled hour, as though it rang from some great distance.

Midnight came and then passed. Hayden began to wonder if in fact Madame Adair had been spared—the Jacobins would not come. But then, before the half-hour rang, he heard the sound of horses' hooves and then muffled voices. Two torches appeared, illuminating men on horseback.

Madame Adair wrung his hand a second and put a knuckle to her lip, but then mastered herself and rose to her feet. Hayden did the same, and she spun and pressed herself against him a moment. Pulling free, she kissed him once upon the lips and then stepped away, crossing the grass towards the gate that led to the lane.

Hayden followed her—he could not allow her to face this mob alone. Just before the gate they paused and watched the torches approaching, riders moving in the bloody light. Too soon these men were at the gate, then through, alighting from their saddles. They numbered a half-dozen—soldiers, Hayden could see.

"Madame Adair?" one of them enquired.

"Yes," she managed, though she could hardly breathe. *"C'est moi."*

"That's him," one of the men interjected. He stepped forward into the dull light—a French naval officer. "Capitaine Hayden of the *Themis*. I would know him anywhere."

Fifteen

He had no coat. He had been hustled away so abruptly that he had left his French captain's coat hanging in his room. The evening was cool, but not cold, and after the harsh nights he had spent in the wreck Hayden was certain he would endure.

He was seated in the back of a small cart, across from him the naval lieutenant armed with a pistol, ahead a driver and an armed soldier. There were men on horseback, including a lieutenant or captain; in the poor light, Hayden was not sure which.

The look upon Madame Adair's face when he did not deny the lieutenant's claim was something he would never forget.

"No, no," she had protested. "He is Capitaine Mercier!"

But he was not, and she had looked at him, first in surprise and then betrayal. He had felt so very low as they loaded him into the cart.

Betrayal of trust seemed to be what defined him, suddenly. He had betrayed Henrietta, then his men by abandoning them, and now Madame Adair, who had given her complete trust to him. For a man who took pride in acting honourably, even at great cost to himself, this was the strangest feeling. Who would think well of him now? Even Philip Stephens might withdraw his support, or so he imagined.

As the cart rolled, the men upon the bench spoke quietly, and laughed occasionally, as did the men on horseback. He had not been manacled or put in irons or even bound, but perhaps they could see he was not strong enough to escape, though it did not stop him from contemplating such a course.

The great worry now was how the local authorities would respond to Hayden's claiming to have been a French sea officer. It was, he realised, a foolish thing to have done and something he would almost certainly not have claimed had he not been so utterly spent and confused when he woke. If the authorities named him a spy and sent him to Paris, he would more than likely not leave that city alive—and he could not claim to be with child.

Rest was the physic for Hayden's present condition, and it was all he could do to stay in his seat. Every part of his being wanted to lie down on the deck of the cart and sleep. It would not matter in the least to him that the planks were hard, the road rutted, and the cart poorly sprung. Looking across at the lieutenant, he could see the man was engaged in the same struggle. He, too, was not recovered from their ordeal.

"What became of Capitaine Lacrosse, if I may ask?" Hayden enquired.

"He survived, Capitaine, but was recalled to Paris." The man shrugged, as if nothing else need be said.

"I am sorry to hear it," Hayden replied, and meant it. Lacrosse was an honourable man, and it did not improve Hayden's mood to learn that he had gone to his death. Fleeing might never have occurred to the Frenchman, or perhaps it had not been possible—he had been taken to Paris rather than simply summoned.

"There was much bad news that day," the lieutenant observed, shaking his head, "though not perhaps for you, Capitaine. Did you know that your ship was taken by English cruisers before it could make Brest?"

"My ship?" Hayden was confused.

"*Oui.* The frigate—*Themis.*"

"Was retaken by the English?"

"So it has been reported."

Hayden could have fallen from the cart. The bad-luck ship had had a bit of good luck for a change? He could hardly credit it.

Over and again, Hayden fell asleep only to catch himself as he slumped down. Brest—if that was indeed their objective—was many miles distant and would probably not be reached before midday.

It was light when Hayden awoke, jounced by a rut in the road. He lay half upon the little bench, across from the sleeping naval lieutenant who seemed to have lost his pistol.

Hayden sat up, groggily, and shook his aching head. For the life of him he could not remember lying down or falling asleep, which he found more than a little disconcerting. One of the horsemen noticed him and prodded the Navy lieutenant with a hand. The man opened his eyes, looked around, and then scrambled to a sitting position, searching the bottom of the cart.

"Where is my pistol?"

The man riding beside the driver reached back and passed the missing firearm to the lieutenant, butt first.

"Luckily, the *Anglais* fell asleep before you or he would have had your gun."

They all laughed, but only briefly. Fatigue had the better of all of them and no one was in particularly good humour, Hayden guessed.

The sea came into view, distantly, as they crested a hill, and it took a moment to realise that this was very close to the parts that he, Hawthorne, and Wickham had traversed when sent ashore by Captain Hart to view the French fleet. How very long ago that seemed!

If that was true, then the Rade de Brest was only a few miles off—but it was a very considerable body of water and it would take more than a day to travel round it.

Within half an hour Hayden realised that this would not be their course, as the little cart and its guard of honour wound down a hillside to a tiny village upon the shore. Here a Navy cutter lay to her anchor, her boat ashore, an *aspirant* awaiting their arrival.

"Is this the *Anglais*? Capitaine Charles 'ayden?" the boy asked.

"It is," the Army officer in charge replied. "You will take him and Lieutenant Nadeau as well."

The Navy lieutenant jumped down from the cart, trying to hide his weakness. "And you must treat him well, you little shit. I will tell your captain. He saved many a French sailor when our ship was wrecked."

The boy looked a little disconcerted by this sudden assault and only nodded in response.

"You must sign my papers," the Army man instructed, climbing down from his horse. "Do not think for a moment that you can escape that."

Signatures were duly scribed, insults traded between the two services, and Hayden and his keeper loaded into the ship's boat and rowed out to the cutter, where they climbed aboard. Men were waiting with irons for Hayden, but Lacrosse's lieutenant stepped in between.

"Those will not be needed, I can assure you."

This did not sit well with the captain of the cutter, an officer only a little older than Wickham, by his appearance. He and the lieutenant stepped away and conferred a moment, and when they returned the captain told his men that the irons could be dispensed with, and he bowed to Hayden.

"You are welcome aboard, Capitaine."

"*Merci.*" Hayden was more than a little surprised, but the intervention of Lacrosse's lieutenant appeared to have worked some small miracle. The anchor was weighed and the little ship got under sail.

There was only a little wind, so the cutter drifted along, the shores of the Rade creeping past.

It seemed cruel that such weather would arrive now. Had the day been clear when *Les Droits de l'Homme* was chased, they would have seen the shore from many miles away and not been wrecked. Yet this spring day seemed almost painfully fair to Hayden. Only a few days previously, he had been wandering along the borders of the land of the dead. Now here he was, sailing upon the Rade de Brest, caressed by a sweet-smelling breeze. Perhaps tomorrow would see him in great danger, but for the next few hours he would be beyond harm.

He wondered what had become of Madame Adair. Had the Jacobins come that night, as she believed they would? Had they taken her away? Certainly, she would be found guilty if so. Her only hope for survival then would be the almost impossibly slim chance that Hayden's seed had taken root in her womb. These melancholy thoughts were so at odds with the day and his present circumstances that he could hardly bear to contemplate them.

He turned his mind to Henrietta and his betrayal. Given that Madame Adair was an exemplary person who did not deserve persecution, Hayden somehow did not feel that what he had done was wrong. Yet he felt a strange sense of guilt over it all the same. The fact that the experience had not been entirely without pleasure seemed to make a lie of his justification.

The whole afternoon was required to cross the bay and arrive at the naval station on the north shore. Here some time was wasted as the captain of the cutter and Lacrosse's lieutenant tried to learn to whom Hayden should be delivered. While he waited, Hayden had an exceptional view of the French fleet and made very careful note of what ships were present and how ready for sea they appeared to be.

Finally, Hayden was handed over to three guards and took his leave of Lacrosse's man, thanking him for his kind treatment.

"Capitaine Lacrosse had a high opinion of you, Capitaine," the lieutenant explained. "I have done this for him."

"I am grateful," Hayden said. "If you meet Capitaine Lacrosse again, give him my thanks."

"I will, sir," but there was, in the man's eye, something that told Hayden he did not expect to see Lacrosse again in this life.

Hayden was led into the citadel, which was both great and labyrinthine. The general direction that they seemed to be going, however, was down. Eventually, they came to the lockup, and it was not a healthful place. After passing a number of large cells occupied by gaunt-looking men, a cell was opened by a guard, and Hayden sent in.

"Why are you putting this Frenchman in with us?" one of the prisoners asked in French.

"You may give it over, Mr Wickham. They smoked me."

"Ah," the midshipman said. "I am sorry to hear it."

Very quickly, Hayden learned that no one knew why they were being held in Brest or where they were going to be imprisoned.

"Certainly, they have prisons for foreigners," Barthe said, somewhat offended that they were in a common prison for Frenchmen.

"They do, Mr Barthe, but perhaps there is some administrative dispute about to which one we should be confined."

Mr Barthe made a growling sound.

To his great relief, Hayden found all of his men from the wreck present but for poor Franks, whose body had washed up on the beach. They were none of them hale, and the youngest of them were not the least affected. Though the cell was not large, Hayden managed to find a moment, when most of the men were sleeping, to speak to Griffiths.

Griffiths, like everyone, appeared frail and stiff, as though still affected with the cold from their ordeal. "I thought Mr Ransome might not survive, but he is on the mend, Captain. All the midshipmen were knocked back, but they are thriving now. Better food would be the best physic, but none of us has any money to buy victuals, as we were all robbed as we lay on the beach."

"I was treated the same," Hayden told him. "And yourself, Doctor? How do you fare?"

"Well enough. I cannot say I thrived, lying exposed to the elements upon the deck of a wrecked ship, but I feel my strength returning . . . If only I could get warm!"

"Everyone says the same. Perhaps a good fever is needed."

The doctor's face turned dark. "Do not even jest about such things. Prisoners are breeding grounds for fevers of all the worst sorts."

"I was not thinking—indeed, my mental powers appear to have been much reduced, as they were by the blow to my head some months ago."

"I am sure we all feel exactly the same, Captain. Another half a day and I believe we would have begun to lose our own men. That is how close we all came to death."

"Rest, I am certain, will do much to restore our vigour. If I could but sleep. Nightmares haunt me the moment I close my eyes—all to do with being trapped in the ship, drowning in darkness." Hayden shivered.

"My own dreams are much the same," the doctor admitted. "I dare say, we shall all suffer from this malady for some weeks or even months."

Hayden had little doubt that the doctor was right—all of the men slept but poorly, moaned in their sleep, and started awake often in the greatest possible distress. The cells in the Brest citadel were deep within the foundations, where daylight could not penetrate. The air was noisome and dank, and the single tallow candle granted each cell did not even send its light so far as the corners. There were tales of men living in such misery for decades, but Hayden suspected that few lasted more than a handful of years; disease and despair preyed upon the inmates as effectively as the guillotine. It was Hayden's hope that his men would be moved to some better place soon, though he dreaded them being marched any distance in their present states. None would go very far before they collapsed.

If not for the distant ringing of the citadel bells marking the passing of hours, time would have appeared to have abandoned its duty. Some effort was made to keep up the spirits of the men. The cell was swept and cleaned as best they could, duties were assigned for water and waste that must be dealt with. Stories were told, even old saws that had often been heard before were brought out and made welcome.

"Tell us about rounding the horn again," someone would say to Barthe at least once a day, and the sailing master would oblige and tell the same story, differing only, from one telling to the next, in the height of the seas and ferocity of the winds. Songs were sung by individuals, and some by everyone who could muster the energy.

When the two daily meals were brought, Hayden would press the guards and ask if they knew what would be done with them or if there was not some official who could speak to him, but each time the answers were the same—they knew nothing and no official wished to climb down so many stairs. Talk began that they had been forgotten. That no one in England knew they lived. They would rot in the dark.

Hayden would cut such talk short and call for a song or a story. The spirits of the men must not be allowed to sink too low. Melan-

cholia was a disease as real as gaol fever, and Hayden did not wish to
see it take hold among his crew.

Several days passed in this way, and then, in the forenoon of a day
no one could name or fix a number to, a troop of guards led by an
officer appeared outside their cell, a gaoler in tow. To everyone's
surprise, the door was swung wide, and the officer beckoned them
out in a manner that appeared almost amiable.

"*Come,*" he said in French, "*you are to accompany me.*"

The sleeping were roused, and the rest gathered their resources
and rose stiffly. "Where are we going?" Hayden asked. "To a prison?"

The officer shrugged. "It is not for me to say, Capitaine. Bring
your men along, if you please."

The British sailors trooped out and, with difficulty, ascended the
many steps, climbing up through the levels of the citadel until they
came out into blinding sunlight, then descended a stair into a gravel
courtyard.

Here they were met by a group of officers and attendants, one of
whom, Hayden was delighted to see, was Capitaine Raymondde
Lacrosse.

"Capitaine Lacrosse," Hayden said in French, "I am pleased to see
you well, sir."

"And I you, Capitaine. So many men were lost. You must have
been touched by God to have survived." Lacrosse smiled.

"Do you know where we are being sent? To what prison? My
men are not yet recovered enough to make a long march."

"You shall make the shortest march possible—a stroll, I should
call it." He smiled. "Down to the quay, Capitaine Hayden, and
aboard a ship."

Hayden was confused. "How far do they send us, then?"

"Not so far. You will be home tomorrow or the day next." He
smiled again. "I have been in Paris working on your behalf, Capi-

taine Hayden. Once I had convinced my superiors that *Les Droits de l'Homme* had a fatal flaw—her lower gun-deck was too near the water for us to open the gunports in anything but a calm—I was absolved of all blame and reinstated to my position. I then set out to convince them that without you and your crew many more lives would have been lost. And I must say they were moved to hear of the loss of your bosun caused by French sailors. It has been agreed, therefore, to return you and your men to England. It took some time to arrange this with your government, but they have now agreed to allow a single transport to carry you all to Portsmouth and return here without being molested by your cruisers. It is, I believe, unprecedented and a singular honour by both nations."

Hayden could not believe what he was hearing. "Do I dream, Capitaine Lacrosse. This seems . . . impossible."

"It is more than possible, my friend, it is a *fait accompli*. You have but to accompany me down to the quay and you will set out this day." He turned to another officer standing by. "Is everything in order?"

"Would Capitaine Hayden object to signing these forms for my records?"

"Would you mind, Capitaine?" Lacrosse asked. "Bureaucrats, you know."

Hayden signed everywhere he was asked, only glancing briefly at the documents, trusting that Lacrosse would not be involved in anything underhanded—he was too honourable.

And so they made their way down to the quay, a few guards in company, though they appeared not at all concerned about their charges and were quite friendly and amiable to all concerned.

"You appear quite hale, Capitaine," Hayden observed. "Given our ordeal, you have recovered rapidly."

"I have been blessed with a strong constitution, Capitaine

Hayden—a great blessing in our profession. Ah, here," he said, gesturing to a small gate. "We have but a brief stop to make here."

They were led in past guards to a barracks.

"I thought you might all desire a moment to bathe. Your clothes
will be taken and washed, and sent with you aboard the ship. The
commander of the citadel has ordered clothing for all of you."

To bathe was a luxury Hayden had dreamt of these last days, for
the bedding in the cells was lousy and they were all bitten and itch-
ing. They bathed and dressed in the clothing supplied—simple
breeches, hose, and a cotton shirt. Still, to be clean and dressed in
fresh clothing did something for their feelings of well-being that
Hayden could hardly describe. They emerged to a table set for them
and were offered all that they might eat. Lacrosse joined them and
was so amused by the looks upon the Englishmen's faces that he kept
laughing in spite of himself.

"I am sorry, Capitaine. Please excuse me, but if you could see the
looks upon your faces . . . No one yet seems to believe their good
fortune—though it stems from perhaps the worst fortune."

"We have gone from believing we would die, to being certain we
would spend some months at least in prison, to being pardoned and
sent home in very short order, Capitaine Lacrosse. It is a great deal
to take in."

"Indeed it is. I myself thought I might end upon the guillotine,
but it seems the man who drew the draughts of *Les Droits de l'Homme*
had some enemies in Paris and so he was blamed and has fled the
country, poor fellow. And instead of ending my days, or at the very
least my career, I am to be given another ship."

"And somehow you have even managed to have us sent home, for
which I can never thank you."

"Capitaine Hayden, it is I who can never thank you. When my
own officers refused to do their duty, to my lasting shame, your

own men stepped forward and took their places. Your sailing master and midshipman piloted one boat safely ashore, and I am certain that your bosun would have done the same had he been given the chance. His death will hang over me all the rest of my days."

"Sir, your position was made untenable by your own government, and you bear none of the blame," Hayden said firmly.

"You are too kind." He tapped his forehead. "Ah, I have almost forgotten to say that I lost everything in my cabin. Had you anything stored there, it would be gone too. I am sorry, but nothing was saved."

"I am sorry to hear it, Capitaine."

They came to a set of steps where a boat was waiting. *"C'est des Anglais pour la* Fortune, *Capitaine?"* a sailor called out.

"Yes, these are the men. You will treat them well. They saved many French lives and lost some of their own."

"We have all heard, Capitaine. Be at peace; we shall treat them like honoured guests."

Lacrosse turned to Hayden. "I must take my leave of you, Capitaine."

"I am in your debt, Capitaine Lacrosse. I do hope when next we meet it shall not be as enemies."

"I hope the same, Capitaine Hayden." He looked at Hayden oddly. "You have no coat, Capitaine?"

"It was lost."

"Then you will take mine," and before Hayden could protest he removed it and pushed it into Hayden's hands. "I will not hear otherwise. It will be cold upon the ship this night. *Bon voyage.*"

He thanked all the English sailors, especially Barthe and Wickham, and not without a show of emotion. The remains of Hayden's crew climbed into the boat and took their places, but before they could push off there came a shout from down the dock to hold the boat.

Hayden looked at Hawthorne, who sat nearby.

"Have they changed their minds?" he asked.

"I do not know."

Three guards came hurrying along the quay, a man held between them.

"Ah, just in time," Lacrosse announced.

The prisoner was Rosseau—Hayden's cook!

Lacrosse put a hand on Rosseau's shoulder, and the little Frenchman looked as though he might collapse from fear. "This member of your crew was mistakenly thought to be French, no doubt because he speaks our tongue almost as well as you, Capitaine Hayden. But clearly he is English."

The manacles were removed from Rosseau's hands and the terrified Frenchman was bundled into the boat, almost too weak to make it on his own.

Lacrosse waved the boat away, and it set out across the Rade de Brest.

Rosseau hid his face in his hands, and his shoulders heaved between deep gasps.

Wickham put a hand on his shoulder. "You are safe. Be of good heart."

"I was . . . on my way to the guillotine . . ." Rosseau managed.

"For God's sake, man," Wickham whispered, "do not speak!"

Sixteen

"Y ou appear very thoughtful this evening, Mrs Hertle," Robert Hertle observed, putting a hand over the fingers she had tucked into the crook of her husband's arm.

Robert had appeared unannounced, as often he did, for no one could ever predict the day a ship would return to harbour, and for the past two days she had been so utterly happy and content that she had begun to wonder if she did not look rather girlish, though in truth she hardly cared.

"Do I, my dear? I must be thinking always how much happiness your sudden return has brought me."

Happiness was in the very air that evening, among the gathered Carthew family and their guests, but not everyone partook of it. She let her gaze wander over the familiar faces. In a room of notably joyful souls, Elizabeth Hertle wondered who, next to Penelope, was least pleased with the proceedings. Mrs Hertle hovered near to her youngest daughter, attempting, largely in vain, to lift her spirits. And though Pen was striving to put on a brave face, far too often she seemed about to weep. Mrs Carthew appeared happier than Elizabeth would have guessed, given the reservations she had recently expressed regarding a match between Henrietta and Frank Beacher. Perhaps her motherly instinct had come to the fore when she realised her lovely daughter was engaged to a gentleman whose character she knew, from long familiarity, was in all ways above reproach.

Elizabeth put this question aside a moment. Who the happiest person was anyone could tell; Frank Beacher looked as though he had been granted every wish he had ever imagined. Miss Henrietta Carthew was to be his wife, and he was transported into a state of near bliss, a smile always upon his lips, his gaze ever returning to his intended.

Poor Pen, Elizabeth thought, such happiness must be like a knife in her heart.

Henrietta, who was capable of a near saintly grace when it suited her, had donned that persona and smiled upon everyone and everything as though they gave her unimaginable joy—but there was, for the briefest second, now and then, a tightening of the skin around her eyes that Elizabeth had come to recognise as distress or perhaps disquiet.

Disquiet was precisely the word that Elizabeth would have chosen to describe her own feelings—not her feelings towards her returned husband, which were never in doubt—but her feelings towards the match that had been announced that evening. Despite the approbation of Henrietta's father and two Carthew sisters—and even Beacher's friend Wilder—Elizabeth felt that a terrible mistake was being made. Not that she thought poorly of Frank Beacher—like everyone in the room, she believed him integrity brought to life. He would cherish Henri and do everything within his power to assure her happiness, she had no doubt of it. *But* . . . she could not feel joy or even moderate satisfaction. She had pushed Henrietta in this direction and now she regretted it most profoundly and she could not even say with certainty why. For no reason that she could explain, she felt that, in time, Frank Beacher, even more than Henrietta, would be made entirely miserable by this union. And then it occurred to her—Henri would never be able to love Frank as he imagined she would. Oh, she might love and respect him and care for his happiness, but there would be always be something amiss—she would never give herself over to him completely, body and soul. And he would spend his life always yearning for a love that could not be. She felt sorry for him already—and for Henri as well.

Mr Carthew cleared his throat, caught everyone's attention, and then held aloft a glass. "Is everyone's glass charged? Then let me propose a toast that I am sure will win Mrs Carthew's approval; may Mr Beacher and our dear Henrietta be blessed with children."

Everyone was willing to drink to such a proposition, and Elizabeth, with Robert at her side, crossed over to Mrs Carthew to say how she wished she would soon have a grandchild. At that moment a servant entered the room, spotted Mrs Carthew, and came immediately to her.

"Pardon the intrusion, ma'am. There is a gentleman caller at the door—a sea officer. He has asked to speak with Miss Henrietta on a matter he describes as of the greatest urgency."

"How very odd," Mrs Carthew interrupted. "Did he give his name?"

"Yes, ma'am. Charles Hayden."

Mrs Carthew put a hand to her heart and, though she opened her mouth three times, could make no words issue forth.

"I will attend to this caller," Robert stated, gently removing his wife's hand from his arm and immediately making his way towards the door.

Mrs Carthew looked at Elizabeth. "Who in their senses would come to our home and make such a claim?"

"I do not know, but whoever it is, Captain Hertle will see him on his way."

And then, without either saying a word, they made for the door in Robert's wake.

"What is it, Mother?" Cassandra asked as her mother hurried past. "Whatever is the matter?"

This caught everyone's attention, and as Elizabeth and Mrs Carthew passed out of the door, half clinging to each other, a general enquiry followed.

As no guests were expected that night, the entrance hall was poorly lit. A man stood inside the door, too stooped and thin to be Charles Hayden, certainly. Elizabeth perceived that immediately.

Robert did not hesitate but approached the stranger directly, his shoulders tight with anger.

"Robert!" the stranger said. "Thank God!"

"Charles . . . ? My God! Charles!"

And the two friends all but threw themselves into each other's embrace.

"How is it you are here?" Robert managed as they pounded each other on the back. "I was informed you had perished. The Admiralty think you dead."

"They did, but no longer. I will tell you the whole story, but . . ."

There was a swishing of gowns behind, and Elizabeth turned to see the remaining family and guests wedged in a little knot, staring past one another at the two murky figures before the door.

The two friends released each other, and Robert noticed all the others staring. "Henrietta," he said, "it is Charles . . . returned to us by what agency I do not know."

It was one of those moments, Elizabeth thought, so completely unexpected and fraught with emotion that no one knew the proper course of action or even how they should feel.

Henrietta gazed, in either amazement or confusion, at the shadow-man standing by Robert, then at the face of Frank Beacher.

Then back again to Hayden. In what appeared to be three strides, she crossed the hallway and threw herself against Charles' chest, her face pressed into his neck. Neither said a word but clung to each other.

Elizabeth turned towards Mr Beacher, who stood looking on helplessly, his mouth slightly open, and she thought for a mad instant that his soul had slipped out of that opening and left him—a husk awaiting a bitter wind.

Seventeen

There was only the feel of her pressed softly against him, the scent of her hair, her chest heaving as she tried to catch her breath or not to sob, or both.

"My letter found you . . . ?" he whispered.

She nodded.

Thank God, Hayden thought, all will be well. Now, if he could only find a few moments alone with—

"Henrietta . . ." an older male voice intruded. "My dear, think of your husband . . ."

Opening his eyes, Hayden saw a gentleman approaching—almost certainly Henrietta's father.

"Henrietta?" the man coaxed a bit more firmly.

Hayden pried Henrietta far enough away that he could see her face.

"*Husband?* Whatever does he mean?"

"I–I believed you had betrayed me . . . And Frank—Mr Beacher— asked for my hand . . . It was only after I had been informed of your death that I received your letter . . ."

"My poor Henri," Hayden whispered. "What have you been through?"

"Henrietta, really," Mr Carthew insisted. "We are happy to see

Captain Hayden alive, but you have engaged your affections elsewhere . . ." Mr Carthew came forward, his gaze now on Hayden.
"Captain, my daughter has been through a great deal. I believe she
needs rest and some time to think . . . Come, Henrietta." He glanced
over at Robert. "Captain Hertle . . . ?"

But Robert, who was never indecisive, hesitated.

"Can you speak with your friend, Captain?" Mr Carthew
prompted him. "Privately . . ."

Reluctantly, Robert turned to Hayden. "Let us walk out into the
garden, Charles . . ."

Henrietta was disentangled from his grasp, though gently, by
both Mr and Mrs Carthew. Robert stepped between Hayden and
the gathered Carthews, though Hayden suspected it was one of the
young men whom Robert intended to separate him from.

Henrietta was led away, though she glanced back twice, so disconcerted that speech appeared to have abandoned her.

Robert gently took Hayden's arm and ushered him towards the
door.

"What in the world has transpired in my absence?" Hayden demanded as they passed out into the night.

"Let me call for my carriage, Charles. There is an inn not too
distant . . ."

Robert stood by a small and slightly unbalanced table in Hayden's
newly procured lodgings. As he poured wine into their glasses, the
table tilted noticeably to his left, the leg "clicking" as it contacted
the floor.

"Elizabeth would be the one to explain all that has occurred in
your absence," Robert began, setting the bottle down so that the
table then tilted back again. "I have it all at second hand from her.

It began with these French *émigrées*—the mother who claimed you had married her comely daughter. Had you really assisted them to come to England?" He passed a glass to Hayden.

"At the request of as eminent a personage as Sir Gilbert Elliot . . ." When Hayden had been led aboard the transport in Brest to be carried home to England, he thought the nightmare he had been living had come to an end. Spring had spread its warmth over that small quarter of the world and all would be renewed. But instead he felt like he had been returned to another part of the nightmare—from which he could not wake.

"I was at sea at the time, as were you, Charles, but I am told these women went about London with such confidence, flashing a marriage certificate, spreading charm everywhere—"

"Running up debts in establishments that would never have extended credit to me, blackening my name . . ."

"Exactly so. News of the claims of these women found its way to Henrietta—and Mrs Hertle as well—accompanied by reports of the alleged Mrs Hayden's astonishing beauty . . ." Robert stopped and looked at his friend expectantly.

"That part, at least, was true—I have seldom seen a more handsome woman—nor had Sir Gilbert, I expect, which led him to make such a request of me. Never have I regretted any favour so much as that one!"

"Henrietta retreated here, to Box Hill and her family. Frank Beacher, who has been a friend to all the Carthews for most of his life, and an ardent admirer of Henrietta almost that entire time, took that opportunity to confess his feelings to poor Henri."

"Taking advantage of my absence, the blackguard!"

"I will tell you, Charles, he is very far from being a blackguard. He is as amiable a young man as you shall ever hope to meet and entirely devoted to Henri, who at the moment he spoke believed you had betrayed her and married another. What happened next, I must confess, Charles, was my fault. I had reports of the loss of the *Themis* and then the wreck of *Les Droits de l'Homme*. It appeared certain that you had not survived. Immediately, I wrote Mrs Hertle and she conveyed the news to Henrietta and her family. I was not present, but Elizabeth assures me Henri was more distraught than can be imagined. Frank Beacher is very dear to her—like a brother— and no doubt, feeling betrayed and wanting to feel safe and protected, she accepted Beacher's offer, though not before she had learned—falsely, it turned out—that you were dead." He looked at Hayden again. "And here you are—alive if somewhat reduced."

Hayden could not sit still but rose and paced across the room. "Do you think Henrietta's feelings could have altered so entirely in my absence? Will she go through with her marriage to this man Beacher?"

"Personally, I believe Henri's feelings more constant than that . . . Certainly, she will not wish to injure Frank Beacher, who is not only a family friend but whose suit is looked upon with great favour by all of the Carthews—though not my good wife, who has strong reservations."

"Then I have one person on my side."

"I am always on your side, Charles. I hope you know that. Had I been in London when these French women appeared, I would not have accepted their claim without hearing it from you."

Hayden felt a tide of gratitude flood through him. "Thank you, Robert. It is a comfort to know that someone did not lose faith in me."

"I will certainly speak on your behalf. There is one matter I must broach with you, Charles. I know it must seem to you that Beacher has taken advantage of your absence in a most dishonourable manner, but it must be remembered that everyone believed you had married and then that you had died. Were you to demand he walk out with you, I do not think you would endear yourself to any member of the Carthew family, including Henrietta. Frank Beacher, as I have said, is like a son and a brother to them."

Hayden did resent the actions of this young man—but he was not unaware that Robert very likely understood the way of things in the Carthew house far better than he. "I take your point, Robert . . . as tempted as I might be. I will tell you, though, I am in such a reduced state I doubt I could hold a duelling pistol steady enough to hit a mail coach. It should be me in fear of him."

"I doubt Beacher will challenge you. Not that I think him to be shy . . . but he has never had reason in his life to discover if he is brave or no. He also knows that Henri is deeply attached to you and that were he to harm you she would not forgive him."

"Then if I could induce him to shoot me I might have Henri turn against him?"

"It does seem a bit rash, however."

"Yes, I have never enjoyed being shot, and I have not got my surgeon here to patch me up again." Hayden stopped, looking out of the window in what he believed was the direction of Box Hill. "Poor Henrietta . . . What has she been through these past weeks? I cannot imagine."

Seldom in his life had Hayden felt like a hypocrite—he was ever scrupulous in his dealings so that he might avoid guilt, which he found a very unpleasant emotion. But now he did feel guilt, if not remorse. He *had* betrayed Henrietta, and with a French woman too, though not the one everybody had supposed—not with the exquisite Héloïse, but with a desperate woman who was both married and a mother. The fact that everyone seemed to feel great remorse at believing the worst of Hayden was not lost upon him. But they had been wrong only in the particulars.

That night, in Brittany, he had never imagined how he would perceive his actions only a short time later. What he felt now was *unworthy*. A liar. An adulterer. And the fact that he was not actually engaged to Henrietta at the time did not make it right. He could not hide behind some legal detail. He *had* betrayed Henrietta and with a French woman, too.

"Charles . . . ?"

Hayden looked over to find Robert gazing at him with poorly concealed distress.

"Do you need a doctor?"

"Do I look so poorly?"

"I have no doubt you have been through a great deal."

Hayden dropped back into his seat and began to tell his friend of the events that had unfolded since last he departed England, leaving out only one incident, upon which he had been sworn to absolute secrecy.

"She has accepted your offer, and so have her family," Wilder found himself expounding to his friend. "Your own father and mother have not yet arranged the details of property and so forth, but that is a mere formality—"

"That does not mean it cannot be broken off," Beacher almost moaned.

"No, but you shall have the right to seek civil action if so."

"Against Henrietta and her family? They have treated me like a son and brother these twenty years. I would not even contemplate it."

"I shall not dispute it with you, but certainly a barrister would argue that you are fully entitled to a settlement."

Beacher waved a hand in dismissal. "I do not care a fig for a settlement. It is Henrietta's hand or nothing." They were in the room where Mr Carthew's collection was slowly being brought to order. Over a half-made primate skeleton laid out upon a table, Beacher turned towards his friend. "Do you or do you not think she will honour her decision?"

Wilder considered this for a moment "She is . . . most fond of you—"

"I am not a complete fool, Wilder! I do realise that her feelings for him are stronger than her feelings for me. Over time I am quite certain that will change, but for now I must sit by like a cuckold fool waiting upon the will of others. I do wish this Navy man would leave. Does he not understand that she is my fiancée? He treats me with utter disrespect, contempt even. I have half a mind to go to his inn and demand he quit Kent immediately."

"And if he says 'no'? What will you do then?"

"I am not afraid of him, Wilder, no matter what you think. And what would it matter anyway? If I lose Henrietta, I lose everything. I should not care to live."

"I am of the firm belief that we should reserve melodrama for the theatre, where all of those who have died in the name of love are reborn at the curtain call. We are talking about your actual life, Beacher, not a fictional one. The man might well shoot you . . . dead. After all, it is you who stands in his way. I do not think you should offer him the opportunity."

"You do think I am afraid of him, do you not?"

"I wish I did. Then I could trust you to do nothing foolish. Do bear in mind, Beacher, that though your courage might well equal his own, your experience does not. Faced with shooting another, his hand will not shake nor will his resolve waver. I beg you, Beacher, as a friend, do not walk out with this man or give him cause to demand satisfaction. There is also this other small matter of the law. After all, he is an officer and may fight a duel, but you are not, and, even should you survive, charges could be brought against you."

"I should not let that stop me, as it is unlikely that any charges should ever be brought where an officer is involved."

"Do not be certain . . ."

Beacher picked up a bone from the table and turned it in his hand. "You are the disinterested party, Wilder—more so than I— you must give me the benefit of your counsel. I do not wish Henrietta to see this man. As her husband-to-be, I feel I am within my right to demand that she does not. Do you not agree?"

It was Wilder's turn to take up a small bone from the table and give it his attention. "It is my distinct impression, from my conversations with Miss Cassandra, that the sisters Carthew are united in their desire never to marry a tyrant."

"But, Wilder, I am convinced that if she speaks with this man . . . I am lost."

"I do not think that forbidding such a meeting will aid your suit. Rather, I think if she speaks with the captain and chooses you, then you may rest assured for the rest of your days that Henrietta Carthew desired you instead of merely settling upon you when the real object of her affection was thought lost."

"Very easily said, but if she does choose the Navy man . . . ?"

"Then it will be time for you to quit this house and make a life that does not include Miss Henrietta Carthew."

"Above all things, she should not be allowed to see this Navy man," Cassandra declared, looking around at her father and gathered sisters. "Above all things."

Mr Carthew nodded his agreement, but Penelope merely pulled at an errant thread in her skirt.

"I believe she *should* speak with him," she offered. "Indeed she must, else she will never know her own heart in this matter." She glanced up at a circle of disapproving faces. "You all know that she accepted Frank's offer only because she was heartbroken. She wanted a man who would never betray her. You know it to be true. However much you might wish Henri to marry Mr Beacher, she only agreed to because she was in such a state. Had she been in her senses, she would never have said 'yes.'"

"Perhaps it is you, Penelope, who wishes that were true," Cassandra said.

"My own feelings are of no consequence in this matter—as has been made perfectly clear to me by everyone from the very beginning."

Anne cleared her throat. "I am of the opinion that this is Henrietta's choice, not ours. I would also like to remind all present that, before the false reports that Captain Hayden had married, Elizabeth, Captain Hertle, and our own Henrietta held Captain Hayden in the highest possible regard. As much as we all esteem Frank Beacher, there is no reason to believe that Henrietta would not be happy with Captain Hayden. I say, do not interfere. It is neither our hearts nor our futures that hang in the balance."

"But there is a matter of propriety," Mr Carthew insisted. "Henrietta has accepted Frank Beacher's offer and should act accordingly. Most certainly, she should not be in contact with her former suitor—it is highly improper."

"Then she should make a clean break with Frank," Penelope informed the others, "so that there are no encumbrances upon her actions."

Mr Carthew seemed most distressed by his daughter's assertion. "I do not believe Henrietta's happiness will be best served by a union with Captain Hayden."

"Perhaps *happiness* is not Henrietta's sole reason for being," Anne interrupted. "She might tell you that other things are more important to her."

"I cannot think what they would be," Mr Carthew replied.

"Such as making a life with the man she loves," Anne said, "whatever the future might bring."

"That sounds very romantic," Mr Carthew answered, making no effort to hide his disapproval. "All well and good before the age of twenty, but a terrible hindrance thereafter."

"It were as though he had returned from the dead." Henrietta lay upon the divan, her mother and Elizabeth in attendance. "What does one say to a man who has returned from the underworld by some unknown path? I knew not what to say nor how to act . . . so I both acted and spoke poorly."

"You should write him a letter, Henrietta," Mrs Carthew said, "and inform him of what has occurred and tell him most directly that another has asked for your hand and that you have accepted."

"If the solution to this matter were only so easily found!" Henrietta responded, glancing at her cousin to gauge Elizabeth's reaction to Mrs Carthew's dictum.

"And why is it not?" Mrs Carthew demanded. "Mr Beacher asked for your hand and you agreed to become his wife. I shall bring you paper and ink."

"You shall not!" Henrietta responded, sitting up and lowering her feet to the floor.

"You do not intend to go back on your promise to Frank Beacher . . . do you?" Mrs Carthew enquired.

"But what of my promise to Charles Hayden?"

"I did not know he ever asked for your hand, my dear. Certainly, this is the first I have heard of it. Did he?"

"No, but we had come to an understanding . . . through our

letters . . . that upon his return he would ask and that I should say 'yes.' Most definitely, 'yes.'"

"He wrote that—most clearly—that he would ask for your hand?"

"Not in those exact words, but we both understood that he would. There was no lack of clarity upon this point."

"If a disinterested party were to read these letters, would they feel the same? Could it not be interpreted as wishing on your part?"

"Mother! Are you a barrister now? Captain Hayden and I had an understanding, whether it was clearly stated or no. We were not in doubt. Had it not been for the lies and duplicity of those French women, we would be happily united and I would be the future Mrs Hayden."

Mrs Carthew looked very grim and disapproving. "So you will break your promise to Mr Beacher?"

Henrietta felt a wave of wretchedness break over her. "I do not know what I will do. I must have a moment to think. That is not an unreasonable desire, given what has occurred . . . would you not agree?"

"Most certainly you must have time to think, my dear." Elizabeth patted her hand. "Through no fault of your own, you have come to an understanding with two different gentlemen. There is no book of etiquette that will offer proper instruction on such a situation."

"I must differ with you, Mrs Hertle." Mrs Carthew rose from her chair and looked down upon her daughter and niece. "Mr Beacher has asked for Henrietta's hand and she has accepted. Captain Hayden might or might not have spoken—we cannot know. I will say nothing more but this—do not forget how wretchedly you felt when told Captain Hayden had departed this life. When next such a report reaches you, it will almost certainly be true. And Frank Beacher? He will have married elsewhere." She quit the room upon this note, leaving both niece and daughter rather speechless.

"You do see my dilemma, Elizabeth, do you not?" Henrietta asked in a small voice.

"Entirely, and there is no escaping that whatever decision you make you will injure one of these gentlemen. Do not think for a moment that there is any course that you might choose that will not lead to disappointment for either Mr Beacher or Captain Hayden. You must make a decision that will see to your happiness."

Henrietta's mood sank even lower. There was no doubt that Lizzie was correct and the idea of injuring either Frank or Charles caused her such distress she could hardly bear it. "Do you think Mama is correct? I have agreed to marry Frank Beacher . . . but I believed Charles lost at sea . . ."

"It is all the most dreadful muddle, Henri. The worst of it is that only you can make the decision that must be made. Neither Mr Beacher nor Charles will withdraw from the field."

"Oh, do not make it sound like a battle, Lizzie. It is not that. It is just the most unfortunate confusion that has ever been. I do not wish to injure Frank, who has been my friend and confidant all of my life. And I cannot bear to disappoint Charles, who was upon his ship fighting for England while his name was blackened and lies spread about him—none of which were the least true. It is Charles who has been treated most unfairly. But to go back on my word to Frank would be most unfair to him."

"You must 'go back on your word' with one of these gentlemen, Henri. I know you do not wish to contemplate it, but that is the truth."

Henrietta was all but overwhelmed by misery. Even worse, somehow she felt this situation was of her own making. If she had only had faith in Charles! But she had been disloyal and foolish. He had trusted her entirely, and she had lost trust the moment anything had been said against him. And who was more loyal and dutiful and honourable than Charles Hayden? She had a strange urge to beat herself as though this self-chastisement was so much less than she deserved.

"I will retire, Elizabeth," Henrietta announced, rising to her feet. "Though I fear I shall do nothing but lie awake all night and swing back and forth and forth and back, growing ever more distressed and miserable. But as you say, I have promised my hand to two gentlemen, and by morning I must decide whose offer I shall accept. Assuming, of course, that either gentleman will still want me by sunrise."

"I do not believe that is a worry." Elizabeth kissed her cousin on both cheeks. "I believe I shall sleep very lightly this night. If you have need of my company—I do not say counsel, for I do not believe I can be of any aid there—but there is often comfort in companionship."

"You are my dearest, most beloved friend, Lizzie."

"And no matter what you decide come morning, you will remain my most beloved cousin and friend as well."

"Thank you, Lizzie."

When Mrs Hertle quit the room, Henrietta did not retire to her chambers but instead began to pace back and forth the length of the floor. At one point she wondered, if one was to continue to do so all night, how many miles one would walk by morning. Not nearly enough, she thought, to have come to a decision.

It was some hours later that Captain Hertle crept into his wife's chamber, only to find Mrs Hertle sitting up in bed, a single candle burning.

"You are very late, my dear," she said as he pressed the door closed.

"I did not expect you to sit up waiting."

"No, no. I have not been able to sleep out of concern for poor Henri and Mr Beacher and Charles as well. Henri is beyond miserable. Given how careful she has always been to not encourage any young man towards whom she did not feel great affection, it is incomprehensible that she has landed in this situation—where she has promised her hand to two different men. How is Charles? He appeared so frail and aged, though the light was so very poor."

"He is frail and aged—though only temporarily, I hope. So few survived the wreck, and those that did lay out in the storm exposed to the worst of cold and icy rain and suffering great deprivation for three days and nights. He seems to have gone so far down the road towards death that only part of him could return . . ."

"Henri said something the same—that she did not know what to say or how to act when he appeared, as though he had come back from the dead."

"Well, as far as we are all concerned, he has done just that. Our own Lazarus. I am at once happier than I can say to have my dearest friend and brother returned, and distressed beyond words at both his state and the situation he has returned to. After what he has been through, he deserves so much better. He should have been most joyfully greeted by the woman he hoped to marry and embraced by her family and his own friends. Instead, he returns to find his intended betrothed to another, his name blackened, and his finances mired in the courts."

"But is he bearing up, my love?"

"He is Charles Hayden, my dear. That has not changed. A much-reduced and quieter Charles Hayden to be sure, but, even so, more formidable than most."

"Is he angry with poor Henri, do you think? She is very worried that he is."

Robert considered a moment. "I do not believe so. Angry with

Beacher, as you would expect, but even there he understands that Mr Beacher did not behave in a dishonourable fashion."

"Charles will not act rashly with regard to Beacher, I hope?"

"I cautioned him most earnestly on that matter, and I am quite sure he understood my point."

"You were a good friend there," Elizabeth said approvingly, "and not just to Charles."

They were both silent a moment. "There was one thing I found most odd in my conversation with Charles . . . I offered to carry a letter to Henrietta, which under the circumstances I believed would be a wise course for him . . . but he declined. Declined the opportunity to declare his feelings at the moment when Henri must choose between him and another."

"Clearly, he is not himself. The Charles of old would never have passed up such an opportunity."

"So I thought. As I left, I told him that it was my dearest hope that Henrietta would choose him, and do you know what he replied? That he was hardly worthy of her."

"He is not recovered from his ordeal. In a few weeks, he would think and act differently, surely."

"I agree."

"Unfortunately, Henri is in her chamber, no doubt lying awake, with two suitors upon her scale. To see Charles appear so near to death . . . it cannot weigh in his favour. A letter expressing the depth of his feeling . . . might have tipped the matter in his favour. Why ever do you think he would not write it?"

Eighteen

Mr Wilder did not lie awake all night wondering, like many others at Box Hill, but slept the deep, untroubled sleep of a young man blissfully unaware that sleep would never come so easily in future years. His awakening, however, was not so untroubled—a loud pounding upon the door of his chamber and a muffled female voice beyond expressing a state of heightened agitation dragged him into the conscious world.

He rolled heavily out of bed, staggered to the door, and opened it a crack. There, red-faced and out of breath, stood Penelope in the greatest possible distress.

"He has taken them!" she cried. "Taken them and gone off on horseback."

"Who has taken whom?" Wilder mumbled.

"Frank! He has taken Father's pistols and ridden off towards the village!"

Without a word, Wilder slammed his door shut and in all haste pulled on the first clothing that came to hand. Penelope continued to hammer upon his door all the while, until a moment later he hopped out on one foot, pulling on his hose.

"You are certain, Miss Penelope? He has pistols?"

"And shot and powder, too. The case is empty in Papa's workroom." She pointed towards a window. "I saw him set off down the lane towards the abbey ruins. And you know that leads into the village as well."

"Bloody fool!" he cursed under his breath. Then, to Penelope: "I will saddle a horse and take the road to the village; that will be quicker. Is Captain Hertle awake?"

"I do not believe so."

"Wake him, please. I shall go straight to the inn and stop Beacher from entering, if Captain Hertle would be so kind as to follow Beacher down the lane . . ."

"I will tell him . . ." And she ran off.

Wilder dashed to the stables, saddled a horse himself, and was just leading his mount out into daylight when Captain Hertle arrived, pulling on a coat. "You are going to the inn, Mr Wilder?"

"I am. By the main road. Will you go after Beacher? Penelope saw him go off down the lane towards the ruin."

"I will. Do not spare your horse, Mr Wilder. Even in his reduced state, Charles is fully capable of shooting Beacher stone dead. Fear will not deter him."

Wilder was on his horse and off at a gallop, the whole way hoping to see Beacher before him so that he might apprehend his friend and put an end to this foolishness. The road, however, was empty but for farm workers going out into the fields, and a few carts carrying wood and wool.

The stillness and beauty of the morning was lost upon Wilder, who pressed his poor mount forward, galloping the three miles and arriving with his horse in a sweat and foaming at the mouth. He passed the reins to an elderly hostler at the inn, who did not hide his disapproval at a horse being treated so.

Dashing inside, he found a naval officer seated at a table about to break his fast. He went to him immediately.

"Captain Hayden?"

The man looked up.

"I am Henry Wilder, Mr Frank Beacher's friend."

"Ah," the Navy man said, rising to his feet. "I wondered if Mr Beacher might send a friend to see me—"

"No, sir. That is not my intention at all. You see, I am afraid that my friend Beacher might be on his way here, and it is my purpose to apprehend him before he can do anything rash."

"Most commendable. Would you care to join me, Mr Wilder?"

"Thank you, sir." Wilder dropped into the chair opposite.

"Have you had a breakfast?" the Navy man asked calmly.

"I have barely had time to dress."

"Then let us call for some more food. Now, why do you think Mr Beacher might be coming here to see me?"

"He left Box Hill this morning with a brace of pistols belonging to Mr Carthew."

"Then apprehending him would be the best possible course of action. Were Mr Beacher to ask me to walk out with him, I should not wish to do it; shooting a friend of the Carthew family, despite the wrong he has done me, would not be to my liking. But I am a sea officer and I am all but obliged to accept a challenge. The service expects it. I should very much prefer not to be put in such a position, for though I might wish to decline it is very difficult for me to do so. Do you understand?"

"Completely. That is why I have all but broken my horse racing here."

"Let us watch out of the window while we dine. If we do see your friend then, I suggest you go out and use all of your powers to dissuade him, if at all possible."

"He should have to shoot me to gain entrance to this inn, Captain Hayden."

"I dare say, Mr Wilder," Hayden said, hiding a hint of a smile, "that is carrying friendship too far by half."

Robert Hertle bent over the neck of his mount, racing down the narrow lane, all the while thinking that he had been a more accomplished horseman when younger. Years aboard a ship had eroded that skill, little by little, until he could hardly call himself a horseman at all.

Dew glittered upon the grass and the spiders' webs suspended between the tallest stalks. Birds flitted from bush to secret bush, filling the air with their songs of love. As Hertle approached the little glen that held the abbey ruin, he heard the sharp crack of a pistol and feared he was too late.

Fully expecting to see Frank Beacher stretched out upon the ground, bleeding away his young life, he broke out of the trees into the grassy meadow. And there stood Beacher, pistol raised. Smoke erupted from the barrel of his firearm, the report an assault upon the stillness of the morning, but his target was not Charles Saunders Hayden. It appeared he had fatally wounded an old hornbeam not ten paces distant.

"Mr Beacher!" Robert called.

Beacher turned towards him, aiming his pistol stiffly down towards the ground.

"Captain Hertle—is it not early to be abroad?"

Hertle dismounted, taking hold of his horse's bridle. "Indeed it is, and early for the slaying of trees as well. May I ask what you are about?"

Beacher looked suddenly embarrassed. "As I thought it possible I might be asked to walk out with a certain gentleman, it seemed most prudent to reacquaint myself with the duelling pistol, as I had not fired one for many years." He glanced up at Robert. "But then, perhaps you have come looking for me in the capacity of Captain Hayden's friend . . . ?"

"Indeed, no. I have come in the capacity of *your* friend. Mr Wilder feared you had taken Mr Carthew's pistols and gone off to the inn to challenge Charles."

"No, only thoughts of preserving my life brought me here."

"Then I should say you have no need of this exercise. I have known Charles Hayden all my life, and I can say with certainty that he will not seek satisfaction in this case. He understands, despite appearances, that you acted only after everyone, including Miss Henrietta, believed he had married another."

"Then he feels no animosity towards me?"

"I think he does feel a certain resentment, but he is above all things a reasonable man. And reason dictates that he await the outcome with as much equanimity and grace as he might muster. I wonder where Mr Carthew obtained such a brace? I have hardly seen a handsomer pair of Queen Annes. May I?"

Beacher passed him the gun, and Robert turned it over in his hands. "Perfectly acceptable for duels," he pronounced, "but of no use in a fight. Turning off the barrels to load them takes half a day. Accurate, though. I have often coveted a pair myself." Checking to be certain the barrel was not too hot, he tucked the pistol into his belt, and then stooped to retrieve the other, which Beacher had laid upon the ground after firing it.

"Let us ride back to the Box Hill. It is a fine morning and I grow hungry. It is my experience that no matter what troubles weigh upon me, a meal will always lift my spirits. Do you not agree, Mr Beacher?"

"I have not always found it so, Captain, but certainly the body requires sustenance even if the soul does not."

"But the soul also needs sustenance . . . of a different sort, certainly . . ."

And so Robert accompanied Beacher back to the home of the Carthew family and avowed that he would not let the other out of his sight the remainder of the day. He would hide the duelling pistols away as well—almost certainly an unnecessary precaution, but he did not wish to leave that particular matter to chance.

A servant was sent to recall Wilder from the inn and the slumber of the Carthew home rose like a blind.

Elizabeth could not return to sleep after her husband was wakened, and so she rose and paced until she sighted Captain Hertle returning with Frank Beacher, clearly unharmed, and just as clearly a brace of pistols tucked into her husband's belt.

Only then did she go in search of Henrietta, whom she found in the library pulling on a light pelisse in preparation for an outing. She appeared to have spent the night in the library without any rest at all, for her beautiful eyes were set deep into blue-grey shadows, and her skin appeared pale and mottled.

"You have not had a moment of sleep, have you?" Elizabeth said upon seeing her cousin.

"Sleep? Who could sleep faced with such a decision?"

"And where is it you go, my dear?"

Henrietta finished pulling on her pelisse and stared at Elizabeth Hertle.

"To speak with Charles," she replied softly.

"And what will you tell him, if I might be permitted to ask such a question?"

Letting out a long breath, Henrietta pushed her lips together in the most dejected manner. "I really do not know. I only know that I must see him and hear his voice before I can decide."

"Then you have not come down on one side or the other? Neither Frank Beacher nor Charles Hayden?"

"I have chosen one, then the other, then the other, then yet again the other, all this night. I have hardly known such a misery of indecision. So now I go to have a tête-à-tête with Charles, and then, if I remain undecided, with Mr Beacher." She closed her eyes a second and put fingers to her temple. "Lizzie? Will you accompany me? It would be unseemly for me to visit Captain Hayden alone."

"Give me but a moment and I shall be at your disposal."

The minute hand upon the mantel clock had progressed hardly at all when Elizabeth Hertle hastened back into the library and the two cousins set out for the main door. The family carriage was waiting, and they were quickly handed aboard and the wheels rolled off across the gravel towards the lane and the road to town. They had hardly gone a hundred yards when Lizzie noticed her husband and Frank Beacher emerge from the stables; both stopped and watched the carriage until it was out of sight.

It took but half an hour to drive into the village, the morning as clear and still as a day of worship. A mourning dove lamented deep within the wood, and a cockerel offered up a heartfelt reply. Henrietta kneaded the hem of her shawl, her fingers unable to remain still.

Elizabeth felt her heart go out to her cousin, who had been through all of the most intense experiences a woman might imagine short of childbirth. Betrayal, death of her intended, a proposal of marriage, and then, miraculously, the return of the man she had hoped to marry—returned and redeemed, as his betrayal had been proved false. And now she must make a choice between two men—two different futures.

"Lizzie . . . ?" Henrietta asked softly. "Is it worth it? All of the time apart? All of the worry—I know there is a great deal of anxiety on your part."

"I could never have married anyone but Robert Hertle. When one has no choice, one accepts the heartache. It is that simple." She gazed at her poor cousin, who appeared ill with indecision. "And what is it you intend to say to Charles Hayden, pray?"

For a moment Henrietta focused her gaze out of the window, and then, without looking at her cousin, said, "I will attempt to tell him that I have chosen another. And if I can form those words, if I can say them aloud, then I will know. If I cannot, then I shall become Mrs Charles Hayden . . . assuming Charles will have me. He must hate me for having so little faith in him."

"He does not hate you, my dear. On the contrary, I believe he is as attached to you as ever. Do not spend the smallest amount of your energies on that matter."

The carriage drew up before the inn, and Henrietta appeared so miserable and weakened by lack of rest that her cousin thought her nerve might fail and she might order the driver on, but instead she gave Elizabeth's hand a squeeze and with only the slightest hesitation allowed herself to be handed down from the carriage, Elizabeth right behind.

Immediately, upon their enquiry, they learned that Captain Hayden had walked out not ten minutes before and was seen proceeding along the north road. Thinking they would catch him up, the two women hurried off, arm in arm.

The north road followed along the edge of a brook, winding under very ancient trees, the leaves of which parsed the sunlight into a jumble of flickering shards. They had no time to stop and marvel at the scene and only rushed along. Twenty minutes on, they were chastising themselves for not employing the carriage, for it seemed that Charles Hayden had outpaced them when Elizabeth caught sight of white breeches climbing up a switchback path and then bits of a blue coat like a jay flitting from tree to tree, its wing patch catching the sun.

They found the entrance to the path but a few paces distant and set off after Charles, neither calling out for some reason they could not explain. The way was not too steep, and in a quarter of an hour they emerged from the trees onto a grassy hilltop, where Charles Hayden stood, hands behind his back, gazing at the scene spread out below.

"Captain Hayden . . . ?" Henrietta attempted to call, but barely a whisper emerged. Her cousin was forced to come to her aid.

"Charles . . . ?" she called, and Hayden turned, clearly surprised to see them.

Lizzie gave her cousin's hand one last squeeze and let her proceed, retreating a few paces herself.

Hayden could not have been more surprised if he had found a pair of wood nymphs calling his name. But there were Mrs Hertle and Miss Henrietta, utterly unlooked for. Mrs Hertle squeezed her cousin's hand, then pressed her gently forward, retreating two dozen steps as soon as she had done so.

Henrietta walked, rather lifelessly, to him, and stopped two paces off, gazing at him with eyes so darkly surrounded that she appeared fevered and ill.

"Henrietta, you do not look well."

"I am not well, but neither am I ill. Sick at heart . . . that is what I am. And you, Charles. What has been done to you?"

"A shipwreck. I shall be myself in a fortnight. No need for concern."

"How many hundreds of men were lost? I thank God you were not among them."

"I had much to return to . . . or so I believed. It was my intention to ask for your hand upon landing in England, and I thought I had reason to believe you might favour me with your consent. Instead, I find you are engaged to another . . . Is my presence here no longer wanted?" Hayden had not meant his words to sound so formal, but given the number of times he had stood before another and not heard the words he hoped for, he found now that he made an effort to escape with at least his dignity intact.

Henrietta looked down, her eyes closing, hiding away that little window into her heart. "It is not that. I have wronged you, I know. I should never have doubted you or believed the stories of these French women—"

"I am not a monument to virtue," Hayden interrupted. "You cannot be blamed . . . given the circumstances."

"You are being very kind . . ." She raised her head and met Hayden's gaze, her lip trembling just perceptibly. "I have learned something of myself by the news of your death—something I have only just realised. I could not bear to hear it twice. I am not made of such stern stuff that I can live my life in constant fear of you dying or being maimed or injured in some unspeakable manner. Lizzie told me that every time Robert goes to sea she sends her heart to war. My heart is not so made. I am not courageous . . . I have come to realise. I lost you once, Charles, and it was more than I could bear. I cannot suffer it again. I am so sorry."

And with that she turned quickly and hurried back the way she had come. Elizabeth came forward a few paces to meet her and then took her off down the path into the trees, looking back only once, her face filled with distress.

Hayden watched her silent retreat, knowing that there was no reasoning with another's heart. There was no argument to be made, no case to be presented that could make a person feel things they did not feel. Either she loved him enough to marry him or she did not—he could not change that with a fine speech. Feeling suddenly unsteady, Hayden sat down upon the grass, his gaze fixed on the path where the two women had gone.

"Come back," he whispered. "Come back."

And so he waited a protracted hour, and when no one returned he rose and walked slowly to his inn, feeling all the while that his feet did not quite weigh properly upon the ground, as though gravity had all but set him free and he might float off into the sky to be carried by the winds, here and there, through the archipelago of endlessly drifting clouds.

Nineteen

The seated officers of the court-martial, all of them plucked from high on the captains' list, regarded Hayden and his gathered crew with something less than ideal detachment. Hayden awaited their judgement with a peculiar sense of inevitable resignation. Having so recently been found wanting by the woman he hoped to marry, he did not expect the captains of the court-martial to be more generous. In truth, despite being a man who believed in reason, he could not escape the feeling that unseen forces conspired to undo him. Perhaps he had been prideful or had committed some other mortal sin—a memory of Madame Adair passed through his consciousness. Certainly, he had spent the lives of others in this war against the French—though never at the cost of his own safety. Higher powers might not care that he put himself in harm's way as often as he did his own men. Higher powers had their own laws, and Hayden was not certain men comprehended them clearly.

Hayden had seen men beset by ill luck before. It was not even terribly uncommon. He had observed the faces of these poor souls, bewildered, injured, not knowing what to do to stem the onrush of misfortune. Wondering what they had done to be so mistreated in this life. And now it was his turn. He had lost his ship—almost lost his life—an act of compassion had led to his near financial ruin and the eventual loss of the woman he adored. And now he stood before the panel of captains to be judged for the loss of HMS *Themis*. Under normal circumstances, this would be hardly more than a formality—he had lost his ship to superior forces after making every conceivable effort to preserve ship and crew. It had merely been bad luck . . . again. Given the direction his life had been progressing, he expected the panel of captains had been chosen by whoever his enemies were within the Admiralty, turning a mere formality into the ruin of his career.

And so he waited, calmly expecting the destruction of the last of his hopes to be announced. Where he would go after his military career had been blasted he did not know. He was accomplished in this single occupation and nothing more.

The presiding rear-admiral, Sir John Harland, settled spectacles upon his nose, raised a sheaf of papers to the light that streamed in the gallery windows behind, and cleared his throat.

"It is the opinion of this court," he began in a soft Irish voice, a voice that did not seem representative of higher powers, "that Captain Charles Saunders Hayden and his officers and crew, in the loss of their ship, the thirty-two-gun frigate HMS *Themis*, conducted themselves at all times with enterprise and courage. The loss of the ship to superior French forces encountered in dense fog cannot in any way be attributed to lack of competence on the part of said captain and crew. The subsequent recognition by the French government of the actions of these men aboard the wrecked French ship of war, *Les Droits de l'Homme*, speaks very highly of their courage and coolness in the most trying circumstances. We therefore find Captain Hayden, his officers, and his crew innocent of any dereliction of duty in the loss of the frigate *Themis*." He lowered the papers and smiled. "You are all free to go."

Despite the fact that everyone believed it would be highly unlikely for them to be held responsible for the *Themis*' loss, there was still a great and palpable dissipation of tension and anxiety at the admiral's pronouncement. The *Themis'* officers and young gentlemen all looked one to the other, their carriages relaxing in ways that were clearly noticeable, and not least among them in feeling this assuagement was their young captain.

The men all began to file out of the great cabin, a low murmuring heard among them, largely words of thanks. As Hayden reached the door, a lieutenant standing there stepped forward.

"Captain Hayden?" the young officer asked. "The admiral desires you attend him, if you please, sir."

"Certainly."

Hayden followed the admiral's messenger as he stepped into the human tide ebbing from the great cabin. Although the tide went to the upper deck and the spring sunlight, Hayden was ushered into the empty cabin of the captain and offered a chair. It was forty minutes before the admiral finished taking his leave of the captains of the panel and seeing to whatever legal duties the proceedings immediately demanded. Hayden rose promptly to his feet as Admiral Harland entered.

"Hayden," the admiral began, "thank you for waiting."

"My pleasure, sir."

Harland bore in his hand a package tied with blue ribbon, and this the admiral proffered to Hayden. "From the First Secretary. I suggest you assure yourself the seal has not been broken, then read the orders immediately, as I was instructed to deliver this as soon as practicable upon the completion of the court-martial."

Hayden did as instructed, the admiral wandering off a few paces and apparently taking in the view from the gallery. It occurred to Hayden that at least someone within the Admiralty had faith in the outcome—a striking contrast to his thoughts of only a few moments before. The package bore the seal of the Admiralty, unbroken, as Hayden assumed it would be. Opening the package, he found, to his

very great surprise, a second letter within, sealed and addressed to
Admiral Lord Howe.

Captain Hayden, the orders began:

> *You are hereby instructed to proceed aboard the sixty-four-gun ship*
> Raisonnable *lying at Spithead and take command of said vessel. As*
> Raisonnable *has been recently refloated from dry dock and her refit-*
> *ting only lately completed, you are to take any or all officers you see fit*
> *from the crew of His Majesty's Frigate* Themis *to fill such positions as*
> *required aboard* Raisonnable. *You are to put to sea at first opportu-*
> *nity of wind and weather and proceed with all haste off Ushant bearing*
> *dispatches of great import for Admiral Lord Howe, who is cruising in*
> *this vicinity in command of the Channel Fleet. As it is possible Admi-*
> *ral Lord Howe might have departed this station, you are to gather any*
> *intelligence from passing vessels as might lead you to discover the admi-*
> *ral and his fleet at sea. As the delivery of the dispatches entrusted to*
> *your care is of the most urgent importance to the success of the present*
> *war you are instructed to press this matter forward with all energies*
> *until such time as you have succeeded or learned that Lord Howe has*
> *returned to England. Once you have fallen in with Lord Howe you are*
> *to consider yourself under his orders until he shall release you.*
>
> *As a valuable convoy of French transports under escort has sailed*
> *from America for unknown French ports and as apprehending this*
> *convoy is one of the objects of Lord Howe's cruise, any information you*
> *might acquire from ships at sea as to the position or expected arrival of*
> *this convoy should be transmitted to Lord Howe immediately upon*
> *joining his fleet.*

The letter was signed by Philip Stephens, First Secretary of the
Admiralty.

Hayden looked up to find Admiral Harland regarding him.
"There is one other small matter, Hayden." The admiral went to a

chair that was turned away from Hayden and took up a package, wrapped in paper and tied with string.

"What is this, sir?" Hayden asked as Harland pressed it into Hayden's hands.

The admiral shrugged. "Here is a note pinned to it; perhaps that will explain."

Hayden opened the note quickly.

I have been informed, Hayden, that you lost your coat in the recent wreck and were forced to wear that of a French captain. That will never do. I send you coats to replace those lost.

Philip Stephens

At the admiral's insistence, he laid the package on a table and opened it, revealing the full dress coat of a junior post captain, and, beneath that, an undress coat for the same rank.

"From Mr Stephens," Hayden said, confused. "But it is a post captain's coat . . ."

"May I be the first to offer compliments, Captain Hayden. I believe it is an honour richly deserved."

"I–I have lost my ship," Hayden said, hardly able to believe what he looked at, "and they grant me my post?"

"God and the Admiralty work in mysterious ways." The admiral appeared to hide a smile. "Given the formality of the recently concluded proceedings, I believe you should wear the full dress."

Feeling terribly self-conscious, as though there had been some mistake, he pulled off his threadbare frock coat and shrugged the new one onto his shoulders.

"It is a passable fit, I should say," the admiral observed. "Nothing even a poor tailor could not put to rights. Would you care for a glass of port, Captain?"

"Thank you, sir."

Port was poured, a toast drunk, Hayden not even tasting the liquid, his mind raced so. When the port had seared its way down to Hayden's nether reaches, the admiral stood. "I know I should not keep you, Captain, as much as I should like to. I have put my barge at your disposal to take you wherever it is you need to go."

"Thank you, sir."

"Good luck to you, Captain Hayden."

Of an instant Hayden was upon the ladder, his ancient coat and undress captain's coat poorly bundled into paper and tucked beneath an arm. He hastened up into the sunlight, where all the persons who had been in attendance at the court-martial were awaiting boats to carry them ashore, the captains of the panel taking precedence over all others.

"Mr Wickham," Hayden said as the midshipman approached him, grinning broadly.

"Sir?"

"Gather all of our officers and warrant officers together this instant. We have been given a ship and will proceed to sea . . ." Hayden looked up at the telltale on the masthead, "this very day, if it is possible."

One of the many reasons Hayden believed Wickham would be a sea officer of great skill one day was that he knew instinctively when questions were required and when they were not. A quick touch of the hat, he spun on the ball of his foot and was calling out the names of the *Themis* men as he crossed the deck. As he was collecting Hayden's officers, the lieutenant, who had earlier led Hayden to his meeting with Harland, approached.

"Captain Hayden? I am to carry you to your ship, sir," he informed Hayden. "My compliments on making your post, sir."

"Thank you, Lieutenant."

In fewer than ten minutes Hayden, his officers, warrant officers, and midshipmen were making their way across the anchorage of Spithead, all of them grinning foolishly.

"If I am informed correctly about the readiness of our new ship for sea, every man will have four hours to have their trunks collected and returned to the ship," Hayden informed his crew. "Any servant or trunk that is not aboard at that time will be left behind. We have a fair wind to St Helens and I do not intend to waste it." Hayden twisted around to find a flag, assuring himself that the small wind was still fair. "We will muster in my cabin as soon as we are in the Channel."

"If you please, Captain," Barthe said meekly. "What ship have you been given?"

"*Raisonnable.*"

"The sixty-four?"

"The very ship, Mr Barthe."

"Did you not serve in her before?"

"As a lieutenant."

Barthe shook his head, glancing at Hawthorne, as pleased as if he had been promoted himself.

"If I may, sir," Hawthorne interrupted, "it would appear you have donned some other man's coat by accident . . ."

"It is my coat, Mr Hawthorne, recently sent to me by a friend within the Admiralty."

Hawthorne turned to the others in the launch and said, "Three cheers for Post Captain Hayden."

And the men huzzahed with a will, their cheers echoing across the anchorage, and so pleased was Hayden that his cheeks coloured like a boy's.

Raisonnable lay to her anchor among ships refitting or having but recently made port. She appeared much as Hayden remembered her—and he let his eye run over her rigging, wondering if she really could be ready to sail that very day. No more than a handful of men were engaged aloft, and that, Hayden hoped, was a good sign. Every second gunport was opened to air the ship, and he could see a bosun and his crew employing a burton tackle to set up the mizzen shrouds.

In very short order, they were piped aboard the sixty-four-gun ship *Raisonnable*. Three lieutenants met them as they came over the rail, the most senior introducing himself.

"Geoffrey Bowen, sir. I was Captain Lord Cranstoun's third lieutenant. May I introduce Robert Stanton Milton-Bell, sir, and James Huxley. We are all honoured to sail with you, sir."

"Thank you, Mr Bowen." Hayden quickly introduced his own officers and enquired into the readiness of the ship for sea.

"She has been both provisioned and watered, Captain Hayden. Shot and powder were put aboard last night and completed this morning. She had a major refit, sir, and has new masts and yards, the better part of a new upper deck, her bottom is newly coppered, and she has been painted from taffrail to beakhead."

Indeed, the ship fairly glowed from the dockyard's recent ministrations. Hayden took the briefest moment to let his eyes run over his new command. There were six carronades on the quarterdeck, replacing the original nine-pounders, four of which remained in the after positions. All of the quarterdeck guns had been repositioned so that the guns beneath the quarter-ladders were shifted aft—something Hayden had once had the temerity to suggest to his captain, whereupon he was informed that when he actually knew something he would be allowed to make recommendations to his commanding officer. The guns beneath the quarter-ladders could not be worked without removing the ladders, which made climbing to the poop difficult—indeed, older officers found it all but impossible. There were nine-pounders on the quarterdeck still.

"I have all the paperwork ready for you, Captain," Bowen informed him, "and will put myself at your disposal at any time to tour the ship. And if you please, sir, I have been given to understand that you are short of midshipmen. There are four likely-looking young gentlemen standing by, sir. None of them have any experience, but two of them are brothers to Mr Huxley and myself and the other two are from good families. I can give them all excellent characters, sir, from being personally acquainted with them for some years, and I believe they would learn their business passably well. I should never presume upon you in such a manner, sir, but given that the Port Captain told me we would sail upon the tide, I thought you might not mind."

"Under the circumstances, Mr Bowen, I should say you have shown excellent judgement. I shall speak to your young gentlemen as soon as you can get them aboard. For now, I will read my commission and then tour the ship." Hayden turned to his crew gathered at the rail. "Mr Barthe, you will see to the masts, sails, and rig. Search out the bosun and put to rights anything that does not meet your approval. When you have completed that, we shall both go down to the hold and find how she is stowed."

The next few hours saw a flurry of activity aboard. Ship and crew were inspected, stores lists, muster lists, etc., were not ignored, for Hayden did not want to discover at sea that he lacked anything essential to the execution of his orders. Permission came from the Port Captain for Hayden to get under way, which he did a scant five hours after first setting foot aboard. It helped greatly that he had served aboard *Raisonnable* before, for she was largely unaltered.

"You will find her fast and able, Mr Barthe," Hayden told his sailing master as the ship gathered way and began to slip across the surface of the anchorage. They stood upon the poop, which gave Hayden a great sense of height compared to the quarterdeck of the *Themis*. "Almost a large frigate, but with a deck of twenty-four-pounders in addition to the eighteens."

"The Advent class was one of Mr Slade's best," the sailing master agreed, patting the broad taffrail with a flat hand. "If this wind bends around but a little, it will carry us out into the Channel, sir."

"For which I would be most thankful."

The wind, which seldom heeded the wishes of sailors, did "bend around" and bore them into the Channel before the day's light had faded. Hayden ordered their course shaped for Ushant and called all of his officers below, leaving a midshipman briefly in command.

As his belongings from the recaptured *Themis* had yet to be delivered to him, and there had been no time to procure any furniture of his own, Hayden collected everyone in the wardroom and bid them sit at the long table. He kept his voice low so that his words would not reach beyond the little enclosure.

"I have been entrusted with dispatches from the Lords of the Admiralty for Admiral Lord Howe and charged to deliver them with all possible haste. To that end, we will shape our course for Ushant in hopes of finding the Channel Fleet on that station. If His Lordship is not to be found in those waters, we are to expend all energies to discover him and perform our duty. I do not know the nature of the Admiralty's dispatches, but it was also noted in my orders that a large and valuable French convoy, under escort, was believed to have left America recently and we are to gather all information we might as to its course or location."

"The Lords of the Admiralty," Barthe spoke up immediately, "are aware, are they not, that a man cannot see across the Atlantic . . . even standing on tiptoe? If Lord Howe has seen fit to leave his station to seek this convoy—if that is his purpose—we might sail the rest of our days and never discover him."

"I do agree with you, Mr Barthe, regarding the size of the ocean. Certainly, we have not been honoured with a simple duty. If you read the report in the *Times* not so long ago of a French convoy consisting of over one hundred transports and escort vessels gathering in the Chesapeake, we must believe that such a fleet of ships will not go unseen even in an ocean as vast as the Atlantic. We shall speak every ship we meet, and if we take a prize, mayhap we shall learn the whereabouts of the Channel Fleet. I know nothing of Lord Howe's orders, but I suspect the Channel Fleet is cruising off Brest or the First Lord would not have sent us there with dispatches."

Barthe made a sound in his throat—a low growl—suggesting that Hayden had more faith in the understanding of the Admiralty than he did himself.

"We shall take up our usual duties," Hayden went on. "Mr Archer, you are first lieutenant. Mr Ransome, second. Our new shipmates, Misters Bowen, Milton-Bell, and Huxley, will make up our complement of lieutenants. We are still short of reefers, but perhaps we shall find some likely men to make up their places. We have no marine captain, I am told, so, Mr Hawthorne, you will be acting marine captain until such time as you are confirmed in that position or replaced. The very experienced Mr Barthe is, as usual, our sailing master, and we are all most satisfied to have Dr Griffiths as our surgeon."

First Lieutenant Archer had made up a watch and station bill with the aid of the lieutenants who had been aboard during the launching and refit, and as Hayden did not yet know the crew, he signed it readily. As this concluded all immediate business, a late dinner was set out by the servants and the residents of the wardroom ate their first meal at sea together with their newly minted post captain as the guest of honour.

"You must be held in very high regard by the Lords of the Admiralty, Captain Hayden," Bell observed. "To be given a sixty-four-gun ship as your first post command is a high honour."

"I should not be surprised to learn this command is temporary,

Mr Bell, and I shall find myself back aboard a frigate in the very near future."

"Was it you, Captain Hayden, who raised the guns to the hilltops in Corsica?" Huxley asked.

"All of my crew, almost without exception, played a part in that particular enterprise, Mr Huxley. Mr Wickham, there, had command of one of the crews himself."

"It must have been a very great surprise to the French when they found batteries erected behind them."

"It was a very great surprise to even the Corsicans," Hawthorne said with less pride than satisfaction. "They assured us that guns could never be raised to those hills. General Dundas was of the same opinion exactly. Only Colonel Moore and Captain Hayden thought it possible."

"I do wish I had been so certain," Hayden admitted. "In the end, it was managed and the French positions overrun by Colonel Moore and his troops."

"And you cut out a new-built French frigate, I am given to understand."

"The French were in the process of scuttling her when we boarded, and she was later refloated. They put up a fight, though— Mr Ransome is limping yet, are you not?"

"I am, sir, but the prize money shall ease the hurt, I am certain."

"It is not the balm for all wounds, you may find," Dr Griffiths felt he should point out.

Hayden thought his new lieutenants showed some promise. They had all been at sea since they were boys—two of good Navy families—and had learned their trade under excellent captains— men whom Hayden knew by reputation. He could not have been more pleased. Notwithstanding a family in trade, Huxley seemed bright enough, though a little retiring. A bit of a bulldog in shape and height, but an English bulldog, and Hayden was not unhappy with that. Bowen's father was a cleric, and he and Smosh immediately fell in with each other, though Hayden expected from what he had overheard that Mr Bowen's father was rather unlike their own parson—not surprisingly. Bowen had that bright-faced, alert manner of the moderately intelligent—true geniuses were invariable misfits of one sort or another, at least in Hayden's limited experience. Milton-Bell—who preferred "Bell"—was of a very good family, but being the youngest son he had drawn the Navy as his career and did not seem perfectly pleased with it either. He was, however, treated with respect by the other lieutenants and the crew, which gave Hayden hope that he was a passable officer.

The new midshipmen, who had been invited to dine, exhibited all of the apprehension one would expect of nonswimmers being cast into a raging river. And Hayden believed it was not nearly fear enough—they really did not understand how dangerous a life they were embarking upon, given that Britain was involved in a war that seemed to be ever-growing in both scale and ferocity.

"Would you care for some wine, Huxley?" Hawthorne asked, nodding to a servant standing behind. And then, "That would be you, midshipman. Your brother will be 'Mr Huxley' or 'Lieutenant Huxley,' but as we cannot have you confused with him when the captain is calling out orders, you will be 'Huxley.' And the same will go for you, Bowen."

"Yes," Hobson added, "we shall call you 'Huxley' as well."

"Mr Hobson!" Hawthorne fixed the midshipman with an indignant stare. "You know very well what I meant. I dare say even Bowen knew, even if he is still damp behind the ears and as green as new-cut oak."

"Despite what you might think," Wickham informed the new reefers, "Mr Hawthorne has not a cruel bone in his body, but he will practise upon you unmercifully all the same. You must not mind, as it is the custom in the Navy to make new midshipmen appear foolish at every opportunity. He will, however, grow tired of it in a few months and leave off tormenting you."

"That is, if you live that long," Hobson interjected. "Most midshipmen are blasted to hell by cannon fire within a month of coming aboard."

"If you live beyond thirty days, however," Hawthorne explained to the new midshipmen, "you will almost always make six months. Never a year—or almost never—but six months is quite possible. I have seen it myself."

"We lost a dozen midshipmen on our last cruise alone," Hobson added, shaking his head sadly. "Terrible mess some of them made on the deck. The worst is to be hit by a thirty-two-pound ball from a carronade. Hardly anything left to put over the side. We just kind of swabbed them up and poured the remains out the scuppers. Mr Smosh said a few words over the bucket and we committed the mush to the sea. 'Midshipmush,' we called it."

"You would never think a midshipman could fit in a bucket, but we've all seen it . . . have we not?"

Everyone agreed, and added what a disgustingly sad sight it was.

"We hope you manage to survive such a fate, but on the chance that you do not . . ." Hobson motioned to a servant, who opened the door, letting three crewmen in. "We had these made up for you."

The hands produced, from behind their backs, three buckets, each bearing the name of one of the new middies in white paint.

The midshipmen had the buckets pressed into their hands, all grinning anxiously, as if uncertain that everything being said to them was not wild exaggeration. The older brothers remained impressively neutral, betraying not a hint of a smile.

"You might find the bucket comes in useful when the sea gets up a little," Barthe added. "I should hang it by my cot."

Hayden's cabin was so barren—merely a cot swinging from the deck beams and his trunk in a corner—that he could hardly bear to remain there. The fact that it was very grand made the lack of furnishings seem even more pathetic. The carpenter and his mates were at work making Hayden a rough table and refitting some old chairs that had been found, so at least he would have a place to do his paperwork and dine. The beautiful table that Wickham's father had given him was sorely missed. It also seemed rather ungrateful to have lost this gift so soon after it had been given. He went out onto the curving stern-walk and stood with his hand on the rail, observing the ship's wake bubbling up aft. He traversed the open gallery from larboard to starboard and then back to amidships. In recent years, he had not allowed himself to even imagine being in such a position—leaning his elbows upon the rail of an elegant stern-walk aboard a line-of-battle ship. *His* stern-walk aboard his own post ship. For a moment, the satisfaction that this engendered overshadowed the almost constant echo of his last conversation with Henrietta. He wondered still that he had stood and watched her walk away without protest. She had seemed so very certain—not the least doubtful—and part of him had felt that she was right. She was meant for better things than waiting at home for her sea officer to return, always anxious. He had lost his own father in just this way and it had been a terrible blow. There was also a part of him that felt he did not protest or make any declaration of his feelings because he *had* betrayed her trust—and he believed that somehow she would learn of it one day. He could not bear the thought of that.

Taking a last look at the sea aft, he returned inside.

Ten minutes of his stark cabin, though, saw Hayden don an old boat cloak and walk out onto the deck. His marine sentry, barely visible in the poor light of a shuttered lantern, touched his hat and said, "Captain," loud enough for the helmsmen to hear. The wheel lay just beyond the door to Hayden's outer cabin and under the shelter provided by the short poop. The helmsmen had only a view forward from such a position but were always directed by the officer of the watch. The two men tending the wheel twisted around and made knuckles. Hayden walked out onto the quarterdeck, which was bisected fore and aft by the companionway that lay just forward of the binnacle, a long scuttle, and a second companionway. Here the bulwark was high but ended abruptly outboard of the mainmast, where hammock netting took the place of a rail.

Hobson and midshipman Huxley leaned against a carronade, but jumped up the instant they apprehended Hayden appearing from beneath the poop. Both touched their hats.

"Your first night at sea, Huxley, is it?"

"It is, sir, and very pleased I am to be here, Captain."

"An excellent night for your first night watch, only enough wind to hurry us along and not a hint of fog. Most pleasant. I trust you and Mr Hobson are employing your time most profitably?"

"Indeed, Captain. Mr Hobson has been quizzing me about the parts of the ship and has begun to teach me my ropes."

"Then what would you name this?" Hayden asked, laying a hand on a long piece of wood seized to the shrouds.

The boy appeared confused a moment and then blurted out, "Is it a 'stretcher,' sir?"

"I am asking you the questions, Huxley."

The boy looked both frightened and embarrassed. "I would call it a stretcher, sir."

"And you would be correct. You might also hear an older sailor name it a 'squaring staff,' and you must know what he means. Mr Barthe has been heard to call it thus, and if he were to use that term and you did not recognise it, he would give you a cuff."

"A 'squaring staff,' sir. I shall not forget."

"Carry on, then."

Hayden gazed aloft. Between the sails, stars glittered among masses of dark cloud. A fresh breeze held steady out of the northeast, pressing the ship down-Channel on the ebbing tide, *Raisonnable* exhibiting her usual turn of speed. What a cruiser such a ship would make, Hayden thought. Two frigates and *Raisonnable* would make a deadly little squadron. Prize money would come rolling in, or so he imagined.

"Captain Hayden?"

It was Archer, appearing out of the darkness.

"You are not standing a watch, are you, Lieutenant?"

"No, sir, it is Mr Huxley's watch. I have just come on deck to take the air. Perhaps it is the motion of the new ship, sir, but I could not sleep."

"Perhaps that is what has brought me up here as well."

"I am very pleased with our new ship, though, Captain."

"As am I, Mr Archer." He did not say that as a young lieutenant he dreamed of being *Raisonnable*'s captain one day. A young man's dream—almost a boy's. Yet here he was, however temporarily, upon her quarterdeck wearing a post captain's coat.

Lieutenant Huxley approached at that moment. "Mr Archer?" and then, realizing whom Archer spoke with, "Captain Hayden, sir. I did not realise it was you."

"What is it, Mr Huxley?"

"A ship, sir. About a league distant. Two points off our lee bow and on about the same heading. Shall we alter our course to come up to her by first light?"

Archer glanced at Hayden, deferring to him in this matter.

"Commonly I should answer, 'yes,' Mr Huxley, but as we are delivering urgent dispatches to Lord Howe I shall not slow our pace to take prizes or to risk our purpose by meeting a ship with a greater weight of broadside. Keep to our course and have the lookouts put a glass on this ship as soon as there is the least light in the sky."

"Aye, sir." Huxley made a knuckle and went off.

Neither he nor Archer spoke a moment but went to the larboard rail to search the dark sea for a light. In a moment they had found it, and Hayden sent for his newly purchased night glass, his old one having been left aboard the *Themis*.

"Can you make her out, Captain?" Archer asked after Hayden had been staring for a moment at the sea and sky reversed.

"Three masts, Mr Archer. Nothing more." He passed the glass to Archer, who held it up to his eye and steadied himself against the rail.

"I imagine I can perceive gunports and then I am quite certain there are none. Lost her . . ." Archer took the glass away from his eye a scant inch, found the lights again, and put the glass back to his eye. "Is she altering course to the south, Captain?" He returned the glass to Hayden.

"She has seen us, I have no doubt." Hayden lowered the glass. "I shall try my cot again, Mr Archer."

Archer turned to him quickly, touching his hat, but then said, "Have you spoken to the doctor at all, sir?"

"But briefly, Mr Archer, and that to do with his concerns regarding a man in the sick-berth with some puzzling ailment. Has he spoken to you about him as well?"

"No, sir. There might be some subject more pressing, sir."

"And what, pray, might that be?"

Suddenly, Archer looked terribly embarrassed.

"I shall have a word with the doctor in the morning, Mr Archer, if you think that might be soon enough . . ."

"Perfectly soon enough, sir."

"Then I will say goodnight to you, Lieutenant."

Hayden went back down to his barren cabin, undressed, and

rolled into his swaying cot. For some time he lay, thinking sleep would not find him. He still could not quite believe he had made his post . . . No doubt due to the efforts of Philip Stephens, though he did wonder if Lord Hood might have made some interest on his behalf. Almost certainly he would never know. How good luck and ill fortune could be so combined in one man's life he did not understand. One day he lost his beloved Henrietta, and hardly a sennight later he made his post. He fell asleep thinking that he would gladly trade both his newly won coats for the hand of Miss Henrietta Carthew.

Twenty

Four and half days were required for the *Raisonnable* to raise the Île d'Ouessant, or as the English preferred it, "Ushant." Hayden did not risk the Four Passage, even with a fair wind. Perhaps the thought of losing his first command as a post captain sent him on the safer course.

The shattered cliffs south of the harbour entrance stood out in the afternoon sunlight like bones bleached and scarred. Even without a glass Hayden could pick out the batteries there, protecting the narrow harbour entrance. A brisk top-gallant breeze swept down from the north, cool but not chill. The green fields of France faded into mist inshore and then disappeared altogether in thickening haze.

"There is a cutter just tacking in the outer water, sir," Wickham informed Hayden. He lowered his glass and pointed. "Do you see her, Captain?"

"I do, Mr Wickham. Is she one of ours, do you think?"

"It seems very likely, sir. Let us ask Mr Barthe if he recognises her."

Wickham and Hayden stood at the rail upon the quarterdeck, the coast of France stretching south beyond Pointe de Raz. They were hardly a few hours' sail from where they had both been so recently wrecked, and the thought of it made Hayden leery of the nearby shore even though the wind did not threaten to take them in that direction.

The sailing master was sent for and appeared a few moments later, waddling up to the rail, colour high, a few strands of brick red hair escaping from beneath a battered hat, which he habitually wore pressed down tight upon his roundish head. His ankle, though still swollen, inconvenienced him less and less—to the point where he had abandoned the doctor's cane.

"Would you quiz this little cutter for us, Mr Barthe, and tell us if you know her?"

Barthe took the offered glass and fixed it upon the vessel, hardly a league distant. "She does bear a strong resemblance from this far off to the *Expedition*, sir. Though I should not wager my savings on it—had I any savings."

"You do think she is British?"

"I should think so, Captain. Holding station here or so it appears."

"Make the private signal," Hayden ordered Wickham. "We do not want to chase her off."

Even as Hayden said this, the cutter tacked and began to beat quickly up towards the rocks at the entrance to the Four Passage, no doubt fearing that *Raisonnable* was a French ship.

The private signal was made, and immediately the cutter answered and changed course out towards the approaching ship. Hayden ordered *Raisonnable* hove to and awaited the cutter, which very quickly ranged up to leeward, rounded up sharply, and backed her headsails, proving Mr Barthe right about her identity.

"I am carrying dispatches for Lord Howe," Hayden called down to the lieutenant in command. "I have orders to deliver them with all possible haste."

"You have missed him by a day, Captain," the lieutenant called back. "We had word from Admiral Montagu by the frigate *Venus* that a French squadron had been dispatched from Brest to meet the American convoy—five ships of the line and two frigates, sir. Lord Howe set out to support Admiral Montagu immediately. The French squadron was believed to be cruising between forty-five and forty-eight degrees north, sir."

"Then Lord Howe has gone south?"

"Yes, sir. With the Channel Fleet. Yesterday."

"And what of the rest of the Brest Fleet?"

"It sailed on the sixteenth day of May, sir, or so we believe. We do not know where, sir, but Lord Howe believed it may also be searching for the convoy."

Hayden turned to Mr Barthe. "Well, that is a bit of ill luck—missing Lord Howe by a single day. It would seem we have no choice but to sail south and trust to sharp eyes and good fortune."

"Aye, Captain Hayden, and hope Lord Howe has not had reason to shape his course elsewhere."

Hayden turned back to the lieutenant in his cutter. "We go south after Lord Howe. If His Lordship returns and we are not in his company, you must tell him we sail with important dispatches from the Admiralty."

"I will, Captain. Good luck to you, sir."

"And you, Lieutenant."

Hayden turned to Bowen, who was officer of the watch. "We will make all possible sail and shape our course due south. Lookouts in the tops. And you, Mr Wickham, might take a glass in a few hours and sit astride the main top-gallant yard and tell me what you perceive. The Channel Fleet and the Brest Fleet are both at sea, as well as French and English squadrons and a convoy consisting of over one hundred transports and escorts. If we cannot find *some* of these ships, then we are either blind or cursed."

The sixty-four-gun ship *Raisonnable* passed swiftly south, leaving the great headland that both created and protected the inner water of Brest Harbour in its wake. The wind remained fair and did not falter all through the afternoon, allowing Hayden to cover a good distance. He had almost forgotten what a swift sailer *Raisonnable* was. There was hardly a frigate that could keep up with her, he thought, and this speed gave him hope. Battle fleets sailed at the speed of the slowest ship, and Hayden had not the least doubt that would be at least two if not three knots slower than he was managing now. As long as Howe did not suddenly change course, Hayden hoped to catch sight of him sometime the next day. Of course, winds did not blow with equal strength over a bay, let alone a vast ocean. Howe might have been becalmed or found a fair wind to speed him on—there was no way of knowing.

Griffiths came up onto the deck sometime before the dinner hour, and Hayden invited him up to the poop, where they might have a conversation in private. Hayden had been admiring the sea— an activity of which he never tired. It had turned all silver-grey beneath the cloud, jagged with ripples. Here and there the sun broke through, illuminating a few acres of water, causing it to glitter and dance so that Hayden could hardly look at it. His mind was ever drawn back and back to his recent visit to Box Hill, still rather amazed by his own lack of action. Was it possible that his attachment to Henrietta was not as great as he had imagined? Or did every man harbour some doubts when it came to asking a woman's hand?

"Have you come to take the air, Doctor?"

"A rumour has wormed its way down to the sick-berth that the French fleet is abroad, and I have come to see if there is any truth to it."

"It is entirely true. Passed through the Goulet but four days ago. There is also a powerful French squadron out here somewhere seeking this elusive convoy from the Chesapeake."

"That does seem like too many French ships by half. Are you concerned?"

"Yes, the French fleet is formidable. But we sail a swift ship, Dr Griffiths. As long as we do not again have the ill fortune to fall in with the French in thick weather, I think we should easily be able to keep our distance." Hayden wondered if this sounded as false as it felt. The French fleet had slipped out of Brest, and that was profoundly disturbing to him. There could be as many as thirty ships of the line—in all likelihood, more than Howe's fleet boasted after he had sent Montagu off to intercept the convoy. He desperately wanted to find Lord Howe before the admiral came upon the French fleet, on the chance that the dispatches he carried held vital information the admiral might require to make informed decisions.

There was also the matter of the gathering invasion force across the Channel—a great unknown, for "Monsieur Benoît" had not been able to say when the planned invasion might take place. What if the Brest Fleet had simply gone into the Channel and taken control of it while Howe searched out at sea? Of course, such a large fleet would probably have been seen by Hayden as he left the Channel, but it was not impossible that they had slipped past him at night.

Griffiths gazed out across the seas, rising and falling, at the retreating dark line that was the coast of Brittany.

Hayden suddenly remembered his peculiar conversation with Archer the previous night. "How fare you, Doctor? We have hardly shared a word since the court-martial began."

"We were all consumed by our own worries throughout that little masquerade. I must say, no matter how often one is court-martialled, one never grows to take pleasure in it."

Hayden laughed. "I dare say, Doctor, you have spoken God's truth. Though I did not mind it so much on this occasion as the last." Hayden was not certain what direction he might take the conversation in, given that Archer had been so utterly vague on the matter. "How fares your patient, Doctor?"

"Poorly. I have been wondering if, when we find Lord Howe, I might consult with the physician of the fleet—Dr Trotter. I might even ask that he take Crowley aboard the hospital ship. Do you think such a thing might be possible?"

"I cannot imagine why it would not be. What other purpose can such a ship serve?"

"Mmm."

They both gazed at the changing sea for a moment, gulls drawn along in the lee of the sails crying out for scraps.

"I do have one small piece of news," Griffiths offered, lowering his voice. "It appears I shall soon be wed."

"My compliments to you, Doctor!" Hayden replied. "I name you a most fortunate man. And who is the lucky bride-to-be?"

"Miss Brentwood," Griffiths answered.

"The young lady you met in Gibraltar?"

"The very one. You appear surprised?"

"Not in the least," Hayden lied. "You did tell me that she was of excellent temperament, and if I may be permitted to observe, she is very handsome. I believe you will be very happy together, Dr Griffiths."

"Thank you, Captain."

A few more pleasantries passed between them, and then the surgeon excused himself and slipped below, leaving Hayden alone at the rail, feeling somewhat low and a little confused. Hearing Griffiths' news of his own pending nuptials brought to the fore that Hayden had no such news—in fact, his news was of the opposite, not that he had spoken of this with any man aboard. Although he made a conscious and concerted effort to push all thoughts of Henrietta from his mind, he caught his thoughts returning there often, despite the fact that was rather like pressing on a wound to see if it healed at all.

The distinctively pleasant voice of Mr Hawthorne was heard speaking to the helmsman. In an attempt to set his thoughts upon a different course, Hayden went forward to the rail, leaned over, caught the acting marine captain's eye, and invited him onto the poop.

Hawthorne fixed an eye on Hayden. "I understand you have been speaking to the doctor, Captain? You have received the joyous news, no doubt?"

"Regarding his coming nuptials? I have."

"And I am certain you gave him your heartiest endorsement?"

"How could I not?"

"Indeed." Hawthorne shook his head. He almost looked angry, Hayden thought. "I doubt she will make him happy," the marine said, "but I do hope she does not make his life a misery."

"Do you think it as bad as that, Hawthorne?"

"It did not begin propitiously—the doctor rescuing her from a gang of drunken sailors and in the company of whores."

"That is true. She was down on her luck, as they say."

"A maid of all work with only one hand, no prospects, no family, and no money at all? She was a step away from whoring herself, if she had not done so already."

"Though it is easy for us to judge who have never been in such circumstances."

"I will not throw the first stone, Captain. I am only concerned for the happiness of our friend. No doubt she sees Griffiths as her path out of the straitened circumstance into which she had fallen."

"Many a marriage has little to do with mutual affection or even respect, and much to do with enlarging one's fortunes. It is hardly a rare occurrence."

"It is not. But one does not like to see a friend snared in such a web."

"Let us hope it is not as it appears and that our friend has attached Miss Brentwood's affections. Though I do think he might have done better than a servant, even a very comely one."

One of the new midshipmen stopped on the quarter-ladder at that moment, not daring to place a foot upon the poop. Hayden could see him hovering there, on the edge of his vision, uncertain if he should interrupt his captain.

"Huxley," Hayden said, saving the boy from indecision. "Is there some matter in need of my attention?"

"It is Mr Hawthorne, sir. One of the marine sentries appears to be ill, sir."

Hawthorne turned towards the boy. "Does he possess a name?"

"I believe they said Stewart, sir. An Irishman."

"From Sligo. Let us go see to him." He touched his hat to Hayden. "If you please, Captain, I have a patient in need of my particular physic."

"We do have a surgeon, Mr Hawthorne."

"If my physic proves ineffective, I shall send the man to the sick-berth."

Hayden watched man and boy make their way forward, Hawthorne almost a foot taller, the child hurrying to stay abreast.

Hayden remembered his first few days aboard ship—knowing nothing. He had been practised upon and bullyragged, made to look the fool and had also been the beneficiary of great kindness. It was not an easy life. These boys were lucky to have Wickham as the most senior midshipman; he would set them on the right course and aid them at every turn. Gould, who was only a few months ahead of them, was also looking out for them, Hayden noticed. He could hardly ask for a more likely group of young gentlemen.

Hayden searched the horizon in all directions for sails—nothing.

He felt a distinct lowering of his mood, as though some oppressive weight settled upon him and pressed him down. His last meeting with Henrietta seemed fixed in his mind, like an echo that never faded away entirely but sounded over and over. He had turned her words over so many times that they had begun to lose all meaning, as though they had been spoken in some other language that he did not comprehend—the language of a woman's heart.

Hayden retreated to his cabin, finally, though he found it so unwelcoming he could barely remain there. He so longed for the companionship of the gunroom—the "wardroom" on a sixty-four-gun ship. Companionship was the physic he required. To sit alone with his wounds in an empty cabin was the most effective way to see them go septic, and he knew it. The wardroom door was no longer open to him without an invitation. Certainly, he could go there on some excuse—to speak with an officer about some matter—but he resisted this perceivable urge. The captain should not appear so weak. Solitude was his natural world, and Hayden would just have to make his peace with it.

For an hour he wrote in his personal journal. Outside his gallery windows the sun plunged into the distant sea, setting the horizon aflame, and then the smoke of night drifted over the sea. Stars flickered into being and overspread the high vault.

Hayden ate a solitary meal, read in a book loaned to him by Mr Huxley, and then rolled into his cot. Despite a deep, aching fatigue, sleep remained just out of reach for some hours. And then some of his fancy twisted off into nonsense and dream swept him away on its own currents.

At an unknown hour, Hayden drifted back into the conscious world and lay swaying in his hammock. He had not heard the ship's bell ring the hour—seamen were never wakened by the bell any more than a household was awakened by its clock's chime—so he did not know if it was late or nearing morning. For perhaps half of the hour he tried to find sleep again, but then gave it up and rose, suddenly fearing that his ship was in sight of a hostile fleet and the lookouts had not seen.

His sentry told him the hour—not yet four—and Hayden climbed to the upper deck just as a little light began to brighten the eastern sky. A breeze of wind blew out of the north, sweeping small seas before it. The officer of the watch was Lieutenant Ransome, who reported all well.

"We have seen but a single light all this night, sir, and she lay hove to, so we believed her to be a fisherman."

"You did not speak this boat, I gather?"

"We did not, sir. I thought it might even be best if they could not give any information about us, as a fisherman in these waters would certainly be French." Ransome now looked uncertain of his decision.

"That was the right thing to do. We have no time to waste. I wish to catch Lord Howe up by noon, if it can be done."

Hayden took a tour of the deck, as much to stretch his legs as to inspect the ship. He stopped and spoke quietly with the men here and there, learning their names, enquiring into their service, and gaining a sense of their character. They seemed a steady lot, though few had been in anything one would call an action. His old crew had been little different when first he had come aboard the *Themis*. He would exercise them at the guns again that morning, though without powder and shot—no need to alert an enemy fleet to their position.

Just as the eastern sky began to gild, Hayden climbed to the tops with his glass, had a word with the lookouts, and then examined the sea at all points of the compass, finding not a single sail.

The head of Arthur Wickham appeared over the edge of the platform, and he seemed rather surprised to find his captain there before him.

"Excuse me, sir," Wickham said, "I did not realise you were here."

"It appears I am, Mr Wickham, but I am not so large that there is not room for you yet."

Wickham had his glass slung over his back, but appeared now afraid to employ it lest this action be viewed as showing signs he did not trust his captain to act as lookout.

"Take a very good look at the Atlantic, Mr Wickham, if you please, and tell me what you find."

The midshipman did not rush his assigned task but covered every quadrant with the greatest possible care. Finally, he lowered his glass. "Nary a sail, sir."

"That is what I thought. If we have not discovered Lord Howe's fleet by midday, I shall begin to wonder if His Lordship has not shaped his course elsewhere."

Wickham raised his hand at that moment and pointed. "Is that a cloud, sir . . . there, on the horizon, south-west by west?"

Hayden raised his glass to examine this faint stain upon the morning sky, and Wickham did the same. "It is very dark, is it not?"

"Could it be smoke, Captain?"

"That is what I am wondering." Hayden lowered his glass and called down to the deck. "On deck, there! Mr Ransome? Shape our course south-west by west."

Hayden saw Ransome remove his hat so that he could see up into the tops.

"Aye, sir," the lieutenant called back. "Is there sail, Captain?"

"Smoke, Mr Ransome. Once the hands have eaten, we will clear for action."

"Aye, sir."

Hayden could hear the buzz this caused among the hands, almost feel the excitement rise from the deck. The men jumped to their places to trim sails and shift yards before the orders had been called, and every eye went to the horizon where the smoke had been seen. Hayden raised his glass again, quizzing the distant blot upon the sky.

"I do think that is smoke, Wickham. Can you hear guns?"

Wickham turned his head a little this way and that. "I cannot, sir. How distant do you think that might be?"

"It is difficult to say; five leagues, at the very least."

"This wind will be carrying sound away, sir, not to us."

"Yes. Well, three hours will tell us something. Have you breakfasted, Wickham?"

"I have, sir."

"Then remain here and see what you can. Do not neglect other points of the compass. I do not want to find a French squadron bearing down from astern."

"Aye, sir. I shall not let such a thing occur."

Hayden climbed down. As soon as he was on the deck, three midshipmen went racing up to Mr Wickham's perch to see this miraculous smoke for themselves, as though smoke had just been discovered.

Upon the quarterdeck, Ransome and Bell were at the rail attempting to see forward, even as the ship turned to take away their view. They leaned out over the rail, each with a glass screwed into his eye.

"Or is it a cloud of the regular sort?" Bell was wondering.

"Captain on the quarterdeck," the helmsman chimed, alerting the lieutenants who were otherwise occupied. They both left off quizzing the horizon, pulled their torsos back aboard, and touched their hats to Hayden.

"May we go forward to allow us a clear view, sir?" Ransome enquired.

"Are you not the lieutenant of the watch, Mr Ransome?"

"I am, sir."

"Then you may go about the deck where your duty takes you. Otherwise your place is here, on the quarterdeck. You are not midshipmen who have never seen a puff of smoke before."

"Aye, sir."

"Mr Bell, you are at your leisure until the change of watch. You may go forward if you wish."

"Thank you, sir." But Bell was now embarrassed to go running forward and instead went below, hiding from his apparently irritable captain.

Hayden followed not long after and ate his breakfast upon his rough plank table. In the brief interval between being given command of *Raisonnable* and setting sail, Hayden had procured what food he could, but that had been little enough, so his diet was going to remain rather primitive until they again made port. This did not help his disposition that morning, which was decidedly peevish, largely from lack of sleep and recent disappointments. Food and coffee ameliorated this condition somewhat and he felt the smallest remorse at his berating of Ransome—not that the man did not deserve it . . . and quite likely more.

He wondered now if Ransome had managed to pursue his suit of Wickham's sister. Certainly, Lord Sanstable would see through Ransome's intentions quickly enough. Fortune hunters must be rather common in Wickham's world.

Immediately Hayden had finished his meal, the carpenters began taking down the bulkheads and removing all the mess tables and benches. Shot and powder were carried up from the hold, and magazines and the guns were cast loose and their tompions removed. When this was done, Hayden toured both the gun-decks and was very satisfied with what he saw—everything in its place, men at their stations, nervous but excited at the possibility of action.

Returning to the quarterdeck, Hayden gathered his officers. "Mr

Archer and Mr Bell shall be on the quarterdeck. Mr Bowen, forecastle. Mr Huxley, you will have the lower gun-deck, and Mr Ransome the upper. We have some very green reefers, so you will have
to watch over them and be certain they give their gun captains the
proper orders at the correct time. We do not know what we might
find ahead, and we should be prepared for any type of evolution.
There is a powerful French squadron and the Brest Fleet abroad, and
we do not want to draw too near either. Mr Wickham reports that
the smoke appears to be blowing off and we have heard no reports,
so I do not think Lord Howe has engaged the French fleet, but we
will see."

Although *Raisonnable* made good speed on the fair wind, the fad-
ing smoke did not appear to draw nearer—in truth, Hayden wondered if they were not chasing after it and never gaining.

Before the beginning of the new ship's day—which commenced
at noon—a lookout called, "*On deck!* There is somewhat on the
water, sir."

"*'Somewhat'?*" Hayden replied. "Would it be better described as
a ship?"

"I don't think so, sir. It disappears behind each wave."

"Mr Wickham, up to the tops with a glass, if you please."

"Aye, sir."

Hayden walked forward to see if he could spot this "somewhat"
the lookout had seen.

"On deck, sir," Wickham called out a moment later. "It might be
debris, Captain."

Wickham left the foremast tops and went scrambling higher for a
better vantage. Hayden watched him fix his glass upon the ocean
before them. A moment later, he leaned out so that he might see
his commanding officer. "I do believe that is what we have here,
Captain—debris."

"Any sign of sail, Mr Wickham?"

The midshipman raised his glass again and could be seen to scrutinize the ocean in a slow circle. Then his arm shot up. "*Sail!* West-north-west."

No one could make out this ship from the deck, and Hayden went aloft with his glass and caught just a glimpse as it disappeared over the horizon.

"No colours, I do not imagine, Mr Wickham?"

"No, sir." Wickham came climbing down to the platform, where Hayden stood with an elbow crooked around a shroud.

Hayden turned his glass back to the south-west. "That is debris, Wickham; you were not wrong."

"Then a ship has been sunk, sir?"

"I should think that most likely . . . But was she one of ours or one of theirs?" Hayden lowered his glass. "Mr Archer!" he called down to the deck. "West-north-west, if you please."

The sail handlers were called and yards were braced round to chase the glimpse of sail that had slipped below the horizon.

"How distant did you judge that sail, Wickham?"

"You could not make it out from the deck, sir?"

"We could not."

"And I caught only a glimpse of half a top-gallant. Four leagues, perhaps five."

"Then we will be most fortunate to come up with them by dark." Hayden raised his glass and stared in the direction of the disappearing ship. "If it is a fleet, they will have outlying frigates. I do not want to find myself fighting a running battle with three or four French frigates." Hayden lowered his glass. "If we cannot come up with them before dark, we will hang back and make the private signal in adequate morning light. Mr Wickham."

Wickham touched his hat. "Sir."

In a moment Hayden was back upon the quarterdeck, where he found Barthe staring up at the sails bellying overhead. "She would almost take royals, sir."

"I have thought the same, Mr Barthe. Will this wind make, do you think?"

"It has shown signs of such an inclination."

"Then let us wait and see if the wind can make up its mind."

"Aye, sir." Barthe shaded his eyes with a blunt hand and examined the debris, now on their port side and still some distance off. "If a ship had exploded, sir, I believe we would have heard it."

"I agree, Mr Barthe."

"If it were a ship of war, then all of the powder was removed before it was burned."

"Or it was not a ship of war."

"And if either were the case, why would it not be made a prize, sir?"

"Well, Mr Barthe, that is an excellent question. A transport would have surrendered to a warship, so it should not have sunk from being fired on. And the magazine of a ship of war would have exploded, as you say. So this burned ship is a mystery."

"I agree, sir."

Hayden found himself staring off towards the area of sea where a few dark objects bobbed low upon the waves, as though something there might suddenly enlighten him

"If I were about to fight a battle, Mr Barthe—even a single-ship action—I might choose not to reduce my crew by sending hands aboard a prize."

"That might answer, sir. But it does not tell us if the burned ship was French or British."

"Does it not? Would the French fleet, which has lain in Brest Harbour most of this past year, be in pursuit of the British or would we be pursuing them?"

"More likely the latter, I should think."

"Then that would mean we have Lord Howe before us."

"We shall certainly know by morning, Captain."

"Unless the French fleet is before His Lordship and a battle about to begin."

"Then let us listen for the sound of the great guns, sir."

They heard no guns that long afternoon; nor did the lookouts discover ships upon any point of the compass. Hayden began to think that the sail they had seen slipping beneath the western horizon was not one of a fleet but only a single vessel, for surely *Raisonnable*, with all her speed, would be within sight of a fleet in a few hours . . . But no fleet appeared.

The day's light was drawn over the western horizon and night was mysteriously upon them. The wind had gone into the north, and upon *Raisonnable* bowlines were hauled and the ship put on the wind as close as she would manage.

Hayden stalked the poop, resisting the desire to call up to the lookouts every quarter-hour to ask if they could not see a light . . . and to be certain they did not sleep. Instead, he swept the sea with his night glass at regular intervals—which the lookouts certainly did not miss. Not wanting their captain to discover something from the deck before they had seen it from aloft would keep them alert.

Finally, Hayden left Ransome the deck and went below.

He took to his cot quickly, believing he would be called on deck shortly, as ships must surely be seen. Darkness brought doubts and he began to wonder if he should have not held his course—that Howe went south yet and the sail he had seen was but a single vessel. What seemed more likely to the reasonable part of his mind was that Howe had taken some ship or ships, learned from them the position or course of the French fleet, and had put about to chase it. That they could outdistance Hayden's ship could only be explained by the variability of wind strength over an area of sea; Howe must have better wind than Hayden, at least for the time being.

As he was not yet fully recovered from his ordeal on the wreck, Hayden slept through the night, but rose before first light and went on deck. The wind had taken off considerably during the darkness and royals had been set.

"Mr Bell. What is our course?"

"North-north-west, sir. But the wind has not held steady from any point, sir, and we have been forced to steer as much as three points south and two north from our present heading. Mr Archer advised me to wake you, Captain, if we were forced three points off our course, but we were not."

"And you have seen no lights?"

"The sea has been most empty, sir."

"Often the case when you wish it were not."

Hayden went to the rail and stared north. The eastern sky grew pale blue-green, pressing back the darkness. Coffee arrived, borne by Hayden's steward, and the newly minted post captain took it braced against the taffrail, where he allowed himself a moment to survey his command with some satisfaction. Making his post had seemed as possible as swimming the ocean not so very long ago, and here he was upon his first command as post captain and it was not a frigate but a sixty-four-gun ship! The thought that it was most likely a temporary command did cross his mind then, and he felt the briefest moment of vertigo.

Hawthorne appeared at the head of the quarter-ladder and at a nod from Hayden walked aft. As he was about to speak, a voice from aloft sang out, "*On deck!* Sail, three points off the larboard bow!"

Hayden returned his cup to the tray balanced on a little bench, took up his glass, and crossed quickly to the larboard side, pressing his hip against the hammock netting. He focused on the area of ocean indicated by the lookout. For a moment he could find only dark ocean, and then a lighter patch of familiar dimensions.

"That is, indeed, a sail." Hayden went to the ladder head and called down to the quarterdeck. "Do you see it, Mr Bell?"

"No, sir . . . Ah, there she is. Cannot say what she might be, Captain."

"Three-master. That is all I know." Hayden lowered his glass. "Mr Bell, we shall beat to quarters. Who knows what ship this might be."

The watch below was turned out and the drummer began his roll. Hayden took up his coffee again and watched the men make the ship ready for action. Archer hurried up the companionway, found Hayden in the poor light, and climbed up to him immediately.

"Have we found Lord Howe, sir?"

"We have found a ship, Mr Archer, and we do not even know what species." Hayden twisted around to look east. "A little more light will tell us something."

"Shall I prepare to make the private signal, sir?"

"Yes. But we will wait awhile yet."

As the eastern horizon turned molten gold, the lookout called again. "*On deck!* Sail to the north of the first. She's hull down, Captain Hayden."

This sail was barely visible from the deck, and only as the ship lifted to a crest.

"Two ships do not a convoy make," Hawthorne intoned. "Is that not an old sailor's saying?"

"It is an old marine's saying, I believe, Captain Hawthorne," Wickham answered as he mounted a few steps of the quarter-ladder to gain a better view.

Hawthorne gazed down on his young friend. "Rather like, 'Pipeclay your belt in the morning, sailors take warning'?"

"Very much like that, Mr Hawthorne, only one can comprehend the meaning."

"Third sail!" came the call from aloft. "Dead ahead."

Barthe had arrived, standing at the foot of the ladder. "We have at least a squadron, Mr Hawthorne," he informed the marine. "Assuming these are ships of war and not transports."

"Let us hope for transports. It is said that the convoy that sailed from America was very rich."

"With powerful escorts, Mr Hawthorne, I might point out."

"You are an eternal pessimist, Mr Barthe."

"All sailing masters are pessimists; that is how we keep you alive."

"Then I encourage you to carry on with it."

Hayden turned to his first lieutenant. "Mr Archer? You have the deck. I shall climb to the foremast tops. Mr Wickham . . . would you care for some morning exercise?"

"I would, sir."

"Carry along a glass."

In a moment, the two were climbing hand over hand up to the foremast tops and pulling themselves up onto the platform.

"This damned topsail is obscuring the entire ocean," Hayden complained, and the two set off upward until they sat astride the topsail yard.

Here the ocean opened up to them, the light growing and spreading west until it caught the tops of distant masts and began to illuminate reddish-brown sails. The slow creep of the light revealed another ship, and then another, and then a dozen and a dozen more, all upon the same course stretched out in two lines abreast, their heading the same as *Raisonnable*'s.

"There is our fleet, Mr Wickham," Hayden announced.

"I do not see a flag, sir . . . ?"

"If I were trying to intercept a convoy or catch a French fleet, I should not fly a flag either. Any small thing that would draw the enemy nearer must be employed."

"Will the French then do the same?"

"Very likely."

"Then we cannot know if this is our fleet or theirs?"

"That is correct. So we must be prepared to fly, Mr Wickham. Remain here and see if you cannot make out anything that would tell us if these ships are French or British." Hayden pointed. "Do you see? They have detached ships to find out if we are friend or foe."

Ships from the rear of the columns were wearing to come upon the other tack, back towards *Raisonnable*.

Hayden climbed quickly down. "Mr Archer!" he called as he made his way aft. "Though we should be prepared to open our gun-ports and fight if it is necessary, I will first require sail handlers to their stations. If this is the Brest Fleet we will wear ship and set our course east by north." He found the sailing master emerging from among the carronade gun crews, a glass tucked under his arm. "There you are, Mr Barthe. Did you hear?"

"Wear and east by north, sir."

"Where is Mr Bowen?"

"On the main gun-deck, sir," one of the new midshipmen answered up promptly.

"Hop down to him quick as you can and ask him who the best helmsman might be."

"It is the quartermaster, Mr Swain, sir."

"How do you know that?"

"My brother told me, sir. 'Mr Swain,' he said."

"Very well, Huxley, find Mr Swain and have him report to me immediately."

"Aye, sir."

Hayden put his glass upon the distant ships, still too far off to distinguish clearly. He would allow them near enough for signals not to be mistaken—and no nearer. Any indication of hesitation or obfuscation of signals by the approaching ship and Hayden would wear and show them his stern. Then the French would see how swiftly a British ship could fly!

There was utter silence upon the deck, by order but also out of mere tension. Every man not engaged in a task had his eyes fixed upon the three approaching ships, which were beginning to distinguish themselves as a frigate and a pair of two-deckers—most probably seventy-fours.

Hayden had no desire to tip Frenchmen to Howe's private signal, so he waited, the ships becoming more distinct and vivid by the moment. Some of the men and even officers began casting nervous glances his way after a time, wondering when he would give the order to make the signal, thinking that these three ships were drawing too near.

Hobson came running along the deck, touching his hat as he stepped upon the quarterdeck. "Sir, Mr Wickham says we have a frigate and two seventy-four-gun ships approaching."

"I can see that," Hayden replied testily. "But are they ours?"

"I do not know, sir."

Hayden turned to find Archer. "Make the private signal, Mr Archer."

The hoist of flags, which had been laid out and ready, were sent aloft, where they could be easily distinguished by the approaching ships.

Hayden fixed his glass upon the three ships, wondering if he should not have made the signal sooner, they looked so large inside the circle of glass. The squeak of cordage stretching through blocks and the common shipboard sounds grew suddenly loud as the human noises were reduced to the occasional indrawing of breath. On the nearest ship, a hoist of signals went jerkily aloft and then fluttered open to the wind.

"She is one of ours," Hayden announced, feeling a flood of relief.

"We have found Lord Howe." He turned to his lieutenant. "Mr Archer? I shall require a boat when we are up with the fleet."

It was some time before Hayden met the three ships, which all wore to escort him back to the fleet. As *Raisonnable* ranged up alongside one of the two-deckers, which proved to be the seventy-four *Audacious*, the captain came to the rail and hailed Hayden.

"I have urgent dispatches for Lord Howe from the Admiralty," Hayden called after they had introduced themselves.

"You may give them to me, Captain," Parker, captain of the *Audacious*, called back over the dividing waters, "I will deliver them to His Lordship."

"I will deliver them myself, thank you, Captain," Hayden replied, feeling his choler rise immediately. The man would deliver Hayden's dispatches in a vain attempt to bring himself to the lord admiral's attention.

"As you wish," Parker called back, realizing that Hayden would not be so duped.

Hayden waved a hand and ordered sail to be trimmed, and very quickly he left the two seventy-fours behind, the frigate making sail to stay near.

Hayden overhauled the ships of the line one by one, until he finally came abreast of the hundred-gun ship *Queen Charlotte*, making the signal for urgent dispatches. Signals were almost immediately made from the deck of Howe's ship, and then she was manoeuvred out of line and hove to quite sharply.

Hayden had anticipated this and had his ship heave to within pistol shot and his boat in the water only an instant later. Two dozen strokes by the oarsmen and Hayden's boat was laid expertly alongside and he was climbing quickly up the side, where he was piped aboard and met at the rail by the ship's captain.

"You have dispatches, Captain?" Sir Roger Curtis said after introducing himself.

"I do, sir."

"His Lordship will speak with you immediately."

Hayden was led down to the admiral's cabin, where he found Admiral Lord Howe eating a boiled egg.

"Will you join me, Captain Hayden? My hens laid these fresh this very morning."

"Why, thank you, sir; I breakfasted but a moment ago."

"Then sit and take coffee. I do wish you had brought me a seventy-four, Captain, for I will tell you I have little use for a sixty-four. None the less, even your little ship may play some part. When did you leave Portsmouth?"

"But six days past, sir. We missed Your Lordship off Brest by a day and have been most fortunate to find you so quickly."

"Indeed you have. Was *Expedition* still on station there?"

"She was, sir, and the Brest Fleet still at sea."

"Yes, the French fleet is somewhere before us," he waved a fork in the general direction of the bow. Finishing his egg, the admiral wiped his mouth most fastidiously, pushed his chair away from the table, and turned his attention to Hayden.

"Let us see these dispatches."

Hayden proffered the package, and the admiral wasted no time in breaking the seal and opening the letters; at the same moment, his servants cleared away. As he read, Howe's lower lip pressed up so that two shallow, wrinkled dimples formed in his chin. Hayden thought the smallest tremor was just perceptible in the admiral's head and hands.

Without looking up, Howe addressed Hayden again. "It appears, Captain, that you were sent to meet with one of our friends in France?"

"I was, sir."

"Do you give credence to this report of a significant invasion force being gathered in Cancale?"

"I was unable to corroborate it myself, sir, but Mr Stephens thought it a matter of the greatest urgency to convey this information to you."

"And when did you meet with our friend?"

"Some weeks ago, sir."

Howe appeared to contemplate this a moment, staring off into the vague distance beyond the hull. "We have known for some time that the French had designs upon Jersey and Guernsey, but it was never contemplated that this might be only their first objective—England we believed out of reach." Again he stopped to consider the information that Hayden's dispatches had added to the great deal of knowledge to which such a senior admiral was privy. "I cannot reinforce Admiral McBride's squadron with the French fleet so near."

It was well known within the service that Admiral McBride had been given responsibility for defending the Channel Islands. Hayden could not prevent his own mind from racing, and he blurted out without thinking, "Is it possible that the French could attempt this crossing without fleet support?"

Howe ignored the impropriety of such a junior captain speaking out of place. "Only if the Channel Fleet could be destroyed or rendered ineffective." Howe glanced again at the letter and then set it upon his table. "I believed the French fleet had put to sea to effect the safety of the American convoy . . . Perhaps that is not their intention at all. Did you speak to this spy yourself, Captain?"

"I did, sir."

"And he could not give you numbers of troops gathered?"

"Only to say more than twenty-five thousand—perhaps many more. No doubt it is detailed in the Admiralty's letter, but I was informed by our friend that there were five or six ships of the line, two razees, five frigates, and more than one hundred and fifty transports. His information was that one hundred thousand troops were to be gathered in the region of Cancale."

"And there was no misunderstanding between you?"

"I speak French as a native, sir. I can assure you that I did comprehend every word he said most perfectly."

Howe nodded, the distant look disappearing from his face. "Thank you, Captain. You understand that you are attached now to my fleet?"

Hayden said that he did.

"Have you copies of our signals?"

"Given me by Mr Stephens, my lord."

Howe considered a moment.

"Sir?"

Howe looked at Hayden and nodded.

"My surgeon, who is an excellent man, has a patient whose symptoms concern him overly. He has asked that I enquire if we might carry this man to Dr Trotter aboard the *Charon*. My surgeon is of the opinion that the man will in all likelihood die if he cannot be properly diagnosed and given proper physic."

"I am certain Trotter would be pleased to take him. Nothing makes the man happier than a medical puzzle."

"Thank you, sir."

Howe acknowledged this thanks with a curt nod. "*Raisonnable* has the character of a swift ship; do you concur?"

"Very swift, sir. I saw service aboard her as a lieutenant and can assure Your Lordship that she is faster than many a frigate and very handy for her size."

"Then I shall have you act as an outlier. Once you have delivered your patient to Dr Trotter, station your ship to larboard of the lead ships in our weather column. If the situation requires, I may signal you to support our advance frigates on the chance that strange sail is descried."

"She is perfectly suited to such duty, my lord, and will not disappoint you in any way."

"It is seldom the ship that disappoints, Captain. You may go."

Hayden made the appropriate obeisance and went quickly out. By the time he lowered himself into the stern-sheets of his barge, the *Queen Charlotte* was already making sail and getting under way. The second he climbed over the rail of his own ship, Hayden was waving for Archer and Barthe.

"Stream this boat, Mr Archer. We have been given permission to deliver the doctor's patient to the *Charon* and then are to take up position off the head of the weather column."

"We are not to be in the line, sir?" Archer asked, not hiding his relief at this news.

"Not at this time."

Hayden looked around at his officers and midshipmen, who had gathered on the quarterdeck. A palpable tension—perhaps anxiety— was apparent among them. Even the new midshipmen understood that a sixty-four-gun ship was no match for a seventy-four. If they were ordered into the line, they would without question meet a vessel of a superior firepower, and the outcome of such an action was beyond doubt—*Raisonnable* would be severely mauled and probably forced to strike. The idea that he could lose his ship—his first command as post captain—and the second ship within a few weeks, was more distressing than Hayden could tell.

"We are in a fleet now," he told the gathered men, "and must look always to the flagship and the vessels that are repeating her signals. Lord Howe is not a patient man and does not suffer incompetence. Let us be about our business."

At the urging of Dr Griffiths, Hayden accompanied the doctor and his patient to the hospital ship, *Charon*. The former forty-four-gun ship, reduced to a single deck of guns and a crew of a little more than a hundred, now bore, upon a former gun-deck, a hospital. Although she was under the command of the Royal Navy captain George Countess, in many ways her senior officer was Dr Thomas Trotter, physician to the fleet. Countess might make all decisions to do with the handling and safety of the ship, but in every other way he was charged to serve the needs of the hospital, and in this he took his directions, if not his orders, from the physician.

It was Countess who met them at the rail, but after the briefest pleasantries Trotter appeared and, upon the completion of introductions, the naval officer retired.

Immediately, Trotter bent over the patient, who had been deposited in his litter upon the deck, took his pulse, and felt his forehead. Very pointed questions were asked, and very succinctly and clearly answered by Griffiths.

Trotter stood and rubbed his small chin as he gazed down at the man, who barely seemed to return his gaze, so removed was he from the activity around him by illness. Motioning to men standing by, Trotter ordered, "Vale, Edwards, into the aft quarantine berth with this man. I shall be along directly to see to him."

The two men, clearly not sailors, took up the litter and bore poor Allen, shivering, below.

Trotter, who was a pleasant-looking man with a high forehead and large, clear eyes, gazed a moment upon Hayden's own surgeon, "Are you the Griffiths who wrote to me some time ago about the scurvy?"

Griffiths smiled. "I am surprised you should remember."

"It was a very insightful letter. I hope you were satisfied with my response?"

"In every way. I believe we are very much of one mind on the subject of the scurvy and the effectiveness of diverse antiscorbutics."

Trotter nodded, apparently satisfied with Griffiths. "Have you a moment to tour the ship? That is, if it would interest you?"

"I should like nothing better . . ." But he glanced at Hayden, clearly wondering if such would be possible under the present circumstances.

"And you, Captain?" Trotter wondered.

"I should be delighted. From Dr Griffiths I have learned that the health of the crew is as important as the powder for her guns and sails for her spars."

"You will find my captain is a modest man, Dr Trotter. He had come to this realization some years before we first met, I assure you."

"If only the Navy Board and the Admiralty were so enlightened." Trotter waved a hand at the ship in general as they went down the ladder. "But here is a great symbol of progress, I believe, and Lord Howe is owed a debt of thanks by all seamen for it."

To Hayden's great surprise, the first member of the medical staff encountered was a woman—one of several nurses, they were informed, just as though they were in a hospital ashore.

"Five nurses, Captain Hayden," Trotter explained when questioned, "under the care of Mrs Simmons, our matron, whom no living man dares offend." A hint of a smile appeared at this. "A surgeon, two mates, three loblolly boys—all of them men, of course—six washerwomen, and the most beloved man upon our ship—Chamberlain, the baker."

In the place of hospital beds, cots were hung in neat rows athwart ship with enough space between for the medical staff to move easily and without danger of being knocked off their feet by swinging patients. There was an actual surgery, and separate quarantine berths for the fevered as well as a locked dispensary with every physic in such abundance that Griffiths could not hide his envy.

Scuttles brought air and light down into the hospital berth, and everywhere it was as clean as a nobleman's house, new white paint everywhere so that one hardly felt shut up belowdecks.

"Fresh air is a physic all its own," Trotter told them. "I am convinced of it. A sick-berth in the orlop contains disease and spreads it easily from one man to another, but fresh sea air is cleansed by nature. Once a ship has gone to sea, and all of the common ailments have run their course, you will find that the crew achieve uncommon good health, provided the scurvy can be kept at bay. Have you not both observed the same thing?"

"I have been upon so few ships where the scurvy has not felled some members of the crew that I can hardly say," Hayden replied. "But for the bad luck of a virulent influenza on our last prolonged voyage, we would have done very well, for the antiscorbutics did keep away the scurvy."

This caught Trotter's interest. "I did hear about that and wondered if it was truly an influenza. I have never heard of one so deadly."

"Nor had I, Dr Trotter," Griffiths told him, "but I was afflicted with it myself and am quite certain it could be nothing else. No other disease, in my knowledge, would fit the bill so perfectly."

The two medical men then fell into a discussion of the particular symptoms and course of the disease, Trotter listening with full attention, as though he might encounter the disease that very afternoon and should be as ready as possible to combat it. Hayden liked the man immediately.

The two medical men could have talked throughout the afternoon, and would have, had Hayden not gently cleared his throat after what he believed was an acceptable time.

Trotter accompanied them up to the deck, clearly a sign of his respect for Griffiths, Hayden thought.

"We get very little news aboard our ship," Trotter said as they stood at the rail. "Has the convoy been intercepted?"

"Not that we know of, Dr Trotter," Hayden replied.

The physician appeared very distressed. "Very many will starve if it does not get through. I know they are French and I should not care, but I would imagine a good number of the victims will be women and children. Starving women and children . . . that is no way to prosecute a war."

And with that he bade them good-bye and safe voyage. Hayden and Griffiths were back aboard their barge and the oarsmen pulling for *Raisonnable* in a moment.

"Well, there was your Dr Trotter," Hayden observed. "Were you pleased with him?"

"In every way. I do wish I could be the *Charon*'s surgeon for a sixmonth. I should learn a very great deal, I believe."

Hayden was less certain. He held his own surgeon in the highest regard . . . and the modesty and desire to learn that he was presently displaying were two of the reasons he felt as he did.

"Do you think the grain coming from America is destined for the French Army?" Griffiths asked suddenly.

"Certainly some of it, but I believe Dr Trotter was correct in saying that the general population will suffer if we do manage to intercept it."

"One hardly knows what to wish for," Griffiths said so quietly only Hayden might hear.

Now you know how I feel at all times, Doctor, Hayden thought, but he did not give voice to this.

Upon Hayden's return to his ship orders were given to take in the boat and then make sail. Very soon, *Raisonnable* gathered way and began to quickly overhaul the ships of the line, one by one. Hayden stood at the rail and admired the ships, some of them first-rates of a hundred guns or more. The stalwart of the fleet, the seventy-four-gun ship, was by far the most numerous and there were at least fifteen of these, though Hayden could not make out all of the ships in the leeward column. Many of the ships he knew by reputation, and more than a few by sight. "Billy Ruffian" sailed in the weather column—the venerable *Bellerophon*. He also passed *Russell*, *Thunderer*, *Leviathan*, *Royal George*, *Invincible*. The pride of the British Navy in two smart columns, sails drawing, a weight of broadside that Hayden could not even calculate lying within the ships' bellies—pregnant with destruction. His own ship—an object of his greatest pride but a short time ago—seemed very small and vastly less powerful. He could not escape the feeling that if Howe did not see fit to put his ship into the line of battle it would reflect badly upon him—as if the failing were his own and not the vessel's. And if the admiral did see fit to place Hayden's ship in the line of battle, great loss of life would almost certainly be the result, if not the loss of his ship. Neither situation was to be hoped for, as far as he was concerned.

He had never seen or taken part in a fleet action, and despite his reservations Hayden above all things was anxious to acquit himself honourably if such a battle were engaged. There were many stories within the service of captains who, sometimes through no fault of their own, were unable to get into the action or only tardily engaged the enemy due to a sudden localized calm, and their careers never recovered. Hayden was determined that such an occurrence would not befall him if Lord Howe put him into the battle. There was no doubt in Hayden's mind, however, that the price for this pride would be paid by his crew, and that knowledge unsettled him terribly.

For two days the horizon in all directions remained empty of sail. There was little communication among the ships, and Hayden felt a growing sense of disquiet; he even wondered if the French fleet had

proceeded into the Channel to support an invasion. Given the recent intelligence he had delivered to Lord Howe, he wondered if
His Lordship was not contemplating this same possibility.

Upon the third day after his joining the fleet, an outlying frigate
made the signal for strange sail, and to his great satisfaction Hayden's
ship was detached immediately to discover what ships these might
be. Orders to beat to quarters were given, and all sail made to support the frigates that lay less than a league ahead.

Sail did appear on the horizon very soon thereafter, though the
ships were hull down for some moments longer. The swift *Raisonnable* managed to catch up with the two frigates as they drew near
the unknown sail. These vessels immediately turned to flee but
within the hour were forced to heave to, and proved to be part of a
Dutch convoy.

This information was signalled to the flagship, and as the British
fleet came up the order was given to heave to. Several of the masters
of the Dutch transports were taken aboard *Raisonnable* and conveyed
with all speed to *Queen Charlotte*. Although Hayden accompanied
these gentlemen, he was not allowed into the presence of the admiral and was not privy to the conversation. Instead, he loitered on the
deck in conversation with two of the flagship's lieutenants, one of
whom was something of an acquaintance of his from early days.

Not an hour passed before the Dutch masters reappeared, and
Hayden took them again aboard his ship to convey them back to
their vessels.

One of the masters surveyed the British fleet carefully and then
reported to Hayden as they stood by the rail, "I believe you are of
equal strength to the French, Captain, though we only observed
them at a distance. They took some of our ships, but we escaped."
He then volunteered the position of the French fleet when it had last
been seen, which meant Hayden was better informed than any captain in the fleet other than the commander of Howe's flagship.

This short meeting heartened him overly, and he repeated the information to his lieutenants and Mr Barthe. A rumour passed around the ship that the French fleet was near at hand, escorting a convoy so rich that every man aboard would make his fortune from prize money. Hayden allowed this rumour to circulate freely, as prize money galvanized a crew and raised their courage more than any love of country or duty, though he hated to admit it. Given his own recent reversals, prize money would not go begging in his life, either, and he was sorry that the convoy was only a rumour.

No sail appeared again that day, and by the supper hour Hayden had the ship, which had been cleared for action the whole day, restored to its more domestic form so that men might eat and sleep, which were as necessary to the prosecution of war as any amount of arms.

The night passed uneventfully, and so did the morning. It was after the ship's bell had rung the midday that the signal for strange sail was again seen upon a frigate and Hayden ordered to make all sail and support the British frigates in their inspection. Upon sight of the British ships, this vessel wore and ran downwind, crowding on sail. Behind her wallowed a dismasted vessel—much smaller— that had been in tow.

Wickham stood by Hayden's side with a glass, as did several other officers, all with glasses raised. "She appears to be a seventy-four, sir," Wickham announced, "and a Frenchman, too."

"Signals on the flagship, sir," Bell called out.

Hayden went quickly to the transom and examined the signal flags while the lieutenant consulted the signal book.

"We are ordered not to chase, sir."

"Are you certain, Lieutenant?"

"Here it is, sir," the young man said, holding up the book.

"Another hoist, Captain," Gould reported.

And indeed a second hoist of flags appeared upon the lord admiral's ship.

"Secure the vessel," Gould said without consulting Bell's book.

A moment later, Bell confirmed this to be true and Hayden ordered his sails trimmed and helm altered to approach the abandoned vessel, which turned out to be a small brig. The officers of this vessel were taken off upon one of the frigates and Hayden never knew what Lord Howe might have learned from them, but the remaining crew were taken off this brig and she was set afire. Immediately after this was accomplished, the course of the fleet was altered to north by west.

All eyes watched the great circle of the horizon, hardly willing to blink. The night passed quietly, and though Hayden had a foreboding that dawn would find the French fleet almost upon them, the sea proved empty yet again at sunrise. The day passed without a single sail to interrupt the vast acreage of blue that spread out to every point of the compass.

That night Hayden felt around him a sense of both disappointment and relief. Certainly, if the French fleet were still abroad they would have discovered it by now. It must have returned to Brest or sailed further south to meet the convoy and escort it . . . into Bordeaux, perhaps. The officers and crew did not know of the other possibility—that the French fleet had gone into the Channel to support an invasion. Hayden was very glad not to be the admiral of this particular British fleet, as any failure might be catastrophic and one's name would be attached to the failure for ever.

Despite the obvious truth that not finding the French fleet might preserve many lives, the crew were also disappointed. An action with a chance for victory and prize money was the dream of many whose service had been less exciting than others. Men went to their hammocks that night speaking sadly of a return to England, perhaps as early as the morrow.

Even so, Hayden slept poorly and was upon the deck at two bells of the morning watch. Light had already begun to wash away the stars and only the brightest struggled to extend their light a little further into the morning.

Hayden's steward and a servant had just brought him coffee when one of the new midshipmen pointed and called out excitedly. "Lieutenant! Signals on the *Niger*, sir."

"'*Strange sail,*' Captain," Bowen interpreted. "'*South-south-east.*'"

Hayden went to the rail; he could see nothing but their distant frigates. Bowen had fetched a glass and stood beside him, aiming that instrument at the appropriate section of the ocean.

"Do you see a sail?" Hayden asked.

"I am not certain, sir." And then, after a moment more: "I do not, but the frigates are much nearer than we."

"Signals for us on the flagship, Captain."

Hayden turned to see the flags stream in the small wind. He drained his coffee cup and passed it to the waiting servant. "We are to follow Admiral Pasley and inspect this sail, Mr Bowen. Sail trimmers to their stations. We will shape our course south-south-east and then beat to quarters."

"Aye, sir. south-south-east and then beat to quarters."

Orders were called. Barthe appeared buttoning his waistcoat, a boy hurrying behind with the master's coat and battered hat. "We have sail, Captain?"

"We do, Mr Barthe, but over the horizon yet."

"*On deck!*" came the familiar call from aloft. "Sail, Captain. South-south-east just as was said. More than one, I believe."

"Mr Bowen. You have the deck. I shall go aloft a moment."

Hayden's glass had already been carried up for him, and he slung it over his back and clambered up to the main-tops, pleased that he did not need to climb further—he could make out sail from that vantage with his naked eye.

"Do you see, sir?" the lookout asked. "Beyond the first ship? More sail."

"Indeed I do, Goodwin. Indeed I do." Hayden grasped hold of a shroud and leaned over the side of the platform. "Mr Bowen!" he called down to the deck. "It would appear we have discovered a fleet—if not a convoy."

This produced a great hum of excitement over the main deck.

Hayden took another long look—more sail appearing as the day brightened—and then climbed swiftly down to the deck. He was on the quarterdeck in a moment. Only the top of a single sail could be seen from this height, but everyone strained towards the south-south-east, trying to conjure up a French fleet or a richly laden convoy.

"Mr Bowen, do not overhaul *Bellerophon*; the admiral will not like it."

"Aye, sir."

Hayden glanced up at the pennant streaming from the masthead. The wind was too light for his liking, though once they had closed with the enemy ships, it would be better to have calm seas, but at the moment it was carrying them towards their quarry at the frustrating pace of a leisurely walk.

"Will they meet us, Captain," Bowen asked, "or will they fly?"

"If it is a convoy, it will most certainly fly from us. If a fleet—I cannot fathom the French admiral's thinking, Mr Bowen, nor can I guess what his orders might be. I do believe, though, that his intentions will be made clear in very short order."

The intentions of the French admiral, however, remained somewhat mysterious for the next three hours until about nine of the morning, when the entire distant fleet wore and went upon the larboard tack, which would bring them in contact with Pasley's squadron by noon or not much beyond, Hayden believed. Not long after that the two fleets would converge.

One thing did become clear—this was not a convoy—three-deckers could be seen, and *Bellerophon* signalled as much to Lord

Howe. This news spread from the quarterdeck throughout the ship like a shiver of anticipation.

As the distance between the fleets remained about three leagues, Hayden took the time to inspect his command and be certain all was in order. He had placed the green midshipmen with one of the more experienced young gentlemen so that they might witness at first hand how to command a battery of guns in the midst of the noise and confusion and under enemy fire. These boys were as pale as clouds and silent as pallbearers, but they all stood their places, and Hayden believed their nerve would hold when they saw the experienced men around them staying to their work even under fire.

Mr Hawthorne had instructed them all to carry the buckets bearing their names to the gun-deck with them, and these had been hung prominently, to the mirth of all the hands and the disquiet of the green reefers. Hayden ordered these taken down and assured the boys that they would not be needing their buckets that day or anytime in the immediate future.

All appeared to be in order, wet blankets hung about the magazines and every man knowing his duty most thoroughly. Hayden returned to the deck to find the French fleet heaving to.

Hawthorne was standing between carronades, watching this evolution when Hayden appeared beside him. "What are they about, Captain?" he asked.

"Preparing for battle, Mr Hawthorne. The admiral is no doubt communicating his intentions to his captains, for, as you know, once the enemy has been engaged it can be near to impossible to make out signals."

"Will Lord Howe do the same?"

"It would surprise me. His Lordship's plan will be very simple— engage the enemy at close quarters and pour in broadside upon broadside until they strike."

Hawthorne laughed gently. "We English do lack subtlety when set beside the French."

"Indeed we do, Mr Hawthorne; fortunately, war is not a subtle art." They both stared off at the distant ships. "Did you really believe it necessary to send the new midshipmen to their stations bearing their buckets?"

"I thought it would be a comfort to them to know their remains would not be lost, should they have the misfortune to be blasted to hell by a cannon ball."

"Mmm. They appeared so frightened as to be nearly paralysed. I had the buckets taken down and hidden away."

A grin overspread the marine's face. "That is why you are a captain and I am not."

"You are a captain, Mr Hawthorne—an acting captain of marines."

"So I am. Clearly, I had forgotten, or I should never have practised so cruelly upon those poor lads. I do hope they all live to see their dear mothers again."

"I wish that for all of us, Mr Hawthorne."

Hawthorne nodded. "How like you our new lieutenants? They seem a likely enough bunch to me."

"We will certainly know their character most thoroughly by the day's end, but I do not expect to be disappointed. And your marines?"

"There is not a man among them who can, from the main-tops, kill a barrel floating twenty yards off."

"Then the enemy barrels may breathe a sigh of relief."

"You make jest of it, sir, but if a boarding party of French barrels comes over the rail we are all done for."

Hayden laughed. He often wondered if Hawthorne felt obliged to make light of battle now that he had gained such a reputation and the obvious admiration of officers and crew for his drollery under fire.

"Sir, there is a great deal of talk among the crew of whether or no we will be put into the line of battle. If not, I believe the men will expire of shame; if so, I understand we are all to expire at the hands of a hundred-gun ship that will blast us to hell with a single broadside."

"Both, I dearly hope, are exaggerations, Mr Hawthorne. Neither will be good for the crew, for they will not want to be left out of the battle, but I dare say, once in it, they will wish themselves elsewhere."

"And what do you hope for, if I may ask, Captain?"

"I believe you know me well enough to answer that question yourself."

"So I thought. God preserve us."

The frustration of watching the French fleet in the offing and the time it was taking to come up with them infected Hayden's entire crew and her officers. There was among all the men aboard a strong desire to undertake this action and to see it done, at the same moment as there was great apprehension. The great expanse of sea that lay between the two fleets, however, was only reduced by the smallest degree every hour, and even Hayden had begun to wonder if darkness would not fall before a general engagement could commence. All that long forenoon he made his presence felt around the deck, urging the men to remain steady, that the French would not escape, if indeed that was their intention.

The small squadron under the command of Admiral Pasley remained some distance before the British fleet, and just as the French fleet again made sail and tacked, the signal was made to harass the enemy's rear.

Sail handlers were ordered to their stations, and royals were set and trimmed to the liking of Mr Barthe and the first lieutenant.

The sailing master found Hayden upon the quarterdeck. "Sir, if we are to allow 'Billy Ruffian' to take the lead, we shall have to spill some wind; we are much swifter than she."

"At this point, I believe we may give our mount her head, Mr Barthe. If *Bellerophon* cannot match our speed, then we shall leave her in our wake. And the same may be said for *Marlborough* and *Russell*."

"Aye, sir!" Barthe replied with obvious approval, and he went about the deck ordering hands to brace yards and trim sails to a nicety, attempting to get every tenth of a knot from his new ship.

Hayden did keep an eye upon Pasley's ship to see if he would be ordered back into place, but no such signal was seen and Hayden turned his attention to the rearmost ship of the French line. Going to the forward barricade for a better outlook, Hayden found several of his officers gathered there with their glasses rising up to quiz the French ship and then dropping down to allow excited conversation.

"And what ship do we have, Mr Ransome?" Hayden asked.

"A large three-decker, sir, but we cannot yet make out her name. Perhaps *Le Montagne* or *Le Terrible*."

"May we send for Mr Wickham, Captain? He might make her out."

Hayden raised his glass. "There is no need for Wickham, Mr Huxley. I am quite certain that is *Révolutionnaire*, of a hundred and ten guns. I have seen her before."

"Her broadside must be treble our own," Ransome announced softly.

"More than treble, Mr Ransome," Hayden took it upon himself to answer, "but if we can slow her progress enough for our seventy-fours to come up, I believe we might earn a huzzah from the fleet."

"And prize money as well," someone said, and everyone laughed nervously.

"Mr Ransome," Hayden said, "let us have the sprit-sail yard sent inboard and all of its gear cleared away so that we may employ our chase guns."

"Aye, sir."

The rearmost ship seemed to grow in size as *Raisonnable* gained on her over the next three quarters of an hour. The fleet, stretched out in a ragged line before her, gradually grew more vivid and detailed and was both a grand and unnerving sight to the crew of Hayden's ship and to Hayden himself. Twenty-six sail of the line and several frigates and outlying vessels meant the two fleets were almost exactly evenly matched. Everyone aboard sensed that this was a moment of enormous gravity in this young war, though few knew as Hayden did that the preservation of England from imminent invasion might depend on the next few hours and the coolness and judgement of Lord Howe and of every jack who manned a gun.

Even with royals set and drawing, *Raisonnable* appeared to gain upon the French only to the smallest degree, though she had opened a noticeable lead over the ships of her small squadron that now lay half a mile astern—making Hayden wonder if these ships were gaining on the French at all. Although he did desire the honour of being the first British ship to open fire on the enemy, he did not want to get so far ahead of his squadron that he might end up in danger. A 110-gun ship was a formidable machine of war, and he would have to rely on the handiness of his ship and the skill of his crew to prevent the *Révolutionnaire* from bringing its broadside to bear upon his own people.

At two-thirty in the afternoon Lord Howe gave the signal for a general chase, and the ships at the fore of the line began to crowd on sail in an effort to catch the advance squadron and get into the action sooner.

A further two hours were required to close the gap sufficiently for Hayden to consider opening fire. He stood by the forward chase guns, attempting to be an example of patience to his eager crew.

Wasting shot and powder to no purpose or effect was foolish, and Hayden was well aware that these valuable commodities should be preserved.

The gun captains at the two forward guns, both of which could be brought to bear, were older seamen named Higgenbotham and Hale—who certainly should have been solicitors. They stood by their guns, firing lanyards in sweaty hands, eyes focused intently upon the chase, quietly ordering a gun elevated or lowered or shifted to larboard to account for the changing distance and bearing of the Frenchman.

There was at that moment a loud report to starboard and Hayden turned to see a cloud of black smoke enveloping the bow of *Bellerophon.*

"They have not a chance of hitting the Frenchman at that distance!" Hale blurted out resentfully.

"Just to be able to claim they fired the first shot . . ." Ransome said with equal indignation.

"At least we shall fire the second," Hayden said. "Gun captains, fire your guns."

Both guns boomed at the same instant, bitter smoke blooming out and blinding them for a moment. Hayden looked up the foretop.

"Both shots fell short, Captain," the lookout called.

"How many yards?"

"One hundred yards about . . . sir."

The guns were quickly swabbed and reloaded, elevated, aimed and fired again, this time Hayden ordering the starboard fired first and then the larboard so that they might have some chance of knowing which gun's ball fell where.

"Starboard gun holed the driver, sir," the lookout called. "Larboard ball a-swim off the larboard quarter—ten yards, mayhap."

Guns were loaded, shifted by crowbar, and fired again.

A *"Huzzah"* rippled down the deck as the first ball shattered a gallery rail, though no one was certain where the second ball had gone.

The wind began making and a smoky haze overspread the azure sky. Hayden began to glance aloft frequently, wondering how long they dared carry the royals. He did not want to have to clear away broken royal masts aloft and finally called for Archer, who arrived with a worried-looking Barthe in his wake.

"I believe we should take in these royals and send down the yards," Hayden informed them. "The wind is making, so I do not think we shall lose much speed."

"Aye, sir," Barthe said, eyeing the small square sails high above. "I do not believe we shall lose even half a knot, Captain." The guns boomed, interrupting conversation. The sailing master winced and then went on. "This wind will make and keep our speed just as it is."

"I do hope you are correct, Mr Barthe. Let us get these sails off her before we have to clear away a tangle aloft."

"Aye, sir."

Men were sent scrambling aloft, and Hayden turned his attention back to the French fleet. *Bellerophon* had come up somewhat and lay upon *Raisonnable*'s leeward quarter about three hundred yards distant. She began lobbing shot towards the aftermost French ship, with reasonable success. Astern, the British fleet was drawing near, with the faster ships coming up quickly now that the wind was making.

Hayden glanced at the sun, which was descending towards the west in its ever-returning arc. Light would remain only a few short hours, and it seemed unlikely that Lord Howe could force a general action in that time, which engendered intense feelings of disappointment in Hayden.

"Mr Huxley?"

"Sir?"

"I will leave you to watch over the chase guns. I want them loaded with chain until we are nearer. If we can damage the rig of this Frenchman, we might slow her so our own ships can come up. We might force the French ships of the rear to come to her rescue or cut her off."

"Aye, sir. Chain."

Hayden returned to the quarterdeck, where he found Archer.

"When we get the royals off, Mr Archer, I want sail handlers at their stations. We will try to rake this rearmost ship."

"Will she not smoke what we are about and bring her broadside to bear, sir?"

"I do not think she will, Mr Archer. Her captain knows that he cannot fall back from his fleet or he will be lost. I believe she will hold her course and be forced to take all we give her, but we will see."

Révolutionnaire began to return fire, though this was concentrated on *Bellerophon*, which was both a larger target and the more dangerous adversary. Hayden's sixty-four was largely ignored as the British seventy-fours ranged up from astern. It was Hayden's hope that he could use this situation to get him near enough to *Révolutionnaire* that he might inflict some real damage and force her to fall behind the fleet. Then they would see if the French admiral would risk a general action to rescue his 110-gun ship or if he would let her be made a prize.

A cheer went up on the deck as the mizzen top-gallant yard on the French ship suddenly swung down in an arc to larboard, the sail flailing and snapping at the rigging all around and the loose spar battering shrouds and stays. "Was that our doing?" Hayden asked his first lieutenant.

"I do not know, sir, but I do think we should make that claim."

The crew of a carronade, forward on the quarterdeck, broke into laughter and the bosun and a mate were on them with rattans of an instant. Archer advanced on this scene to take names and to impress upon these men again that silence on deck was imperative.

"What was that about, Mr Bellamy?" Hayden asked the bosun as he passed.

"I cannot say, sir. A bit of drollery, I should wager. Those men well know that they should keep their traps shut. I don't imagine you'll be hearing from them again, though, Captain."

Hayden well knew that a bit of humour relieved the tension as the ship went into danger, but silence on the decks was imperative. Orders must be heard.

Gould came hurrying aft, touching his hat as he came onto the quarterdeck. "Sir, Mr Huxley has asked me to inform you that the Frenchman is mustering musket men on the quarterdeck. He believes they will be sent aloft, sir."

It was the practise of the French to put marksmen aloft with instructions to concentrate their fire upon the quarterdecks of the enemy, and most especially upon the officers.

"Pass the word for Mr Hawthorne, Mr Huxley, if you please."

"Aye, sir."

The acting captain of marines was very quickly found and sent aft.

"I have gathered my best men, sir, in anticipation of them being required," Hawthorne said as he hurried up,

"Let us have them on the foretops, Mr Hawthorne, and order them to concentrate their fire upon the French musketeers." Hayden gazed a moment at the distance between ships. "We are five hundred yards yet, Mr Hawthorne, but if the Frenchman loses more spars his speed could alter quite quickly. We might find ourselves upon him rather suddenly. Have your men stand ready, but tell them not to waste shot and powder."

"I will go aloft with them, sir."

"I would rather you sent a reliable corporal aloft and remained on deck, Mr Hawthorne."

Hawthorne looked surprised by this. "Aye, sir." He touched his hat and hurried forward.

Hayden did not wish to lose his captain of marines when a general fleet action was very likely in the offing. Hawthorne would be wanted then to repel boarders or to board the enemy.

"Mr Archer," Hayden addressed his senior lieutenant, "we shall bear off and fire our first broadside at a cable's length."

"Aye, sir."

The stern of the French ship began to loom over Hayden's *Raisonnable*, such was the height of her decks. Against the hazy sky, the silhouettes of men clambered aloft with muskets slung over their backs, and a moment later, the flash and smoke of their fire could be seen and Hawthorne's men returned fire. The French were attempting to kill the crews manning the chase guns forward, making the forecastle the most dangerous place aboard for a moment. Hayden sent word to clear that deck but for essential crew and Lieutenant Huxley. It always surprised him that young men would brave gunfire unnecessarily rather than appear shy to their comrades. It was one thing to not have enough sense to come in out of the rain, but to not have sufficient reason to come in out of a hail of lead balls was beyond foolhardy.

It was far into the evening before Hayden's ship ranged up to within a cable's length. He had worked his ship to weather as he could to allow them to bear off and fire without then having to work their way back to windward.

Hayden turned to the sailing master. "Mr Barthe, brail up this mizzen and up mainsail. I shall order us to bear off the moment your gear is cleared away."

"Aye, sir."

The aft sails of the ship would resist a turn downwind and must be taken in or, if urgency demanded it, the sheets let fly before such a turn could be made.

"Bear off, Swain," Hayden ordered the helmsman. "Bring our starboard broadside to bear. The instant our guns fire, Mr Barthe will set the mizzen and we will come back to our present heading." Hayden turned to find his sailing master. "Do you hear, Mr Barthe?"

"We shall haul out the mizzen the instant the guns are fired, sir."

Hayden was quite certain Barthe knew his part without any instructions from him, but it was always better to have every detail stated clearly so there was no misunderstanding. Barthe had spent a long, eventful life at sea and there was little he could learn about the management of a ship in all weathers from a young captain—even a young post captain.

For some minutes Hayden gazed, almost without blinking, at the first-rate ship before them. He gauged the wind direction and how constantly it blew.

"Mr Archer."

"Sir?"

"Let us port our helm and fire as soon as we can bring guns to bear."

"Aye, sir. Swain—port your helm, if you please."

The helm was put over, and the ship began to bring the wind aft. Despite being a handy ship for her berthen, *Raisonnable* appeared to take some good part of the evening to finally bring her broadside to bear.

"You may give the order to fire, Mr Archer." Hayden, who stood upon the quarter-ladder, quickly climbed the last three steps and hastened aft to be as clear of the smoke as possible that he might survey the effect of his gunners.

And an instant later, the two decks of guns and the guns on the quarterdeck boomed, spewing smoke and fountains of flame. This smoke drifted away forward, and Hayden was gratified to see much of the Frenchman's mizzen rigging carried away so that the severed shrouds and stays swung forth and back in the wind. The stern gallery shattered as raking fire swept down the Frenchman's deck.

In the deep silence that followed, Archer ordered the ship put back on her course. The mizzen brails were released and the sail set more quickly than Hayden believed he had ever seen, the men galvanized by the firing of guns. He walked forward to see the guns being rapidly swabbed, reloaded, and run out. They could almost have been fired twice.

Raisonnable came back to her course, and though she had lost some way, the speed of *Révolutionnaire* was equally reduced by the loss of her mizzen sails, the last of which were being cut away in an attempt to save the mast.

Across the water a cheer carried to them from *Bellerophon*, which was now gaining rapidly on the rearmost ship.

Hayden put his hands on the rail and leaned over to speak to his first lieutenant. "Mr Archer. I believe we should do the same again as soon as we have worked but a little to weather."

"Aye, sir. We are more weatherly than she," Archer replied, his face flushed with excitement.

"You approve our new ship, then?"

"Most heartily, sir."

"I do wish Mr Landry were here to give us his opinion."

"If I never see that man again, I shall not be sorry, sir. It is enough that I see him proven wrong in his opinion . . . yet again."

Hayden could not help but smile. The former second lieutenant of the frigate *Themis*, a man they had all come to despise, had one evening differed, in terms less than polite, with Hayden about the sailing qualities of the Ardent class sixty-fours—despite the fact that Hayden had served aboard one and he had not.

Hayden turned and examined the fleet ranging up in his rear, and wondered if Landry was serving aboard one of these very ships. Pity the captain who has that man for an officer, Hayden thought. He returned his attention to the French fleet just at the instant a signal went up on one of the ships in the van—a signal repeated by various ships down the line.

In the few short months since Hayden had come into possession of a French signal book, the enemy had changed their signals so that he could not decipher them—it had been an advantage short lived. There was little mystery to this signal, however, as ships began to shorten sail so as not to leave *Révolutionnaire* and several slower ships behind.

Hayden looked up at the quickly retreating sun. There was yet time for a general action, though it would have to commence almost immediately. *Bellerophon* continued to fire her chase guns, as did Hayden's crew. With the French ship's speed so reduced, Hayden could see that *Bellerophon* would be able to bring her broadside to bear in moments. *Thunderer, Marlborough,* and *Russell* were coming up very fast.

"Mr Archer?" Hayden called down to the quarterdeck.

"Sir?"

"I believe we shall have the opportunity to fire a single broadside more, and then we shall have to give way to our seventy-four-gun ships."

"Well, no one can say we have not done our part, Captain."

"Let us hope that is true."

The helmsman continued to work the ship up whenever the wind veered but a little—Hayden missed having Dryden at the wheel, for he had been the best helmsman aboard the *Themis,* after Mr Barthe, but Swain was quickly gaining his confidence in this. He stood with one hand upon the wheel, as far out from beneath the poop as he could reach, and quietly gave his mates orders. "Half a spoke to leeward. Up, up, bring her up now."

Barthe, who stood with his hand upon the companionway rail-ing, glanced up at Hayden and gave a nod of approval. Working a ship to windward was an art that not every sailor could master, Hayden had learned. Even though an excellent sailor such as Barthe might stand by and give the helmsman orders, there was no substi-tute for feeling the pressure on the wheel, watching the wind on the water, and keeping an eye upon the telltales and the set of the sails.

Before *Bellerophon* could bring her broadside to bear, Hayden managed a second raking fire.

"That will do for her mizzen, Captain, I would wager," Mr Barthe called as the smoke cleared away. "It will not stand half an hour."

Bellerophon opened fire then, and, at same instant it seemed, *Révo-lutionnaire* fired her three decks of guns. Smoke enveloped both ves-sels, and as it cleared away Hayden could see that both had inflicted much damage upon the other. Sails were flailing and thrashing on *Bellerophon*, and Hayden could see that her standing and running rig was much cut up.

It hardly seemed to have been noticed by the gun crews, for Hayden saw the muzzles run out, and before the French could do the same, a second broadside exploded, the sound itself violent and unnerving.

Gould came pounding up the ladder to the poop, touching his hat as he reached the top. "Signal for us on the lord admiral's ship."

Hayden turned to find *Queen Charlotte*. Indeed, *Raisonnable*'s number floated aloft.

"We are ordered to break off our engagement, sir," Gould re-ported without reference to the signal book.

"Have Mr Archer confirm that signal, Mr Gould." He did not for a moment believe the midshipman wrong—he appeared to have memorized all of the common signals—but this was not a matter in which a mistake could be made.

But a moment later, Archer, signal book in hand, informed his captain that they were indeed ordered to break off the engagement.

Barthe came up and stood by his captain. "We could easily have poured in another broadside, sir, if not more."

"I agree, but a one-hundred-ten-gun ship is a formidable ship of war, Mr Barthe. Too much for a single seventy-four, in truth. I am sure the admiral would preserve us for our present duty—as we are much faster than any of his ships of the line." Hayden also wondered if his apparent inexperience was the real reason he had been ordered back, but was not about to say so. Barthe, who knew the service as well as any, was no doubt entertaining the same thoughts.

Seeing *Thunderer* coming up astern under a press of sail with *Russell* and *Marlborough* in her wake, Hayden ordered his course altered so as to be well clear of them and to not impede them in any manoeuvre they might wish to perform.

Archer came up the steps to the aft deck. "Shall we return to the line and find our place, sir?"

"We will if we are so ordered, Mr Archer, but until such time I will hold our position here in the event that our assistance is required. Mr Barthe, arrange gear to take a ship in tow."

As preparations were made to take a ship in tow, *Thunderer* came abreast and slowly passed, her captain taking his hat off to Hayden, who returned the gesture.

Archer looked around at the British ships engaged in the fight, or about to be so. "Is there a ship in need of our assistance, Captain?"

"Not at this time, Mr Archer, but let us be prepared for any eventuality."

"Aye, sir." And Archer went off with Barthe to arrange the gear for towing.

Thunderer drew abreast of *Révolutionnaire* and immediately opened fire, the French ship responding with her own massive broadside, both ships hidden in dense cloaks of smoke. Even before it blew off, a second broadside erupted from the cloud, flame boiling out of the rolling mass.

The men upon Hayden's ship all stood transfixed by this, to a man wondering if the French would wear and come to the rescue of their besieged ship, which action would open a general engagement between the two powerful fleets.

Out of the storm of smoke *Thunderer* materialized, falling off to leeward, her gear damaged.

"*Bellerophon* is signalling, sir," Gould called up to Hayden. "She has a wounded mast, Captain."

Indeed, *Bellerophon* was dropping back, her crew swarming aloft to effect repairs.

Russell, however, was quickly overhauling the damaged French ship, her gunports open. The ships were becoming silhouettes as the day's light appeared to ebb into the west. Despite all British hopes, the French fleet showed no sign of coming to the rescue of its now isolated ship, which was unable to carry sail on the mizzen and had ruined gear hanging aloft and men working to clear whatever had fallen from the decks.

Russell ranged up alongside and tore open the air with her guns just as *Révolutionnaire* fired her own broadside. Through the pall of smoke Hayden could see the mizzen mast of the Frenchman slowly lean, accumulate speed, and then plunge into the drifting cloud of smoke. Hayden's crew cheered.

A second broadside was fired by the *Russell*, and the mainsail yard of the French ship dropped to the deck. With her gear so cut up and sails torn away, *Révolutionnaire* lost way while the British ships attacking in succession were able to keep up an almost constant fire while sustaining less damage.

Marlborough was next to fire and then *Thunderer* took her place, the French returning fire, but each broadside was reduced in strength as her guns were dismounted and crew killed or wounded.

Audacious and *Gibraltar* overhauled the three British ships and opened fire on the French vessel, which to the credit of her officers and crew answered every three broadsides with two of their own. As smoke drifted off, Hayden saw the Frenchman's mainsail yard swing down and then drop to the deck. A moment later, her main topsail yard did the same. She was still firing raggedly at the British ships, but she was almost wallowing and had lost steerage, her head blowing off.

Audacious and *Gibraltar* did not stop to see her colours struck but passed by in chase of the fleet stretched in line ahead.

"We are prepared to tow, sir," Archer reported. "Though it appears that only a Frenchman will be in need." Archer turned and gazed at the stricken vessel in the gathering gloom. "Will she not strike, Captain?"

As Hayden was about to reply that she had no flag left flying, *Révolutionnaire*'s guns fell silent. "It appears she has struck, Mr Archer."

There was a moment of silence on the deck of *Raisonnable* while everyone waited for the French ship to fire again, and when she did not, three cheers erupted and were echoed across the waters from the other British ships.

Hayden went to the stern and in the sea dusk saw a hoist of flags float aloft on the *Queen Charlotte*, quickly repeated by outlying frigates and ships in the line. There was no need to consult a signal book—it called for a general recall and to form a line.

Hayden was about to transmit orders to this effect to his officers when a second signal appeared—and this was for his own ship and the frigates, which were ordered to maintain contact with the enemy fleet.

Hayden walked forward to the rail and called down to Archer, whose features were quickly being lost in the dimming light. "Do you see the signal, Mr Archer? We are to maintain close contact with the French fleet."

"Are we to remain at quarters, Captain?" Archer called.

"Yes. We shall have to feed the hands at the guns."

"I shall see it done, sir." Archer went forward on the darkening deck. "Mr Barthe? We shall make sail and keep close contact with the French! Mr Huxley! We shall remain at quarters, but the men must eat."

"I will go down to the cooks straight off, Mr Archer, and I will muster the mess stewards," Hayden heard Huxley reply, though he could not make him out.

It was here that Hayden missed his former command—a frigate had a berth-deck where no guns were lodged. When a frigate cleared for action, the living space of the men was left unaltered. Aboard a sixty-four the men lived on the gun-decks, their mess tables taking up the places between the guns, their trunks stored there and hammocks hung in the same space. All of this must be cleared away to fire the guns, and to build it all again so the men might eat required no small amount of work. Men would have to remain at their stations and eat and sleep and live as best they could without the few comforts that frigate crews kept always to hand.

In the very last light of the day, against an opalescent sky, *Raisonnable* overhauled *Révolutionnaire*, which lay rolling to the swell, her mizzen gone, yards shot away. At that very moment, a group of Frenchmen came to the hammock nettings bearing something between them, and then with a slight heave sent a body tumbling limply through the air where it plunged into the dark, unfathomable sea.

Until the sea shall give up her dead. The words came unbidden to Hayden's mind. He had a vision of the dead, rising out of the ooze and floating towards the surface through the dim waters, like sleepers slowly waking. His own father would be among them—perhaps even Hayden might find a place in such a corps.

Révolutionnaire looked beyond forlorn. A few hours ago, she had been both formidable and awful—a machine of ruinous beauty. And now she was silent, drifting with the small wind, falling and sending at the sea's whim. Had it not been for the men moving slowly about her decks, she could have been a hulk, lifeless and hollow. How swiftly her ruin had been effected.

"If you please, sir . . ." It was Wickham at the ladder head.

"Come up, Wickham."

"*Audacious* sails on, Captain. I wonder if she did not see the lord admiral's signal?"

"Fire a gun to leeward and repeat the signal."

"Aye, sir."

Wickham went quickly down to where Gould and the new midshipmen were already laying out the flags to be hoisted. The forward chase gun was fired—devoid of iron ball, and the signals run up into the damp, night air.

Hayden had little hope of *Audacious* seeing this but thought it likely someone aboard would realise that other ships were returning to the line or reducing sail to allow the fleet to come up to them.

Guns began firing aboard *Audacious* at that very moment—as she had drawn within range of the aftermost French ship.

In the east, stars came into existence, blotted by a thin haze. Night was victorious. Lanterns were lit around the ship and festooned the British fleet.

Twenty-one

The men lay scattered among the guns. By the scant light of lanterns they appeared insensible rounded mounds upon the unmerciful planks. It almost pained Hayden's heart to see one man of every crew sitting upon the gun carriage, hands upon knees, arms limp, staring blankly, barely conscious, hardly able to keep himself from falling, but somehow willing himself to remain awake for his watch.

Hayden stood a moment in the shadow of the afterdeck, the men at the helm unaware of his presence. Four days and four nights they had remained at quarters—neither hands nor officers having refuge to their hammocks or cots. Even Hayden laid on a paltry mat upon the gun-deck planks. His own exhaustion had crept into his mind, breaking off his thoughts often so that they began with purpose but then lost all way and drifted into a void as featureless as a flat, calm sea.

He found Lieutenant Bell slumped down on the quarter-ladder, his head hanging.

"Mr Bell?" Hayden whispered as he emerged from the shadows.

The young lieutenant staggered up, startled. "I was not sleeping, sir."

"Indeed you were not—unless you can perch upon a ladder and sleep without falling. Are the French still in sight?"

"A thin haze has settled all around, Captain, but *Niger* has signalled at every bell—fired a gun, sir—indicating that they have the fleet yet in sight."

"But we have not?"

"No, sir."

"Then we will make sail."

"Shall I call all hands, sir?"

"No, we will make do with the hands upon the quarterdeck and the forecastle. Have them stirred, though I am loath to do it."

The men were stirred, and not easily, coming dully to their feet, surly and truculent. Hayden took charge of this evolution himself, sending men to unfamiliar stations. Slowly it was managed by the limited numbers, but sail was made, and the ship pressed forward in the small breeze. When yards were braced, sails trimmed, and all the ropes coiled, Hayden allowed the men to return to their unwelcoming beds, and he climbed up onto the afterdeck to stare into the liquid darkness.

It was the type of haze that could almost not be detected on a moonless night. Overhead the stars were only very slightly obscured, and the thin mist hanging low over the sea blended into the darkness, only raising the horizon a little.

He could just see the lights of the most forward vessels in Lord Howe's roughly formed line, and before his own vessel the lanterns of two frigates that had been ordered to remain in close contact with the French fleet. His own ship was to support these and relay signals were it to become necessary.

Hayden wandered back to the stern rail and leaned heavily against it. He would have given all he possessed to be allowed to lie upon the deck and sleep. It took all of his will to keep his feet beneath him. The ship's bell counted seven—half three of a morning. Daylight was not distant.

Thinking that he might find wakefulness easier to maintain if he moved, Hayden set off to tour the decks, beginning down the starboard side. Slowly, he went down the ladder and padded quietly forward, stepping, here and there, over somnolent men who were not stirred by his passing. The men seated upon the guns rose as he advanced and made a knuckle, whereupon Hayden motioned them to resume their seats. Once or twice he paused to whisper quietly with a waking man and to speak with the lookouts posted upon the ship's four quarters. Almost painfully he hauled himself aloft onto the foremast top and, after consulting with the lookout, gazed out over the misty sea, hoping to discern the rear of the French fleet—but could not.

With equal difficulty, Hayden returned to the deck and continued his rounds. Upon the larboard gangway a gaunt figure approached.

"Dr Griffiths. Is it not early to be abroad? Is there some errand upon which you are called?"

"I am habitually awake at eight bells—four of a morning. I am taking a turn around the deck to clear my mind."

"As am I, Doctor. Shall we continue together? I will reverse my orbit and accompany you." They walked only a pace before Hayden enquired, "How fare you, Doctor? Have you found a little sleep, I hope?"

"More than many, I should think," the surgeon answered quietly. "My mates and myself have slung cots on the orlop, where we have moved the sick-berth—but the hands, Captain . . . They cannot bear up to this much longer. Human endurance has limits."

"I agree, Doctor. If only this damned French admiral would stand and fight, but instead he remains just beyond our grasp. Each time we appear to have finally forced an action, he finds some way to slip out of our hands and we are back to chasing after him—waiting. For ever waiting."

"I do not claim any particular knowledge of such matters, as you well know, but I am surprised that we have been four days since the French were sighted and yet there have been only skirmishes and not a general action."

"It is peculiar," Hayden agreed, "and I am most confused by it. It is almost as if the French do not try to escape yet they will not give battle. I do wish they would do one or the other. But if the wind holds, I believe we shall finally have the weather gauge and then Lord Howe may force an action at his pleasure—assuming the sea fog does not again intervene."

Griffiths removed his hat and ran fingers through his grey hair. "I hold less enthusiasm for a general action, I fear, as all of the wounded come down to me." He waved his hat out towards the distant fleets. "Think of the great number of men who could be killed or maimed. I almost wish the French could slip away."

"The war will most likely only last that much longer if battle is averted," Hayden replied, and not without some sadness. "There is no war to be wished for, but a short one, no matter how violent, will always see fewer lives lost than a war that drags on for years. Perhaps a significant naval defeat will put an end to the Jacobin government's designs to spread their revolution across all of Europe."

"Perhaps." The surgeon considered this a moment—very sadly, Hayden thought. "The Jacobins are fanatical, Captain, and fanatics make decisions based on belief, not reason."

"I spent half my young life among the French, Dr Griffiths, and I can tell you that the Jacobins cannot last for very long among such a civilised people. They are an anomaly—almost an abomination."

Griffiths shrugged as if to concede the point, which Hayden had stated with more passion than he intended.

The actions of the present government were a deep source of shame to Charles Hayden—which, as an officer in His Majesty's Navy, he could not admit. But it was true—the Jacobins and their infamous Committee of Public Safety caused him many hours of mortification. He thought of Madame Adair, coupling with a stranger in hopes of eluding the guillotine. Of the sound of the men coming for her in the night—and then, at the last instant, being persuaded to go elsewhere by the doctor who certainly was about to be condemned to the guillotine himself.

"*On deck!*" The familiar call from above stopped both men. "Sails, north–north-west, two leagues."

Hayden hastened to the quarterdeck and crossed to the starboard side. Men bestirred themselves from among the guns, rubbing eyes and massaging shoulders sore from their hard-plank bed. A midshipman hastened up quickly with a glass, and Hayden scanned the horizon.

"Yes," he said softly, "there—on the larboard tack." Hayden passed the glass to Griffiths and turned in a slow circle, quizzing the sea at all points of the compass. The eastern horizon grew faintly opalescent; the sun would soon overtake them yet again.

The men separated as Hayden turned away from the rail and went immediately to the quarter-ladder that led to the top of the roundhouse—the poop. As he reached the afterdeck, he realised that Griffiths had followed and now hovered on the top step.

"Come up, Doctor, by all means."

Griffiths ascended to the short afterdeck, looked around as though to be certain no one was near.

"If I may, Captain . . ." Griffiths almost whispered.

"Speak up, Doctor. You know I value your opinion in all matters."

"The men have been at their stations four days and five nights. They are all as exhausted as we. They will fight much better upon full bellies."

"I could not agree more, but I dare not light our stove when we are at stations. The admiral would see me sent ashore for the rest of my days."

"Can you make a cold meal, then?"

"That I can do, and I will if I must, but Lord Howe is no fool. He will have come to the same conclusion, I believe."

"I hope your faith is not misplaced. If you will excuse me, Captain, I shall repair to my station." The doctor turned towards the ladder, then stopped and turned his head back. "Luck to you, Captain Hayden."

"Luck to all of us this day, Doctor."

As he watched the surgeon descend the ladder, Hayden gazed out towards the line of sail and felt his pulse quicken. Lord Howe finally had the weather gauge and the sea fog was, if anything, dissipating. The French fleet was but six miles distant and the days would hardly grow longer—they had many hours to catch and engage the French fleet. This would be the day, for good or ill. A great battle would take place, the first of the present hostilities, and he would be part of it. If Lord Howe had decided what Hayden's part would be in the affair, he had not seen fit to let Hayden know. The thought came to him then—he hoped he would live to tell the story . . . whatever occurred.

Upon the deck of his ship he could see crews mustered at the guns, boys with buckets coming to each bearing water for the men to slake their thirsts. The midshipmen, some of them so green they had been but a fortnight at sea, were gathered on the gangway, gazing off at the great fleet, and fairly bouncing up and down with excitement and fear. The older boys like Wickham, and even Gould, had been in actions before. They had seen the decks slippery with blood, and even their friends killed. They were much more subdued—resolute, but already sorrowful, Hayden thought. Those boys knew what was coming—for the others it would be a terrible shock. For a moment Hayden thought to send them all down to the lowest deck—to shelter them from what was to come. As though they were his own sons. But it could not be done. This was their chosen profession—there was no protecting them from the truth of war.

Archer appeared at the ladder head at that moment and Hayden waved him aft. Archer was pulling on his coat and looked even more dishevelled than usual.

"My apologies, Captain," he began, his voice still hoarse with sleep. "It was my watch below, and I had fallen into the deepest sleep."

"A great accomplishment under the circumstances, Mr Archer. I hope you are rested, for I believe we shall finally bring the French to battle this day."

"We have been ready in every way for this moment for several days, sir, but I shall inspect each deck to be certain that nothing has been forgotten."

"Take the new midshipmen with you, Lieutenant. They should comprehend all of our preparations." Hayden looked up. "Order those men to leave off wetting sails. They will be dry long before we meet the French. We shall wet the sails when battle is near—not before."

"Aye, sir." Archer went off at a near run.

"Mr Smosh," Hayden said, perceiving the clergyman upon the quarterdeck. "Come up, sir. The view is better from here."

"Thank you, Captain." The corpulent little parson clambered quickly up the ladder.

"I see you are not wearing your ecclesiastical collar, Mr Smosh?"

"I intend to assist Dr Griffiths with the wounded, and you know how superstitious the men are about clergymen in the sick-berth— they feel just as strongly about us in the cockpit, I have no doubt."

"I did hope you would lead the men of each deck in a short prayer. Many would find it a comfort."

"Nothing would give me greater pleasure, Captain Hayden. When shall I begin?"

"If now is not inconvenient . . . ?"

"Not in the least. I shall begin upon this very deck, if I may?"

The men on the upper deck were quickly mustered onto the

quarterdeck, and standing upon the poop, Smosh led them in a brief but moving prayer. He then explained to the men that it was his custom to aid the surgeon in the cockpit but he would not be there in his clerical capacity, and that he had done so upon his previous ship and the men had all accepted his aid without question or concerns. Hayden was not certain the men of *Raisonnable* were entirely comfortable with this idea, but he did not believe any would attempt to hide their wounds due to superstitions about parsons in the sick-berth.

The sky continued to brighten as Smosh descended to the upper gun-deck to repeat his prayer.

"*On deck!* Captain Hayden, sir?" the mizzen top lookout called down.

Hayden gazed up at the man, who stood up grasping a backstay to stare down on his commander, who came out from under the mizzen to see him clearly.

"I've counted the French ships three times over, sir. Appears they have repaired all their damaged ships, somehow, sir. I count twenty-six sail of the line, sir."

"Thank you, Pierce. I will send Mr Wickham up the mainmast." Hayden turned to find the midshipman. "Mr Wickham . . . ?"

"I am on my way up, Captain," the boy called back, and Hayden spotted him making his way to the larboard shrouds. In a moment he was in the tops.

Hayden walked forward to the rail, where he could see Wickham with his arm locked around a shroud and his glass screwed into his eye. For a moment he braced himself against the small roll of the ship, then he turned and found his captain on the deck below.

"Pierce is correct, sir," the sharp-eyed midshipman called down. "But I would wager some of the French ships were too damaged to have been repaired."

Hayden waved the boy back down to the deck. Lieutenant Huxley stood gazing up at Hayden, quizzically, from the quarterdeck. "It is difficult to imagine," Hayden said to him, "but there can be no explanation but a French squadron has found the fleet. Ships do not rise out of the depths, after all."

Huxley nodded.

This observation by the captain was repeated down the deck in a whisper and then circulated below, like a small breeze finding its way down the companionways.

By five the French fleet was fully visible to the naked eye, in an orderly line upon the larboard tack. The wind held true, showing no signs of backing or veering. The afterdeck was now populated by other officers, whom Hayden kept near that he might give them orders. A few midshipmen had also been allowed upon the captain's private preserve, and they were hanging upon the words of the officers and quizzing both fleets constantly.

"Signals from the flagship, sir," Gould reported, pointing excitedly. "We are ordered to steer north-west."

The signal book again proved the midshipman correct, and all and sundry commented upon Gould's prodigious memory—though the other reefers did exhibit signs of some jealousy.

Men jumped to their places with a zeal Hayden could hardly remember witnessing. Yards were braced, the helm turned, and they were upon the new course in but a moment.

The signals were repeated up and down the line and the fleet performed the same evolution.

"Very smartly done," young Bowen observed. "Did you not think, Mr Archer?"

"I am gratified to see that you have become an authority in so brief a career," Archer observed.

The boy coloured noticeably and fell silent thereafter.

"Is that our number?" Gould then asked.

A new hoist of flags jerked aloft aboard Howe's ship.

"Indeed it is, Mr Gould," Hayden replied. "Do you know it?"

"Are we ordered . . ." But then the midshipman fell silent, biting his lip. "I do not know it, sir."

"We are ordered, Mr Gould, to take our place in the line of battle . . . directly astern of *Brunswick*, I believe." The words brought with them a distressed silence. "Who has the signal book?" Hayden enquired, hiding his reaction to the order.

Lieutenant Huxley was in possession of this valuable document and quickly confirmed Hayden's reading.

The young gentlemen glanced one to the other. They had been told the meaning of this, and Hayden could see it frightened them terribly.

"Mr Archer? We will spill wind and allow the fleet to overhaul us. Let us take our place in the line with all speed but no misadventures. The ships aft of us will have to make room, so we dare not barge in until they have made us a place."

The news travelled the length of the ship and down to the decks below in less than five minutes, and Hayden could see the effect of it.

Barthe came up onto the poop and, after staring a moment at the French line, growled quietly to his captain, "Let us hope we are not placed opposite a first-rate ship."

Hayden pretended not to hear. But Barthe was right—one broadside from three decks of a hundred-gun ship would put paid to *Raisonnable*, Hayden was quite certain. Clearly, Lord Howe had decided that even a sixty-four might inflict some damage on the enemy. Oddly, Hayden felt a little as he had as a child when pressed forward to fight some bully twice his size. There was no hope of success, but to gain a reputation of being shy . . . It was unacceptable.

Most of an hour passed before Hayden was able to work his ship into the line by a process of backing and filling, and even then he thought himself too near the seventy-four forward of him.

It was perfectly clear to every man aboard at that point that an action was inevitable that day. The French showed no signs of scud-ding, which would be their only hope of escape.

Raisonnable had just found her place when the flagship signalled that it would attack the enemy line's centre. Though the enemy fleet was still three miles distant, perhaps a little more, the ships suddenly loomed very large—larger than Hayden's sixty-four-gun ship, which he believed the smallest ship in either line of battle. He could see the hands all staring at the French line, and he wondered how many were counting to see which ship would be opposite their own.

"Mr Archer?"

"Sir?" Archer was slightly paler than usual, and very solemn. He was no fool, Benjamin Archer, and knew what lay in store for them as well as any man could.

"I shall make a quick tour of the decks."

"Aye, sir."

Stepping quickly down the ladder, Hayden went from gun crew to gun crew.

"It is no secret, boys, that a seventy-four has a greater broadside than we, but we all know that twenty-four-pounders can be fired at twice the rate of thirty-two-pounders, so who will pour in more iron, a Frenchman or our own stout ship?"

It was a speech that contained a small amount of fiction, but it had the desired affect. The odd mention of prize money did not hurt either. After he had passed along the upper deck and then both gun-decks, Hayden ran up the steps to the poop in time to see a hoist of flags go aloft on the now nearby flagship.

"Signal thirty-four, sir," Gould reported. "Break through the enemy line and engage from leeward."

"Well, Mr Gould, it is exactly what I expected from His Lord-ship. There can be no half measures in battle."

No sooner had this signal been made than the signal to heave to followed, leaving Hayden, and he guessed others, somewhat confused. But Lord Howe quickly followed this with a signal to feed the crews, of which Hayden heartily approved. Mess tables could not be set up, so the gun crews went down to retrieve their food one by one, and food was consumed in any position men found comfortable. The ship's boys went around collecting wooden plates after, and the men were all fed and mustered to their guns in little more than half the hour. Only minutes after that the entire fleet again got under way, and at eight thirty in the morning Admiral Lord Howe sent aloft another hoist of flags.

"Signal thirty-six," Midshipman Huxley called out, clearly attempting to best Gould. "'Each ship is to independently steer for and engage her opponent in the enemy line.'"

"Mr Gould?" Hayden said quietly to the midshipman.

"That is correct, sir. Are we not to pass through the line, then?"

"I believe as long as we place our ship alongside our opposite number in the line and do our utmost to overpower that vessel no fault can be found with us, whether we are to leeward or windward." Hayden turned to find his senior lieutenant. "Mr Archer? Pass the word for Mr Barthe, the bosun, and all of our lieutenants."

"Sir."

Hayden's senior officers hastened onto the afterdeck a moment later and gathered in a knot, facing their captain. "We all know what we are up against, but I have an idea that will give us half a chance. Here is what I shall attempt." Hayden pointed at the French line. "Do you see the ship that is our opposite? The second aft of the flagship?"

"The eighty-gun ship, sir?"

"No, Mr Huxley, aft of that—a seventy-four. We will steer for it as though we will engage her to windward, but as we draw near her larboard quarter I will order all of our guns fired at once—even before we can bring them to bear. With this small wind the smoke will not carry away swiftly, so for a moment we shall be utterly concealed, and in that moment I will order the helm put up and we will pass astern of the seventy-four. It is my intention that we will fire both batteries at the ships in the French line as we pass through, so reloading with all haste will be required. Our fire must be concentrated on the enemy's lower gun-deck to do as much damage to her great guns and their crews as can be managed. We will then come up to leeward of our seventy-four and engage her with our larboard battery. It is an evolution that must be managed with great precision and no hesitation. As we are hidden from them in smoke, so will they be hidden from us. We will make our turn blind so can have no errors in either judgement or execution. Mr Barthe, the mizzen sail must be brailed in with all speed. We dare not do this before we have fired our broadside, or the French captain will comprehend our intentions and turn downwind to stop us from raking him." He stopped for an instant to see that comprehension was apparent in all of the faces. "Mr Bowen, you must find me a reliable hand of very steady nerve to man the beak-head and call out our distance to the sternpost of the seventy-four. Another man must crouch behind the barricade to take his place in the event that he is wounded."

"I will do that, sir," Wickham volunteered.

"You will be in charge of a gun battery, Mr Wickham," Hayden informed the midshipman. He turned his attention back to Bowen. "We will station men to relay the distance from the enemy back to me on the quarterdeck—in yards, if you please, Mr Bowen."

"I have just the men, Captain."

"Does everyone understand their part? We will fire each gun as it bears, but do not begin until you have had the order from me." Hayden gave everyone a moment to ask any question they might have and then said, "Some few of you have not been in a close action before, but do not be concerned; you will be equal to the test. The men at your guns will not fail you, nor will you fail them. Luck to each and every one of you."

The men returned to their stations after Hayden ordered Barthe and Mr Archer to attend to the sail handling, while he would give the order to put the helm up. The gun captains stood ready, firing lanyards in hand, all eyes fixed on the French ship, which appeared to grow larger and more formidable by the moment. The man sent out to the beak-head had to be made of very stern stuff, as he would certainly come under musket fire.

As these things often went, closing with the French, who were sailing almost at the speed as the British, took an unbearable hour. It was not until after three bells that the first shot was fired, and that by the French at the leading British vessel—the eighty-gun ship *Caesar.* Very quickly firing became general, though the British ships held their gun crews in check until they were almost within musket range.

Hayden observed the smoke from each broadside and was given some hope that his plan might answer, as the dark clouds clung to the ships and blew off but slowly. All the while he kept his eye upon the two ships where he must pass through, measuring the distance between them, noting that now they closed and then separated. Hayden realised that if the ships closed as he approached there would be no room for him to break through the line and he would have to go broadside to broadside against a far more powerful ship. An iron ball scraped through the air then, tearing into the mizzen overhead, causing the boom to swing wildly about.

"Mr Archer?"

"Sir?"

"Detail three guns to fire alternately chain or bar and then grape up into the tops of our Frenchmen. Let us sweep the musket men from the rigging."

The French musketeers were overly effective at killing English crewmen on the exposed upper deck, especially officers, sometimes leaving a raw lieutenant in command, much to the detriment of the ship. Hawthorne had also been ordered to send his marines aloft to shoot their opposite numbers in the tops before any fire should be directed at the French ship's deck. The failure of other captains to do this, Hayden believed, was an attempt to demonstrate to the hands that the officers would brave all dangers—for the French musket men targeted the officers first. To Hayden's mind, this was a foolish conceit. He had proven his courage often enough not to believe his men would question his motives for killing the musketeers.

A ball found the upper quarter-gallery, causing audible cries from the men below, who then came dancing out onto the quarterdeck, staring aft in horror. Of an instant, Hayden was down the ladder and found the gun crews dodging this way and that as a red-hot ball rolled dangerously among them, threatening to blow them all to hell if it touched the powder cartridges. Snatching Bowen's speaking trumpet, Hayden caught the ball up in it as it rolled past and then he emptied it out the nearest gunport.

"Return to your stations!" he ordered sharply, thrusting the brass speaking trumpet back into a surprised Bowen's hands. "Do not leave them again until you are ordered to do so."

Hayden went back up the ladder. His ship was coming under increasing fire, and though he did not like it, he resisted the urging of his crew to return fire, instead ordering the bosun to keep the men silent.

"Do you see the name, sir?" Gould asked, aiming his glass at the stern of the ship they were to engage. *"L'Achille."*

"Then we shall have to wound him in the heel," Hayden replied.

A broadside from *Achille*, aimed at the *Queen Charlotte*, obscured the French ship entirely.

"Let us hope they fire as we approach," Gould said, noting the same thing.

"I do believe they will preserve their fire until we are abeam—though we shall try to rake them first."

The reports of the guns were like thunder that grew nearer and nearer. *Raisonnable* passed through the fire of one ship into a brief area of calm, and then into the fire of the next. Their rigging was being shot away, and Hayden took a moment to gaze aloft, assessing the damage. Losing masts in battle left one at the mercy of the enemy ships that could still manoeuvre—and Hayden was not expecting mercy.

Hayden could see on the forecastle Hawthorne with a company of marines, muskets at the ready, just waiting until they were within range.

"Only a moment now," Hayden whispered, though no one could hear above the din.

He had hardly given voice to this when a marine standing but two feet from Hawthorne toppled backwards to the deck. Hawthorne raised his cutlass, gave the order, and fire was immediately returned.

They were almost upon the larboard quarter of *Achille*. Pounding down the ladder lest his orders to the helmsman be lost in the crashing of guns, Hayden pulled up in the centre of the quarterdeck, within three yards of the helmsman.

"Your name?" he asked of the senior man at the wheel—for there were two and another pair standing by.

"Bullfinch, sir."

"Well, Bullfinch, do not turn before I give the order. But if I am shot, you must make your turn just after our broadside is fired and bring us through on such a slant that we might fire both our batteries into the enemy ships while not becoming entangled with the starboard vessel."

"I'll manage it, sir."

"*Seventy yards, Captain,*" came the call from the man on the beakhead, and this was echoed back along the deck by the appointed hands.

Hayden gazed forward at the tip of the jib-boom. He could see his officers staring at him nervously—but none of them spoke. The ship aft of *Achille* was now almost abreast, but she had just brailed up her sails, believing *Raisonnable* was to engage her, so she quickly dropped back, opening the gap Hayden hoped to pass through.

"*Sixty yards, Captain.*" The word passed aft.

Still, Hayden delayed, watching both ships, estimating their speeds, measuring in his mind.

"*Fifty yards from the tip of the jib-boom to sternpost, Captain.*"

Archer kept glancing at him with apprehension, but Mr Barthe appeared as intent as Hayden and showed no signs of doubt.

"Ten yards, do you think, Mr Barthe?"

"That will be shaving it very near, sir. Her mizzen boom must overhang five yards, at least."

"Fifteen?"

Barthe glanced at the ship aft of *Achille*, which they had passed now. "I believe you are right, Captain. Ten yards."

"*Thirty yards, Captain,*" the word passed back again.

Musket fire had reached the quarterdeck now, and Hayden did his best to ignore the deadly thwack of lead balls piercing into oak.

In a lull in the gunfire, Hayden heard, "*Twenty yards, Captain!*"

Still, Hayden delayed. Then, "Mr Archer? Fire both batteries."

"Aye, sir." Archer lifted his speaking trumpet to his mouth and gave the order.

Men positioned to relay the orders called down to the decks below, and two decks of guns fired only an instant apart, the sound almost knocking Hayden off his feet. The great blossom of smoke roiled up and obscured everything beyond a dozen paces.

Hayden gazed up at the men brailing in the mizzen, which had to be done before the ship could turn downwind. The instant it was completed, Hayden nodded to the helmsman. "Port your helm."

The ship began to turn. Hayden could not see the bow of his own vessel clearly, and the stern of the Frenchman was not visible at all. He waited for the sound of his jib-boom being torn away, but it did not come. Hurrying to the larboard side between carronades, he leaned out over the water, the open gunports visible below. The smoke began to clear, but there was no French ship. Had she comprehended his intentions and turned as well?

"Mr Archer!"

"Sir?"

"You will order the starboard guns fired when you can bring them to bear on the next ship aft in line."

Raisonnable continued to turn, justifying Hayden's claim of her being handy. And then, just visible through the smoke, the great bulk of *Achille*'s stern, officers at the taffrail calling out and pointing aft.

"Too late," Hayden whispered. He watched as his own crews traversed their guns, and when he saw them come to bear he called out so loudly that the cry pained his throat, "Larboard battery . . . fire as she bears."

The French ship was not forty yards distant, and the destruction wrought upon her was monstrous. The first few balls stove in her galleries, and the next screamed the length of her gun-deck, wreaking terrible destruction and death. The gun crews forward were in a whirl of motion to load again, and a few of the guns most forward fired a second time into the stern . . . and then they were past

At that instant the starboard battery finished firing, and Hayden turned to see the tip of a jib-boom emerging from a cloud of smoke. Most likely the crew of that ship had not been able to discern *Raisonnable* since the moment she fired her first, obscuring broadside.

Hayden turned to the helmsman. "Bring her up in the lee of *L'Achille*, Bullfinch. Mr Barthe! I do not want to fly past our chase."

"We shall not, Captain Hayden. Don't you worry," and he went off shouting orders to the sail handlers. There was a notable excitement and even relief in the master's tone. He understood that they had done what they could to even the odds.

The starboard guns of the French seventy-four began a ragged fire at that instant. Hayden had ordered guns concentrated on the lower gun-deck of his enemy—where the largest guns lived and which could be levelled at Hayden's own ship in such a way as to cause the greatest damage. Now, if he could keep his ship near enough, the quarterdeck and forecastle guns of the seventy-four could not be brought to bear on his own upper deck, or so he hoped. It was what remained of the lower gun-deck and the upper gun-deck with the French equivalent of twenty-four-pounders that worried him.

His own crews fired and reloaded and fired again in fury of activity. Smoke blinded everyone and Hayden employed all of his senses, attempting to gauge which ship gained the advantage. The aftermost quarterdeck gun—a nine-pounder—was struck by a ball and thrown out of its carriage upon three of its crew. Hayden hurried immediately aft.

"Take up your crowbars," Hayden ordered, snatching a bar from a man's hand. "You, take the bar from the starboard gun. No, not under the cascabel—here under the muzzle, where the burden is less. One, two, *heave!*"

The gun was raised just enough that the wounded men were slid out from beneath, all of them crying out in pain.

"Secure this gun, then carry these men below to the doctor."

Hayden hurried back to his place just as the mizzen topsail yard came swinging down, broke free, thudding down on its boom-iron, then crashing upon the starboard gangway and hammock netting, striking no one. All around him a storm of devastation raged. Splinters spun across the decks and ruin rained down everywhere. Through the smoke Hayden could see men thrown down on the deck, broken and unmoving, and the massive shot of the enemy's thirty-two-pounders crashed through the side of his hull. Hayden felt as though he stood in the middle of a hurricane and would be swept off at any second.

Through the dense smoke and deafening thunder of guns all around, Hayden could just make out *L'Achille*, men at the guns and clearing away wreckage. The French were fighting with great ferocity, and though Hayden had done damage to her lower gun-deck and killed many men, he was sure, these guns were now being manned and fired, if slowly. Each shot at that range crashed into Hayden's hull, shaking the ship from end to end.

A few feet away, Hayden could make out Archer, who glanced his way, his face smoke-stained and grim. There was no mistaking the message written there: *We are losing.* Hayden was not certain that Archer was wrong.

"Bullfinch, a point to port. Do not let the Frenchmen alongside."

Hayden did not know if it was by intent, but the French ship was turning to starboard, and Hayden did not want to repel boarders, as the French possessed greater numbers.

Through the darkening veil Hayden saw a man on the gangway stagger three steps, then topple limply to the deck below. An unseen ball struck just aft of the mizzen mast and killed all the men manning one side of a carronade in an instant, then tore through the hull again on the starboard side. Hands manning the starboard gun opposite pulled the shattered bodies away and took their places. The sight of the mangled bodies lying in a heap was so horrifying that Hayden could not bear to look that way again.

But wherever his gaze lit, men fell at the guns and were replaced immediately by their opposite numbers from the starboard battery, which had no target at that moment. Forward, the bosun mustered a crew and slid the fallen yard overboard, men with axes cutting away rigging and jettisoning it the same way. Boys wove among the men, bravely bearing powder for the guns. For an instant Hayden thought to admire them—children, among all the destruction and mangled men, performing their single duty. Frightened, yes, but bearing up to it.

Firing from *L'Achille*'s forward guns appeared to have ceased, and then his own gunners paused. The smoke cleared a little and the enemy ship was not to be seen.

"Captain!" Bullfinch called out. "The helm, sir. It does not answer."

A glance up told Hayden that the wind was now almost dead aft. The head of his ship had been blown off course and *Achille* had shot ahead.

"Pass the word for the bosun!" Hayden called. He went immediately to the wheel and pulled on the tiller ropes, one of which slid up without the wheel responding. "Lost a tiller rope . . . and no more, I hope."

He was down the companionway steps, pushing by men coming up. Racing aft, the cause of the problem was quickly seen—a severed tiller rope.

"Thank God it is not the tiller smashed," he observed.

"Where has our Frenchman gone, sir?" Huxley asked.

"Shot ahead when we lost our helm, Mr Huxley."

Huxley realised immediately what Hayden meant. "Rope! We need rope!"

The bosun came hurrying through the fog, bearing a coil of thick rope.

"I shall leave this to you and the bosun, Mr Huxley."

Hayden went bounding back up to the deck, and then up the quarter-ladder to the stern-deck. At every point of the compass he could see ships, smothered in black silken skeins drawn to leeward on the breeze—ships locked in pairs and threes and fours, a relentless cannonade assaulting the ears and nerves. Masts fell in tangles while other ships appeared to burn. Fire and horror and death were everywhere, carried from ship to ship by screaming, iron balls that sounded like nothing so much as a horde of ungodly banshees.

A hundred yards off he found *L'Achille*, her mizzen and main gone, her crew cutting masts away and setting sail upon her foremast. Not distant, all but obscured in a dusk of smoke, three ships fought, and the centre vessel bore the pennant of Lord Howe.

"Sir!" Archer appeared from beneath the poop. "Our helm answers."

Hayden pointed at the flagship. "Take us across the sterns of those three ships, Mr Archer. We shall assist Lord Howe if we are able."

Archer turned and stared only a moment, then touched his hat, words lost in the booming of guns. Immediately his ship began a turn to larboard, and Hayden saw Archer at the ladder head communicating their intentions to the lieutenants commanding the batteries below.

Hayden leaned over the rail and shouted at the top of his lungs, "Mr Archer! You comprehend the situation? A French ship, then the *Queen Charlotte*, then the French admiral's flagship. We will rake the first ship as we cross, reload, and do the same to *Montagne*."

Archer nodded vigorously. Barthe had climbed up to the afterdeck, face red, out of breath.

"We have a great deal of rigging shot away, sir. Larboard lower shrouds of both fore and main are a shambles. We're risking both our masts on this tack—even in so small a breeze. We're hauling cables aloft to brace them, sir, but it will take some little time."

Hayden gazed up at the forward masts. "Will they stand for five minutes, Mr Barthe, or will they not?"

"I cannot say, Captain, but let us pray they do. I would not dare tack until we have cables taut."

"Then we will have to wait to come about. Let us hope they hold."

Barthe turned to face him, his hat gone and coarse, red hair standing out at all angles. "Our ship is in ruins, sir. If we had not broken it off, all of our masts would have been lost. We've many men killed and hurt. A very great many, sir."

"I know, Mr Barthe, that seventy-four all but did for us. But while we can steer where we will, it is our duty and obligation to engage enemy vessels, no matter their weight of broadside."

"I know, sir." Barthe nodded. Hayden thought the man might weep. "I know . . ." he said again, then reached up to touch his missing hat and retreated forward to oversee repairs.

A little cat's-paw rippled the water, and Hayden felt his hands take stronger hold on the rail. With his naked eye he could see the few shrouds remaining stretch, though the familiar sound was hidden beneath the firing of guns. The three ships were not a hundred yards distant, he was sure, but the shrouds might not bear them so far.

Hayden turned in a quick circle to be certain that no ship had singled them out or slipped up from astern. Smoky clouds, thick and clinging, drifted low over the waters, and in each Hayden imagined an enemy ship, cloaked and deadly. The firing of the ships ahead was so intense that single shots could not be distinguished in the din. Only a terrible, unbroken thunder, pealing on and on without respite.

The little cat's-paw increased; Hayden felt it on his face and saw it flow over the water. If a gust caught them now, the masts would not stand. He could see the men in the tops, risking their very lives, working with great energy, all their movements sure and without hesitation. Smaller ropes were used to haul the cables aloft. They ran through notch-blocks rigged for that purpose alone, men on the deck hauling with a will, the larger cable stuttering aloft, four feet to each *"Heave!"* One cable had reached the tops already and the bosun was there with a mate to make up a temporary seizing. It was dishonourable to think it, but Hayden was not unhappy that the bosun was not the late Mr Franks, who was not nearly so competent as Mr Bellamy, as much as Hayden esteemed his other qualities.

Archer looked up at Hayden from the quarterdeck. "If these masts do not fall, sir," the lieutenant informed him, "it is because some saint's invisible hand holds them up."

"Why, Mr Archer, you have found religion at last."

"Not entirely, sir."

"Mmm. Mr Archer, order those marines out of the foretops, if you please. If that mast goes by the board, they will all be in the sea—if they are not broken upon the deck."

"Aye, sir."

"What is Mr Hawthorne about?" Hayden complained to Gould, who stood three paces off. "He should have had those men on the deck before now."

"I saw Mr Hawthorne being helped below, Captain," Gould said, almost too quiet to hear.

Hayden looked sharply at the midshipman. "Not too badly hurt, I hope?"

"I do not know, sir. He was not being carried, but only aided, so perhaps it was not too bad a hurt. The doctor will put him to rights, I am certain."

The sterns of the great ships were suddenly drawing near, all but smothered in thick, acrid smoke.

"Mr Archer. Go forward, if you please, and be certain the guns are fired into the French ships and not our flagship."

"I will, sir."

Hayden's eyes stung from powder-smoke, and if his face resembled those of his crew, it was stained with sweat-smear as well. On the forecastle, Archer stopped where he could look down to the gun-deck below yet still gauge the position of the enemy ship. The lieutenant's hand raised, hovered a moment, and then cut swiftly down, his cry lost in the explosion of guns.

Raisonnable sailed close across the sterns of the trio of ships, blasting away in the fog of smoke, as though they were half in this world and half in a dusky Hades where the light of day did not penetrate. As they passed the first ship, an opening in the cloud revealed a sailor with musket tight to his shoulder, tracking Hayden's ship as though it were a stag. Before he thought, Hayden pulled a pistol from his belt, thumbed back the cock, and shot the man through the neck so that he fell back into the all-consuming smoke.

The sterns of the ships were hardly visible then. Hayden threw up an arm as though it would ward off the sight-burning smoke. *Le Jacobin*, Hayden realised—when he had seen the musket man the name of the ship had been visible—*Le Jacobin*.

The guns aft fired and Hayden could make out the crews below him, swabbing and ramming cartridges home. The first ship passed, but the second he could not find in the searing smoke, not helped by the fact that his eyes watered terribly, but he dared not wipe them for fear of making matters worse. A bit of gilded rail, perhaps a square of gallery window appeared in the blear—the *Queen Charlotte*, Hayden thought.

He thumped quickly down the ladder to the quarterdeck and fell over a powder-monkey in the smoke; picking himself and the child up at once, he sent the boy on his way. He pushed forward to the edge of the gangway, where for a moment he could not find Archer in the gloom. But there he was, standing in the chains, one hand grasping a shroud, the other atop the anchor stock, leaning out and trying to distinguish the transom of the enemy. Suddenly, he vaulted back over the barricade, waved to the men at the forward gun, and ran to the pin-rail in the waist. He called down to Wickham, whom Hayden could just make out, and immediately *Raisonnable*'s forward guns began to fire—the first, then the next, then the next again, all the length of the ship, the tolling of a thunderous bell.

The damage inflicted was lost in the pall, but then *Raisonnable* sailed free of it, only a few ghostly swirls eddying behind the sails. Hastening to the rail, Hayden leaned out and gazed back at the battle still in progress, though the French ships certainly were firing less frequently since being raked. Their topmasts were almost all that was visible, and then one of these went by the board—*Queen Charlotte*'s, Hayden realised—and the French flagship surged slowly ahead. In a moment, the French ships had both outdistanced Lord Howe's vessel, and stood on.

Hayden called for a glass, and when he fixed it on *Queen Charlotte*'s quarterdeck, he found Admiral Lord Howe, his hat gone, but standing undaunted near the helmsmen, surveying the scene at all quarters.

"There is the admiral," Hayden said, surprised at how relieved he was to see the man—a near stranger.

The hands around him gave three mighty "huzzahs," a few leaping up to the rail so that Hayden ordered them back to their stations. Archer returned along the gangway with all haste.

"Sir," he said as he came onto the quarterdeck, "what shall we do now?"

"We have lost our opposite number," Hayden replied, trying not to sound relieved at this, "so, Mr Archer, we shall employ our guns elsewhere. Let us make a quick survey of our enemies and who among our friends might need us most."

Hayden went up the ladder to the poop with Archer and Gould, who was running Hayden's orders, upon his coattails. The fighting was not concentrated in any one place; nor was there any semblance of "a line of battle" to be found anywhere. Spread over a few acres of heaving blue were any number of small actions, few involving more than two ships or three. Here and there unengaged ships, like *Raisonnable*, appeared headed for one action or another, and yet more ships lay wallowing, their masts gone or slanting half over the side, guns silenced.

Hayden fixed his glass upon the French admiral's flagship, which appeared to be gathering a small squadron in its wake. *Queen Charlotte* was already engaged in another action with what appeared to be an eighty-gun ship.

"Shall we go to His Lordship's aid, sir?" Archer wondered.

"I do not think he requires our assistance as much as some others." Hayden pointed. Although he would not shy away, engaging another larger ship, broadside to broadside, Hayden thought would be their undoing. His ship answered her helm but was in ruins, many dead and injured, guns thrown out of their carriages.

"Sir?" Gould said nervously. "Captain . . . ?"

Hayden glanced aft, where the midshipman stood staring.

"Are these French ships, sir, bearing down on us?"

Archer gave a start as he turned. "Where in blackest hell did they come from?"

All three moved quickly aft. Two ships of the line—seventy-fours, Hayden believed—appeared to be making directly for *Raisonnable*; indeed, one fired a chase gun at that moment and the crow-jack yard fell to the deck where Hayden and Archer had been standing but an instant previous.

"We will scud," Hayden said to Archer. "It is our only hope."

Archer flew to the smashed rail, clambering over the crow-jack yard and its gear.

"Mr Barthe! Call hands. Make all possible sail. Helmsman, put her dead before the wind."

Hands came welling up from the gun-deck and yards were quickly braced and sail made. Hayden watched this evolution anx-

iously, praying the rig would stand, but it did, and they were heading slowly downwind, not the swiftest point of sail, but the
converging seventy-fours left Hayden no choice.

One of the helmsmen appeared from under the afterdeck, looked
around for Archer, who had gone forward, and then spotted Hayden.

"Sir, there is a dismasted Frenchman dead ahead. Shall we leave
it to larboard or starboard?"

Hayden turned and looked back at the chasing ships, measuring
their speed and the speed of his own vessel. Both French ships were
bracing yards and drawing the wind aft, sailing perhaps sixty yards
apart. Hayden turned back to the helmsman.

"Leave the hulk to larboard. Where is Mr Archer?"

"On the starboard gangway, sir.

Hayden turned to his runner. "Mr Gould, go to Archer and tell
him I want twenty men on the poop the instant yards are braced and
sails trimmed."

The midshipman touched his hat and climbed over the fallen
yard in such haste that he stumbled down the ladder, catching himself at the bottom. Hayden found an axe and began cutting away
ropes on the crow-jack, though he left anything he could. Archer
and two dozen men came onto the poop as Hayden was sorting out
a fallen rope.

Thrusting the rope at one of the hands—a man named Pierce—
Hayden said, "I need a run of ten fathoms—mind all of it is sound.
Mr Archer, we will slide this yard over the side in but a moment."

"Fifteen fathoms, sir," Pierce quickly reported.

Hayden took one end and tied it off to the tip of the fallen yard.
"Take the end and run it outside of all to starboard, outside the
transom, back inboard to larboard, and make fast. You," Hayden
pointed at a man he did not know, "feed the rope to Pierce."

The starboard brace had torn away from the forward shroud, and

Hayden sent two men down onto the quarterdeck to sort it out, coil it, and carry it up to the poop.

"What are you intending, sir?" Archer asked.

"It is a desperate plan, Mr Archer. We will let this French ship on our larboard quarter—the swifter of the two—all but catch us. Just as we pass by the dismasted ship—which I pray has struck and will not fire into us—I intend to push the crow-jack yard over the side with all of its attendant gear. It will drop astern and pull up short on these ropes, which will check our speed. The ship to larboard will be forced to pass the hulk to larboard. As our speed is checked it will shoot past, and we will cut away the crow-jack, turn to larboard across the bow of the hulk, and rake the Frenchman as he passes."

Archer considered this only a second. Hayden half expected him to express doubts, but instead he asked, "What of the other chasing ship, sir?"

"If we catch him by surprise, he will not turn quickly enough and we will be away. If he does make the turn. We must either luff and rake him from forward or run. I hope he will not make the turn in time and we will be away."

Archer nodded. "Shall I cut away the hammock netting so it does not interfere?"

"By all means, Mr Archer, do so at once."

Hayden realised then that Barthe was standing on the ladder head, listening over the firing of guns all around.

"Mr Barthe, we must slow our speed a little. For this plan to work, we will almost certainly have to take a broadside. Once we are up with the hulk, sufficient hands to brace yards and make our turn to larboard will be required. It must be handsomely managed."

"Aye, Captain." He glanced down at the fallen yard. "I shall let some sheets run, sir, to slow us a little."

"If you please, Mr Barthe."

Barthe climbed stiffly down onto the quarterdeck and took up his speaking trumpet.

Hayden watched the French ships in their wake. His plan depended so much on timing and accurately measuring the speed of each vessel to a nicety that he could hardly bear to think of what would occur should he fail. Two seventy-fours would be on them of an instant, and though his crew would not lose their nerve, the larger ships would destroy them. He had struck his colours once in the last weeks; he did not intend to do so again.

"Captain Hayden . . . ?" It was the one of the bosun's mates calling from forward. "Ship forward of us, sir, is displaying a Union Jack."

And indeed it was, laying the flag over the stern to indicate it had struck.

"Do you trust them, sir?" Archer asked.

"I cannot see that we have any choice, Mr Archer. Trust does not enter into it."

"Yes, sir."

Hayden turned to the men, who awaited his orders. "Take hold of this yard. We will slide it out to starboard but keep the outboard end up; if it catches in the water it will cant aft and the inboard end will swing forward and make a great deal of mischief, I fear."

The French seventy-four to larboard fired its forward guns at that moment, balls screaming overhead through the poor mizzen and several burying in the oaken hull below. Hayden could feel the tension of the men around him. One cursed under his breath.

If the French managed to take down one of Hayden's masts now his plan would come to nothing, but there was no choice. The spar over the stern would only check *Raisonnable*'s speed to a degree. If the French ship was not almost abeam when they reached the hulk, slowing their ship would not work and they would be broadside to broadside with the powerful seventy-four with a second bearing down astern.

They were very quickly coming up on the dismasted vessel, and Hayden was relieved to see that the chasing ships would split, just as he had assumed, the faster taking the opposite side to *Raisonnable*, hoping to fire a broadside as they sailed clear of the bow.

"Handsomely, now. Slide it out."

A second report from the French ship and the rail at the forward end of the poop shattered not a yard from Hayden. All of his men held their places.

The heavy yard resisted a moment but then began scraping slowly—too slowly—over the side.

"Push, men! Push!"

And push they did, the yard finally releasing its hold on the deck.

"Everyone aft of the yard!" Hayden ordered. "Put your weight on it."

They all pushed down as they could, but finally the yard tilted down, caught the water, and swung round, even as it slid overboard, and though it struck the mizzen backstays it did not tear them away.

The yard floated clear of the ship, falling aft. First the larboard rope came taut, then the starboard. The spar was not quite square to their travel, but even so it did check the ship's speed. Hayden glanced right and found the crew of the dismasted vessel watched their passing in sullen silence.

"Take up this axe, Pierce. When I tell you, cut the yard away."

"Aye, sir."

The chasing ship, which had been all but abreast, now surged ahead down the other side of the drifting vessel.

"Is this going to work, sir?" Archer asked suddenly.

"I do not know, Mr Archer. Go quickly down to the helmsman and be certain we make our turn the instant I give the order."

Archer went down the ladder without so much as touching his hat. He took up position where he could see both Hayden and the men at the wheel.

The stricken French ship appeared to slide aft, and very quickly they were up to its bows.

"Cut it free, Pierce!" Hayden called out and took his own axe to the rope, but made a poor job of it on the first try and had to cut again. The rope slid quickly aft and was gone. He ran forward a few steps.

"Helm to starboard, Mr Archer."

Archer gave but a nod to the men at the helm, and Hayden felt the ship begin a quick turn, Mr Barthe calling out orders to sail handlers. To his horror, Hayden saw the French ship only a little ahead and immediately they began firing into *Raisonnable*'s bow.

"Down on the deck!" Hayden yelled over the din. "Have the men lie down on the deck!"

Hayden went quickly down the ladder to the quarterdeck and stood some yards before the helmsman, ready to take the place of either man at the wheel in the event that one was shot. Archer was yelling through his speaking trumpet down at the lower deck, and around him the men threw themselves flat between the carronades; many covered their heads with their arms.

Raisonnable slowly turned. Hayden could see the men handling braces and sheets, all crouched down as low to the deck as they might, but hauling on ropes all the same. His ship continued its turn, the tip of its jib-boom threatening to tangle in the enemy's shrouds. Fewer of the Frenchman's guns could be brought to bear now, but even as Hayden turned to larboard, the French ship began a turn to starboard.

Hayden's jib-boom all but tore into the other ship's mizzen sail, they came so close to collision.

Going himself to the wheel, Hayden began to turn the ship now to starboard, that he might cut squarely across the other ship's stern.

"Up, Mr Archer. Back to stations. We will fire the starboard guns as the enemy bears."

Archer went running along the gangway calling down to the decks below. Reaching the forward gun, he pointed to the gun captain and it reared back in a torrent of smoke. The guns below began to fire at that instant, one by one by one. Hayden continued to turn his ship to match the manoeuvre of the French seventy-four. Overhead he heard someone let the mizzen sheet run.

The transom of the French ship was being methodically destroyed, and Hayden could but imagine the destruction along the decks, the lives being lost.

Hayden handed the wheel back to the helmsmen. "Continue your turn," he instructed, and he went forward to where he could see what transpired. As he did so, he realised that French ships were going to run afoul of one another and the ship that had been in Hayden's wake was turning to avoid collision.

And then they were past, the main and mizzen masts of the French ship toppling slowly to leeward.

"Luff and touch her, Bullfinch." And then to the men on the poop, "Sheet the mizzen close; we go hard on the wind now."

Hayden climbed back up to the poop and surveyed the field of battle, ships still engaged here and there, many others drifting with masts gone or lying over the side. To the west, ships were forming what appeared to be a line. Finding his glass, Hayden fixed it on this gathering.

"Mr Archer!" Hayden called.

"Sir?" Archer had just returned to the quarterdeck.

Hayden raised what he realised was a painfully stiff arm and pointed. "The French are forming a line. Do you see?"

Archer took a moment to find a glass but then replied, "It is their flagship, Captain. She is signalling." The lieutenant climbed up to the poop.

Other French vessels were shaping their courses to join their admiral's ship.

"What are their intentions, sir?" Archer wondered.

"They will wear and return to the action." Hayden made a quick count of ships in the French admiral's line and those sailing to join him. "Eleven sail of the line, Mr Archer." Hayden began searching among the field of ships, fearing that he would find Lord Howe's vessel disabled. But then he saw her, just as signals were being hoisted.

"Mr Gould? There you are." Hayden thrust a glass at the midshipman. "Do you see the admiral's signal?"

The midshipman raised the glass for only a second. "'Form a line as convenient, sir, astern of the flagship.'"

"Mr Archer, we will hold this course until the lord admiral's intentions become clear. We dare not tack—our rig will not bear it—but if needs be we will wear to join his line."

"Aye, sir."

They both stood watching Lord Howe's ship and the few British ships that appeared to be making for her.

"Have you been down to the gun-decks, Mr Archer?"

"I have not, Captain."

"Do you have any idea of our losses?"

"It will not be a small number, sir. *L'Achille* did a great deal of damage, and we were all but raked in this last action."

Hayden was silent a moment. "Water in the hold?"

"The carpenter reports we took no shot below the waterline, sir."

"We have had some luck this day."

"Both good and ill, sir."

"I have seen luck run ill out of all proportion, Mr Archer; I shall gladly accept an equal share of either. And even more gladly on a day such as this."

"I agree, sir. Ill luck is like the intermittent fever—once it has its hooks in you, it returns again and again. Few men shake it off."

Hayden did not much like this diagnosis, as he had certainly endured his share of poor luck—more than his share, he often thought.

Across the watery field cannon fire reverberated yet, and dense creatures of smoke rambled low over the waves. Ships with all masts standing, if not engaged, were making their way towards their respective flagships.

"Sir?" Archer said, and pointed off to the north. "Is that ship one of ours?"

Farthest from the centre of action lay a three-decker, dismasted and drifting north-east. Hayden fixed a glass on her a moment.

"Where is Mr Barthe?"

"Forward, sir," Gould reported, "overseeing repairs to our rig, sir."

Hayden proffered his glass. "Jump down to him, if you please, Mr Gould, and ask him if he knows that ship."

"Yes, sir."

Gould went quickly down the ladder and forward among the working crew. Hayden tried to count the disabled ships, but there were battles still being fought and smoke obscured much even yet.

"Captain Hayden, sir." Gould came pounding up the ladder, glass in hand. "Mr Barthe believes it is the *Queen*, sir."

"Does the king know that his queen is consorting with sailors?"

Turning about, Hayden found Hawthorne stepping awkwardly onto the poop, with Doctor Griffiths' cane under employment. His white breeches were stained crimson.

"Mr Hawthorne, it would appear you have been wounded, sir," Hayden observed.

"A musket ball in my leg. Mr Smosh has bound it up nicely and it hardly seeps at all. The doctor will remove the lead at some later time. Perhaps on the morrow when there are fewer pressing matters for him to attend."

"Should you not be below in a cot?" Hayden asked.

"I believe I can be of use on deck—unless running is required. Give me a musket and corner to wedge myself in and I will put paid to the careers of a few Frenchmen, I am quite certain."

"Mr Gould . . . fetch Mr Hawthorne a musket, if you please." Hayden gestured aft. "You may wedge yourself in either corner against the transom, Mr Hawthorne. There are small benches there to sit upon, if you so desire."

"Thank you, sir." Hawthorne reached up to touch his hat— gone—and then limped aft.

Gould appeared a moment later bearing a musket, powder, and shot. He also took Hawthorne his own glass, for which the marine gave markedly heartfelt thanks, the thoughtfulness of this gesture affecting him greatly.

"Do you know, sir," Archer began, "the French appear to be forming a line of ten or eleven ships. Lord Howe would appear to have no more than five or six, including our own ship, sir."

"Can our own ships not see the signal? Look there." Hayden waved his glass. "It is being dutifully repeated on a frigate."

"So it is, sir. I believe a number of our ships are engaged in securing prizes."

"Prizes they will be in danger of losing if the French can bring eleven ships against five."

Hayden could see *Queen Charlotte* begin to stand down towards the approaching French.

"Make ready to wear ship, Mr Archer. If we cannot find a place in the line near to the flagship, we will take up the rear."

Hayden watched as the men went to their stations. Exhaustion festered like poison in all their limbs, and every movement was a conscious and trying effort. Even his officers' faces were blanched beneath the smoke stain, eyes red-rimmed. Hardly a soul aboard had slept more than a few hours at a stretch these five nights past, the hands lying on the deck at the guns. The excitement and fear of the battle had given them much energy, but now they were spent, utterly. And Hayden realised that he was little different—his mind was fogged, thoughts coming with difficulty, and he felt as though he dragged his limbs along, barely able to keep his feet beneath him. How much longer he could demand his crew fight he did not know. They were past the point of endurance now, functioning on nothing but desire and a sense of duty. Even so, the French could be little better off; his own crew could not shirk when the enemy did not.

Something caught his eye at that moment. "Mr Hawthorne? Can you see that ship?" Hayden pointed. "South of the two that still fire their guns?"

"With just the stump of a foremast showing, Captain?"

"The very one. Fix your glass upon her, if you please. Does she sit low in the water? I cannot be certain at such a distance."

Hawthorne twisted around on the little bench, leaned an elbow upon the cap, and scrutinized the ship Hayden indicated.

The marine looked over at Hayden in surprise. "She appears to be almost up to her gunports, sir."

"Is she one of ours?"

"I could not tell." The marine lifted his glass and examined the ship again. "I cannot say, sir," he informed Hayden after a moment, not lowering his glass.

"Does any ship come to her aid?"

"Not that I can tell, sir."

"Captain . . . ?" It was Archer. "Should we wear, sir?"

Hayden glanced back to Lord Howe's ship. "By all means, Mr Archer. Immediately."

As the wind was brought across the stern and yards braced—perhaps not as smartly as commonly—Hayden took up his own glass and went to the rail beside Hawthorne.

"I do believe that ship is sinking," Hayden observed after a moment.

"Not unheard of, I should think?" Hawthorne said.

"No, but almost so. Whatever could have happened to cause that, I wonder?"

"Will frigates not come to her aid?"

"So they should, but whose frigates? Ours or theirs?"

Hayden was forced to tear himself away to concentrate on slipping his ship into the line, which required some backing and filling. Fortunately, it was a line formed in haste and hardly a model of such endeavours, so the distance between ships was greater than seen commonly.

The small breeze carried the British ships down towards the French, though not swiftly. Every ship had some damage to sails and rig, and so were handicapped to a greater or lesser degree.

To the north, the French had worn and made sail towards the disabled three-decker Barthe believed was the *Queen*, and Howe was shaping his course to intercept them.

"This is an unequal fight, Captain," Hawthorne observed.

"Howe will not abandon the *Queen* to the French."

"But is he not in danger of losing even more ships? There are eleven French ships of the line, and we have but five."

Hayden cast his gaze around the field of battle. There certainly were more British ships with their masts standing and not engaged in action. "If things turn against us, I believe the captains will see and come to our aid."

"If they can take but a moment from lining their pockets with prize money." Hawthorne looked around, his face blanched beneath the grainy grey of powder smoke. Hayden was quite certain the marine was in considerable pain. That he had come back onto the deck to take up a musket affected Hayden greatly. To have been blessed with such officers was a stroke of inestimable good fortune.

Hayden turned away from the marine and fixed his attention on what was clearly now eleven French ships bearing down on the crippled *Queen*. The five ships in the wake of Lord Howe sailed towards that same object and the two squadrons could not help but meet, though the French would almost certainly gain their prize first. Howe would never give up such a ship without a fight and Hayden would surely be expected to take part fully, and though he would not shy from it, the thought of the losses he would suffer could not be ignored.

And so the two lines of ships slowly converged, gunports open, men at their stations. Hayden's own crew were barely standing, all of them stooping, shoulders sagged and arms hanging limp. They looked as if a small breeze would knock them all down. It was only meagre comfort that the French could be little better off. The battle had sucked the life out of his crew; they were little better than ghosts now.

"Two adversaries at a duel," Hawthorne observed quietly.

"Neither can back away," Hayden replied.

"Honour will not allow it." Hawthorne looked over at Hayden, his face very grim. "Although Lord Howe will never be called shy, I fear he might be making a terrible error."

Hayden could not say it but he believed the marine was more than likely correct. "Hold your musket ready, Mr Hawthorne, I believe you shall soon have employment for it."

The leading French ship fired a gun at the disabled *Queen*, which had not struck, though she could hardly defend herself.

"That seems rather unsporting," Hawthorne said, clearly offended. "Who is the captain of the *Queen*? Will he return fire?"

"That is Rear Admiral Gardner's ship—Hutt is the captain. Perhaps, seeing us attempting his rescue, he will fire. Otherwise, he would have no choice but to strike, and would be a fool to attempt otherwise."

"I do not much care for the odds." Hawthorne stood—one-legged, supported on the rail—the better to see the nearing French.

Hayden did not reply. It seemed suddenly possible that the outcome of this battle might hinge upon this very action—and the British were outnumbered better than two to one. Hayden glanced around to see if other British ships were hastening to this spot and to his horror could not discover a single ship so engaged.

He did find several ships sailing towards disabled French vessels, apparently with intention of securing them as prizes.

Hayden turned back to the French ships, clearly going to win this race and take the *Queen* before Howe could intervene. Another bloom of smoke from the French ship, and the sharp report carried over the water. A gun was fired aboard the *Queen Charlotte*, merely a show of resolve, as the flagship was too distant to have any hope of hitting an enemy vessel. A hoist of signals was sent aloft on the French admiral's ship, and suddenly they turned away, one by one in succession, bracing yards and sailing hard on the wind back towards their own disabled ships.

"They have broken off," Hawthorne said, his voice hoarse with fatigue and perhaps disbelief. "Is it a ruse?"

"I do not believe it is. Villaret-Joyeuse has decided that preserving his own disabled ships is more important than taking a single British ship—even a first-rate. Now, can Lord Howe gather enough ships to give chase . . . ?"

But once he came up with the *Queen*, Howe made the signal to break off the chase. Hayden was about to order his ship hove to so that they could effect repairs, but was reminded of the ship he had seen that appeared to be settling down. Hunting over the sea of stricken ships and debris, he found the ship. A quick perusal with a glass confirmed his earlier impression.

Archer appeared at the stair head.

"Orders, Captain?"

"Bring us near to that ship." Hayden pointed with his glass. "We will offer assistance."

"Is she one of ours, sir?"

"I do not know, Mr Archer. I only know that she is sinking and many souls are in peril. Make ready to launch our boats, Mr Archer."

Hayden looked once more around the scene of battle, the drifting, dismasted ships, bodies floating everywhere he looked, all of them given animation only by the sea, staring down into the depths where they would soon make their beds.

Upon his own deck he could see officers sorting among the wounded and the dead, bearing men down to the doctor, some of them limp, faces bloodless. Exhausted men cleared away the boats and rigged tackles to hoist them out. It was almost more than they could do—but hoist them out they managed, though dropping them heavily into the sea. The youngest men were not the least affected. Indeed, many an older seaman manned the oars, and Hayden sent marines and lieutenants down to man the boats. By the time they were near enough to send the boats away, the stricken ship—French—was down below her gunports and sinking fast.

Having witnessed the scene aboard *Les Droits de l'Homme* after she was wrecked, where panic had sunk a boat and seen the death of a hundred—including the ill-fated Franks—Hayden watched the boats approach the sinking ship with great apprehension. But the captain of this ship stood upon the rail without so much as a cutlass and ordered the men to board the boats in an orderly fashion. A second British ship had launched boats, which were rapidly approaching the sinking vessel.

Looking around the watery field of battle, Hayden saw the French line retreating, sweeping up what ships they could but leaving many behind. Miraculously, it was over. And he was alive and largely unharmed but for a fatigue so great he could barely stand.

Hayden's boats bumped alongside, French sailors heaving themselves over the rail and then helping those behind. The ships' boys had been sent away first, but Hayden saw no signs of wounded—they had been left until last, the captain choosing to save those most likely to survive. A hard choice.

The frightened French sailors slumped down upon the deck, and though the British marines trained muskets upon them, they were too exhausted to fight or even to stand.

Hayden went down to the quarterdeck, where he found the eyes of the Frenchmen upon him, as though they wondered what their fate would be.

Gould appeared at his elbow, and Hayden could not recall if he had been there all along or had come back just now. "It appears we will have a hundred prisoners or more, Mr Gould . . . Mr Gould . . . are you well?"

Gould covered his eyes with a hand and turned away; his shoulders heaved twice and then he recovered himself.

"Prisoners, sir," he mumbled.

"Yes. What has happened?" Hayden demanded.

"It is Mr Wickham, sir. They carried him down to the doctor."

"Wickham . . . ? How badly hurt?"

"I cannot say, sir. He was not sensible . . . and bled horribly."

Hayden felt himself sag down onto a carronade slide. For a moment he could not speak; nor could he seem to think. And then he saw the eyes of all the French sailors upon him—haunted as though they had just peered into the underworld, and then been drawn back from the edge.

"Be at peace," Hayden heard himself say to them. "You are safe. Be at peace."

Twenty-two

I have observed these cliffs so often, Mr Barthe, that I believe I know them better than I know my own countenance." Hayden lowered his glass.

The sailing master leaned upon the forward barricade with one hand and held the doctor's cane in the other. Like Hayden he stared off towards the cliffs that lay to either side of the entrance to the inner waters of Brest. "I am more pleased to see them this time than many another, sir."

Hayden lifted his glass again, watching the stern of the last ship as it entered the Goulet. One by one, the entire French fleet—what remained of it—was swallowed into the long shadows of late afternoon.

Lowering his glass, Hayden stared but a moment more. Lord Howe had sent *Raisonnable* in company with two frigates to be certain the French fleet returned to port, which it had now done.

"Well, Mr Barthe, that is our part completed. The frigates will stand watch, and we," he took a deep breath, "are for England." He turned to the midshipman hovering three paces behind. "Pass the word for Mr Archer," he ordered.

"I am here, sir." Archer was standing in the foremast chains, observing the retreating French fleet. Quickly he clambered back over the rail.

"We will round Ushant before dark, Mr Archer, and then shape our course for Portsmouth."

"Aye, sir," Archer responded, approaching his captain. "And what becomes of us then, I wonder?"

Hayden felt himself shrug. "That is for the Lords Commissioners to decide, Mr Archer, not mere mortals such as ourselves."

"I do know," Barthe growled, "that we shall arrive in Portsmouth after Lord Howe has carried his prizes there in state and he and his captains have been awarded jewelled swords and even knighthoods . . . as though we had no part in it."

The same thought had occurred to Hayden, but then he had so little to draw him back to England—disappointment, threatening bankruptcy, legal troubles . . . He hoped that he would be sent back to sea—and the sooner the better.

"At least we can tell our grandchildren that we fought in the first great sea battle of the war," Archer observed.

"And had nothing to show for it," Barthe added.

"Mr Archer . . ." Hayden prompted.

"Round Ushant and shape our course for Portsmouth, aye, sir." The lieutenant went off at a run, passing a limping Hawthorne as he made his way forward along the gangway.

"Have I missed the French retreating into Brest?" the marine officer enquired.

"I am afraid you have, Mr Hawthorne."

"Damn. I had so wanted to see what an admiral looked like with his tail tucked between his legs."

"Should you really be walking, Mr Hawthorne?" Hayden asked. "Did the doctor not order you to stay in your cot?"

"Were those his orders? I must have misunderstood . . ." Hawthorne gazed a moment at the last French ship disappearing between the cliffs. His face became more serious of a sudden. "Do you ever wonder, Captain, how many lives were lost on both sides?"

Barthe eyed the marine oddly. "You *have* been in your cot too long, Mr Hawthorne, if your thoughts have taken such a melancholy turn."

"I suppose . . ." Hawthorne said quietly.

The hands came hurrying to their stations in preparation to shift yards and wear around. None of them spoke as they did so, but only went to their places and set soberly to their duties. There was something in their faces, illuminated by the golden light of the westering sun. They, all of them, appeared older, Hayden thought. Not aged, but older in some mysterious way.

"I do not know how many died, Mr Hawthorne," Hayden finally replied. "A very great number, I fear."

"The Lord knows." It was Smosh, just arriving on the quarterdeck. He waved a hand out towards the open sea. "And now they await His mercy."

Hayden looked out towards the horizon where the sun was just settling into the vast ocean. "'Until the sea shall give up her dead . . .'" he said softly.

No one responded for a moment.

"Amen," Mr Smosh intoned.

"Amen," Hawthorne whispered thickly. "Amen, sir."

AFTERWORD

The French seventy-four-gun ship *Les Droits des L'Homme* did sink much in the manner described in the book, though later in the war. A large number of the crew were rescued when the storm moderated, unlike fictional events in the book. There were British seamen aboard, though I believe they were merchant sailors (and very likely one woman) and they were returned to England in thanks for their efforts and discipline aboard the sinking ship. The swamping of the ship's boat happened much as described, and the loss of discipline among the crew is documented.

As far as I know, there was no sixty-four-gun ship at the battle of the Glorious First of June, but most of Hayden's exploits here are fictional. I did take pains, however, to give an accurate depiction of the battle itself. Anyone interested in a single-volume account of the battle would do well to read *The Glorious First of June 1794: A Naval Battle and Its Aftermath*, edited by Michael Duffy and Roger Morriss.

ACKNOWLEDGEMENTS

As usual, I have numerous people to thank for their generous assistance. Rif Winfield, who kindly answered questions for me and whose magnificent *British Warships in the Age of Sail* I refer to regularly. I would like to thank Brian Vale for answering all my questions about Dr Thomas Trotter and the hospital ship *Charon*. Mr Vale's wonderful *Physician to the Fleet* (written with Griffith Edwards) deserves to be widely read. Robin Manson for reading an early draft (and getting the oil canister back on my marine diesel when I thought only a contortionist might do it).

When I was looking for information about Hayden's new ship, *Raisonnable*, I came upon a scale model of *Agamemnon* (*Raisonnable*'s sister ship) built by Roger Antrobus. Not only was this a fantastic model, but it was photographed in such a way that you could believe you were looking at a full-sized ship. I used these photos of the model to help plan and imagine the action aboard *Raisonnable*. Anyone interested in seeing this model might find it online at roger-antrobus.magix.net. Many thanks to Roger.

I would also like to thank another Rodger—my good friend Rodger Turner, who created and looks after my site for me and also answers technical questions whenever I have trouble with my computers. I suspect he has no idea how much I value his contribution.

I have to thank my fantastic agents in the United States and the United

Kingdom—Howard Morhaim and Caspian Dennis, and my ever-thoughtful editors, Alex Clarke and Rachel Kahan.

Last, but first in my heart, everlasting thanks to my wife and son, who put up with all of my writer's eccentricities and manage to take it all with the best of humour.